LIGHTNING STRIKES THE SILENCE

THE LANE WINSLOW MYSTERY SERIES

A Killer in King's Cove (#1)
Death in a Darkening Mist (#2)
An Old, Cold Grave (#3)
It Begins in Betrayal (#4)
A Sorrowful Sanctuary (#5)
A Deceptive Devotion (#6)
A Match Made for Murder (#7)
A Lethal Lesson (#8)
Framed in Fire (#9)
To Track a Traitor (#10)
Lightning Strikes the Silence (#11)

IONA WHISHAW

LIGHTNING STRIKES *THE* SILENCE

A LANE WINSLOW MYSTERY

TOUCHWOOD

TouchWood Editions
touchwoodeditions.com

This book is a work of fiction. Names, characters, places, and incidents are either products of the author's imagination or used fictitiously. Any resemblance to actual events or locales or persons, living or dead, is entirely coincidental.

Edited by Claire Philipson
Cover illustration by Margaret Hanson

CATALOGUING DATA AVAILABLE FROM LIBRARY AND ARCHIVES CANADA
ISBN 9781771514323 (softcover)
ISBN 9781771514330 (electronic)
ISBN 9781771514347 (audiobook)

TouchWood Editions acknowledges that the land on which we live and work is within the traditional territories of the Lkwungen (Esquimalt and Songhees), Malahat, Pacheedaht, Scia'new, T'Sou-ke, and W̱SÁNEĆ (Pauquachin, Tsartlip, Tsawout, and Tseycum) peoples.

We acknowledge the financial support of the Government of Canada through the Canada Book Fund and the Canada Council for the Arts, and of the Province of British Columbia through the British Columbia Arts Council and the Book Publishing Tax Credit.

This book was produced using FSC®-certified, acid-free papers, processed chlorine free, and printed with soya-based inks.

PRINTED IN CANADA

28 27 26 25 24   1 2 3 4 5

For Eva, my grandmother . . .
a life of joyful kindness cut short

PROLOGUE

―――――

"**LOOK WHAT YOU'VE DONE, YOU** pig! Why don't you go back where you came from!"

He barely had time to form an answer when he was pushed so violently that he stumbled backward, falling in a heap, slamming his hip on the rough ground. In a fury, he scrambled up and lunged at his attacker's feet, knocking him over so that his head fell hard on the rocks.

"Say that again!" But the boy didn't move.

"Say it again!" he yelled, swiping at the boy to make him move, and then struck him hard. "Say it!" he was screaming now. "Go on!" He kicked the downed figure, feeling the blood pounding in his own head. "Don't you play dead with me! For the rest of your life, you look behind you, 'cause I'll be there! Do you hear me?"

He was deafened now by his own rage. He heard nothing —neither the woman screaming nor the man yelling—until he felt himself being lifted off the ground, someone shouting from a distance, "Stop! For God's sake, stop!"

1

CHAPTER ONE

June 11, 1948

THE EXPLOSION WAS DEEP AND resonant, and so unfamiliar that the residents of King's Cove who were outside, which was most of them on a beautiful June day, looked upward thinking it was odd to have thunder out of so clear a blue sky.

Lane Winslow, reading under the weeping willow, frowned, closed her book, and struggled up from her folding canvas chair. Where had the boom come from? Having dismissed the idea that it was thunder, she turned her mind to her neighbours. Had an explosion accidentally ignited in someone's coal cellar? It seemed to be coming from up the mountain a little south of her. The Hughes family lived up there!

She dropped her book and ran into the house to seize the car keys off the hook by the inside of the door, jumped into her little Austin, backed it hurriedly onto the road, and then swung it around and made for the fork that led on up the hill toward the Hughes house. She turned left and bumped as quickly as she could down the rutted road that ran alongside their fenced field, her tires sinking into the muddy pools still left from the torrential rain of the night before. She saw their two milking cows cowering under a tree, and she tried to go faster, conscious of the deep ruts causing the centre hump to scrape the bottom of her car. In the driveway, she stopped and gazed around her.

Not a bloom out of place. The magnificent flower borders maintained by the grande dame of the family, old Gladys Hughes, flowed around the fruit trees, and the curved patches of lawn were the luminous green of early summer. Drops of moisture on the plants dazzled in the mid-morning sun. No smoke, no fire. Just a gentle mist as the sun evaporated the remains of the night's rain. But the two cocker spaniels were definitely kicking up a fuss. She saw what she had missed initially. At the edge of the apple orchard, all three Hughes women were standing with their hands shielding their eyes, looking west up the mountain. Then Mabel, the elder of the two "girls," both in their fifties, leaned over and tried to hush the hysterically barking dogs.

Lane got out of the car and hurried along the final bit of grassy drive to where they were standing.

"You heard it too," Gwen, the younger daughter, said, turning to greet Lane. "The dogs have gone mad."

"I thought it came from here," Lane said. She too gazed in the direction of the hill above the orchard where they had been looking.

"Good of you to come," Gladys said, glancing at her. "All tip-top here. It came from up there somewhere." She

3

pointed to where the thickly treed mountainside climbed steeply above King's Cove. "I thought it might be those Sons of whatever they are, those Freedomites blowing things up again, but there's nothing up there to blow up. It's just bush. Do you think some hound is blasting up there looking for silver? That would be the bloody limit!"

"Language, Mother," Mabel said, then pointed up the hill. "Is that smoke?"

The dogs took up their chorus again. "It is, I think," Lane confirmed. "I wonder if anyone is up there and been hurt."

"If whatever it is sets the forest alight, we're all for it," Gladys said grimly. King's Cove had lived through the fire of 1919, which had destroyed several houses and most of the orchards in the north part of the settlement. "We'd best telephone the authorities." She started back to the house.

"How far up do you think that is?" asked Lane.

Gwen considered. "It's hard to tell from here. We sometimes hike up that way with the dogs; it's a good forty minutes to where we go, but that smoke is much farther still. There's a rocky outcrop with a marvellous view of this arm of the lake and the mountains. There's not really a proper trail there, though."

"Higher up than forty minutes?" Lane was becoming more uneasy. The smoke was rising blackly above the thick blanket of trees and was rolling over on itself. "I think I'd better go up and make sure there's nobody there."

"Mother can do the phoning. We'll come with you. Let me run and get my first aid kit," Mabel said. "I know the way. I still keep the kit in good nick since the war, though it won't do much if someone is badly burned."

4

Lane waited impatiently, keeping an eye on whether the smoke patch was getting larger. Finally, Gwen and Mabel came, Gwen carrying a Thermos and Mabel a shoulder bag.

"The damn water is patchy again," said Mabel. "All I got was a blast of air when I turned on the tap. That's why it took so long. It's been a bit dodgy for ages, but it's just got really bad. I've got to get Harris to go check the lines. There must be a hole or air pockets in the pipe somewhere. Right, off we go."

With that Mabel strode off, leading the way, the dogs bounding around her, excited about the adventure.

THE JEWELLERY HEIST must have been so noisy that Darling could scarcely believe the thief was even sane. He stood in front of Harold's Fine Jewellery and Watch Repairs looking through the window into the chaos inside. No one had spotted anything amiss that morning when they were rushing off to work or shop. It was the ill fate of Mrs. Harold, the jeweller's wife, to find the devastation when she'd come in to work at ten thirty in the morning. The streets were full of people to-ing and fro-ing, and the café was right across the street, all the window seats occupied by people having their morning break. Seeing the police and a clearly distraught Mrs. Harold had caused all those in window seats to gape out at the scene. It *would* happen on a Friday, Darling thought. It would keep them all busy all weekend.

The store normally opened at eleven. Mrs. Harold always came in early, she explained. "Why did the thief have to break the place up like this?" she asked Darling. "It's wicked! Ron is away in Vancouver. He's going to be beside himself when I tell him. How am I going to cope on my own?" She made as if to go back in. She had evidently taken one look at the mess and run off to get the police.

"I'm sorry, Mrs. Harold, you can't go in now. We're about to go in and see what we can find."

"Ron's going to be sick. It's everything we own!" Her voice was beginning to rise.

"I understand. I've got a constable coming along to talk with you. He can take you back to the station and get you a cup of tea. Please tell him anything you can about your inventory. Where do you keep the records? I'll get them out so you can give an accurate account, but let him know if there is anything unusual or of extraordinary value."

Mrs. Harold came marginally out of her state of panic under the influence of Darling's calm manner. "In the back, in the office. My inventory records are in the desk, in the drawer on the right." She fumbled in the pocket of her cardigan. "Here's the key. This one is for the back door, and this is for this door."

"Right, thank you. We'll lock the front for now," Darling said. "My constable will be along in a moment."

My inventory records, she'd said. Like so many businessmen's wives, she must be the chief accountant and record keeper. Mrs. Harold nodded unhappily and looked in the window at the chaos.

Ames and Darling stepped out of earshot. "I'll talk to nearby merchants to see if anyone was working last night and might have heard anything," Ames said, readying his notebook. He shook his head in wonderment. "I was just in there yesterday."

Darling glanced at Ames, allowing only the slightest twitch of an eyebrow, then went to peer in the window while Ames went to the first store south of the jeweller, a tobacco shop. The interior of the Harolds' store was full of glass from broken display cases. Someone really had taken something heavy to the cases, Darling thought. It looked to him like it had been done with a sledgehammer. He frowned and examined the front door. It had been locked when Mrs. Harold had come in that morning.

So, the thief had broken into the back of the shop, performed a sort of smash and grab and escaped the same way, into the alley.

Ames came out after talking with the tobacconist. "Sorry, sir. He knocked off early because it was his wife's birthday yesterday."

"No joy, then. The front door was still locked, so let's assume the back alley. All the display cases are smashed to smithereens. It looks like whoever it was just scooped up what he could."

"It must have been an unbelievable racket."

Darling looked back at the shop. "Yes, indeed. Well, keep at it. I'm going in the back to get the inventory records while Mrs. Harold talks to Terrell."

Someone had come out of the café and had a hand on Mrs. Harold's arm, consoling her where she stood, her arms tightly crossed as she looked miserably at the two policemen.

"Right, sir. I'll try the bakery next door. They come in pretty early, and for all I know stay late."

"Good. If Terrell gets here before I come back, get him to take Mrs. Harold to the station and scare up a cup of tea for her. Her husband is away, so she's having to cope on her own."

He started to walk toward the end of the street and then turned and stopped, looking closely at Ames. "You were in there yesterday? A present for your mother?"

Ames's cheeks became pink, and Darling waved him on. "Get on with it, then."

Making his way up the hill the half block to the alley, Darling had no difficulty recognizing which rear door belonged to the jewellery store. It was open, and a small canvas bag was lying on the ground, no doubt dropped by the thief in his flight. He picked up the bag and was about to open the drawstring when he saw that there was a smear of what looked like blood, darkening now in the warmth of the morning. The perpetrator must have cut his hand on all the glass. Not surprising considering the mess in the shop. He gingerly pulled the string and looked inside. Several gold chain bracelets. When he went through a dark short passage into the dimly lit office, he was surprised to see that it too had been ransacked. Any normal thief, he had reasoned, would have got into the display cases, seized whatever he could, and then fled. But now this. Why take the time to pull the office to bits?

As his eyes adjusted to the dim light, he scanned the office, noting the open metal filing cabinet with papers spilling out, and books swept off a low shelf. As he turned to the desk, he nearly jumped out of his skin. Certainly not in Vancouver, but slumped face down at his own desk with something very wrong with the back of his head, was Mr. Ron Harold himself.

Rushing forward, he placed his fingers on the victim's neck, and then nearly snatched them away because it was so cold. No heartbeat. The acrid ferrous smell of blood assailed Darling's nostrils. Nearly gagging and wondering why this man's wife thought he was away, Darling pulled the chain on the desk lamp, but no light resulted. The wall switch was equally unforthcoming. He should have asked Mrs. Harold if there was an alarm. Perhaps the thief had cut the wires to prevent it going off. Ledgers forgotten, Darling pushed the back door wide, letting more light into the murky space, and looked for signs that the owner struggled or fought, though these would have been difficult to distinguish in the disarray of the open drawers and spilled books and boxes. Still, no chair or shelf was overturned as might indicate a physical struggle—and, after all, there was Ronald Harold himself, looking like he'd just put his head down on his desk for a nap. In the better light, Darling saw what was wrong with his head: the back of his skull had been smashed in.

He looked as closely as he dared, decided that more intense scrutiny was a job for Gilly, and took the set of keys out of his pocket. The floor was aged and much-scuffed wood—pine, he guessed—and he could not discern anything in the way of a useful footprint, had one even survived his own tramping in and out. Outside, he stopped to look at the ground, hoping that the rain of the night before would have made a muddy base for a telltale size ten boot, but again there was nothing to be seen. If the killer had left while the storm was still on, the rain would have washed away any traces.

He located the key that fit the back door. It was then that he saw that the wire that fed electricity into the shop from the main line was severed and hanging against the back wall. He locked the door and went around the building to Baker Street. They would have to secure the scene and call electricians to fix the hazard.

He was not surprised to see that a crowd had gathered in front of the store, and people were talking animatedly about the break-in. Well, they'd be shocked by what really went on, he thought.

Darling was about to push his way through but stopped. "If anyone heard or saw anything early this morning, or sometime in the night, can we get you to come to the station?" he asked. A general shaking of heads indicated there'd be little business resulting, and Darling sighed. He caught sight of Terrell walking Mrs. Harold back toward the station and pulled Ames away from the crowd. Ames had come back from the baker with an empty notebook.

"I've asked people to come to the station if they know anything. You get down to the station, quick as, and ask Terrell to come back here and secure the scene, then get Gilly here as fast as you can," Darling said.

"Yes, sir." Ames gave a quick surprised look at the store and then back. *Secure the scene* would be appropriate for a robbery, certainly, but Gilly? "What's happened?"

"We have a problem. Owner, Mr. Harold, has been killed. Ask O'Brien to attend to Mrs. Harold in one of the interview rooms; keep her quiet and in the dark for now. Then phone the city to send someone out to deal with a live wire at the back of the shop."

"Sir."

"Make it snappy."

Infected now with Darling's sense of urgency, Ames hurried across the street and down toward the station.

"Sergeant O'Brien, could you relieve Terrell and make sure Mrs. Harold has everything she needs," he said as he burst through the station door.

Something in Ames's demeanour caused the usually ponderous O'Brien to almost leap from his stool. "What's happened?"

"There's a body," Ames said in a low voice.

Raising his eyebrows with a shake of his head, and sighing at the sinfulness of man, O'Brien disappeared into the interview room. In the next moment, Terrell came out. "Sir?"

"The boss needs you up there to secure the scene right away. Dead guy. And keep people out of the alley. There's a live wire hanging off the back of the building."

"Sir." Constable Terrell, ex-military police as he was, just managed not to salute his superior officer, but was otherwise crisp efficiency and dispatch. He was out the door in seconds.

Waiting for Terrell, Darling thought about the sequence of events. The thief had come in the back door, found the owner at work, killed him, and then . . . torn the office apart and gone through to the shop, creating a din and helping himself. Then he'd run out the back door. To a car he'd parked right behind in the alley? Or had he killed Harold, gone through to the display cases, and then torn the office apart on his way out? But why did it look as if there'd been no actual struggle? It looked for all the world

11

as if Harold had been dispatched while he was quietly finishing up some paperwork.

It was at this point that he remembered Ashford Gillingham, their usual medical man, had inconsiderately gone off on holiday with his wife.

Terrell appeared by his side.

"Ah. Good. Come with me," Darling said, and led the way around the block and into the alley behind the shop. Pulling the keys from his pocket, he opened the rear door and led Terrell to the office where Mr. Harold sat, his head collapsed on the desk, the blood from his final experience of this life congealing around the wound in his skull.

"Do you know this man, sir?" Terrell asked, standing with his hands behind his back, as if to remind himself not to touch anything.

"I do. It's the owner of the store, Ronald Harold. His wife thinks he's in Vancouver."

"It looks like he came in at night, or the early hours," observed Terrell.

Darling saw at once what he meant. The dead man was wearing a trench coat over his suit, and furthermore, it was still a bit damp, as if he'd been in the thick of the downpour. He'd been so focused on the damage to the victim's skull that he hadn't noticed his clothing.

"Yes, well done. I expect you're right. When did that downpour stop?"

"I couldn't say, sir. But I did wake up around 4:00 AM and it had stopped by then."

"So, he comes in last night, planning to work. Someone kills him before he has time to take off his coat. Unless he

12

was keeping it on because it was cold, or he only wanted to stay a short time. He was supposed to be going to Vancouver. Does it look to you like there was a struggle?"

Terrell looked around the shambolic office. "At first sight, yes, sir, but I see what you're suggesting. It's not really like the man and his killer had wrestled. It looks more like he was killed where he sat and then the killer started looking for something."

Darling grunted agreement. "Lock up and go round the front to keep people away from the temptation of peering in the windows. Gilly's away. We have to get someone else."

"Yes, sir."

BACK AT THE station, Darling called Ames into his office. "How's that man's poor wife?"

"Well, she's upset about the robbery still. Even O'Brien's famous bedside manner will not do any good when she learns about her husband."

"Hmm," Darling agreed. "I've just remembered Gilly's away on vacation. We'll have to find someone else."

"All done, sir." Ames looked at a small piece of notepaper in his hand. "The hospital has someone on hand, as it happens. There's a Dr. Miyazaki who is visiting from Lillooet, and he actually has experience with this sort of thing. They just called back a moment ago, and he's on his way here."

"Oh, well then," Darling said, a little surprised. It was only a short time ago during the war that Japanese Canadians were *personae non gratae*, as it were. "Good. That's lucky. By the way, sharp-eyed Terrell noticed his raincoat was damp. That might help us with placing the time."

13

Ames had a proprietary interest in Terrell, underling and newish though he was, because he considered him something of a friend. He was also Nelson's first Black police officer. "Good catch on his part, then."

"Yup," Darling said, but noted with approval that Ames seemed genuinely pleased and was feeling no jealousy about Terrell's often trenchant observations.

"You're sure it's him, sir?"

Still trying to collect himself after the gruesome discovery, Darling resisted the urge to be sarcastic this time. "I am. I bought my wife's engagement and wedding rings from him. Of course, we'll need Mrs. Harold to identify him officially, but not until Dr. Miyazaki has had a look."

Darling turned to the pressing matter of telling the poor man's wife. How to say it? He imagined going back for the ledgers and going over the inventory with her, without telling her just yet. No. He shook his head to clear the nonsense. He was being ridiculous. He would have to tell her at once. He just dreaded it, as he always did when he had to tell anyone that a loved one had died, especially in so gruesome a manner.

"When Dr. Miyazaki comes, get O'Brien to let us know. We have to go and talk to Mrs. Harold."

"Yes, sir," Ames said, relieved that delivering such terrible news was not his job this time.

Pulling firmly at the hem of his jacket, Darling led the way downstairs.

CHAPTER TWO

"I **T CAN'T BE HIM! YOU** must be wrong. He's on his way
to Vancouver! No, he's there by now!" Mrs. Harold
was clutching her cup of tea on the table with both hands
as if to anchor herself, but her hands began to shake, and
tea splashed over her fingers. She pulled her hands away
and put them in her lap. "Please! You must check again!"
Shaking her head, she asked, "What was he even doing
there? He was supposed to be on the road."

The interview room, while hardly welcoming, was the
only place Mrs. Harold could have some privacy. Darling
was sitting kitty-corner to her at the small table. "I know
your husband, Mrs. Harold. I'm afraid there is no mistake. We will, of course, have to have you make a formal
identification."

She wheeled on him. "But how? How could he just die
like that?"

Darling struggled with what to say next. It was patently
obvious how he died; however, the victim had not undergone

a post-mortem, so Darling did not, strictly speaking, have complete information.

"Was it his heart? He has a bad heart. The doctor *told* him to slow down. And he smokes way too much. I'm sure it's bad for you, whatever people say. That's why I didn't want him going off to Vancouver like that, but he said he had to, for the business."

"We're not sure of all the details as yet, Mrs. Harold. It does look as though someone . . . struck him," Darling said after a pause.

The blood drained from Mrs. Harold's face, and she looked for a moment as if she would faint. She reached for the edge of the table as if she were making a great effort of will not to pass out. "Struck him?" she croaked. "What do you mean, 'struck him'? Who's going to strike him?"

"We aren't sure at the moment. Is there anyone with whom your husband has had a disagreement?"

"My husband doesn't have disagreements. He gets along with everybody!" As if the news was only now beginning to reach her awareness, tears welled up and she seemed to sink into the chair. "I've never seen him have a disagreement with anyone in my life," she said in a low voice.

"Who can we ask to come and be with you, Mrs. Harold?" Ames asked. He had been sitting opposite her taking very discreet notes.

She shook her head miserably. "My cousin's wife, I guess. She's up the hill past the hospital. I . . . I don't drive. Barbara Dee."

At that moment there was a soft knock on the door; Ames opened it and turned to nod at Darling.

"I'll leave Sergeant Ames here to look after you. May I telephone her?"

"Her number is 344X."

Ames nodded. Darling said, "The medical examiner is here, Mrs. Harold. I may be able to tell you more soon."

Mrs. Harold stood up, shaking the table slightly. "Can I see him now?"

"Not just yet. We'll need to go over the scene as closely as possible so that we can try to understand the sequence of events. Do you mind talking with Sergeant Ames? Just tell him as much as you can about his movements, his associates, his friends, any other family members. Anything might help."

Back upstairs, Darling found Dr. Miyazaki. He was of a slight build with receding dark hair and had a long face with a generous mouth. He wore a grey suit and stood perfectly still, watching Darling.

"Dr. Miyazaki, it's so good of you to come. I'm Inspector Darling, Nelson Police." Darling offered his hand, which was taken up by Miyazaki briefly.

"Masajiro Miyazaki. I am only too happy to help where I can." He smiled suddenly. "Luckily I have my camera." He held this up. "I often take pictures as part of my analysis."

"Excellent. You clearly have experience with this. Where have you come from?"

"Lillooet. I am here to meet with one of your local doctors on a toxicology case. He has the expertise I don't have. Tell me about your victim."

"I can do better than that. Come. He's just up the street." He led Dr. Miyazaki out the door. "Your practice is in

Lillooet?" Darling asked as they made their way to the jewellery shop.

"And anywhere horse, truck, or train can take me. I've been there since the war. I was interned nearby at Bridge River, and when the only doctor in the area died, they asked me to come and take over. Not everyone has been happy, as you can imagine, but I am grateful to the imagination of whoever it was that didn't want to waste the skills of a practitioner on a faulty principle. I am an osteopath, but I've done some of everything, including pathology. I always imagined such a place when I was a boy in Japan. We had these ideas about the 'wild west.' It has not disappointed! Well, not completely, of course. I did not expect citizens would be interned by the government. But a wonderful place, nonetheless."

"It must be very hard going in the winter. I've heard the roads can be impassable," Darling commented.

Dr. Miyazaki smiled. "I have devised a sort of ambulance from one of those single rail-track cars. It's been useful many times when the roads are blocked!"

"An inventor as well," Darling said with admiration. "This way." He indicated the store across the street.

They arrived to find that the crowd had dwindled to a few curious passersby who stopped to stare at both Terrell and the store he was guarding. Tom Booker stood on his own with his hands in the pockets of his filthy overcoat, his mouth working under his ragged beard.

"What's goin' on?" he called out to Darling, his words slurring.

Darling stopped and excused himself and came as

close to Booker as he dared. "Have you been up all night, Mr. Booker? Did you see anything?" He tilted his head toward the store.

"Not me, no sir. I mind my own business." He turned and shuffled down the street, flapping a hand dismissively.

Darling shook his head at the insoluble problem of the Tom Bookers of this world, spit out broken by the Great War and left to rattle through the rest of their days on the edges of society. He sighed and returned to the doctor. "Dr. Miyazaki, this is Constable Terrell, our newest recruit on the force."

Terrell offered his hand, and nodded to the slight bow the doctor made as they shook hands. "How do you do, sir?"

"Very well, thank you, Constable. How are you enjoying Nelson?"

"I'm very happy here, sir. It's a good community. Well, I mean usually. Not for poor Mr. Harold in there, I'm afraid."

"No indeed," agreed the doctor.

"We'll go around the back, Doctor," Darling said, taking the set of keys out of his pocket.

"Sir, I think we ought to get the window boarded up. Anyone could go in at night and take what's left. If you're here for a few minutes, I'd like to arrange for someone to come from Dean's Lumber."

"Good idea. Get a No Trespassing sign as well. Off you go, then. And get the van boys lined up to get Mr. Harold out of here."

Darling led Dr. Miyazaki around into the alley and thence to the office. The sun was nearly directly overhead now,

19

and Darling pulled the curtains back from the window in the office to let in more light. "Electricity off, I'm afraid."

The doctor stood looking at the victim. Harold had fallen straight forward when he'd been struck, and his forehead rested on the desk. Blood had trailed through his hair and down his neck and dried in uneven black lines on his skin. Darkening stains showed where blood had dripped onto the collar of his white shirt. Dr. Miyazaki took out his camera and shot several pictures of the scene as a whole.

"He was hit very hard with something that cratered his skull here," he said, pointing to where the wound gaped a little to the right of centre on the upper part of Harold's head. He looked toward the door. "Perhaps the assailant came through the door over there and hit him before he was aware someone had come in. The victim would have passed into unconsciousness almost immediately. I expect it did not take long for him to die. There was a robbery, I suppose, judging by the mess. What time do you guess this took place?"

"Last night some time, we think. It was raining heavily, and his coat is still damp."

Miyazaki nodded and looked at the floor. "Nothing clear in the way of footprints." He reached into his pocket and pulled out a pair of rubber gloves. Mr. Harold's hands were resting on the desk, on either side of his head, as if he'd been leaning on both elbows when he was struck. Dr. Miyazaki gently lifted the man's fingers and then gave the foot under the chair a light kick. "As you can see, there is still some give in the fingers and the feet from the ankle, so complete rigour has not set in. It is not an exact science, I'm afraid, whatever Sherlock may say; however, I would say this man died somewhere between ten last night and, say, two in the morning?"

Ten, Darling thought in surprise. "His wife said he was in Vancouver. She can't understand why he was here, or how he came to die here. At ten," he added. "What was he doing here?"

"That must be a rhetorical question, Inspector. I'm afraid no medical science can answer it. What I see is that he was perhaps working at his desk, concentrating so that he did not hear his attacker's approach. It doesn't look to me like more than one blow was delivered here." He took up a pencil from the desk and parted some of the blood-caked hair to one side so that Darling could see. "You see here? These shattered edges are all from that one strike, and it was powerful enough to have driven in a good two or three inches. A right-handed blow, judging by the location just right of the midline here."

Darling closed his eyes for a moment and then peered at the unsavoury mix of smashed bone and brain. The one thing about Gilly was that he didn't require so much participation, he thought. "I don't think a hammer would have done that," he suggested. "Unless it was wielded by Paul Bunyan."

Miyazaki smiled almost cheerfully. "Ah yes, the American folk hero. I learned about him while I was at medical school in the United States."

"He might not be American after all. I read that the real-life person was a French Canadian lumberjack. But this was not an axe," Darling suggested, getting back to the task at hand.

"No. That might have cleaved his skull. I am going to suggest something like a cobbler's hammer. Not a regular hammer, I don't think. The claw of the shoemaker's tool is longer than that of a normal hammer. You see, it has gone in quite far. Failing that, an upholsterer's tack hammer? The wound is the right size and shape, but the instrument would have been wielded with a great deal of force because it is relatively light. A geological sample pick, perhaps? They have the right sort of shape but are heavier. Whatever it was accomplished the task in one blow and made a second one unnecessary. I hope I can tell you more after my investigation."

"I CAN'T UNDERSTAND it," Gwen said. "There's absolutely nothing up here. I can't think what would explode like that."

Lane, who was puffing slightly from the steady uphill climb through dense and still-wet underbrush and thick forest, noticed that neither Gwen nor Mabel was breathing heavily at all. They had been climbing for almost half an hour, winding through the trees and stepping through bracken and years of accumulated twigs and branches. "Do you come up here often?"

"Mabel more than I do. She comes up with the dogs and sits on that outcrop over there like one of those swamis." Gwen pointed through the trees to where, about twenty yards farther, the dense growth of trees thinned, and the sky brightened the edge of the shadowy forest.

"You can laugh at me," Mabel said, "but it gives me perspective. You ought to try it sometime."

They had been keeping a steady pace. Even with the path Mabel and the dogs had made, it was rough going. It was steep in parts, and trees made it difficult to see if they were going in the right direction.

"There's a clearing up ahead. We should be able to see where that smoke is coming from."

Lane was relieved to be out in the full daylight and she took a breath. The smell of burning hit her suddenly.

"We must be close! I can smell the smoke." She looked over the tops of the trees across the clearing. "Over there!"

Although it was no longer as thick and black as what they'd seen from the house, there was still a trail of smoke rising a little to the left and above them.

They hurried across the clearing and plunged back into the trees toward the smoke, now without the benefit of Mabel's path.

"It must be close," Lane began, when they all heard a faint cry.

They stopped in their tracks. After a long silence in which there was nothing but the soft rustling of the trees, it came again.

"It sounds like a child!" Lane said, horrified. She plunged ahead toward an open area where the dark billows of smoke they'd seen from below were dissipating into a thin coil of yellowy vapour. The cry had come from the far side of what looked like another clearing.

The cocker spaniels, low to the ground, coursed through the underbrush. The scene that greeted the party was hellish. A deep cratered rend in the earth, with trees blown down in an arc, splintered and tangled, and scorched underbrush. The rank smell of the explosion struck Lane at once. Not just the charred flora but something more chemical. There were little licks of flame scattered in the blast area coming out of a considerable pile of ash. The previous night's rain looked to be keeping the flames from spreading.

Lane looked desperately for the source of the human sound, but all she could see was the destruction of this bit of forest. She saw the dogs flit forward and stumbled after them. Pushing through the underbrush, she saw her—a little girl of no more than nine or ten years lying on her side, looking as though she'd been tossed there by a careless giant.

"She's almost passed out," Lane exclaimed, kneeling beside the little figure. She was reluctant to touch her until she'd ascertained what sort of injuries she had. It was an enormous relief to see that no limbs had been blown off, but her left leg lay unnaturally, and her foot was badly burned, as was a good deal of her right arm. She was wearing a pair of shorts and a little cotton T-shirt with orange and red stripes that was badly burned and torn by the explosion. There might be more burning under that, Lane thought. The girl's thick dark braids appeared undamaged, though her eyebrows and the fringe on her forehead were singed. Her shoes were nowhere to be seen, and the undamaged foot had only a sock hanging off it. Then Lane frowned. Some of the damage on her legs looked like it had been caused by shrapnel. Wartime wounds. She looked around briefly. Surely not? But shrapnel could shatter a bone, which might explain her obviously broken leg.

"She looks Chinese," Gwen said falteringly. "Why . . . ?" She looked around at the vast empty forest in puzzlement.

"Canteen," snapped Mabel.

Gwen fetched it out of the bag and handed it to Lane, who very gingerly placed an arm under the girl's neck and lifted her head to try to induce her to drink. At the feel of the water the little girl's lips moved, and they could see that some was slipping down her throat.

"I don't think there's much in my bag that can do any good just now," said Mabel.

"You're all right now," Lane said softly to the child, though she was herself very unconvinced of this. An explosion, she knew, could do untold internal damage as well. "We'll get you to help."

"Look," said Gwen, taking off the enormous denim shirt she wore over her clothes most days. "The two of you could carry her out of here, at least to the track along the upper orchard. You could make a sort of sling out of my shirt. I'm going to stamp out those flames here and then get back down to call Robin Harris—"

"Oh, he's going to be no end of help," Mabel said.

"Wait, if you don't mind," Gwen continued with asperity. "I'll get him to meet you at the road so he can drive her back to the house. I'll also call the ambulance. That's going to take at least an hour, if not more, from town, but it will take time to get her out of here."

"Good thinking, Gwen," Lane said. "Before you go, could you just look around the perimeter of this crater to see if there is anyone else? I can't understand why this little girl is here on her own." Gwen nodded and set off around the edge of the burned area.

"On second thought," Lane said, as they laid the shirt out next to the injured girl, "my car is at yours, so I could drive her into town with no wait at all."

"There's no one else here," Gwen called. "It's very peculiar. Why *was* she here alone?" She set about putting out what flames could be seen in the centre of the crater, though most were dying on their own in the dampness of the morning. "This is peculiar too. It looks like just a pile of paper caught fire. I guess everything else is too wet."

Mabel and Lane discussed how best to use the shirt and settled on laying the girl across the middle of the shirt so that there was a sleeve and a shirt tail at either side of her head and feet. Grasped tightly together, these would make a fairly stable hammock for the trip down the mountain. The little girl was painfully slight and had made no sound since the cry that had alerted them to her being there. Lane wondered if she would have the strength to survive whatever had happened.

"And, Gwen, my husband has some kit from his flying days. It's on the top shelf of a little cupboard in the hall. A khaki bag. Could you get down to mine and pick it up? I don't know what's in it, but maybe something to protect her hand and foot while we get her to hospital. Here are my car keys." She realized that what Gwen was proposing about Robin Harris and his tractor made sense; Lane's car would never get onto the rough track at the upper end of the orchard. He could drive their little patient down to the house. "And do get Harris as quick as you can. And here, take my bag."

Gwen hurried off, the bag bumping against her side. "Come on, you!" she called to the dogs. The two spaniels looked up from where they were sniffing, and one obediently trotted after Gwen, but the other had moved farther afield and had his nose to the ground.

"Come on, Eddie. Leave that!" Gwen barked. She'd started down the hill but turned again. "Eddie, no one needs you here. Come!" With evident reluctance, the spaniel gave a bark at some ravens that had settled in a nearby tree and trotted after his mistress.

LANE GAVE THE little girl more water and talked soothingly to her. Then she said, "What is your name? Mine is Lane, and this is Mabel."

The girl didn't open her eyes, but her lips moved fractionally.

"Now, we're going to put you into a nice little hammock, and we're going to carry you down as gently as possible. I want you to tell us if anything hurts too much, all right?"

The girl still did not open her eyes, but it was possible that she had nodded almost imperceptibly, or had Lane imagined it? Had the blast somehow affected her eyes or her hearing? Lane wondered. She was clearly in shock. They would have to hurry.

Wishing she'd worn a cardigan or jumper she could cover the child with, Lane positioned her arms under the girl's shoulders and hips while Mabel supported her legs so they wouldn't flop around, and they lifted her as slowly as they could. "There we are," she said softly, but the girl began to whimper as soon as she was raised. "Just another second, dear," Lane responded. Then, with relief, they settled her into the middle of the shirt.

Lane wanted to let the child rest for a moment, to briefly recover from the ordeal of being moved, but she knew they had no time to waste. She nodded at Mabel, and the two of them each took up their end of the impromptu stretcher and began the slow journey down the hill.

Gwen had not seen under the mess of felled trees and bushes when she'd been stamping out the fire. In fairness, the dead woman there was completely invisible underneath it.

CHAPTER THREE

"TELL ME ABOUT MR. HAROLD. Did you meet him here?" Ames asked.

Mrs. Harold kept glancing nervously at the door, but she did finally turn and look at him. "Yes. I was born and brought up here. Ronald's family came from the old country before the Great War. He moved here when he was a little boy. I met him in 1921. He was so handsome." She stopped.

Ames waited. It was as though the truth had finally come through that her husband was dead.

She looked up at him, her eyes reddening. "You have to find the person who did this," she said. And after another long pause, "Why was he there? If he hadn't been there, he would be alive." She shook her head. "He likes to make the trip at night because there's less traffic on the roads. I . . . I didn't know he was stopping at the shop."

"What time did he leave your house?"

"Twenty after nine, maybe. I was going to stay up and listen to the news on the wireless. Maybe Marty . . ."

"Marty. Who is he?"

Mrs. Harold nodded, as if in tacit approval of this change in direction. "Martin Humphries. They met in the army. They were in the same unit. I can't remember now. They both came from Cornwall, you know, on the coast. Funny thing was, they discovered they were distant cousins. Second once removed or something. I never understand that sort of thing." She hesitated and appeared about to cry again. "We were going to go back to visit, but we never did. In fact, he'd been talking about going just in the last few months. I never met his people." She paused. "Well, except his little brother, Bill, but he signed up in '39 and was killed when the ship he was going over on was torpedoed."

"So, he had no other family here?"

She shook her head.

"Martin Humphries is the locksmith," Ames remembered suddenly.

"That's right. He has a little place near the jam factory on Vernon. Oh! He has to be told. He'll be wild. They were inseparable," she said, wringing her hands. "I don't think I . . . I don't think I . . ."

"It's all right, Mrs. Harold. I'll want to talk to him in any case. He may be able to help us."

He was going to have to ask, he knew it. "Mrs. Harold, can you think of why your husband might have gone to the store?"

She looked up at him, and Ames could see from her expression that she couldn't even understand the question. What she couldn't understand, he knew, was her husband's behaviour, his death.

30

"Tell me about his trips. Was it usual for him to go out to Vancouver as part of the business?" Ames tried.

This seemed to pull her back from the brink. "Yes, that's right. He would go on buying trips. The longer ones were a couple of times a year, out to Vancouver, you know. Well, during the war. It was harder to get stock. It used to be more like once a year. And then, of course, he'd make the rounds of the local towns."

"The rounds?" Ames asked. He could understand buying trips to a large city, though he wondered if the volume of jewellery sold could really require two such trips. But why to smaller communities?

"Yes, you know, to meet with other jewellers and so on. Day trips, like. I suppose to discuss trends and trade a bit. That's how he explained it. Of course, most of his business in town was jewellery and watch repair, that sort of thing. Sometimes he had shorter trips to deliver things he fixed to people with no car who had a hard time getting into town. I stay here to hold the fort."

Ames nodded. "He did good work. My mother had a necklace repaired by your husband. He restrung a pearl necklace when it broke. He did a very nice job."

"Oh, yes," Mrs. Harold said. "That's always a very time-consuming repair. He would have to put a knot between each pearl to really make sure all the pearls wouldn't be lost if the string broke." Relating the details of the repair seemed to calm her slightly.

"And you worked in the shop?" He wasn't sure where this line of questioning might lead, but he never learned the answer as there was a knock on the door frame.

"There's a Mrs. Dee here, Sergeant, for the lady," O'Brien said quietly, nodding in Mrs. Harold's direction.

Ames rose and thanked him. Hovering just in the hall was a tall and not unattractive woman of middle years, wearing a pale green, light summer coat and an almost-matching brimmed hat of some twenty years' vintage, which still looked smart on her. "Mrs. Dee?"

"Yes. Dear God, how is she?"

"She'll be happy to see you, I'm sure." She struck Ames as a no-nonsense sort of woman, who might be just the ticket for this situation. "Come on through."

"Wait. Has she seen him yet?"

"Not yet. They are still investigating the scene. The medical man and Inspector Darling."

"With your permission, I'd like to take her home and look after her. When you need her for anything, you can call and we'll come back."

Ames felt that he'd run the course on his interview for the moment and could not envision how long it would take for the pathologist to get the body to the morgue and do whatever it was those people did. He agreed with Mrs. Dee's plan, and then mentally crossed his fingers that he was right.

As the two women were leaving, Mrs. Harold gave herself over completely to tears of grief and confusion.

Ames sighed and stretched, then went up to his office to compose his notes onto his foolscap pad. Harold had no enemies, as far as his wife knew, and his best friend was Martin Humphries, who was some sort of cousin whom he met during the Great War. Harold had moved to Canada as a child, and he had had a much younger brother named Bill who signed up in '39 and was killed when the ship taking them overseas was torpedoed. No other immediate family alive. And he had left his home at quarter to ten.

Ames looked at what he'd written. The thing he found surprising was how often the jeweller was away "for the business." There were a couple of trips to Vancouver a year, and then, Mrs. Harold had said, a number of smaller trips to small towns around the province. She'd acted as if these were perfectly normal, but Ames couldn't see why a jeweller needed to travel to all these other places. So, Mr. Harold had managed to spend a good deal of time away. Ames wondered why.

"OF COURSE, THE poor tyke probably can't really hear anything," Mabel commented as they picked their way back down the mountain. The edge of the upper orchard was just visible below them.

"No, you're right. I've been near blasts, the London bombing, you know, and it can take a little while for the hearing to come back." Lane knew people who'd suffered permanent loss of hearing and earnestly hoped that would not be true for this little girl. How close had she been to whatever had blown up? And what the heck was it that had exploded? She looked up. The temperature had increased and a few wisps of clouds floated overhead, as though it were just any other lovely day.

Their progress was slow because they wanted to jostle her as little as possible. Lane looked at the girl constantly and wanted to stop and make sure she was all right, but she knew it would be better to get her to safety quickly. Long before they arrived at the orchard's edge, they heard Harris's tractor toiling up the hill and then stopping.

Suddenly the girl made a sound like a small animal cry, and both women stopped. She lay deep in the fold of their makeshift stretcher, her face just visible, and her dark eyes were open, staring at Lane, wide and uncomprehending.

"You're awake," Lane said softly. "You've had an accident, and we're getting you to help. You're going to be all right." She nodded at Mabel. "It's not far now. Just close your eyes and try to rest." She demonstrated by closing her own.

Robin Harris, King's Cove's grizzled curmudgeon who lived near the turnoff up to the hamlet from the main road, was standing beside his tractor waiting for them with a damp, shredding, hand-rolled cigarette between his lips. The minute he caught sight of them, he threw the cigarette down, ground it out with the toe of his boot, and hurried forward holding his arms out.

"Here, give that to me."

"Careful," Mabel said. "She's in a bad way."

Scowling at her admonition, Harris took the whole bundle in his arms, and looked at the girl as the shirt fell away. He shook his head. "It's too bumpy on the tractor. Mabel, drive the tractor back; I'll carry her to the house. And we'd better hurry. Poor kid." He started immediately in the direction of the Hughes house, taking long strides in his rubber boots between two rows of apple trees.

Lane trotted after him, trying to keep an eye on the girl's face, but she had closed her eyes again.

34

They moved quickly without speaking through the upper orchard, across a strip of sunlit meadow grass, and into the next orchard. The apple trees were already covered in the tiny green beads that would grow to become King's Cove's main source of revenue by September.

When they came out into the garden, they found Gwen waiting with a canvas bag in hand and a raised umbrella, which she hurried to hold over Harris and his young burden to block out the sun. Lane rushed to her car and then opened the door so that the girl could be placed on the seat in the back. "I'm going to drive her in; it will take far less time than waiting for the ambulance. Gwen, let's see what's in the bag. I think there might be burn gloves with some sort of ointment or something."

Lane unclasped the bag, finding what she might expect: rolls of gauze, various bottles of pills, and then boric acid ointment for burns. Should she put this on her? She cast her mind back to her first aid training. Cover the burns with clean gauze, no ointment. Pulling more things out of the bag, she found big folds of gauze. There was a pair of yellow gloves coated on the inside with something. Darling had talked about the importance of these as part of an airman's kit. The gloves and ointment would have been for airmen wounded in crashes, far from help. Deciding against them, as the girl would be helped at the end of the hour it would take to get her to town, she opened the folds of gauze and placed them gently over the angry burns. She watched the girl's face. She did not respond. This caused Lane to anxiously feel for her pulse. Still beating.

"She seems to be unconscious. Merciful, under the circumstances," she said.

Gladys had come from the house and now stood holding a couple of blankets. "You'll want these," she said.

Lane took the blankets. "I want to be able to keep her warm for the shock, but I don't want to put anything over those burns besides the gauze." She carefully positioned one blanket over the upper part of her body, leaving the burned arm free. "That's going to have to do. I'd better get off."

"I couldn't believe what Gwen was telling me," Gladys said. "Why would she be up there by herself?"

"Can you call the hospital and tell them to expect me? Tell them she is unconscious but has a steady pulse, and that she has a badly burned foot, likely a broken leg, a burned arm, and possible other damage. Tell them she was near an explosion." Lane got into the car and immediately wished the blankets didn't smell quite so robustly of mothballs.

Mabel came from the house with the army canteen, which she'd refilled. "Hope it doesn't spring a leak." She handed it in to Lane.

Harris had come around to the passenger door and was looking at the girl. Gently he reached over and tucked the blanket a little more securely around her. "Canteen!" he commanded, holding out his hand.

Lane handed it over and Harris, with infinite care, lifted the girl's head enough to feed a little water onto her parched lips. He gave a brisk little nod of satisfaction at watching the water trickle into her mouth. He gave her a little more and capped the canteen, backing out of the car and putting it on the passenger seat. "She's not unconscious, but she's just holding on," he said. "Now, you stop on the way a couple of times and give her water," he ordered.

She nodded. Harris's peremptory manner was reassuring; he sounded as if he knew what he was doing, and she was grateful. Perhaps he was drawing from his own battleground experience, distant though the Great War now was.

Gladys shook her head and turned back to the house, when they had watched Lane disappear down their driveway. "Who the devil *is* she?" she asked no one in particular. "I've got the kettle on."

Harris leaned his elbows glumly on the kitchen table while Gwen poured hot water into the teapot. He'd equipped himself with another hand-rolled cigarette, and it rested on his lip, smoke lazily rising to the ceiling. "Who'd let a little thing wander by herself in the forest?"

Mabel looked at him in surprise. She'd poured some milk into a creamer and was putting it on the table. He sounded positively gentle. "You're taking it a bit hard," she said. He didn't respond but sat up straight and drew on his cigarette and then knocked the ash into an ashtray.

"What would someone like that be doing out there on the mountain anyway?" Gladys asked.

"Someone like what?" Harris surprised them all by asking. His tone was combative. That, at least, was normal for him.

"Well, you know, a little Chinese or Japanese girl, whatever she is. The Japanese must have all left those camps by now and gone back to the coast, and there are no Chinese families anywhere around. Not around here. They're more up near town."

Harris, already looking thunderous, said, "What does it matter what she is? She's a little girl. Someone's going to have to find her people. She's all alone just now."

"All right, all right," Gladys said, trying to pacify him. "I didn't mean anything by it. I just don't understand."

"That doesn't surprise me," Harris said morosely.

"Mother, what did the police say when you called?" Gwen said, wanting to change the subject, though she, like her mother and sister, was very surprised at Harris's attitude. She'd never known him to express concern for another living human out loud, for all he helped them with the orchards, and came to their aid with plumbing and house repairs whenever they needed it.

"They told me to call the RCMP as there's some sort of crisis on at the police station, and the Mounties said they were on a case up Lardeau way and couldn't get out right now. They wanted to know if there was any danger of fire, and I said I didn't think so. There wasn't, was there?"

Mabel shook her head. "The ground was soaked. Gwen stamped out the few flickers of fire. It was barely even smoking by the time we got there."

ONCE LANE HAD cleared King's Cove, she went as fast as she dared on the gravel main road to Nelson, crossing her fingers that she would not be stuck behind logging trucks or tractors, impediments that could add a good twenty minutes to the nearly hour-long drive into town. Praying that the girl would not die—indeed, was not already dead—Lane rested her left arm on the window ledge. She had time, at last, to think about what on earth could have happened way up the side of the mountain, where nothing and no one were meant to be.

TERRELL AND SEVERAL passersby watched the boarding up of the jewellery store's window. Both the greengrocer and someone from the laundry were outside, leaning on their door frames, arms crossed. "What happened?" asked a young mother with a baby asleep in an expensive-looking pram.

"Break-in, ma'am."

The woman frowned and looked around. "In the middle of the day?"

He shook his head. "Last night."

"Poor Mr. and Mrs. Harold! It's shocking that something like this could happen in Nelson."

"I agree. It's surprising." Terrell was indeed surprised. He'd come to know Nelson as a small and more or less tolerant town where this sort of thing ought not to happen.

"Well, I hope something is being done about it," the young woman said, walking on, as if suspicious that the police, or Terrell in particular, might shirk their duty.

"Yes, ma'am." Terrell nodded and touched the rim of his cap, wondering what she'd think when she learned that Mr. Harold had been found dead in his office.

That news did not take long to get around when the hospital van was driven around the corner and into the alley. The man from the laundry said something to someone inside and bolted up the street and into the mouth of the alley to watch. He was not alone. The progress of people walking down toward Baker Street was arrested by the urgency of the activity behind the store, and they stood, watching and murmuring.

"Someone broke into the store, but that van means someone's maybe been hurt."

They were rewarded in due course by the appearance of a shrouded figure on a stretcher carried by two men, who loaded it into the back of the van.

"'Scuse me, move please," someone said, pushing through. It was Dillon, the photographer from the *Nelson Daily News*. He sprinted toward the van with his camera and began to take pictures of the van, the body disappearing into it, the back of the store, and then of Inspector Darling and Dr. Miyazaki emerging from the back of the shop. Darling locked the door and prepared for the journalist's assault.

"What's happened here? Someone been hurt?" Dillon asked. His camera now loose and hanging by its strap on his neck, he'd taken out a notebook. "Is it true someone broke into the store?"

"Well, if you saw *who* broke into the store, that would be helpful," Darling remarked.

"Sorry. Who's that?" The journalist nodded at the now closed rear doors of the van.

"I'm afraid I can't say at the moment," Darling said, gently touching Dr. Miyazaki's elbow to guide him past the throng and back toward the police station.

"And you are?" Dillon said to the doctor.

Under normal circumstances, Darling would not have bothered to answer any of Dillon's rude questions, but he didn't want the doctor badgered. "This is Dr. Miyazaki, the medical examiner who is helping in our investigation. Thank you."

"*Medical* examiner?" Dillon said, staring at Dr. Miyazaki.

Darling indicated the conclusion of the interview and said no more. On the street, he caught Terrell's attention and jerked his head in the direction of the police station. Once they were safely inside, he gave a slight sigh. "O'Brien?"

"Yes, sir. Mrs. Harold has been collected by a friend and will be available to identify the body when you are ready."

Darling nodded his thanks and turned to Dr. Miyazaki. "I'll run you up to the hospital now. We have a little morgue here, but you might be more comfortable there, so I've sent the van there."

"Thank you, Inspector. I am happy anywhere, I assure you. You would be quite astonished at the places I have done my work!"

Darling smiled. "I'm sure I would. O'Brien, let Ames know I'll be back shortly. Doctor?"

Dr. Miyazaki nodded courteously to Sergeant O'Brien and followed Darling out to the car.

Shaking his head, O'Brien watched them out the front window. "Well, I'll be," he said out loud. "Seems okay."

CHAPTER FOUR

L ANE DROVE THE WINDING STREET up to the hospital, and pulled to a stop as close to the doors as she could. A van had beat her to the very front of the doors, but she squeezed next to it, and taking a look at her passenger, her fingers crossed that she was still among the living, she ran inside to the front desk.

The young woman looked up when Lane, not waiting for a greeting, said urgently, "I'm Lane Winslow. I have a young girl—"

"Oh, yes!" the young woman said, taking the phone. "They're expecting you." She spoke into the receiver while Lane looked out through the glass doors at her car. The last stop they'd made, to wait for the ferry, had been encouraging. Lane had drizzled a little water between the girl's lips, and again, it seemed to go down. She wasn't unconscious. Lane was sure that she had done absolutely everything you shouldn't do for someone in her state and wondered if she'd been foolish not to wait for an ambulance. She shook her head slightly. It really could have taken ages for them to get there, especially if it were on another call. She thought about her own field experience with explosions. She had done what she remembered a medic doing when Layla had been badly hurt by the hand grenade in the farmhouse in Bretagne. Why couldn't she remember the name of the village?

"Miss Winslow, you made good time." A tall angular woman was addressing her as a gurney was wheeled toward the doors. "Dr. Edison."

"Of course, Dr. Edison." Edison was the only female doctor at the hospital. A woman doctor was unusual in itself, but Dr. Edison herself was unusual; during the war she had commanded an Air Force medical unit. Now she seemed most involved with emergencies and urgent cases brought into the hospital. "Yes, we were lucky. No trucks. I don't know what sort of condition she's in. I'm afraid I sort of ran on instinct and memory, but I've probably done all the wrong things. I'm sure treatment for shock and burns has progressed since the war."

She hurried out to the car and opened the door so they could get the girl. Dr. Edison nodded, waiting while the girl was put on the gurney.

"Room three," she ordered and turned back to Lane. "Thank you, Miss Winslow. If you wait a bit, we can give your blanket back. Do you know the girl's name? She could be Japanese or Chinese."

Lane shook her head. "I'm afraid we know absolutely nothing about her. I don't think anyone at King's Cove has ever seen her."

"And what sort of explosion was it?"

Again, Lane shook her head. "No idea. We were so anxious to get her to safety we didn't really have time to look around. It was right out in the bush, halfway up a mountain. By all rights there shouldn't have been anything up there at all. Even at that distance it was very loud. It reminded me of a bomb more than anything. I thought I saw traces of shrapnel."

"Shrapnel?" Dr. Edison sounded surprised. "I had wondered if it was kids playing, getting hold of something they shouldn't, but shrapnel suggests something quite different."

Lane shrugged. "I don't know about kids. As I said, she is not a girl from our little hamlet. King's Cove only has three children, and none of them was up there, as far as I could tell. They'd have been in school. I can't make out why she was out there on her own."

"I'll telephone you when we know more. Can you tell Miss Cathcart there anything you can, and leave me your number?"

"Of course. Thank you, Dr. Edison." Lane watched with gratification as this competent woman hurried after the gurney. If anyone could save the little girl, it would be she.

"My word. It's been busy today!" Miss Cathcart said, shaking her head, getting ready to take Lane's information.

Lane was giving whatever information she could to Miss Cathcart and had just supplied her phone number when she was surprised to hear her husband's voice behind her.

"Darling, what's happened?" he asked her. "Has someone from King's Cove been hurt?"

"It's a little girl," she said, wondering how to compress the story. After all, he must be here on police business. And then she realized her little girl *was* police business. "Are you something to do with the van?" she asked before beginning her story about the girl.

He nodded and took her arm, pulling her away from Miss Cathcart, who had given up all pretence of being busy and was now staring intently at them. "We've had a homicide," he said, *sotto voce*. "I brought the medical examiner up here to examine the body."

"Doesn't Gilly have an office here at the hospital?"

"He's on holiday. Another fellow, a Dr. Miyazaki, is visiting from Lillooet, and he's offered to do the honours. Now. A little girl—so, not one of our Bertolli boys." Angela and David Bertolli, friends of Lane's and the resident Yanks, as the older residents of King's Cove called them, had three energetic school-aged boys.

"No, thank goodness. I don't know who she is, but she's been hurt in an explosion way up the mountain behind the Hugheses'. Dr. Edison is not sure if she is Chinese or Japanese. The Hugheses didn't recognize her. You know, I think I'd better follow you down and make a full report. I was thinking it was an accident, but the circumstances are so peculiar that I must report it. Gwen did call the RCMP, but they hadn't any men available just now."

"We already have work, no need to keep finding more," Darling said with a shade of a smile, holding the door for her. "I'm staying here to await the outcome of my corpse, found by me, by the way. I'm sure Ames would be happy to take your information." *Happy*, he knew, wouldn't cover Ames's thrill at taking a statement from her. "See you at home?"

Lane gave a rueful smile back and nodded. A murder in Nelson would not be a small thing, and the whole force, such as it was, would be engaged, and possibly the RCMP as well.

As she pulled up in front of the station, she wondered if the RCMP had some sort of specialized unit for bombs. Dr. Edison could be right; perhaps the child had been playing with a gas can or something. But that did not account for the shrapnel. She had a moment of wishing she'd had a better look at the site, but of course the little girl's life had trumped everything else. But who was she? Lane understood that she herself, still relatively new to the area, might not know her, but it was puzzling that neither the Hughes ladies nor Robin Harris had ever seen her before. Now that she was safe in the hospital, they had time to consider where her family might be.

"MRS. DARLING. GOOD to see you. We're having a busy morning," O'Brien said, and then glanced at his watch. It was past noon. He was very conscious of his mealtimes and longed to see everyone disposed properly so that he had a moment's peace to pull out his lunch box. He was sure his wife had packed him a nice chicken salad sandwich.

"You are indeed. I met the inspector up at the hospital, and I'm afraid I'll only be adding to the workload."

"That's all right, ma'am. The inspector called down. Sergeant Ames has been detailed to take your statement. Little lass, I hear."

"That's right. Very strange business. Good afternoon, Sergeant Ames." Ames had by this time bounded down the stairs and was now holding the gate open for her.

"Miss Winslow. Hello. Please come up. I bet you could use a cup of tea. I don't mind saying I could."

O'Brien nodded. "I'll send Terrell up with it," he said.

Once settled in Ames's small office, Lane looked at him and shook her head. "I honestly don't know where to start. Well," she said, deciding suddenly, "I'll start with the explosion."

Ames's eyebrows flew up. "Explosion! Right." He had his notepad at the ready.

Lane closed her eyes for a moment, saw herself sitting in her canvas chair under the weeping willow in the morning sun, and then began. "At about quarter to ten this morning . . ."

WHILE LANE HAD been driving to the station, Darling was waiting outside the morgue until Dr. Miyazaki signalled that he could come in.

"It is exactly as we surmised, Inspector Darling. Mr. Harold died from a single penetrating injury through the scalp and skull in the parietal region to the right of the midline. There is an almost square defect measuring a half inch by a half inch that suggests a small one of the tools I spoke of earlier—something like some sort of hammer with a thicker claw. In some ways, he is lucky the assailant did not elect to use the hammer end of the instrument, as it would have taken a more sustained assault to render the man dead. One blow is all that was required with the pointed end. Strong person, right-handed. The victim will not have felt anything after the first instant. There are other more technical details about blood, brain tissue, and the length of the wound track that I will write up in my report, but you have the essence."

"I see. It is difficult to imagine who would attack a jeweller with such violence and such efficiency."

Miyazaki shrugged. "That is, of course, what must be discovered. I have done my job at this terminal end of the story. It is for you to put together the narrative that has led to this sorry outcome."

"Are you going back today, Doctor?"

"I think I must. The hospital has given me an office to write up my report. I have a large and far-flung practice in Lillooet and the surrounding area, and I fear I may already be needed there. It has been a great pleasure meeting you, Inspector."

Suddenly having an idea, Darling said, "Before you go, Doctor, may I ask for your thoughts on another matter? My wife brought a little girl in a short time ago who has been injured in some sort of explosion. She is Asian, but she has not spoken, and we don't know if she is Japanese or Chinese. If she is Japanese, perhaps there is a tiny chance she is someone from one of the families you were interned with, or another family that you know."

Miyazaki shrugged. "I could see, certainly."

In the ward, Dr. Edison shook Dr. Miyazaki's hand and led him to where the girl lay, occupying so little space in the middle of the bed.

Dr. Miyazaki, hat in hand, gazed at the girl and shook his head in pity. "Poor thing. I could not say for certain if she is Japanese, but I don't think I've ever seen her before. Have you found her family? Has anyone been looking for her or contacted the police?"

Both she and Darling shook their heads. "Not yet," Darling said. "Not by the time I left the station. I hope to God they do."

OUTSIDE, THEY SHOOK hands, and Darling saw Dr. Miyazaki off before heading to the station. He did not know how a doctor of Japanese descent had found a place in society during and even after a war that had been so punishing to Japanese Canadians, but he rejoiced at it. He wondered how much other talent was being squandered by prejudice and lousy laws.

Only when he pulled into the place so recently occupied by his wife's car did he turn his mind back to her and the little girl.

At least, he thought, pushing open the station door, Lane had not found someone dead. That had been her usual practice. But a strange girl in an explosion in the mountains above King's Cove—that was going to be a story, he knew. He sincerely wished that Ames had cautioned Lane to stay away from the damned site, because he knew she'd be up there the minute she got home, but he knew that Ames would have done no such thing. His sergeant worshipped the ground Lane walked on and would not dream of being so peremptory. He hoped Lane's intrinsic good sense would prevail and could almost hear his own mental "harrumph" of doubt.

"What now, sir? The formal identification?" O'Brien asked his boss, who was standing irresolutely by his desk.

"Yes," Darling said. "I never enjoy this part."

"No, sir," O'Brien responded, shaking his head sympathetically.

THE MINUTE LANE got back to King's Cove, she drove straight to the Hughes house. She knew they would want news of the little girl. "She was still alive when I dropped her off, and that wonderful Dr. Edison received her," Lane told them. She had found the three women working outside, Gladys in the borders, Gwen shovelling the chicken coop, and Mabel reorganizing the root cellar. Now they were standing under the cherry tree at the edge of the garden, next to their defunct and rusting blue 1925 Ford. The garden had that glorious green smell that rose up as the ground dried after a rain.

"Who the devil is she?" Gladys asked. "Aside from that noisy gang of Bertollis, we've no children here."

"And why was she all the way up there?" Gwen asked.

They all looked up in the direction they had travelled; though it was mere hours ago, it felt like days had passed.

"Anything get worse up there?" Lane asked.

"Nope. We've been keeping an eye on it. It's like it never happened. There'd be trouble if something were smouldering, but I stamped everything out pretty well. I expect the rain was our friend here."

Lane turned to look at them. "So, she's no one you've ever seen before?"

"No, never. I mean, I think I know most of the children over in Balfour from the church fetes, but none of them is, you know, Eastern." Gladys dropped her voice as she said this word in a slightly conspiratorial way. "Anyway, I'm certain I've never seen this girl. And Balfour is more than three miles away. Any houses between here and there are those summer cottages down on the lake. It beggars belief that a child could have got from the lakeside up to the wilderness on her own. It would be miles of dense bush between Balfour proper and here, up at that elevation. I should think only hunters would attempt it, and they'd be on horseback," Gladys said.

"She still couldn't talk when I dropped her off, so she couldn't tell us her name, provided she even remembers it. A blast like that can wipe out your memory, at least temporarily." Lane sighed and turned back toward her car. "I'd best get home. The hospital is going to call me when they have news."

She trundled down the rutted road and then pulled onto the grass just inside her gate, leaving room for Darling to park his car when he got home. With a murder on, it would be unlikely he'd be home for supper. Which was fine. She could do him a cheese omelette and some toast using one of Mabel's magnificent loaves of brown bread. She really must begin to bake her own, she thought, getting out of the car.

It was then that she remembered that when she'd been reading peacefully in the garden all those hours ago, she'd been waiting for her washing machine to stop sloshing the clothes about so she could put them through the mangle and then hang them outside. She strolled to her front door, looking up at the sky. It should be all right to hang them outside on the clothesline. It didn't look like there would be a repeat of last night's rain. The work would keep her mind off the child.

The work did nothing of the sort. She thought of nothing but the child as she turned the handle on the roller and then slid the wrung-out clothes into her washing basket. She took them onto the little porch off the kitchen to hang them, something she quite liked doing. But her mind went to the little girl's clothes. A pair of shorts and a striped T-shirt. Her thick hair in braids. Those braids. What was it about the braids? They looked . . . not neglected, exactly, but as if she'd had them for a couple of days. But that might have been because she played in the bush; even the most carefully plaited hair would become dishevelled as a child ran about in the underbrush. And God knew what the explosion would have done. Certainly, it had singed her hair.

She pinned the last towel and rolled the line out to catch the maximum amount of late afternoon sun and then looked out at the lake. The community of King's Cove, the proper King's Cove as they all thought of it—those summer beach houses way down the hill along the lakeshore, empty most of the year and then filled with strangers during the summer—was up the hill, above the road to Nelson. Several of the properties had magnificent views of the lake and the Selkirk Mountains beyond. Hers was among them.

She shook her head and looked at her watch. Nearly three. The whole business of the morning seemed to almost be from another time. Her decision was made before she was aware of making it. She had time. She knew she was unlikely to hear from Dr. Edison for a while yet.

Lane left the laundry basket with the cloth bag of clothespins on the porch and collected her car keys in the hallway. She knew Darling would disapprove of what she was about to do, but, she reasoned, whatever was going to explode had already done its business, and the good solid rain of the night before had evidently taken care of any fear of fire. She could drive up the short stretch of track, just past the Hugheses', above the upper orchard that had been created by Harris and his tractor. There would still be plenty of daylight left at this time of year. She really had to get a look at the site and try to understand where on earth that little girl had materialized from and what on earth had exploded like that.

CHAPTER FIVE

MRS. DEE STOOD IN THE hospital morgue with her arm around Mrs. Harold's shoulders. She nodded at Inspector Darling, and he lowered the sheet on the corpse, exposing it to the clavicle.

"Is this your husband, Mr. Ronald Harold?"

Mrs. Harold looked for only a moment and then jerked her head away with a little gasp, but she managed to nod and then stammer out a "Yes." Shuffling in her handbag for a handkerchief, she looked at Mrs. Dee. "I . . . I want to go now."

Darling nodded at the friend and then covered the dead man and left him in the care of the attendant. He hurried forward to open the door for the two women. There were some uncomfortable chairs lining the wall of the anteroom, and Mrs. Harold tottered to one of these and sat heavily, looking down at her hands.

"It doesn't seem real till you see someone like that," she said, lifting her chin toward the closed door of the morgue.

Darling nodded, and her friend squeezed her hand. "Come on, Bertha dear. Let's get you home."

Mrs. Harold looked up, her eyes wide. "Oh, I don't think I want to, I don't think I can go home just yet. There would be reminders everywhere . . . he was such a good man. We shared everything. I can't bear . . ."

"Then," said Mrs. Dee firmly, "you'll come to ours. I've the spare room all set up, and you'll be most welcome. Come on." She helped Mrs. Harold up and then looked inquiringly at Darling.

"We will need to try to understand what Mr. Harold was doing here when you thought he was in Vancouver, and of course, how . . ." He let the sentence trail off. "May we contact you again, Mrs. Dee? We'll have to speak again to Mrs. Harold once she is able."

"Yes, of course." Mrs. Dee dropped her friend's hand and snapped her handbag open, extracting a card, which she handed to Darling. "The number is there. I have a small cosmetics business that I run out of my home."

"Thank you," Darling said, impressed. He was relieved Mrs. Harold had such an efficient, businesslike sister-in-law. She'd need Mrs. Dee's steadiness.

"THE BOYS ARE across the way, sir," O'Brien said by way of greeting when Darling came through the front door of the station.

"I think I'll go along myself. Showing the dead to their loved ones is draining. Anything for you?"

"Just about time for my tea and cookies, sir," O'Brien answered, patting the top of his lunch box.

"Right you are." Darling went back onto the street and stopped for just a moment to close his eyes and breathe in the fresh warm air, so especially fragrant after a rain. Wrongful death always seemed to carve a little chunk out of the universe, and he felt it could never be filled in until he knew what had happened. And of course, there was that tiny soupçon of guilt he felt at such moments, that he could rejoice in still being alive himself. He'd faced the alternative several times during the war and had come close during the course of his job. He tried not to relish quite so much the prospect of a piece of whatever pie was going in the café and the companionship of, really, a couple of very decent men.

Both the decent men looked up and smiled when Darling came in. Ames scooted over on the bench at their table by the window to give their boss room. "Apple today, sir," he said, indicating his own nearly empty plate.

"Good," Darling said, hanging his hat on the hat stand and plunking himself down. He waved at the waitress, who had also looked up when he'd come in, only she wasn't so glad to see him. She famously resented customers.

She came and stood over him with one hand on her hip. "Yes?"

"Good afternoon, Marge. Could I have a piece of that excellent-looking pie and a cup of coffee? Thanks." Darling had taken to following the lead of his two underlings in attempting to soften her up with a winning grin, but it made him feel undignified, and it never had any effect.

She turned without a word, and he shrugged. "At least she doesn't actually withhold the pie and coffee," he said.

"Identification done, sir?" Ames asked.

"Yup. It's him all right, not that I wasn't already sure. Poor woman is in a state, of course. Her sister-in-law is taking her to her house because she can't face going home just yet."

Terrell suffered that little bit more because of the notoriously cantankerous Marge. She'd been brought out of retirement and not only was difficult to deal with but also was not April McAvity. April had worked in the café until recently, and then had gone off to Vancouver for a summer course in policing. She'd sent him three letters, which even now, as he thought of them, warmed his heart. She said very little except about the course, but he felt sure that the fact she wrote to him at all meant something. The only real problem was that she addressed these letters to him through the police station, so he'd taken a certain amount of guff from his colleagues over them. Perhaps this was the reason he was so careful and neutral in his responses. He shrugged.

"The whole thing is strange," he said, thoughtfully turning his coffee cup around and back again. "He was supposed to be on his way to the coast, but he went into the shop before he left. Didn't his wife say he liked to make the drive at night? He was wearing his coat because it was a particularly cold night. I think it got down to forty, and there was that downpour. I suppose he kept his coat on because it was cold in his office."

"And Dr. Miyazaki said he'd been dead since at least ten, if not sometime after. Someone knew he was there and hopped around the back to do him in. Does he have a business partner?" Ames asked.

"Good question," Darling said. "I don't think so, besides his wife. I don't actually know anything about him. It's funny: you go along dealing with all the merchants and whatnot without any necessity of knowing anything at all about their personal lives until someone hits one of them over the head. All we really know is that Martin Humphries, the local locksmith, was his best friend."

"They're chums from the war, actually," Ames said. "Met in England during the Great War, came back more or less together. I think Humphries immigrated when the war was over because of his friendship with Harold. His wife told me they discovered they were some sort of distant relations."

Darling looked at Terrell's empty cup and plate and then at his watch. "Constable, could you go along to the locksmith? He should still be open. You may have to break the news to him, though I'm sure it's all over town by now. His place is by the jam factory down the hill near the train station. Find out what you can about their relationship and anything he might know about Harold's movements. He may know if Harold had any enemies, though this looks like a heist gone very wrong."

"Yes, sir." Terrell got up and reached into his pocket. Darling held up his hand.

"I'll get this," he said.

When Terrell had left, Ames said, "That's mighty nice of you, sir."

"I'm getting his, not yours," Darling said. "Now, what did my wife have to say?" He leaned back slightly to let Marge slap down his pie and coffee. "Thanks very much. Could my sergeant have a refill, please?"

Marge looked daggers at Ames, who beamed at her, and stomped off to get the pot.

"Well, sir. It was quite a story." Ames told Darling what Lane had said about the explosion and finding the little girl.

"Thank God she's alive," Darling said of the child.

"And where's her family?" Ames added.

"Where indeed? That worries me, and so does something exploding in the middle of nowhere." Darling took a forkful of pie, and then said, "I don't suppose you told her to stay well away from the scene, did you?"

"I did, as a matter of fact, sir." He coloured slightly. "I know she likes to get involved."

"Well, I'll be. I may yet pay for your pie. I bet she hasn't listened to you, though. If it's any consolation, I doubt she'd listen to me either." And, he conceded, but strictly to himself, she might find something useful. She usually did.

LANE STOPPED THE car and looked up the hill. She could see the faint path they'd followed in the morning disappearing into the trees. She would have no difficulty retracing her steps. She climbed steadily, surprised at how far they'd come that morning. This only increased the mystery of how the little girl came to be so far from anywhere all by herself.

At last, she began to smell the faint odour of charred bushes, and something else . . . a chemical smell. She knew she'd smelled it before but couldn't put her finger on what it was. As she approached the site, there was a great squawking and flapping as several ravens flew up from somewhere across the crater, disturbed by her arrival. She watched them flap upward and then settle in the trees about fifty yards away. It was a murder of crows, she knew, but what about ravens? Then it came to her: a conspiracy. About what had they been conspiring on the pile of shattered brush? She stopped at the edge of the devastation and had a good look.

The damage was about five feet across, possibly four feet deep. It seemed such a small range for the amount of destruction caused. But she'd seen this sort of devastation in London from unexploded bombs that had not been safely detonated. The explosion had splintered trees and sprayed out and exposed the reddish-brown soil that supported the canopy of lodgepole pines and underbrush. That's when she spotted what looked like the remains of a large amount of burned beige-coloured material on the far side of the crater, the edges black and uneven. Some sort of parachute? Though it looked more rigid than that, more like very stiff paper.

She walked around the crater, skirting the splintered trunks of slender pine trees and the spray of dirt, and leaned down to examine the ashes. It was paper all right, but it was thick, yet somehow pliable, almost like a fabric. It seemed to have some kind of coating. The scene of devastation could be any bomb crater she'd ever seen but for this strange paper. She could not understand its presence here. Up close, she could see that there was a seam where two sections of paper had been overlapped and glued. Did this have something to do with what caused the explosion? Someone might know. She found a small scrap of the material the size of her palm and, knocking off the worst of the char, slipped it into her pocket. She carefully moved farther into the crater, looking for anything that could explain it. The blast had done a thorough job, but she focused her eyes on the ground and at last began to distinguish what was there: metal shards. Shrapnel, metal bits of a bomb even. That's when the smell came to her. Gunpowder. Picric acid. Then, as if they'd suddenly decided to make themselves visible, she began to see tangles of wires and more bits of metal. It certainly looked like a bomb. She stood upright and gazed at the surrounding forest. Why would there be a bomb here, far away from anywhere? If it were England, she'd have assumed it was an unexploded bomb left from the Blitz, but here?

The girl must have found the strange object lying in the forest, touched something, the paper perhaps, and it had gone off. Looking at the damage now, she was amazed the girl hadn't been killed outright. Perhaps the explosion had blown her back. She climbed out of the indentation and continued her circumnavigation, climbing over downed trees and wading through the splintered underbrush until she was opposite where they had found the child. Her eye was drawn to something white, and she looked down. The remnants of some sort of heavy white cotton sacking. She picked this up. There were grains of sand stuck in the weave. She leaned over to look closely at the ground, pushing away the burned grass and twigs. More sand covered the small space under the fabric.

Straightening, she shaded her eyes and looked up, as if she might be able to retrace the trajectory of this strange object.

She'd have liked to stay and look more closely at the bomb site, find a bit more that might tell her something, but her mind was on the girl. Where had she come from? Lane put her hands on her hips and looked for anything that might explain her presence. Perhaps there was a cabin in the woods no one knew about? It was possible. There were several abandoned cabins closer down to the lake, but way up here? She could not hear the babble of any nearby creek, which would, she thought, have been necessary to sustain anyone this high up.

She caught sight of what might be a little path, grass slightly flattened, and she started toward it. She'd been looking ahead, trying to see if she could follow it into the forest, when her foot hit something soft. She reeled back with a gasp. There was something very wrong with the consistency of what she'd touched, and in the next second, she was down on her knees.

A woman's outstretched arm lay where she'd almost stepped, the rest of its owner concealed by splintered trees, fern, and bracken underbrush. She understood why Gwen had not found her. She'd been completely covered.

"No, no, no, no!" Lane cried out loud. The woman was face down, her head turned at an awkward angle, her dark hair singed, revealing a badly injured face. Lane put her fingers on the woman's neck. Nothing. Lane sat back on her feet and closed her eyes for a moment. This was surely the young girl's mother. She stood up and moved the bushes so she could see the woman's whole body, and again had to step back, recoiling and choking back a gag at the sight of the stump of a wrist where a hand had once been.

Her heart beating fast, she forced herself to look for anything else that might be important. The woman was

62

wearing a flowered dress that was now in tatters, and a pink rayon silk slip had ridden partway up her legs. One shoe had been blown off. There was nothing anywhere that might give a clue as to who she might be. Lane paced the area looking for a handbag, wallet, anything that might reveal something about her. Even in the late afternoon, it was still hot. She glanced at her watch. Already nearly five. The smell of drying blood assailed her, as if she'd inhaled the smell when she was leaning over the body, and now could not rid herself of it. She had to force herself to continue the search. But of course, if you were going for a walk in the forest with a child, would you carry a handbag? More like a sack with some lunch or some fruit. But there was nothing in evidence. She came back and squatted next to the woman, hand over her nose. She wanted to see her face more clearly, but she knew she mustn't touch anything more than she had. The woman had a fine gold chain around her neck, but whatever medallion it carried was pinned under her, out of sight. She sat on her knees and said a quick silent prayer to the sky, thinking of the child waking up finally, wondering where her mother was.

Racing down the hill toward the upper orchard and her car, she wondered why she was running. No amount of hurry was going to do that poor woman any good. But then she thought about ravens. Scavengers. She didn't have any idea what other kinds of scavengers there might be in the forest, but the idea of it spurred her on.

It took several rings before O'Brien answered the phone. "Nelson Police Station. Sergeant O'Brien."

63

"Hello, Sergeant," Lane said, wishing she were not sounding so breathless. "It's Lane Winslow. Is the inspector there? I'm afraid I've found someone else at the site of this morning's explosion. Not alive, I'm afraid."

"I'll put you through, Mrs. Darling. Are you all right?"

Lane was touched by the kindness in the voice of the usually brusque sergeant. "Quite, thank you. It's so kind of you to ask."

"I'll put you through now."

"Lane," Darling's worried voice came over the line. Her head was tilted up so that she could speak into the horn of the ridiculously old-fashioned telephone that still hung on the wall in their hallway. She held the earpiece against her right ear.

"I'm all right, darling. Don't let Sergeant O'Brien make a fuss. But I've been back to the site of the explosion this morning—"

"Of course you have," Darling interjected with a sigh. "And you've found someone dead, I suppose." He meant it as a sort of dark joke. She had been a regular finder of corpses since they'd met almost two years before.

"Don't interrupt. I have, yes. It's a young woman, dark haired, Asian, like the little girl. I think it might be her mother. And I was able to determine that there had been some sort of incendiary device. I could smell the gunpowder, and there were bits of metal like shrapnel and tangled wires sort of strewn around. I think the device . . ." She stopped. Could this be possible? "I think the device, a bomb maybe, might have been delivered with some sort of paper parachute. That poor woman. Her hand . . ." Lane stopped. It was one thing to have seen it, but it was quite another to say it out loud, to make it real by naming it. "She didn't stand a chance. It's a miracle the little girl survived."

"I'm sorry, darling, what a dreadful thing for you to see. The RCMP has some bomb people with expertise. I'll call them and get them out there. Now that there's a casualty, they'll be able to get some men on it."

"I'm worried about the woman. I mean, she's dead, but I scared a bunch of ravens away when I arrived. I'm worried about scavengers. How soon can someone get out here?"

Darling was silent for a moment. This was a critical juncture. "Listen, I hate to ask you this, but could you take something up to cover her with? A thick blanket that we'll never use again. That khaki one we keep in the barn will do. Then get back to the house. You'll need to show whoever comes out how to get up to the site."

"Right you are, darling. It might not be you, then?" She'd have to hurry to get all the way back up and down again before the Mounties arrived.

"It might not. This murder and break-in has all hands on deck. I don't know when I'll get back. And I have a feeling the Mounties will want full control."

65

CHAPTER SIX

LANE DROVE WITH THE MOUNTIES, who'd introduced themselves none too warmly as Sergeant Fryer and Officer
Anthony, to where they could park the car.

"We have a way to walk. It's about forty minutes up, if
we move quickly," she told them, eyeing their heavy jackets.
Late as it was, it was still warm and she was glad, on this,
her fourth trip up to the site of the day, to be wearing a
sleeveless cotton shirt. It would be almost eight by the
time they got up there.

"That's fine, ma'am," Sergeant Fryer said.

The corpse lay under the khaki wool blanket that Lane
knew she and Darling could do without ever using again
and looked mercifully undisturbed by scavengers.

The three of them stood over the body. Anthony had
his hat off and was wiping his forehead. "Did you touch
anything?" Fryer was bordering on curt.

"Aside from putting the blanket over her, no. It looks to
me as if this was likely some sort of bomb. You can smell

the gunpowder and picric acid, and see those wires and the metal just there. The smell suggests TNT was used. I believe the paper there might—"

"Yes, thank you, ma'am. I think it's best you leave this sort of thing to us. I'll ask you to stand over there." He pointed back the way they'd come.

"Unless you need me any further, I'll go back down now." She'd be damned if she was going to stand around at their beck and call. Not that they were going to either beckon or call, judging by their treatment of her.

"Suit yourself, if you can make it back on your own." He barely looked at her. "Oh, and ma'am? I'll thank you not to discuss this with anyone."

Charming. She wanted to tell him that besides the police, the whole of King's Cove would be in the know by now, and who knew who else? But she would caution people not to discuss the little girl. Her privacy, at least, might be preserved.

"DO YOU THINK we ought to call Harris?" Mabel asked. She'd pulled the Saturday lunch pork roast out of the oven to give it a baste. The cracklings were going to be delicious, she could see already.

"Whatever for?" her mother asked. "It's after noon. He'll have made his own." The ructions of the day before had put everyone's normal schedule behind.

"Mabel's right, Mother. He was very good in yesterday's emergency, and we've a nice lot of pork here."

"Well, suit yourself. He won't thank you." Gladys sat at the kitchen table, rolling cigarettes, cutting them, and putting them into her battered cigarette tin.

Mabel put her spoon down and wiped her hands on her apron, making for the hall. She rang the exchange and asked to be put through to Robin Harris.

Lucy, who worked the phone lines out of Bales's filling station and general store at the top of the Balfour road, said, "Right away. Is it true what I heard?"

Mabel had little patience for the girl, who was renowned for her nosiness. "I don't know what you heard."

"Well, a big explosion, to start with."

"Yes, there was an explosion. Could I talk to Mr. Harris, please?"

"No one was hurt, I hope," the girl said.

"Mr. Harris, if you please."

"Yes, all right. You can't blame me for being curious."

Mabel could, but she decided not to respond in the hope of ending the conversation and being put through to Harris.

"Yes?" Harris barked.

"No need to take my head off. It's Mabel. I've got a nice bit of pork roasting here. Why don't you come up for lunch?"

"Why? What do you need?" He sounded suspicious.

"We don't need anything just now, Robin. We've all had a hard day yesterday and I thought you'd like to join us, that's all."

There was a long silence. "All right, then." Another silence. "Have you heard anything more about the little girl?"

It was Mabel's turn for a spell of silence. There was Harris, sounding uncharacteristically kind again. "Miss Winslow, Lane, came by to say she'd made it alive to the hospital." She modulated the raspy tone she used with him.

He grunted. "All right, then. I'll be up."

Mabel hung up and went into the kitchen, where her sister and mother were at work on the vegetables. "There. That's done. Though I must say, Robin is behaving very strangely. Does anyone else think that?"

Gladys shrugged as if she would expect nothing less than peculiar behaviour from Harris, but Gwen nodded. "Maybe he has a soft spot for children."

"A soft spot, my aunt Nora! He's never had the time of day for Angela's boys. He hasn't had a soft spot for anything but that bloody noisy, smelly tractor for as long as I've known him. I'll go out and collect some early scallions," Gladys said, pushing herself up with her gnarled fists on the table.

"I wonder if Lane has heard any more this morning. No, she'd have told us. She's usually so good," Mabel said, throwing herself onto a kitchen chair, and then getting up again. "I'd better get a jar of beans." The Hughes ladies kept a full root cellar of bottled vegetables and fruits, jams, and boxes of apples and baskets of carrots and potatoes. Gwen had bought a small fridge and they were using it more, but nothing could convince them or their mother in particular that it could ever replace a good root cellar.

"I'll get that," Gwen said when the phone rang. Mabel was into the hallway so quickly that Gwen muttered "Fine, you do it" under her breath and went out for the beans. Their mother was on her knees among the early vegetables in the garden, the two spaniels lying nearby on the grass.

Mabel came and stood on the steps, holding open the screen door. "You'll never guess!" she called loudly so that her mother in the far bed could hear. The dogs, alerted to the tone in Mabel's voice, both trundled up, shook themselves, and gave their full attention to her.

"Shut the door!" Gladys commanded, getting slowly to her feet. "What's the bloody point of a screen door if you're going to let all and sundry fly into the house? Now what's the fuss?"

Gwen had come out of the root cellar and stood holding the jar of beans. "What?" she asked.

"That was Lane on the phone. She's found someone dead up there. A woman. Apparently, the Mounties came yesterday evening and are there again. She showed them where the body was."

"That's impossible!" Gwen said. "How did we not see it?"

"How did we miss the Mounties banging around the place? I suppose they parked well above the upper orchard on Harris's track," Gladys said, looking in that direction.

"Lane went back up there to see what happened and she found the woman. She suspects it's the little girl's mother," Mabel said.

"Oh, no. That's dreadful!" Gwen exclaimed. "Did she say anything about the little girl? How is she?"

"She said she was going to telephone the hospital to see what she could learn. She's going to tell them about the woman."

"Damned bad luck," Gladys said, shaking her head. She'd collected a handful of slender scallions and was now striding back toward the house.

"Apparently the inspector won't be back tonight until late, if then," Mabel added.

"Well, get her back on the line," Gladys commanded. "She can come up to join us for lunch. We've got masses of food."

"Yes, of course!" Gwen said, making for the door.

Lane, who was still feeling disgruntled at her treatment by the Mountie constable the evening before, was glad to get the invitation, especially as Gwen had said she could bring leftover pork roast back with her for when Darling did finally make it home. She looked at her watch. It was nearly one. "You're eating late. Don't you usually have this sort of lunch on a Sunday?"

"It's all the excitement. We're off to Trail tomorrow to see a film about the Russian ballet, so we're doing it today."

"Good luck for me, then. I'll be right up."

ROBIN HARRIS PULLED on his boots and went into his barn to get the tractor. He'd stopped driving the green Ford that he'd picked up across the line in '23. For all he knew, it wouldn't even run anymore. It didn't matter. He could get anywhere he liked on his tractor, and he could count on the steamer, or Gladys or Mabel, to run him up to town if he ever needed to go. He stood by the tractor now, one hand on the steering wheel, but looking out the barn doors to the late afternoon shimmering of the lake through the trees, he was aware of an almost forgotten feeling. He couldn't even put a name to it. It was a combination of longing and pain. He was seven again. He closed his eyes, trying to remember.

"YOU CAN'T GET me!" Robin hung upside down on the highest branch he could reach.

"Can too!" Betty was already halfway up, shinning her way to the first branch so that she could swing up and use the branches to climb the rest of the way. The oak tree stood like a solitary sentinel in a field between the cottage and the village, and it was their favourite place. In the tree they were above everything. Above the mud stirred up by the cows in the field, above the cottage, above the miserable temper of her father, who drank more than he worked.

"Hurry up. He'll find you," Robin said. Now that Betty was eight, she was expected to do the work in the cottage. Cooking, cleaning, the washing.

"It's all right. He's asleep," she said, climbing the next set of branches. She threw her bare leg over the final branch, pulled herself up next to him, and slumped forward, elbows on knees, looking at her hands.

"What's the matter?"

"That horrible Mr. Slater came and took Benjie. Didn't you see? They had a big fight. Pa almost hit him with a shovel."

Robin shook his head, his eyes wide as he looked in the direction of the cottage. It looked peaceful enough, a thin stream of smoke coming out of the chimney. "But what about the cart, and the wood he sells? How is he going to drive it around?"

Betty shrugged. "Dunno. Mr. Slater said Father owes him money."

A fear welled up in Robin. Betty was all that he loved most. He had never seen her unhappy like this, and it frightened him. He put his hand on the rough bark of the branch they were on. "Maybe he'll get another horse," he said. "Then it will be all right."

Betty shook her head. "He can't get another horse. We couldn't even get any hay for Benjie."

The mention of food made Robin's stomach growl. "I wish we had a bun from Mrs. Sawyer's. One of those ones with raisins in it."

"Me too," Betty sighed. "I like the way she puts sugar on the top that kind of sticks to it."

"Can you remember your mother?" Robin asked suddenly.

Betty shook her head. "I was a baby. There was that picture Pa used to have, but that's not like remembering."

"Why did he take the picture away?"

"He said there wasn't no use for it since she's dead."

Robin kicked his legs back and forth. "I can remember mine sometimes. She had black hair. I wish I could remember her face. Sometimes when I'm going to sleep, I can see her standing at the end of the bed. Never my father, though. I don't remember him."

"No, you can't see her," Betty objected. "If she was there, I could've seen her too." She fell into silence. "I wish Benjie was there." Her voice shook.

Robin could feel tears burning his eyes, and he swiped at them with his hand.

The fear in his chest felt like it would spill out. He wished it would stop. Even talking to Betty didn't stop it this time. He knew she was afraid too.

BETTY'S FATHER SLAMMED his glass down on the table and took up the spoon. They were eating bowls of grey potato soup. There should have been bread, but there wasn't any.

"You can't stay here," he said suddenly, still holding his spoon midway between bowl and mouth and looking at Robin. "I don't know why my brother thought it right to land you on me. I can't afford it no more."

Robin stared at him, his stomach compressing. He felt as if night flowed into his head and filled it all up.

"What do you mean, Pa? Where is he supposed to go?" Betty had put her spoon down and blurted this out, then had to shrink back in her chair because her father raised his hand with the spoon as if to hit her.

Robin sat rigid, fear engulfing him, watching Betty's father, waiting for the hand to come down. It made him feel like he was shrinking, becoming smaller and smaller. But her father's hand didn't strike.

"Look," her father said, putting his spoon into the bowl. He sounded less angry. "It's not like he's going down the mines. We have a cousin out in Canada. He can go there. He should have gone there right at the start, when Leila died, and his pa. You'll be better off," he said to Robin. He tried to infuse a note of kindness into his tone but failed. He could feel his own failures as if they were rags hanging off his body for the world to see. "I can't afford it no more, that's all."

HARRIS STARED UNSEEING at the wall behind the tractor. He had not thought about Betty since the Great War. For all he knew, she was already dead then. He tried to remember the actual leaving, where he must have gone from the farm, with whom. And then there was the sea. It came to him now as a heaving watery dark universe, grey-blue and opaque, dividing forever that child from this remembered moment. He put his hand on the steering wheel and then stopped again, trying to bring Betty to mind, but she'd only hovered near his memory when he hadn't tried. Now he could not see her face or remember her voice. It was as if he'd gone into the fevered sleep of the very ill when he left England, and when he'd awoken, he'd been here, with Kenny and John, running through the orchard in the sun, shouting and hitting the young apple tree trunks with sticks.

"Now, why the blazes?" he said out loud to himself. He sat for a moment and pulled out the tin of cigarettes he'd made up. He fumbled opening it, and he saw that his fingers were shaking slightly as he extracted one. He parked it between his lips, closed the box, and pocketed it, fishing for his brass lighter. It took several tries before a flame leaped up, and he lit his cigarette and inhaled, forcing the world to right itself.

He found Gwen and Mabel in the kitchen and could hear Lane and Gladys in the dining room, laying the long dark oak table. He'd imagined they'd be having lunch in the kitchen as they normally did when it was just him and the Hugheses. The roast was out, the enamelled roasting pan sitting on the kitchen table. Potatoes surrounded the sizzling meat, golden and crisp. The smell was something he remembered from when he'd come as a boy. The kitchen at the Armstrongs' when they lived at that Winslow woman's house. He'd been amazed at first by the amount of food to be had. He frowned at the intrusion of yet another memory and removed the cigarette stub from his mouth. He walked over to the stove, lifted a ring with the iron lid lifter, and tossed it into the fire.

"You had to come on that infernal machine. Lane somehow managed to get up the hill on foot," Gladys said, coming through. "Wash your hands. You'll be carving."

"WELL," LANE SAID when the dishes had all been passed around and they'd helped themselves, "I called the hospital yesterday and got Dr. Edison before she left for the evening. The little girl is, she thinks, going to be all right. She has a badly burned foot and arm, and her leg is broken in two places. There are burns and cuts on parts of her torso, and her shoulder was dislocated. She will be some time healing. She is no longer unconscious, but she is heavily sedated and has not spoken. Dr. Edison was horrified to think that poor woman I found might be the girl's mother."

Harris had stopped eating and dropped his fork, so it banged on the edge of his plate. "What?"

"Oh, I'm sorry," Lane said. "Of course, you wouldn't have known. I went back up to the place we found the girl and discovered a young woman, dead. I don't absolutely know that she was the girl's mother, of course, but she is also Asian, and the right age. And, of course, they must have been there together when the explosion happened."

Harris jerked his head sideways, looking toward the parlour where a fire crackled in the grate. The movement was sudden, and it caused the women to look at him in surprise. Usually, a meal with Harris meant looking at the top of his head the whole time because he bent over, shovelling food into his mouth. He was not a man who believed in dinnertime conversation.

"Is she sure?" he asked, turning back to look at Lane.

"Is who sure of what?" Gladys asked, ever impatient.

"Is she sure the girl is going to be all right?"

"She said so, didn't she?" Gladys said.

"She's a woman doctor," Harris said.

"Oh, for Pete's sake," began Mabel.

"I think Dr. Edison is quite sure," Lane interjected to prevent a row. "She was an Air Force medic. I imagine she's had a good deal of experience with just these sorts of injuries."

"Hmm," said Harris skeptically. "Who's the girl got, then?"

"That's the question, really, isn't it?" Lane said. "Until she can talk and at least tell someone her name, we can't really know. But maybe someone will be missing her and go to the police."

They ate in silence for some moments. "This is absolutely delicious," Lane said. "I shall never be able to produce a bit of roast pork like this."

"Nothing to it," Mabel said. "Score the top, bung it in the oven, cook it slowly, and remember to baste."

"That girl can't be on her own," Harris said.

"She's not on her own, Robin. She's in the care of the exemplary hospital staff," Lane said, surprised. She also couldn't remember Harris ever showing the slightest concern for another human being.

"What I don't understand," Gwen said, "is what she was doing there. There's absolutely nothing up there but forest. There were all those Japanese up in New Denver and Kaslo and Sandon during the war. Is she from there, do you think?"

"What did the Mounties do?" Mabel asked Lane.

"I assume they got the woman out somehow, poked around the blast area, and ignored what I said about the chemicals used in the bomb. Ordered me away and told me in no uncertain terms to stay away. I think the real question is yours, Gwen: What were they doing up there in the first place? Where did they come from? I wonder if there's a way that the Mounties can check lists of who might have been held where. Only, of course, we have no idea what her name is."

"Where's that poor tyke going to end up? That's what I want to know," Harris said, addressing no one in particular. He stabbed a piece of pork and lifted it to his mouth. "This is all right," he added ungraciously.

"They'll find her people, don't you worry about that," Gladys said. "Anyway, it's no concern of yours, or ours for that matter. What does matter is that our water isn't running properly. Any chance you could pop up tomorrow and have a look, Harris?"

"I knew it," was all he said.

CHAPTER SEVEN

"WHAT ARE YOU GOING TO do today?" Darling asked. They'd moved their scrambled eggs and coffee onto the porch to take advantage of the mild and fragrant morning. He was hoping it would wake him up a bit. It had been nearly one when he'd finally come home, exhausted and puzzled. At least the drive up to town would be quicker on a Sunday.

"I shall certainly be calling the hospital to see about that poor girl, in the hope of learning who she is. And I might go back up the mountain to see if I can figure out where she and her mother, assuming that's who she was, came from."

"Let's hope the hospital tells *us* who she is before the general public," Darling said.

"Am I just the general public, do you think?"

"I do. There is no special status conferred on you by being married to the police. And you are not to find any more bodies. The RCMP has kindly informed us that the corpse and the bomb are to be considered matters of the strictest security and we are to stay out of it. They will be sending someone out who knows about incendiaries. It will very quickly not be a local concern. The Canadian government might become involved, concerned that perhaps our new enemy, the Soviets, have found some novel way to harass peaceful democracies. They haven't said the words 'national security' yet, but if they find you mucking around, you can bet they will. I haven't got room for you in my cells. They are even concerned that Japan might be involved."

"Hmm. I wonder if they found something on the bomb, or does the danger come in the form of that girl and her poor dead mother? Have we not made peace with Japan?"

"Perhaps the RCMP have not yet made peace with them. And there's the Doukhobors. That breakaway group, the Sons of Freedom, is creating plenty of difficulty with its protests."

"Anyway, you do have room in your cells," objected Lane. "You've not arrested anyone for the murder of the jeweller yet, have you? And surely the Mounties must have their own cells. I told them what the damn thing was made of. I thought I could save them some trouble."

Darling looked at her and shook his head, smiling. "They must have loved that."

"Not particularly, as it happens. Quite dismissive, really. Told me to run along."

"I know how they feel," Darling said, slurping back the last of his coffee and getting up. "Must be off. Oh. Did I tell you Dr. Miyazaki stayed on an extra couple of days? He's having a look at your corpse now, on behalf of my mounted colleagues. I really do caution you against finding any more. I'm sure he'd like to get home to Lillooet."

At the car, he kissed her fondly, a fondness perhaps enhanced by his tiredness and his longing to just stay in King's Cove and enjoy the day along with his agrarian neighbours. "I'm not going to be able to stop you from snooping around up there, but mind the bears. What do they do here about that?"

"Gosh, I didn't even think about bears! A tin can full of rocks is the usual remedy. Apparently shaking it constantly keeps them away. It's like hanging garlic against vampires. If you never see a vampire, you assume it's working."

"Vampires. That's all we need. And stay away from the Mounties."

She smiled sweetly. "Of course, darling. Have a lovely day."

REASONING THAT THE hospital must have morning routines that should not be interrupted, Lane decided she would call in the afternoon. By then, perhaps, the girl might be speaking. Anyway, she ought to get up the mountain early to avoid running into the Mounties. She tidied up, slipped on her plimsolls, and set off. Deciding to go on foot to avoid attracting attention, she climbed the hill toward the Hughes driveway, and then, instead of going to their house, took the rough tractor track up past the top orchard until she found the trail back up to the blast site. After all the trips taken by her and Harris and the Mounties it was very visible now.

The morning was glorious—sweet smelling, cool, and golden. Her favourite time of day. She loved it for its newness and the silence. What she relished above all else in King's Cove was the silence of the country, encompassing birds and the gentle swaying of trees and ferns in the breeze coming up off the lake. It was a shame the Mounties would soon be cluttering the place up, but, she supposed, needs must.

When she reached the bomb site at last, she could see that they had further shuffled about among the remains of the blast and had set any metallic bits to one side, including a very distinct, and very familiar, bomb tail. She was astonished to see something so familiar and unlikely in the mountains above King's Cove. The bomb must have been at least a twenty pounder, she reckoned, or possibly thirty. Not huge, but it could pack a good wallop. What was it doing out here? They had roughly folded what remained of the strange paper and placed it alongside the other debris, and then they had marked the area out with stakes and string. Lane stopped to looked again at the paper. It really was a remarkable material. She had never seen paper like it. Fighting an urge to kneel down and look more closely at it, she stood as close as she dared to the string barrier they'd put up. It had a texture to it; it was thick but flexible. She knew some papers were made from cloth fibres. Perhaps that accounted for its characteristics. She still had her little scrap of the paper. Maybe there was someone in town who could tell her about it. That printer in town, perhaps. He dealt in all kinds of papers.

Was Darling right? Could it be the Soviets? It would be a strange method of bomb delivery. She thought of them as being more in the rocket line. At any rate, delivering a bomb to Canada would be an act of war. Certainly there was a state of war of sorts between the Soviets and the West. Cold War, she'd heard it called. She'd understood that the Soviets had exhibited an interest in atomic bombs. A little TNT affair like this was surely not up their alley—but if not theirs, then whose?

Careful not to touch anything the RCMP had laid out, Lane skirted the edge of the crater and moved toward the place she'd found the body. The Mounties had no doubt scoured the place looking for anything that might lead to identification, but Lane stopped and began to go very methodically over the area.

Parting the underbrush, she looked along the jagged edge of the crater. Tiny scraps of cloth from the woman's dress clung to the torn shrubs, and then another fragment of sacking, this one burned but clearly with sand clinging among its rough weave. After a thorough search in a five-foot arc around where she'd found the body, she straightened up. What else had she hoped to find? A handbag with the woman's driver's licence? But, she remembered now, there had been that gold necklace around her neck. That must be at the morgue now. She wished she could ask them about that. Maybe, because of the child, they might be willing to answer questions about it. Because the woman had been face down, she hadn't been able to see what the chain held. Perhaps initials? A locket?

She looked into the forest. Was there a faint trail the mother and daughter had come along that fateful day? If they didn't walk this way regularly, there'd be nothing, and the rain might have obliterated any trace. Deciding that there was the faintest of trails, she began walking up the hill and into the forest. She'd not gone twenty feet when she nearly tripped over something. A thick black rubber hose snaking down into the woods to her left. She looked back in the opposite direction. Where had it come from? In that direction, but at a considerable distance, lay the upper creek from which the Hugheses, Mathers, and Armstrongs got their water.

She followed the hose away from the distant creek and found that it began a drop down a gentle slope toward the south . . . right to a faucet outside a very small log cabin lying about 150 yards down the slope and set in a slightly inclined clearing. How far was she from King's Cove now? Three miles over rough terrain? It felt like more. She would have to ask if the Hugheses knew of it.

"I'll be!" she exclaimed out loud, and hurriedly made her way down the hill.

"Hello?" Lane called. "Anyone home?" She approached slowly, looking to either side of the cabin. It had been built in a different era and surely consisted of only one or two rooms. Someone more recently had set about making improvements. New windows, larger, she suspected, than the original windows; the frames had been recently mortared, and a new door had been added, set snugly into its frame—critical if anyone were to winter over here. In the shadow of the trees behind the cabin, an outhouse had been built some thirty paces away. A considerable garden had been marked off with stones directly in front of the cabin and was filled with orderly rows of well-tended young vegetable plants. Is this where the little girl and her mother had lived?

Calling out again, Lane approached the door. The brass knob turned easily, and the door swung open. "Hello?" But she knew already there would be no answer.

Inside, the single room had a stillness that had the feel of abandonment, and a slightly musty smell—and yet, if Lane was right, the little girl and her mother had been here only two days before. The room inside was tidy. There was a single bed, made, and a table with two folded napkins, a little glass saltcellar, a chipped mug, and a pile of scribblers and some books and pencils stacked neatly at one end. Along the front wall of the cabin there was a waist-high shelf, and on it an enamelled wash basin was turned over, and a dishtowel hung on a nail. At the very end, against the wall, were three kerosene lamps and a coffee tin containing several boxes of matches. The little window had a wire strung across the top sill with a faded green cloth that served as a curtain. A half loaf of packaged bread, now hosting a stream of small black ants, and jars of peanut butter and Robertson's strawberry jam lay on the counter, both more than half finished. There was a row of canned soups and evaporated milk next to these.

Where did she cook? Lane had become used to the dim light and saw now that there was a small cast-iron stove, not unlike her Franklin, against the south wall. On it sat a kettle, and next to the stove, a cast-iron frying pan and a small, battered aluminum pot hung on nails hammered into the wall.

She saw two weathered apple boxes under the bed and hesitated a moment before pulling them out, struck by some atavistic desire not to snoop through someone's private things. Both boxes contained neatly folded clothes. Most touching of all was a pile of three children's books on top of the clothes in one of the boxes, the topmost being *Babar*. Leaving these for the moment, she stood up. There must be something, some sort of document somewhere to say who they were. Looking at a shelf set above the bed, she saw a metal box and two piles of books. Up close, she was surprised to see these were legal texts of some sort. Feeling more than ever as if she was trespassing, and now blatantly disobeying the RCMP, she took the heavy metal box and went back out into the sunshine, happy to get away from the claustrophobia induced by this sad, cramped, and abandoned place.

The box was about five inches wide, ten inches long, and three inches high. The lid had a little latch but no lock. Inside were several folded documents, the topmost of which proved to be a birth certificate. Lane read it with excitement.

Sara Himari Sasaki Harold. Born November 10, 1939, St. Paul's Hospital, Vancouver. Six pounds two ounces. Mother's name, Ichiko Sasaki Harold. Father, William James Harold. Where was William James Harold, then? Had they run away from him? Was he a prospector and still away somewhere? Had he died in the recent war? No need yet to go down further dark roads, she told herself. She was elated to have the child's name, at any rate. She refolded the birth certificate and pulled out the next paper. A similar-looking document, only completely, she guessed, in Japanese except for the date, 1915. Had Sara's mother been born in Japan? The third document down was something from the Dominion Government of Canada, indicating the immigration of the Sasaki family in 1917. So, Sasaki was the woman's maiden name. Under the final document were two photographs, one of a slender young woman holding a baby so that both she and the baby were turned toward the photographer. The woman had one side of her hair pinned back, and had a big open smile, as if, at this moment, she was delighted with the state of things. The second was a much older one of a mother and father with a toddler, all Japanese. By the clothes, she would say it had been taken in the early '20s. It looked to her as if it was Canada. She wondered if it had been taken in Vancouver. Underneath the final paper, she found what had given the box weight: a gold pocket watch. Pulling this out, with its heavy gold chain, she turned it over. The back was a beautiful, simple clamshell design. The whole thing fit nicely into the palm of her hand. Lane carefully opened the cover. The watch face, like the watch itself, was elegant and had a chronometer dial in the lower half. Vacheron & Constantin, Geneva. She closed it and looked around the spare arrangements of the cabin and felt sad. This watch, beautiful as it was, would be all that poor girl would have instead of her mother.

Lane felt a wave of darkness for the mother and her child. She carefully replaced the photos along with the other papers and then held the watch irresolutely.

She should give these documents to the RCMP, she knew. Or perhaps she should replace them and pretend she hadn't seen them because the Mounties would no doubt find their way to this cabin eventually. No, that would be disingenuous, not to say dishonest. She knew she was tampering with evidence, but for the girl's sake, she thought her best course of action would be to keep the box and go to the hospital with the child's documents—at least they would have a name for her. Then she could head down to the RCMP detachment, own up to her misdeed, hand it in, and provide a description of the location of the cabin. She'd let the chips fall where they may with the RCMP. But, she decided, she would keep the photos and the watch. She could not risk the only photos of the little girl's family disappearing into an evidence drawer somewhere. She felt a certain amount of guilt at disobeying direct orders, and God knew what Darling would say! Anyway, now the RCMP could get cracking, looking for the girl's father.

Thus determined, she started back toward the ridge, and then she thought of the little girl's books. They surely could not be implicated in any national security threat! She turned back, collected Babar and his friends, and gave a quick look around for a teddy bear or something similar. With a pang she wondered if the child had taken it with her on the walk that fateful morning. She should keep her eye out for it. On the way past the table, she put what she had down and looked more closely at the scribblers and three books—a grammar, an arithmetic book, and a science book—all geared toward a child in about grade six or seven, if she remembered her brief period as a schoolteacher. There were two pots of ink, several nib holders and a box of nibs, plus several pencils in a jar. The books meant Sara—she was so happy to know her name—might be working a couple of years ahead. Underneath the table was a wooden apple box with a stack of papers on top of more books. She picked up the top sheet of paper and found it to be covered in what she assumed must be Japanese writing, the same symbols over and over, as if Sara had been practicing. A small, lidded box revealed a hard black slab and a couple of brushes. Beneath these practice papers were some schoolbooks for younger grades. Had they been here long enough for Sara to have progressed through several grades' worth of material?

She stacked the schoolbooks back up. Perhaps later, when the girl was better, these might be of use. Picking up the box of documents, the watch, and the children's books, she was outside again. She closed her eyes and breathed in a great draught of air, perhaps of gratitude to be among the living.

How long had this woman and child lived here? The morning sun on the meadow gave the place a peaceful air so out of step with the tragedy of the people who had called this home. Lane walked past where a clothesline had been strung between a tree and a pole that someone had buried in the ground. She was struck with the poignancy of seeing clothes hanging on the line, moving gently in the slight breeze. Sara's mother must have done a wash the morning she died.

Setting down the box and books, Lane took the clothing down and folded it, taking it back into the house. She placed the two pairs of shorts, a T-shirt, a worn blouse, a pair of trousers, and several pairs of underwear on the table. Of course, she should have left them for the RCMP.

Outside again, she looked around. The whole place had a strange feeling of being temporary, yet permanent. Certainly the well-established garden, and even a few young fruit trees, suggested a sense of homesteading. On the other hand, one could only get to it on foot, there was no electricity, and the only water was from the outdoor faucet. Surely no one thought this arrangement was suitable for a child in this day and age?

She turned the faucet on, and water tumbled out. She stopped the gush of water and looked back at where the hose disappeared up the incline and thought it would be interesting to follow it all the way back to the source of the water. The cabin was oriented so that the front door and its front window were facing toward the lake, which wasn't actually visible from this meadow. Around the south side, she was surprised to see quite a well-worn path heading down a gradual slope. Where would this go? If one kept going in this direction, would one hit the road and Bales's store? She thought of the bread and the tins of food. Did she walk down to the store for these things? If that was the case, someone must have known they were here.

Tempting though it was to follow the path, Lane decided she would talk to Bales himself later. In the meantime, she'd best head back and get this new information to the people who needed it. With the box and the books under her arm, she set off home.

"Hello!" she called when she reached the Hugheses' yard, eliciting an excited response from the spaniels who hurled themselves at the screen door and bounded out to sniff Lane's feet when Gladys threw open the door.

"You're out early," she said. "We've just finished our breakfast. There's still tea left."

"Gosh," Lane said, looking at her watch. "I'm sorry. I bashed off this morning after Frederick left and didn't think about the time at all. I've discovered something." She followed Gladys into the house, where she found Mabel doing the washing up and Gwen putting things into the pantry.

"Not another body, I hope," Gladys said, her expression belying her words.

"No. But I found a very small sort of refurbished log cabin just south of the bomb site. The little girl and her mother were living there. I brought these out with me, as I thought she might be happy to have them." She held up the books. "I was hoping to find a teddy bear or a doll, but no luck. I'll stop by Hudson's Bay and find a nice teddy bear for her. And we know her name now! Sara Himari Sasaki Harold."

Gwen came out of the pantry to look at what Lane had put on the table. "Harold? That's not Japanese. Are you sure?"

"It's right on the birth certificate. Father's name is William James Harold. God knows where he is, though." Then it hit her, saying that name out loud. Wasn't Harold the name of the jeweller who'd been killed? She would have to ask Darling.

"But that's appalling! How can a young girl like that have been living up in the bush, and no one knowing about it!" Gwen went straight for the photos. "What a pretty young woman. How old is the child there? Two? That poor creature, having to carry on her life without her mother!" She turned the picture over, but there was no date. "This one might be her grandparents, maybe?"

Mabel shook her head. "My word. How were they even getting up there? I never saw them going past us."

"No, you're right. I found quite a well-worn path going down through the forest toward Balfour. I didn't follow it, so I don't know how far down it goes. The cabin is as far up as the bomb site, but a bit south from us, so maybe it would be a mile, mile and half to Bales's store? Did you know it was there?"

"I didn't," Mabel said. "Never went that far up in my walks. How were they getting food?"

"She had peanut butter, bread, jam, and tins of things. She might have got them from Bales. I'm going to go up to town later with this lot, and I'll stop and ask him. But that's not the only thing. When I was up at the crater this morning, endeavouring not to touch anything the RCMP had so carefully laid out, I discovered a heavy black sort of garden hose. I followed it down, and that's how I found the cabin. That's how they were getting water."

CHAPTER EIGHT

"**SHE MUST HAVE BEEN MUCH** nearer the blast," Dr. Miyazaki said. It was early Sunday morning. He'd wanted to finish the job and get started home. He'd washed his hands and was now drying them. He shook his head. "It was definitely the explosion that killed her. Many of those wounds were caused by shrapnel. If I didn't know better I'd say it was an anti-personnel bomb. I'll write something up for the Mounties." He put the towel on the rack. "If that little girl I met is her daughter, she might like this." He held up an envelope and opened it for Darling to see inside. "A gold chain and a charm with S.H. on it."

"That's something, anyway. We've no identification for her as yet. I'll be going upstairs in a minute to see if the girl has been able to talk. I can't imagine what they'd have been doing up there in the bush. It's quite a way up a mountain behind where I live along the lake, at King's Cove. There's really nothing up there but pine forest."

"Have you seen the bomb itself?"

"No. I was busy here with our dead jeweller, but my wife, Lane, and some of our neighbours found the child two days ago. Lane went back up yesterday, just to have a look around, and that's when she found this woman. We are assuming she's the mother, but who knows? My wife did say she could smell quite a simple mixture of gunpowder and TNT, and some picric acid. Interestingly, there was some paper. She said it looked as though the bomb had come down with some sort of paper parachute."

"Your wife made these observations? She sounds very interesting," Dr. Miyazaki said appreciatively. "A woman with skills."

"She is that," Darling said. "The RCMP don't appreciate her much and have warned her off. They have taken up the investigation. They seemed to be concerned it might be a security matter."

"Hmm," Miyazaki said. He moved to the coat rack where he had placed his grey hat and then turned to Darling. "How does your wife know so much about explosives?" he asked with genuine interest.

"My wife seems to know a good deal about a lot of things. Something to do with the war, I suppose."

Dr. Miyazaki smiled and nodded. "It does not surprise me that the Mounties don't want anyone near the bomb site. Perhaps it involves the Sons of Freedom. Is there something up there that might have been of interest to them?"

"Not a thing. It's completely wild up there," Darling said.

Miyazaki nodded. "I suppose they will find out and we will never know." He held out his hand. "This time I really must be on my way, Inspector Darling. I wish you luck with both these matters." He nodded toward the morgue and made a slight bow.

Back at the police station, O'Brien said, "Had a call from your missus. She's found something she thinks might be of interest and will help identify the young girl. Has she thought about officially joining the force, sir?"

"Thank you, Sergeant," Darling said repressively. "Anything else?"

"Ames and Terrell have gone off to talk to the locksmith. They are planning to go through the office of the jeweller but wanted to wait for you. Can I ask, sir, if there's any word on the condition of the girl?"

"She is conscious but not talking. At the moment they are happy because she is eating."

"I'm glad to hear that. Poor thing. A horrible thing to happen."

TERRELL HAD GONE to Humphries's Locksmith first thing, but it was closed. He'd found a home address in the directory, but no one had been there either. Perhaps they were off for a Sunday drive. On Monday morning, he and Ames were making another stab at it. The locksmith occupied a tiny shop on Vernon Street. It was so small, Ames thought, that it looked as if it would not fully accommodate both him and Terrell. They found Mr. Humphries behind a counter. He looked up at the sound of the door opening and stood.

"Morning, gentlemen."

"Good morning," Ames said. "I'm Sergeant Ames, and this is Constable Terrell. Mr. Humphries, is it?"

"That's me. How can I help?" But then he shook his head and sighed, looking crestfallen. "Oh, of course, this will be about poor Ron. His wife telephoned me, and of course it's been all over town that a body was taken out of his store." He shook his head. "I can't believe it. I've known that man for nearly thirty-five years. Wouldn't hurt a fly. In fact, a little too kind, if you want my opinion. Poor Bertha must be beside herself. I asked if we could go see her, but Barbara said she wasn't quite up to it yet."

Ames nodded. "We're hoping you might be able to tell us something that would help. Constable Terrell stopped by yesterday, when we didn't find you at home."

Humphries nodded. "The wife and I were visiting her sister in Castlegar for the weekend. Got back late. A horrible thing to come home to." He shook his head. "We've been friends since the Great War. Heck, we're even third cousins. Found that out during the war, if you can believe it. It's a real tragedy. You couldn't find a nicer guy."

"Do you have time for a few questions? We'd like to know a little bit more about him," Ames asked.

"Sure. However I can help."

Terrell took out his notebook and leaned against the wall near the door, surveying the shop. There were various sorts of padlocks and other locking devices in boxes along a low shelf. Humphries's work counter was very tidy, with tools laid out along one side to the right of where he'd work. There was a cash register and wooden inbox with receipts or orders in it next to the wall. On one wall, next to a selection of uncut keys, there was a framed photo of a much younger Humphries with a woman and two small children. The extreme tidiness of the place impressed Terrell. He returned his focus to Humphries. He was one of those easygoing, unperturbable types. Always had a smile for the customer, Terrell decided.

"Very organized shop, sir," he commented.

Humphries smiled. "That's the wife. I'm hopeless. She comes in once a week and gives the place a going-over. Let's slap the Closed sign on the door so we won't be interrupted," he said. "Now, what can I tell you?"

This was always the question for Ames—where to start, what questions might build a picture of the man. "You're English yourself," he observed.

Humphries gave a brief smile. "It's that obvious, is it? You'd think after all this time I'd have lost some of it."

"You said you've known him for thirty-five years. You first met in the army?"

"That's right. It was the darnedest thing, really. We weren't in the same unit, but we met one night at a pub when we were on leave. We took to one another right away. So much so that I decided to come out here, he made the place sound so good. Lots of space and opportunity. Beats the East End of London all to hell." He waved his hand to indicate his shop. "It was the right choice. I've done really well between my shop and my investments."

"You mentioned that you discovered you were distant relations."

"I always wondered if that's why we got on so well. Blood tells, sort of thing. His grandmother and mine were first cousins, it turns out. We found out by accident when we were in England."

Ames nodded. "And more recently, would you say you have remained close?"

"Oh, yes. He and the missus and me and mine are often together. We even went on holiday together a couple of times. Once down across the line to Montana, and another time out to Victoria. Even a road trip didn't break our friendship! In fact, we were planning to all go to England together, maybe in the fall." Humphries gave a quick laugh, and then stopped, as if he recalled the somber business they were on. "I'll miss him, and that's the truth. It won't be the same without him. We got on like a house on fire. I've never had a closer friend."

"Did he have any enemies? Or any kind of business troubles?"

Humphries set his mouth in a grim line, and then twisted it into an expression of doubt. "I don't think so. Not really. I mean, he is, was, the only jeweller in town, so not much in the way of competition. He . . ." He paused. "Now, mind you, he travelled a good deal. I know he visited a wholesaler in Vancouver quite a bit. Did something go wrong there? I don't know. He never said."

"Can you remember the name of the wholesaler?"

Humphries took a thoughtful breath and then shook his head. "I'm not sure I ever heard it. But it'll likely be somewhere in his records of purchases. Bertha will know." He shook his head. "Poor Bertha."

"Did you and he drink at the Legion, or anywhere?" Ames asked.

Humphries nodded. "Oh yeah, sure. The Legion. Not once a week or anything, but pretty regularly, say, every ten days? The girls weren't keen on being left out, so we'd go to the ladies' bar at the Dade every now and then, just to keep the peace. But honestly, we were happier on our own at the Legion. Being with other veterans is, I don't know . . . you just sort of feel at home. I don't think the girls ever really understand that sort of thing."

"Do you have children, Mr. Humphries?" He wasn't sure why he asked this, and he could feel rather than see Terrell look up at the question.

The locksmith didn't seem surprised. "Yes, two boys. Grown up now, of course." He waved a hand at the family photo. "One has gone out east to Halifax, and the other one, believe it or not, has gone back to the old country. He's staying with my nephew in London." He shook his head. "Says it's a right mess and he wants to come home. The Harolds never had any kids, but that kid brother of his stood in for one. It was a real shame. He died almost the minute he shipped out."

Terrell took notes. "What was his name, sir?"

"That was Billy. William. Ron doted on him, very proud. He was at the university when the war started. It was a real blow, losing him like that."

Ames nodded. "Is there anything else that you think might be helpful?"

Shaking his head, Humphries said, "I can't understand any of it. He was a kind and generous man, and I don't know anyone who even disliked him, let alone would want to kill him."

"Well, thank you, Mr. Humphries. If you think of anything else, give us a call at the station."

"Will do. Thanks, Officers."

Terrell closed his book and pushed it into his breast pocket with the pencil and touched the brim of his cap, and then followed Ames out the door. He'd just stepped onto the sidewalk when he turned. The door was still open, and Humphries was flipping his Closed sign around. "You said at the beginning that he was 'too kind.' What did you mean by that?" Terrell asked him.

"He was always helping some poor person in distress. He'd give his last penny or piece of bread to some of the poor folk in the French villages that had been flattened. He was always helping someone." He shrugged.

"Who, do you think?" Terrell asked.

"Well. That's me just guessing. I don't actually know of anyone. I expect he gave pretty freely to charity, helped out the odd homeless veteran here as well. I think it's why he worked so hard at his business. A bit over the top, if you ask me. His missus complained to mine more than once about how hard he worked. He doesn't need to, sorry, didn't need to. He was quite comfortable. I tried to get him to invest from time to time, do something for himself for a change, but he was cautious to a fault."

Terrell touched the brim of his cap again, and he and Ames made their way back to the station.

"What do you think?" Ames asked him.

"I'm not sure. I just think it anomalous that a man who has no enemies and is 'too kind' has a cobbler's hammer buried in his skull."

Ames smiled slightly and pushed open the station door. "Sergeant, quick. Use the word 'anomalous' in a sentence," he said to O'Brien.

Sergeant O'Brien looked up from his paperwork at the ceiling. "Nine-letter word meaning 'aberrant.' Anomalous."

"Ha. And I thought those crossword puzzles were a waste of time! Constable, can you write up your notes, and don't use any nine-letter words!"

"Sir."

DR. EDISON LOOKED at the birth certificate and sighed. "Sara. A lovely name. We are no nearer to hearing from her. She is awake, and eats a little, and she looks around a good deal, as if she is hoping to find something that is not here. Her mother, I should think. What a lovely woman she looks!" She handed back the photo. "She—we can call her by her name now, Sara—seems to like one of the nurses. Sister Evans is the only one she will put up being bathed by. It's a terribly painful procedure with a burn, and she has several places where shards of metal were removed." She held up the teddy bear Lane had brought. "This is very nice. Here. She is awake just now. Would you like to see her and give it to her?"

"Oh, yes indeed. I didn't like to ask. Of course, she won't know who I am."

"But she will know you are someone kind. While you do that, I will get the details on this birth certificate copied down."

The little girl was in a large room with three other beds, all of which were empty. There was a chair beside the bed that almost highlighted the sad fact that no one came to visit. Someone had put a vase of flowers, perhaps left by another patient, on the table next to the bed. Lane stood at the doorway holding the books and the teddy bear for just a moment.

Sara lay on her back with her arms outside the covers. One of them was bandaged heavily. Lane could see, from the disparity in size of her legs under the covers, that her left leg was in a cast. Stoic, she thought. The kind of stoicism only a child would have, caught in a situation she could have no control over and could not understand. That was the expression on Sara's face. She had been looking up at the ceiling when Lane had come to the door, and now, without moving her head, she had turned her eyes toward her visitor, as if the cast and bandaging had limited all movement but that of her eyes.

Lane approached the bed and sat down. "Hello, Sara. My name is Lane. And this fellow is called Teddy for now, but I know you will want to give him a name yourself." She put the teddy bear along the inside of the unbandaged arm and patted its head. "He's very good company and was very excited to come here and get to know you."

Sara swivelled her eyes so that she was looking down at the bear and moved her arm just slightly, as if she might pull the bear into a hug.

"I was at your cottage and found some books I'm sure are yours. If you like, I could read one to you. How about *Madeline*? It's one of my favourites." Lane held the book up. She had thought of reading *Babar*, but a story about a baby elephant whose mother is shot seemed appalling under the circumstances. The girl looked at Lane, her dark eyes like liquid shadows, and then looked past her, at the door. Lane's heart constricted. "Right." She put down the two other books, *Babar* on the bottom, and opened *Madeline*. "In an old house in Paris that was covered in vines, lived twelve little girls in two straight lines . . ." She leaned forward and held the book so that Sara could follow along and was rewarded by seeing that the little girl's eyes were on the pages.

When she was finished, Sara had closed her eyes and appeared to be asleep, the bear still nestled in her arm. Lane closed the book, put it on top of the two others, and stood at just the moment Dr. Edison appeared in the doorway.

In the hallway, Lane shook her head. "If someone does read to her, I don't think they should attempt *Babar*. The poor fellow's mother is shot by hunters right at the beginning. Too close to home."

Smiling, Dr. Edison shook her head. "My father used to read me the original Grimms' Fairy Tales. It's a bit shocking what we expose our children to. I think I'll ask the nurse to just put *Babar* in the cupboard. Did she have clothes and things?"

Lane nodded. "The trouble is the police, the Mounties I mean, have more or less warned me off. But I'm on my way down there now with these papers. I'll ask if I may bring out some clothes. It might be comforting to have her own cardigan and so on nearby. How long is she likely to be here?"

Edison shook her head. "We aren't completely sure about any internal injuries. She does eat, but not much. That could be indicative of something. She moans when she is picked up for the bath, but since she can't tell us if it's the burns, her broken leg, or something inside, it is difficult to know. But just the visible damage would likely keep her here a couple of weeks. The leg is broken in two places. I expect she'll limp a bit for the rest of her life."

While it wasn't good news that she would have to be in the hospital all that time, it did, Lane could see, buy some time for the authorities to sort out if she had family other than her mother, or where her father might be. Perhaps members of the Sasaki family had returned to the coast. "Thank you, Dr. Edison. I'll come back tomorrow, if I may. I have some books from my own childhood that I think are less lethal, although I'm not even sure of that now! I shall pre-read them to make sure they are soothing. I must say, I remember feeling sad about Babar's mother when I was a child, but by the time he got a nice set of clothes I'd quite forgotten he was an orphan."

AT THE RCMP detachment on Stanley Street, Lane approached the front desk. "Is Inspector Guilfoil here?"

"Who shall I say?" asked the young officer. He could not have been more than twenty, Lane thought, noting his slicked-back hair and the earnest expression of a young man who wanted to impress with his diligence.

She smiled. "Lane Winslow Darling. We met earlier in the year. He might remember me."

One did not, evidently, smile in the performance of one's duty. "What is this regarding?"

Here she was stumped. She would have liked to speak with Guilfoil in confidence, but she was not sure she would get past this dutiful officer. "It is to do with the explosion up at King's Cove."

"I see. Wait here, please."

Lane waited and looked at the list of the wanted on the wall. The photographs were browning with age and vaguely malevolent. She wouldn't like to meet any of them in a dark alley, she thought. But in the next moment she looked more closely. Some were so young, and in one she saw not evil so much as fear. But the rest had a disturbing lack of expression. She turned at the sound of footsteps. To her dismay she was being approached by Sergeant Fryer, who had been particularly dismissive at the bomb site.

He looked down at a piece of paper. "Yesterday you told us your name was Winslow. I see here that you have added Darling."

Lane tried for a pleasant smile. "Yes. I use my maiden name for the most part, but I am married to Frederick Darling, the inspector at the police station. It is how Inspector Guilfoil knows me."

He was not to be won by a smile or a reference to his boss. "What can I do for you, Mrs. Darling?"

"I had hoped to talk briefly with Inspector Guilfoil—"

"If it is to do with the business at King's Cove, I am in charge."

"Yes, I see." She took a breath. "I stumbled on a cabin that I think might belong to the victims of the bomb, and I did find some documents, including a birth certificate for the girl and the mother. I've been to the hospital to share the information. Now, I've brought the documents to you and"—she hesitated—"a watch." She held up the metal box.

He took the box, bristling. "When I said that you were to stay away from the area, what did you take that to mean?"

That you are a patronizing weasel, she thought. She attempted to look chastened. She hoped she was succeeding.

"Instead, you've been tramping all over the evidence and destroying a crime scene. This is a murder investigation, and if I find you've destroyed evidence, I won't hesitate to charge you as an accessory after the fact. I don't care whose bloody wife you are."

"The little girl will be in hospital at least a couple of weeks. I'm hoping that you will be looking into who her people are. And that watch. It should go to the little girl, you know, eventually. Can you make sure?"

"Staying away, Mrs. Darling, includes not telling us how to do our job. Good afternoon."

CHAPTER NINE

"WHAT SURPRISED ME WAS HIS saying it was a murder investigation. I mean, someone has died, to be sure, but murder?" Lane and Darling had taken their dinner of meatloaf and mashed potatoes onto the French cast-iron table on the porch and were enjoying the lingering warmth of the evening as Lane caught Darling up on the events of the day. "On the basis of what, exactly?"

"You've become quite adept at this meatloaf business. I look forward to my sandwich tomorrow," Darling said, pointing his fork at his dinner. "Soon I'll be like O'Brien, with a lunch box and some homemade cake to look forward to every day. So, you've been told off by the Mounties yet again. I wish I had their courage," he added wistfully.

"Stop being silly. I'm serious."

"Oh, all right. It might be a long shot, but they may try to make the case that whoever put the bomb there can be accused of the murder of, let's call her Mrs. Ichiko Harold, since you went to all the trouble of messing up the crime scene to get the information." He sat back and looked out at the lake. "Harold is the name of my victim, the jeweller. You're right to ask if they might be related. We'll need to find out. It's quite a coincidence, and with two people named Harold dead, one has to wonder if there is some more lethal connection."

"Strange indeed. I suppose it's a common name. Was his first name William?"

"No, Ron. Now, I think he did have a younger brother called Bill, but he was killed right at the start of the war. I'll contact the police in Vancouver and see if they can get some information about this Ichiko Sasaki Harold."

"That would be remarkable, and quite sinister. I wonder if Sara and her mother were a secret family Ron Harold was keeping from everyone."

"Blast! That would put the dead man's wife in the frame," Darling mused. "I shall get on to Vancouver first thing tomorrow. He was making secret trips to Vancouver, and the child was born there. But no. That doesn't work, not if they're here."

"Or maybe Ichiko's William and Ron Harold's Bill are one and the same, in which case . . . well, I don't know in which case what," Lane said, sighing. "Luckily, you're a police officer. You can find out all about it."

"If only you'd let me do that," Darling said.

"By the way," she continued, "the cabin wasn't the crime scene. It's at least a quarter mile as the raven flies from the blast site. And if I hadn't gone, we still wouldn't know who the girl is."

"I do see your point, darling, but I see theirs as well. I mean, what if someone decided to go past the tape I've put up at the jewellery store to have a scrounge about in the shop? Investigation is a methodical business. Even if someone found something we'd missed altogether, it wouldn't justify their action, and more importantly, it might lead to the loss of valuable information. Those photos you kept back, for example."

Now feeling genuinely chastened, Lane sat back. "All right. I do see the point. But I was thinking about Sara. And it has helped that she has a name now. But I see what you mean, I really do. Still, it's a situation of a wrong resulting in a right. I'm worried about that watch. It belongs to Sara now. I want to make sure she gets it. Anyway, I promised Sergeant bloody Fryer I'd stay away."

"Excellent. What's for afters?"

Lane turned to him. "Does this mean that he knows who put the bomb there? Or he suspects someone?"

"Nothing then," Darling said sadly. "Except a large helping of your persistence. All right. Let's see. It could mean that. They may have found something when they were collecting their bomb detritus that gave them a clue as to the origin. You only have to read the papers to know they are contending with a rash of bombings and arson by the Sons of Freedom. From what I have heard, the traditional Doukhobors are upset with this Freedomite splinter group, as it is their schools that are being burned, and, of course, it tars them all with the same brush."

"But that's not here. It's out toward Grand Forks, isn't it? I mean, they target actual buildings or electric structures, don't they? There's absolutely nothing up the mountain that would be of interest to anyone."

"Perhaps they have reason to believe the child's mother was herself a target."

"But they didn't even know who she was till I found the papers!"

Darling shook his head. "Perhaps, or they might well know who she is. Alas, they have not shared anything with me. But I would suggest you do as you're asked. I'd ask you to help out with the murder of poor Mr. Harold just to distract you, but no one is Russian, so I won't need you to translate, and you didn't find his body, I did, so we are going to have to stagger on somehow without you."

"You are very sweet. Just for that I will produce a vanilla cake I picked up at the bakery in town. It is quite handily across the street from Hudson's Bay where I got the teddy bear for Sara."

"That's the stuff! Now we're talking."

At that precise moment of Darling's anticipation, the phone rang. They both waited. Two longs and a short. "I'll get it," he said. "You wrangle up that cake." He got up and stretched and then went into the hallway. "кс 431, Darling speaking," he said into the horn.

Lane could hear Darling's end of the conversation as she cut two pieces of cake and put them on plates. She was just licking the icing off her fingers when she heard, "You'd better talk to Lane. She's been there today." He called down the hall, "Darling, it's Harris asking about the little girl."

"Your cake's on the table. If you're a gentleman, you'll wait till I get there."

He smiled broadly, handing her the earpiece. "I'm not."

"Hello, Robin," Lane said. She was a little surprised that he would telephone during the generally agreed-upon King's Cove dinner hour. She couldn't recall his ever having done it before.

"What's going on with the kiddie?" he asked without preamble.

"She seems to be doing as well as can be expected. I did discover what her name is. It's Sara. Sara Himari Sasaki Harold. I found the little cabin where they have apparently been living. I also found a few children's books and I got her a teddy bear. They let me see her."

"Sara," he said, followed by a longish silence. "The bear was a good idea."

"I actually have a copy of a book from my own childhood here, *Doctor Dolittle*. I might take it up and read it to her."

Another long silence. Then a statement that surprised Lane as nothing else could. "I could do it."

The silence now was on her side, as she weighed whether a snarly old man smelling strongly of tobacco would be welcome to sit by the dazed child's bed to read to her. Then, shrugging, she thought, Why not? He was of a grandfatherly age, if not demeanour. "I think that's a really nice idea, Robin. Why don't you come up with me? I'm not sure who they are letting in to see her, but I've been allowed, so we might both get in. I'm going up again tomorrow a little after lunch. Would you have time then?"

"I have to fix the damn water problem at Gladys's, but I'll do it first thing. You know where I live."

"Yes, Robin, I do. See you then."

Darling, of course, proved to be a gentleman after all, and had cleared the dishes and now sat at the French table with the plates of cake and clean forks.

"Well, if that doesn't take the biscuit," Lane said, sitting down. "Harris wants to come to town and read to Sara."

"Frighten Sara, more like. Shall we?" He picked up his fork.

"Yes. Did I mention you are very sweet?"

"You did. I'll thank you not to let it get about."

"I'm actually really worried," Lane said, after her first bite. "This is quite good. Is it as good as homemade? I wish we had one of Mabel's to compare. I'm worried because Sergeant bloody Fryer said absolutely nothing about whether they would be looking for Sara's father or relatives. She's got two weeks, maybe a little more in the hospital, but that's not very long if it's going to be complicated. I suppose they will. They have to, don't they? It's just maddening not to know."

"You're already quite mad enough, in my view, if you plan to take that bad-tempered old man to scare a child in poor health. I tell you what, I'll call Guilfoil tomorrow and see if he'll let me in on what they're up to." Inspector Guilfoil had been tasked with the investigation into Darling's conduct earlier in the year when allegations of corruption had been brought against him. They'd come to respect each other through the process.

"Oh, would you, darling? You are an absolute love."

"Am I? I know at least one way you could prove it," he said, leaning across the table for a lingering kiss.

HARRIS WAS UP early the next morning, and the denizens of King's Cove, an early-rising bunch, were nevertheless surprised to hear his tractor lumbering effortfully up the hill past the Hughes house before seven. He stopped the machine at the top of the upper orchard near where the heavy rubber hose that carried water to the Hugheses' lay, now buried in the growing grass and underbrush. He dropped his cigarette and began the tramp up the mountain toward the creek, following the hose.

He arrived a good thirty or so minutes later, frowning and short of breath, at a surprising sight—a junction where another smaller hose had been spliced onto the one he was following. He dropped to his knees to look. He could not immediately see how the business had been done because the whole thing had been expertly duck-taped and, for good measure, bound up tightly with cloth. Someone was tapping the main water pipe. And he could see why they only started noticing it in the last while: the whole thing had sprung a leak, and water had been dribbling out onto the ground under the splice.

He stood up and contemplated the direction of the smaller hose.

With a sigh he started back down the hill. He would need the roll of duck tape he had in his barn workshop to fix it. He could do it the next day. For now, he'd go home to ready himself for the trip into town.

Lane, having cleared the breakfast dishes, contemplated the growing pile of laundry and decided against any involvement with it, and then thought it might be high time to bring the Armstrongs up to date. It was already after nine, so a respectable time, and she was quite ready for the cup of tea she knew she would be offered in return for the latest news. On the way, she wondered how Darling's conversation with Guilfoil would go.

Her musing was joyfully interrupted by Alexandra, the Armstrongs' Westie, who had been waiting for Mrs. Armstrong at the door of the root cellar. She ran around Lane, yapping happily, and then sat directly in front of her, her whole bottom wagging. Lane obliged by picking her up and saying a few affectionate words.

"She only greets you like that," Mrs. Armstrong said, ducking to come through the root cellar door. She was carrying a bowl of potatoes. Her dazzlingly white hair, something she achieved with regular bluing, was pinned in a roll, and she wore a flowered apron over her neat pre-war dress. Nothing, Lane thought, would ever go to waste in this cottage.

"Come on, leave her alone," Eleanor said to Alexandra, who'd embarked on a campaign of face licking. "Tea?"

"Only if you're not busy."

"Have you any news?"

"Yes, some."

"Well then, I'm not busy. Put the dog down and go call Kenny from the garden."

Lane obeyed and found Kenny Armstrong working on one of his espaliered plum trees. "Good morning, Kenny. I'm to bring you in for a cup of tea."

His face brightened immediately, and he snipped the twine he was using and pushed the roll and the scissors

114

into the pocket of his overalls. "Good, then. How are you? Inspector get off all right?"

"He did, thank you. Your garden looks delightful as always. I don't think I'll ever manage to create anything as wonderful as this. It's like paradise."

"It's all I do. You have other responsibilities, which I hope you will be discharging over our tea, yes?"

Lane smiled at the insatiable appetite this man had for news, and all of Darling's cases in particular—or as the Armstrongs thought, Lane's cases.

In the kitchen it had been the work of a moment to produce a pot of tea because a full kettle always simmered on the wood stove. Eleanor had already pulled open an old George V and Queen Mary coronation tin to reveal a tempting pile of her ginger biscuits.

"I'm not sure I know enough to warrant this cup of tea. I went for a bit of an explore the day before yesterday, after the explosion. I met some Mounties at the site and was more or less ordered off. But I was anxious to see where the little girl might have come from, so later in the afternoon I went up again and I found their cabin."

"You never! A cabin?" Eleanor's cup was halfway to her mouth, and she put it down again. "They were living up there in the middle of nowhere? What were they doing for water?"

"There was a hose coming down from somewhere, and a tap outside the cabin. It was a very complete little homestead, with an outhouse at the back, a vegetable garden, and I think very possibly a path going down toward Bales's store. Oh. I meant to talk to him and ask about whether the woman shopped there. I was so focused on getting Sara's birth certificate to the hospital it slipped my mind." Lane described the discovery of the books, watch, and papers belonging to the pair, and her visit to the hospital. "I took the papers and the watch to the Mountie detachment and got told off again, but they didn't *say* exactly that I couldn't continue to visit the girl. Harris and I are going in to visit her this afternoon." Lane knew this would be astonishing news, but decided to present it as if it were the most normal thing in the world. "I didn't tell them I'd kept back these." She reached into her pocket and took out the photos.

"Oh, she's lovely!" exclaimed Eleanor, taking them up. "Fancy her last name being Harold. Do you think she's anything to do with the poor dead jeweller? There's a story there, I'm sure. What a dreadful loss! And this must be Sara's mother as a little girl with her own parents."

Kenny was also interested in the coincidence of the names, but he was not to be denied his astonishment. "Did you say you are taking *Harris* with you to see her?"

"I am. He wants to read *Doctor Dolittle* to her." Lane had known this bit of news would amaze, and she wasn't disappointed.

Both Armstrongs put their cups down with a clatter.

"My cousin, Robin Harris? That Robin?" Kenny asked.

"He's gone mad," Eleanor declared. "It's the only explanation." She sat back, shaking her head, then abruptly leaned forward again. "They'll never let him in. He's an appalling specimen. He'll frighten the poor little thing to death. What's got into him?"

116

DARLING AND GUILFOIL were sitting in the café, having somehow wangled some coffee out of Marge.

"I must say, I miss the nice young woman," Guilfoil said, watching Marge abuse a customer hoping for a cup of tea at the counter.

"We all do. Miss McAvity has decided she wants to go into police work and is doing a course in Vancouver."

"Is she, by Jove? I think she mentioned that to me when I was in here earlier in the year. I didn't think she'd follow through. Good for her. You could use a pretty girl around the place."

"You couldn't use a woman officer?" Darling asked, raising a brow.

"Well, you know. We have a matron we can call on to deal with any women prisoners. Luckily not too much trouble with the fair sex, so she's mostly idle. But policing, it's not a woman's game, is it?"

Darling smiled and shrugged. "I don't know why not, when you think of what women did during the war."

"Really, Darling, taking over a few assembly lines in factories and running the gas stations while the boys were away hardly qualifies them to take on men's work."

"Quite a few worked out on the front, as I understand it," Darling said. He knew he'd make no headway, and he rather liked Guilfoil, whom he considered an honest man, so he'd sooner not have an argument. And Guilfoil held the prevailing view, he knew. Women ought to be at home, looking after house, husband, and children. He wondered if there was a Mrs. Guilfoil toiling away on his behalf somewhere.

"I heard about that. I don't know how much of it is true. Couriers and that sort of thing. Still not the battlefield, is it? Anyway, you've brought me here for this excellent cup of coffee and exposed me to that woman's wrath. What can I do for you? I don't doubt it has something to do with your good wife. The boys have told me about her showing them the site." He leaned forward and added, "I must say they were surprised she seemed to know a bit about the contents of the bomb in question. I dare say she's one of your war women."

"Alas," Darling said, "she has not taken me into her confidence, but I can tell you what she is concerned about, and I'm wondering if, in this one respect, we might give a hand. The little girl in the hospital at the moment is without known relations. We likely have a couple of weeks during which she is recuperating in the hospital. Does your investigation include that aspect, or could we perhaps help here? We could check among the Japanese in the area and contact the Vancouver Police to see if they can find her father or any member of her extended family. I know my wife turned over the paperwork she found. Another important consideration is that the girl's surname is the same as that of the man we found murdered in his shop. Cases could be connected."

Guilfoil set his mouth in a line and looked out the window. Before he could speak, Darling spoke again. "What sort of investigation are you doing? Is this linked to the other disturbances from the Freedomites?"

"Look here, Darling," Guilfoil began. "We're all in the same business, and in this town at least we've been working together pretty well, so I don't mind telling you. We are, of course, looking at this in the light of the other bombs and fires. It's hard to imagine there are two lots of bombers operating in our small area. And we have some very suspicious activity nearby by a known member of the organization. The two things certainly suggest a link. We're bringing someone out who really knows about bombs to have a look. This doesn't look like the usual sort of device. As you can imagine, that raises the alarm. Are they getting bombs and weapons from another source, maybe even a foreign source? My guess is they set it off up there to try it out, before turning it on their usual targets. Not much more I can say, I'm afraid." His tone let Darling know he begrudged telling him even this.

"My wife said she's seen something like it in Europe. She suggests it's at least a twenty pounder."

Guilfoil shrugged. "Best left to the professionals, I think. I understand my men told her to stay away from the site."

"Absolutely, but you know she and a couple of other women found the child, and she subsequently found the mother. She had ample opportunity to look around before your officers were able to get out there and warn her off. At any rate, it will be interesting to see what your expert has to say. She does not in any way want to interfere with your work in that regard." Darling mentally crossed his fingers. "But she is most concerned about the little girl, who is apparently still in shock. She has not spoken and does not yet know her mother is dead. She'd like to go and get anything that might be of help to the girl from the cabin, if she may."

"Yes, yes. Quite right." Guilfoil thought for a moment. "I tell you what, the whole business of the girl is a distraction we don't have the manpower to pursue just now. Certainly more appropriate for your wife to be concerned about the child than bombs she knows nothing about. I'll have the men photograph the documents and bring them along to you, and you can see if you can scare up some relations for her. She's called Sara, I believe. Dreadful thing to happen to a child."

"Thank you. I'll get someone on to it. My wife will be very pleased." Darling's teeth were clamped tight as he watched Guilfoil leave. "Dolt," he muttered under his breath.

CHAPTER TEN

"I **'M NOT SURE SHE CAN** have so many visitors," the floor nurse said, looking suspiciously at Robin Harris. Much to Lane's amazement, Harris appeared in a pair of black trousers, shiny with age, an almost respectable belt, and a clean white shirt. She'd never seen him without his grungy coveralls, even on Sundays. But, of course, this nurse had never seen him in his natural habitat and garb, so she wouldn't recognize this as an improvement.

She could feel Harris shift impatiently next to her, so she put her hand very quickly on his arm to keep him from speaking. "We have a new book to read to her. Is Sara awake?"

The nurse shrugged. "She is. She's had a little bath and some lunch, but she's still not talking. You're the only person who visits her."

"Well, then, I think having another visitor might be rather nice. Is she enjoying her teddy bear?"

The nurse's expression softened. "We had a job getting her to leave it behind for the trip to the bath. In the end we had to promise he could come and sit in a chair waiting for her. She seems to understand all right, so that's something. I don't think she could hear well at first, but that seems to be coming back." The nurse appeared to be recovering her aplomb.

Another chair was brought around so that Harris could sit next to Lane by the bed. Sara turned and looked at them both and pulled her bear a little closer. Lane tried to ascertain if she looked better and decided that her wide-eyed stare was perhaps an indication of recognition. And she did have a bit more colour in her face. Her hair had been brushed and braided. In the sun from the window, it had reddish highlights. Maybe that was what she'd seen when she'd first found her and had noticed something about her hair.

"Sara, this is Mr. Harris. He helped when we found you, and he very much wanted to see how you are getting along. I brought this book that I used to have when I was a little girl." She held up *Doctor Dolittle*.

Sara looked at the book cover for a long while and then at Robin Harris when Lane handed the book to him. She did not change her solemn expression, but she had the air of settling in to be read to.

"WOULD YOU LIKE to go into the supermarket before we start back?" Lane asked. "I wouldn't mind picking up a couple of things myself."

"I'll sit in the car."

"Are you sure, Robin? They have lovely things."

He sat for a couple of moments after she parked across the street and gazed at the store. Finally, he opened the door and stepped out. "Fine."

"Here, we can get a cart. You can put your things in the top, and I'll use the bottom."

"I can get what I need at Bales's."

"Right you are." Lane proceeded to the meat counter and picked up a chicken. She had become a reliable roaster of chicken, and it gave them a couple of meals. There were some hams hanging along the back wall and she asked the butcher for a cut. She contemplated the packaged bread and then thought of the bread she ought to be learning to make. She would buy milk and a block of cheddar cheese and perhaps some crackers. A couple of cans of mushroom soup, because she had read that chicken pieces could be cooked in mushroom soup. Should she get rice? Oats? Perhaps she could learn the secret of Eleanor's oatmeal cookies. A lettuce, some carrots and potatoes, and some frozen packets of vegetables, several tins of salmon.

In the bakery section, she took a Hovis loaf, a white loaf—she couldn't *always* depend on her neighbours—and contemplated a small walnut cake.

"Robin, you've been so kind coming into town to read to Sara. Let me get you something. I'm thinking of that nice-looking walnut cake. I can ask them to split it and you can have half for your tea."

He was not, as it turned out, insensible to the lure of cake, and he grunted his assent.

The grocery bags stowed, they began their trip home with a short wait at the ferry.

"You really read so beautifully. She was entranced."

"Why shouldn't I? I suppose you thought I couldn't read because I'm a yokel on a tractor."

"I didn't think that at all," she said pacifically. "But I hadn't expected you to read so perfectly to a child, I suppose. The way you stopped and showed her the pictures of the animals and so on. I could see she was following you avidly. And that was certainly close to a smile she gave you at the end. She hasn't done that for anyone else!"

Harris made his usual harrumph sound, but there was an element of being pleased about it. He was silent all through the ferry ride and for some miles after they'd bumped off. "She reminds me of a friend I had as a boy," he said finally.

"Does she?" Lane said, in a way that she hoped would show she would like to hear more.

"I was seven. We were separated by poverty and circumstances. It doesn't much matter anymore."

"Is that around the time you came over here?"

"Yup. My parents were dead. Was sent to live on a miserable farm with an uncle. Dirt poor. Don't know what became of the girl."

"What was she called?"

"Betty. We both didn't have a mother. I had no father either, so we lived with her father. He was a brute, but she seemed to be able to look after him. He couldn't afford me, so he packed me off here at the Armstrongs' expense, Kenny's parents, you know. Girl's father was a drunk and he was lazy. I swore I'd never let myself get into that state. Treating a child the way he treated her. Both of us. But she was his blood." He said this with disgust and turned to look out the window. "I imagine she worked herself to death looking after him."

Lane nodded, and wanted to reach over and pat his shoulder, but knew at once it would not be welcome. He'd been married, she remembered, before the war, and his wife had got pregnant while he was overseas and had disappeared by the time he'd come back. He'd never married again. The pregnancy had led to very bad blood between Harris and Reginald Mather, she knew that.

"Thank you, Robin. Maybe you'll come with me again?" They were parked at the bottom of his driveway just before the turn up the hill toward the rest of the houses in King's Cove. Harris stood holding his paper bag from the grocery store. He had his half of the walnut cake along with the bottle of milk and the loaf of bread he'd finally agreed to.

"What's gonna happen to her when she gets out of there?" His gruff manner made the question sound accusatory. Or maybe he meant it to sound that way.

"I'm not sure. I've asked my husband to see if there is any way we can speed up finding her relations. I'll let you know."

"If you don't find anyone, she can stay here. I have lots of room." This was delivered in a brusque manner as well. It did not diminish the surprise this statement elicited in his hearer.

Unable to imagine any circumstance in which a mute little girl would be delivered for safekeeping into the hands of a single, old, and cantankerous farmer, Lane struggled for a moment with a response. "That is a lovely offer, Robin. Thank you. I'll keep you up to date on the developments.

We've a couple of weeks yet, I think."

On her way up the hill, Lane's mind turned on the whole matter of the unexpected new Robin Harris. The tender-hearted—that was not an exaggeration, she decided—kindly Harris who had suddenly emerged in the crisis of the lost child. Where on earth had that come from in him? Then she remembered she wanted to stop at Bales's to find out if Sara's mother had ever been in there. She unpacked her own groceries and put them away, and then got back into the car for the trip to the filling station.

IT WAS A task that had to be done, Darling thought, tapping a pencil on his desk. Someone had to go through the inventory at the jewellery shop and discover what had been stolen. The best person to do it was Mrs. Harold, but that would require going into the shop and going through the mess of destruction. She might well not be up to it; perhaps her efficient friend Mrs. Dee could help her. And he could certainly assign Ames or Terrell to do the heavy lifting. At least on the shop floor. The office was a different matter. And all of this was assuming robbery was the motive. Once Mrs. Harold had figured out what items had been stolen, he could get Terrell on to the pawn shops in nearby towns.

When a death occurs during the commission of a robbery, it is typically because the burglar is surprised, challenged, perhaps even attacked. Most burglars, in his experience, were not killers unless forced into it. He wondered if the murder itself wasn't the main event because there had been so little evidence of a struggle.

But of course, there was the theft, from display cases and drawers in the shop, and the ransacking of the office, looking for . . . what? Had the search been the main object?

He had a feeling that the killer did not find whatever it was he'd been looking for. But again, all the documents would have to be gone through with Mrs. Harold who, as part-time unpaid secretary and bookkeeper, would be in the best position to know what might be missing. There was nothing for it. Without understanding a possible motive for Harold's murder, it would be harder to track down the killer.

Time was of the essence. Terrell and Ames had been to see the locksmith, Humphries. He wanted to hear what they had to say but wanted to contact Mrs. Dee to see if Mrs. Harold was still staying there and might be up to talking. Ames could write up the interview notes and Terrell could get a start on looking for the weapon, though he had very faint hope there. He would send him to the hardware store, and any stores providing industrial supplies to tradespeople, assuming Miyazaki was right about the shape of the weapon. And he could find out if Lane's William Harold was related to their dead man.

MR. BALES TURNED his mouth down and frowned. "A Japanese woman? I don't think so, no. I mean, there's Mrs. Wong, who has a mending business down by the ferry, but she's not Japanese, and she's been here for years. Not that I'd know the difference, really."

"I suppose you know all your customers pretty well, as the only grocery store and gas station in Balfour."

He nodded. "That I do, for the most part. Now mind you, in the summer we get quite a few people I don't know, and in the last year and a half, since the ferry terminal went in, I'll get people going or coming from Kootenay Bay." He sighed. "That new ferry caused a lot of disruption and pretty well destroyed our nice peaceful little bit of heaven here with traffic, but it hasn't been bad for business. There's that café down there that's booming, expanded in the last year to cope with the travellers. But no one Japanese around here."

Lane nodded. The ferry landing was nearly finished by the time she'd arrived after the war, and a ferry called the *Anscomb* had been making the run to Kootenay Bay the whole time, so she didn't experience it as a "new" thing the way Bales did.

"Blast. She must have been getting her groceries from somewhere," said Lane. "There's no road to her place, and there's a path that leads down the mountain more or less in this direction. It's close enough to walk, I think, at least when it isn't snowing. It's three miles from the King's Cove turnoff along the road, but it might be shorter coming directly down the hill."

"This is about that woman that was found dead, isn't it?" Lucy, freed from her responsibilities at the telephone exchange by a lack of custom, was standing in the doorway listening. She had been, Lane realized, since she'd come into the shop. There certainly was no secret that was safe from this young woman's nosiness and gossipy nature.

"Yes, that's right," Lane said, resigned.

A car had pulled up to the gas pump, and Bales made a motion with his head to excuse himself.

"Is it true there was a little girl too?" Lucy asked.

"It is. How on earth did you find out?" Lane knew Lucy would not be offended by the question. Quite the contrary.

Indeed, Lucy leaned in with an almost conspiratorial expression. "Well, Mrs. Hughes up the hill called someone in town and mentioned it. I couldn't help overhearing."

I bet you couldn't, Lane thought, as a man came in and perused the contents of the ice cream freezer. He was followed in due course by Bales, who began to ring up the gas purchase.

"I'll have this too," the man said, holding up a Popsicle.

Lucy had made a *pas devant* movement of her eyes and slipped back into the exchange room, where several lines had lit up.

"See what I mean? I don't know that man from Adam, but he's been in a couple of times. I think he goes back and forth on the ferry," Bales said to her when his customer had left. He looked at his watch. "It's been about five minutes since the ferry landed. You can see the steady stream of cars heading up to town."

TERRELL WAS PUT to looking again for the weapon while Ames accompanied Mrs. Harold and Mrs. Dee to the store. He went up and down the alley, looking in bins and under the bushes, ground he'd already covered. He had little hope of finding anything. Any self-respecting murderer would have thrown the thing into the lake. He'd gone to the hardware store to see if they carried either shoemaker's hammers or upholstery tack hammers, but both tools were too specialized, especially as the shoe repair already had tools and the nearest upholsterer was in Castlegar. He also had nothing in the geological line but was able to direct Terrell to a miners' and prospectors' emporium just off Front Street. It was a bigger operation than he'd imagined, as it included some large industrial-looking mining equipment.

"Morning," the proprietor said when Terrell went in. He scratched his neck and watched Terrell scanning the small tools he had along one wall. "Can I help you find something?"

"Yes, good morning, sir. Constable Terrell of the Nelson Police." He held up his card.

"Rockford," the man offered. "Rocks are my business." No doubt his standard joke.

"I'm not entirely sure what I'm looking for. I think a hand-held tool, perhaps the size of a hammer with a sharp point?"

"You'd want something like this." Rockford walked to a bin. "It's a sample pick. Hammer one side, pick the other. I sell them to geologists and prospectors. You planning to take it up?"

Terrell smiled. "No, sir. But I'm wondering if you have a record of who you sell these things to?"

"I do. What's up?"

"Could I see the list?"

Rockford sighed. "It's not a list. I have copies of the receipts. I'd have to go through them and make a list for you. Say, is this about that murder?"

Well, that was all over town now. Terrell nodded. "How long would it take for you to make that list?"

"If it's not too busy, I could give it to you by the end of the day. It might not tell you much, though. These things get passed around, sold privately. People get enthusiastic and then when it doesn't pay off, they quit. Boy, they could do quite a bit of damage to a man!"

"You're probably right. But I'd appreciate the list. Thanks." Terrell felt not much further ahead after all this. He headed for Deacon's Shoe Repair, the proprietor of which looked up in surprise to see Terrell.

"Morning, Officer. Shoes need fixing?"

"Good morning, Mr. Deacon. No, thanks, but I wonder if you could help me. Could you show me the sort of hammer you use for your work?"

"Yeah, sure. Why?"

"I'm just conducting some research," Terrell said vaguely. Deacon went to his bench and came back with a hammer that in most respects looked to Terrell like a regular hammer, but with a claw that was longer and thicker at the top, narrowing down at the end. He turned it over. This sort of thing could do it. "How many of these do you have?"

"Just the one. I got it from my dad. He used to run a place in the old country."

"Where would someone get such a thing?"

Deacon sighed. "I couldn't tell you. I imagine Vancouver, maybe?"

"And you've never lent this one out?"

"No, Officer, I haven't. It's my most precious possession. What is all this in aid of? Wait . . . is this something to do with that murder? It's all over town." Deacon just managed to cloak his eager curiosity with an overlay of concern.

131

Terrell smiled and handed the tool back. "Thanks, Mr. Deacon."

AN ELECTRICIAN HAD been called to reconnect the electrical wires that had been cut outside the store, so they could turn on the lights. The shop looked like a bomb had gone off in it. Ames was impressed with Mrs. Harold's bravery under the circumstances. She stood now with her hand over her mouth, shaking her head. "It's worse than I ever imagined." But then she seemed to gain resolve. "Right, well. We'd better get at it. Come on, Barbara." There were two rows of glass cases, and she took a broom out of a narrow cupboard in the rear hall that led to the office. "I'll just push this glass off to the side."

Mrs. Dee and Ames began gingerly picking the glass out of the cases. Ames had found an empty cardboard box in the office, and they threw the shards into it. After a few minutes, Mrs. Harold stood with her arms hanging by her sides, looking into the glass case. The displays of watches, which mainly occupied this rear case, had been tipped over. Tears formed in her eyes.

"You know, all the most expensive watches are gone." She wiped her eyes and made an effort to pull herself together. "They left some of the cheap ones, anyway. They must have taken the velvet bags to put them in. We keep a stock of those to send the good jewellery home in."

They proceeded to the two cases that had held rings, necklaces, bracelets, and brooches, and here Mrs. Harold stopped and looked into the case. Among the shards were five small velvet boxes designed to hold rings. They'd been emptied, and some rings lay scattered among the glass. She picked through the glass carefully and pulled out three rings, which she lined up on the wood frame. She turned to Ames. "There are about ten watches missing, and quite a few rings—maybe ten." She looked miserably around the store. "He knew what he was doing. He picked the most expensive rings."

"Ten? What was their value?" Ames asked.

"Just these three are left, the least expensive. Most of the ones taken are priced around 300 dollars. I had one at 450. You can pay even more than that, but we never brought one in. No one wants to buy a ring that costs the same as a house!"

"Whew! That's a lot of money," Ames said. He certainly hadn't paid 300 dollars for the ring he'd bought.

CHAPTER ELEVEN

"HELLO, INSPECTOR," CHIEF CHAMBERLAIN SAID. "How's things out your way? Say, I think we have a young woman from your part of the world here now. She's in our training course. The only girl this time around."

"I know the young woman. April McAvity. She has a good head on her shoulders," Darling said. "We have a murder and a missing family here. But the weather is very nice for the time of year."

"I know what you mean." The chief of police in Vancouver chuckled, sounding a little tired. "How can I help?"

"I need some help locating a Japanese Canadian family." He went on to explain about Sara Harold and her mother.

"Those Russkis, eh? Never think about the effect of their bombs. Do you have anyone for it?"

"That is for the RCMP to discover, though I'm doubtful about it being a Freedomite bomb. There is absolutely nothing up there to target."

"Might have been trying it on for size. Just bad luck for them. So, you want us to find some relations. You're going to have trouble with that, I'm afraid. The Japanese who lived here haven't been allowed back. Nothing to come back for. Anything they had is gone. Damn fool business, there you are. What's done is done. And I'm a bit pressed here, Darling. We're after gambling. It's like a cancer. In every basement. Bookies everywhere. In fact, bookies stitching up other bookies so they can take over. Got my hands full." He paused. "She won't find much, but I suppose I could put your girl on to it. She won't find any Japanese, but she might be able to talk to neighbours if she gets an address, or the doctors at St. Paul's for that birth certificate you found. You think she's up to it?"

Darling was staggered to learn the internees were still forbidden to return to the coast this long after the war. Had it been in the papers? No doubt it had, but like most people he paid most attention to those concerns closest to home. He cleared his throat. It wasn't this man's fault, after all. "I'm sure she is. It won't interrupt her course?"

"It'll give her some practical experience. I wouldn't normally pay any attention to the kids on the course, except that she's the only girl, and I heard she's pretty sharp."

Darling nodded. "Can you give her the resources she needs?"

"Well, she's hardly going to make arrests, but we can make sure she has a temporary card so she can get questions answered."

"Thanks, Chief Chamberlain. Can you have her call me?"

"I'll talk to the sergeant in charge of the course. Good luck."

"Thanks. I appreciate the help."

LANE SALTED THE chicken, put it into the baking tin, and pushed it into the oven. She was beginning to rather like cooking, she decided. Or at least to like the outcome. Sitting with Darling at the table, exchanging descriptions of their days—and plenty of nonsense. She wondered now how she grew up so careless of the pleasures of food. There were those terribly tense dinners in her father's house. She and her sister had sat on either side of their father, and she often would not have one word addressed to her during the whole course of the formal meal, except by Lina, who served at the table. Lina always had a smile and a kind word. The exception to her anxiety about food was her incursions into the kitchens where Mrs. Sarma always had something baking. She sighed. It was probably why she had a terrible weakness for baked things even now. She remembered Mrs. Sarma with overwhelming fondness. She also remembered that Mrs. Sarma was extremely plump. She'd best take note.

It had been completely different at her grandparents' house, where mealtimes had been so pleasant. There was always a coterie of single ladies of a certain age who were distant relations, or their own governesses, and once in a while a diffident, overly grateful man with a moustache who might have been a stray lonely cousin or a spare uncle collected by her grandmother. All of them found a welcome at the table. And of course, her grandparents were kind to everyone, though her grandmother had not been above gently sending up the German governess, Fräulein Schmitt, because she was so intensely serious all the time. It was the people Lane remembered now, gathered around that table so long ago, though the food must have been good as well. Then there was the war. It was no earthly good thinking about anything good to eat then.

Really, she thought. It was King's Cove that was teaching her. The growing, the preserving, the baking, the fresh eggs she got weekly from Gladys Hughes.

She wasn't completely sure about the tins of mushroom and chicken soup, but today she would not be employing either. Darling had been having a beastly week, and hers had been quite as harrowing. They deserved a proper roast chicken and a bottle of wine. And, of course, walnut cake. She had just returned to the contemplation of what the wages of liking cake quite so much would be when the phone jangled in the hall. She waited. Two longs and a short.

She picked up the earpiece and began to speak her name and number, but she was interrupted immediately in desperate Russian. "Oh, Miss Lane, they have arrested Andrei! They will tell me nothing!"

"Slow down, Mr. Barisoff. Tell me everything from the start. How dreadful for you!"

"He has been here, visiting me. You know how it is. He rarely comes because he is always angry at me about something. He has been staying in the little house I keep for him, you know."

Lane did. When she had first met Peter Barisoff, who lived in New Denver, he had given the house to a Russian refugee, which had infuriated his adult son, Andrei, who had subsequently moved to live with another Doukhobor family. Andrei had finally settled near Grand Forks with his new wife. "How was he arrested? Why?"

Barisoff was silent for a moment. "He was not exactly visiting me," he admitted. "He told me he was, but he was away all the time, meeting with people, he said. I wanted to ask him who he had all these meetings with. With everything going on, I worried, but I knew I would only inflame his anger, so I kept quiet. Now maybe I am proven right. He is up to something."

"You don't know that for sure. Perhaps he was arrested by mistake. That is certainly not uncommon. Was he arrested with other people?"

"Yes, yes, yes. That is the point. He was with some 'friends,' he called them, but I'm sure they belong to the Sons of Freedom. They were all arrested somewhere just outside Nelson. They accused them of bombing something. They say someone died. They will be charged with murder. My son is an idiot, but I don't think he would be bombing anything. He has a wife and child. Anyway. He is angry all the time, I know, but he is not a murderer. You have to help me, please, *dorogaya* Miss Lane! You will know what to do."

Lane listened to this recitation, alternating between helplessness and puzzlement. She didn't for a minute think she would know what to do. She wondered if Andrei had been allowed to call his father. But of course not. His father was not on the telephone. Barisoff would be calling from the store and filling station in New Denver. "How did you learn this?"

"The sister of one of the men went to the RCMP to find her brother; she was sent away but she learned the names of the men. She called my son's wife, and she called the store. Hiro was working at the store and came to tell me."

"Did she say when they were arrested?"

"Sometime last night. They were all staying in the same farmhouse. They said . . . they said they found explosives there."

"Oh," said Lane. This could be very bad for Andrei and his friends. "A bomb went off a few days ago right near here. A woman was killed by the blast. It must be that."

"Dear God," Barisoff said. "Dear God."

She wanted to tell him that she did not really think it was a Freedomite type of bomb, but she didn't want to give him false hope. After all, what did she know, really? The RCMP might be thinking the organization had found a new source of explosives and was trying them out. They would compare the explosives they found with the bomb remains they'd recovered from the site. On the other hand, the explosion had been in the middle of nowhere. The Freedomites were in the business of trying to disrupt. There was nothing to disrupt up the mountain behind King's Cove.

"Mr. Barisoff, I will try to find out what I can, but the Mounties are not very happy with me, so I'm not sure they'd let me see him. I'll go in first thing tomorrow. I'll see if they will allow you to visit."

"Thank you, thank you," Barisoff said in a tired voice.

THE RECRUITS STOOD outside on the street in front of the station. Eight men and April. This demonstration about how to arrest a suspect who'd been stopped in a car was delivered by a tired Sergeant Bailey, who had given it many times before.

"Right, Jones and Dayton, get in the car. The rest of you—obviously not you, young lady, this will never come up—get into your pairs. Approach the driver side and passenger side from the rear, like this. One of you on either side to determine the perps aren't armed, then open the door, and get them to put their hands up. If they get argumentative, secure them by bending one arm around the back, like so. That way it's painful to try to twist out.

"Ow!" said Jones.

"You had to try it, didn't you, Jones? Moron," Bailey said wearily. The other men laughed.

"You're going to search them now. Place them forward against the side of the car, hands on the roof where you can see 'em, and legs apart. Spread 'em, gents."

"Do we do this when we arrest girls too?" one of the men said, smirking at April. Another laugh. April felt her cheeks go red, and she continued taking notes.

The sergeant ignored this. "Now, why do we have the suspect in this position?"

"To pat them down?" said one, hopeful.

"Okay." The sergeant waited.

April put her hand up tentatively.

"Yes?"

"Because they are slightly incapacitated, and it makes it harder for them to make a sudden move."

The sergeant looked around at the men and then back at April. "You read your text. That's exactly right, Miss McAvity. Now, the pat-down." He demonstrated this with Jones. "You, Barnes, pat down Dayton, like I showed you—arms, waist, up the legs."

"Wouldn't mind patting you down like that," Barnes said to April as he approached the car. "No fun doing this to a fella."

"Get on with it, Barnes, and stop being an ass," Bailey said.

LATER, IN THE station, Sergeant Bailey approached April. "Sorry about them, miss. Boys will be boys. If you ever do enlist, you won't have to put up with that sort of thing where you'll be working." He winked.

He was turning to go into his office when she said, "I was hoping to become a full-fledged police officer, you know, on the beat, in a squad car, and all that."

"Listen. You've been working hard. In fact, you've got more brains than this rabble put together. But I don't see women ever taking that sort of role. Not built for it. And no one would trust having a female partner in a squad car. I couldn't ask it of them. When you get this out of your system, you should go on home. Who knows? Maybe marry a policeman. You could support him because you'd know what he has to go through."

"AH, MISS MCAVITY. Please sit down," Chief Chamberlain said.

April, her heart pounding with anxiety, sat very straight, right on the edge of the chair, her hands clenched in her lap. Had she done something wrong? Were they going to ask her to leave?

"How are you finding things? People treating you well?"

"Yes, sir. Very, sir." As well as could be expected, she thought. She couldn't think what she might have done. She'd been meticulous in every class and with every test because she felt she would have to be better than the young men training with her to even be noticed. As it was, the other trainees treated her with varying degrees of amusement and barely cloaked disdain, or tried to flirt with her as if she were just a girl who was supposed to bring them coffee. She had retained an exaggerated professional distance from them so that she might never be open to an accusation of impropriety. Perhaps they interpreted this as unfriendliness and were offended. A summons for some failure would justify their views.

"Sir, have I—"

"Relax, Miss McAvity. I've got a job for you."

She felt her tension ease slightly. "Oh."

"We need you to look into what used to be the Japanese community here and try to find someone. There's a little girl back in your hometown who's been orphaned by a bomb blast, and they want you to see if you can track down any of her relations. You know Inspector Darling?"

She nodded. "Yes, sir. He's the head of the Nelson Police. A bomb, sir?" She'd not heard this alarming piece of news from anyone at home. She'd be calling her father immediately.

As fire chief, he must know something about it. She was a little cross he hadn't told her already.

"I don't know any details, but he's the one asking, and we don't have time right now, and this seems like a job a woman could manage. So I'm giving it to you. You've wanted some experience on the street. Here you are." He pushed a card over. "We've made this up as a temporary warrant card so people will answer your questions. I've written down the details from the child's birth certificate. Kid was born at St. Paul's. They might know something." He watched her. He knew his attitude about women in the force was not in keeping with the more modern ideas, but he was the son of a former police officer, and he held firm views very much like his father's. Women in the home, men in the police. When she didn't get up, he barked, "Dismissed."

Newly kitted out in a dark blue uniform that was a tad too big for her, with the addition of a smart cap and a pair of sensible shoes, April made her way to the bus stop from her rooming house. Mrs. James had pronounced her "handsome in that getup" and sent her off with good wishes, all the while opining that policing wasn't something a woman ought to be doing. Not in the natural order of things. Not ladylike. April sighed and hopped on the bus to Burrard Street. She could feel eyes on her and was conscious that her uniform fairly shouted its newness, as if she were in a Halloween costume or had put on clothing to which she was not fully entitled. She tried to harden her face and look nonchalantly out the window, and then remembered what her father always told her when she thought people

143

might stare at her: "People are way more concerned about themselves than you." The truth was, she was nervous. Would she be able to ask the right questions? What if they refused to answer? What if she failed? She wondered if Constable Terrell ever felt like this.

"YOU CAN GO upstairs to the administration office. I don't know that they'll be able to help you," the woman at the hospital's front desk told her, after April explained why she was there. It was a warm day, and the wool uniform felt scratchy as she mounted the stairs.

She put the paper with the birth certificate information on the counter. "I need information about this family and this birth," she said to the young man who had been detailed to talk to her.

He took the paper. "Sara Sasaki Harold. Sasaki. That's Japanese," he said, looking at it impassively.

"Yes. I need any details about the birth of this child. Is there anyone who might remember? And any information about the mother, Mrs. Ichiko Harold, or the father, William James Harold. He doesn't seem to be in the picture."

"Father could be dead, I guess."

"Well, can you find out?"

"Are you seriously a policeman? What a waste!"

"Woman, policewoman. Can you help or not?" April realized that patience was going to have to be one of the tools in her police tool kit.

"All right, all right. Keep your shirt on. Japanese all got deported or something during the war. Don't know what we'll find. Sara Sasaki Harold, 1939. I'm not going to find

144

it in a second, you know. It was almost ten years ago."
He moved off into another room and came back without
information only a moment later. "I got one of the ladies to
look in the files. You can sit down over there, if you want.
I don't know how long it will take."

"Thank you," April said and composed herself on a
wooden chair. There was no one else waiting, and she took
heart from this. She should not have.

After half an hour she was tempted to get up and ask
how much longer it might take, but she did not want to
irritate the young man. That wasn't quite true—she did want
to irritate him, because he was dismissive and supercilious,
but she didn't think it would be useful.

At about the forty-five-minute mark, a middle-aged,
very official-looking man in a suit came around the counter
and stood in front of her. "Miss? You are inquiring about
a Mrs. Ichiko Harold?"

April stood up, relieved that something was finally going
to happen. "Yes."

"My name is Mr. Bright. I'm the administrator here.
Come into my office, if you will."

Newly anxious at what felt like another official summons, April followed him and took the chair he offered
across his desk.

"May I ask why the police need this?"

April explained what she knew of the situation and
emphasized the importance of finding any relation for
the wounded child.

Bright shook his head. "Very unfortunate for the poor
little girl. We were able to locate a file. It doesn't say much,

145

really, except the name of the attending doctor and that the birth was difficult."

"Oh, might I be able to speak to him?"

"He was an intern then. He's gone off to private practice. I happen to know his father, so I know he's in town here. Dr. William Bowring. Let's just check . . ." Bright pulled the phone book out of a drawer at his side and ran his fingers down the pages. "Here we are. He's on Powell Street." He wrote the address on a piece of paper and handed it across. "Right where Little Tokyo used to be."

April took the paper. "What was Little Tokyo?"

"Japanese all lived around there—you know how immigrants cluster in one place. Understandable, I guess. They were all moved out in '42 when we went to war against Japan."

April frowned a little. "But the war is over. Why haven't they come back?"

Shrugging, Bright said, "I never thought the whole thing was entirely fair in the first place. Lots of those people were actually born in this country. War may be over, but not for them. Still can't come back here. I think all their property was auctioned off, so they've nowhere to come back to anyway."

"So where have they gone if they can't come back here?"

"Search me. I heard a lot of people moved down east to Ontario after the camps broke up. Here's an address for the mother, but that was ten years ago. Maybe the people who live there now know something, but I very much doubt it."

"THAT'S IT," BERTHA Harold said finally. "They've left a few baubles. Everything of any value is gone." She put her hand on a case, and then, fearing the glass, removed it quickly. She looked close to tears. "I just don't understand how someone could do this to us! We could never make up the losses. We've never done anything to anyone. Can I go into the office?"

Ames hesitated and then nodded. Maybe she would know something about what somebody wanted to find so badly. "It's a pretty big mess, Mrs. Harold, and—"

"I know. Poor Ron." She walked to the door and pushed it open, flicking on the light switch, though the afternoon sun coming in the rear window revealed the chaos very clearly. She stopped dead and put her hand to her mouth. "It's malicious! Someone just out to destroy us!"

Ames stood next to her. "We think, in the case of the office, that someone was trying to find something—an important document, perhaps."

She wheeled around, frowning angrily at him. "An important document? What 'important document' would we have in here? I know this office backward and forward. There's nothing here that isn't directly related to our business." She moved into the office. "Oh my God, look at this place. It would take me weeks to refile everything!"

Ames wondered at her use of the word *would*. Was she thinking of not refiling? "You didn't keep wills or deeds to the shop or the house or anything like that here?"

"Whyever would we? We have a place at home where all the papers are for the house and car, and the will is, of course, at the lawyer's office, where we drew it up." She shook her head. "Oh, dear. I'm going to have to see him about the will, aren't I?"

147

Ames acknowledged this with a nod. "I suppose, yes. You don't think there might be something unusual about it?"

"About the will? Certainly not. We have no children; everything is left to me. In the case of my death, some was meant to go to Ron's little brother, but he's dead, of course. I don't think Ron's even changed his will since Bill's death, now I think of it. No, wait. He did write a note to Padgett. I don't know what was in it, but I dropped it off at the law office last week. He must have finally changed it. I should go see him, but I just can't cope with paperwork right now. I guess now it's mine I'm going to have to make up my own will." She said this almost to herself. "My sister has a girl, but I haven't gotten on too well with my sister, ever, if the truth be known. It never occurred to me I might be leaving anything to any child of hers!"

Ames made a mental note that they, at least, should go see Padgett, even if Mrs. Harold wasn't up to it.

CHAPTER TWELVE

L**ANE HUNG THE EARPIECE BACK** on its hook and leaned
against the wall, her hand on her chin. What could she
do about Andrei Barisoff, really? If he was accused of the
bombing, she would be way out of her depth. And what if
he had, in fact, been involved? It was natural for a father
to say his child would never do such a thing, but might
even he be in the dark? The daily coverage of the Sons
of Freedom in the *Nelson Daily News* described them as
"insane" and said they were perpetrating crimes against
their own "simple and credulous countrymen." She knew
that the Freedomites had been accused of burning down
their own schools and staging nude protests, and there had
been several instances of sabotage.

If one just read the paper, there was a general sense
that all Doukhobors were the same, but she knew from her
experience with Peter Barisoff that that was not at all the
case. She remembered him telling her they had emigrated
to Canada to live lives of "pacifism and toil."

Leafing through the copies of the *Nelson Daily News* piled by the Franklin stove, she finally found what she was looking for. The reporter had asked someone what the protests were about and was told that the Sons of Freedom did not want to send their children to provincial schools. They wanted them educated at home, in the pure practice of their faith. It was, after all, what they had come all the way to Canada to do: get away from government demands that they enlist in the army and put their children in public schools where they would learn ungodly things.

She closed the paper in disgust. Even non-protesting Doukhobors cannot have felt good about being called "simple" and "credulous."

She would have to telephone Darling. No, she would stop in and see him, because she wanted to go and visit Sara. She would buy another book for her. Barisoff had said it was the RCMP who had arrested Andrei, so perhaps Darling could suggest the right Mountie to talk to.

"NO, NO, NO, and no," Darling said. "You're an absolute menace, leaping to the aid of every Tom, Dick, and Harry. I hadn't heard anyone was arrested for this, but I know for a certainty the Mounties will not be the least bit interested in talking to you about it. They won't even talk to me."

"Hmm. That's unfortunate. I thought you had a bit more pull."

"Not the tiniest pull, I'm afraid. What are you going to do?" Darling knew Lane would not give up, so this question was asked with genuine, and anxious, curiosity.

"Mr. Barisoff is not every Tom, Dick, and Harry. He's

my friend, and he deserves the same respect and answers any family should get when one of their number has been arrested." Lane bit her upper lip. "I'll go back to the detachment and ask to speak to Guilfoil. I was rebuffed last time, but what else can I do?"

"You could leave well enough alone," Darling suggested. Then he sighed. "I suppose I can give him a call and let him know you'd like to see him. We had a cordial conversation about Sara Harold when he handed the matter of finding her family off to us." He did not mention Guilfoil's disparaging remark about her.

"Oh, would you?"

"I should warn you that he is not particularly in favour of women being involved in police work. He thinks your proper sphere of influence is the kitchen."

"He obviously hasn't eaten my cooking. Anyway, this isn't me being involved in police work; it's me helping a friend find out what happened to his son. That's all I really want."

"You can tell yourself that all day long," Darling said, picking up the phone receiver.

"I CAN CONFIRM he's been arrested with three other people," Guilfoil said to Lane. "I don't know that I'm able to say more." He smiled across the desk, his hands folded on top of a closed file as if he were guarding it.

"Is this for the explosion up by King's Cove?"

"Mrs. Darling—"

"Only, are you sure? I don't know what sort of explosives the Sons of Freedom have been using, but that looks very like a wartime bomb. I saw plenty of them in Europe.

Guilfoil actually allowed himself a slight indulgent laugh. "Goodness, you are persistent. We do know what we're doing, Mrs. Darling, and someone has died, as you know perfectly well, since you found the poor woman. Now, if you are here to ascertain if Mr. Barisoff might visit his son, I *might* be able to arrange that; however, he will have to travel to Prince George to our facility."

Lane sat back. She suddenly saw the whole thing from Guilfoil's point of view. She imagined herself during the war, focused, planning, executing an operation, and then some civilian coming along to tell her how to do it better. She sighed and nodded. "Yes, of course. I'll let him know. Would he need some sort of letter of permission from you? Would you expect any difficulty if he made his way there?"

In answer, Guilfoil pulled a notepad forward and unscrewed his fountain pen. He scribbled something on it, signed it, and blew on it. "You've taken an interest in the young girl, I believe. How is she doing?"

It was a peace offering, and Lane knew it. "She seems to be slowly on the mend. She hasn't spoken yet, but we visit her and read to her, and she appears to enjoy it. The main thing is to find a family member before her time in hospital is up; otherwise I don't know what will become of her."

Guilfoil looked genuinely sympathetic. "You see what tragedy that bomb has wrought. I understand your husband is contacting the police in Vancouver to see what can be done. It is very kind of you to take an interest, Mrs. Darling. I'm sure the little girl needs a woman's touch." He stood up, smiling, and offered the note he'd written for Peter Barisoff.

"This should do it, but it may depend on the mood of the people in Prince George."

"Thank you, Inspector. I know he will appreciate this very much." She smiled and nodded, starting toward the door. She could feel herself on the verge of wanting to talk about explosives and began to turn back. No! she said sternly to herself. Not now. No point in alienating this man. She'd got a note of passage for Barisoff out of him. That was victory enough for now.

Out on the street she tried to still her annoyance. He was a good man, she knew that, as far as goodness went. But he could be won by a smile and a nod, and a show of compliance. She opened her handbag and slipped the note in, and then saw the scrap of paper she'd taken from the bomb site. If only he knew how very uncompliant she was feeling just now.

DARLING, TERRELL, AND Ames sat in Darling's office, listening to the sound of traffic on the street below through the open window.

"So," Darling said at last. "We've nothing of use from witnesses, we've not found a weapon, and he was such an awfully nice man that no one would want to kill him. Any joy from looking for likely weapons?"

Terrell held up a short list. "The hardware store does not carry either cobblers' or upholsterers' tools, as they are of no use to the general public. He told me geological picks could be bought here at an outfitter on Front Street. The man there showed me several geological sample hammers. Here are all the people he's sold the sample tool to. I've started to track them down. Most live away from town. He did point at one man whom he said would be a very likely candidate to hit someone over the head, but that person has been in the Yukon for four years now. He also said anyone could have been given one by someone giving up on prospecting. A lot of those guys go bust and give up. Ditto Deacon the shoe repair man. The cobbler's hammer is a likely looking candidate, but he has only one that he inherited from his father." He paused. "I did check it for blood, but it really didn't look like it had been used for anything but shoes. I did, by the way, check his whereabouts, and he was where he said he was: at the Legion and then home."

Darling nodded. "That doesn't really narrow anything down. Even if our killer didn't pop out to a local emporium to buy or borrow his weapon, he could have had one from his own work or that of anyone he knew."

"Mrs. Harold is asking for the body, because she'd like to get on with a funeral," Ames said.

"One question, if I may, sir, is the number of times he's been away. As you've said yourself, it is an extraordinary number of buying trips for a small-town jewellery store," Terrell said.

"Let's start there," Darling said, pulling his notes forward. "Mrs. Harold said he did business with Vancouver Jewellery Wholesale. Constable, can you get hold of them and find out if anyone can tell you how often he was there, say, in this last year? Ames, we need to go through the papers in the file cabinet, and the desk, and any damn place he might have squirrelled paperwork. Find out what the killer was looking for, because judging by the state of the office, it's possible he didn't find it."

"Mrs. Harold says they kept nothing in the office but stuff for the business. Any personal legal documents are either at their home or with the lawyer," Ames said.

"Well, he might have been keeping something she knows nothing about."

Ames nodded. "Which the intruder might have known about. That suggests it maybe wasn't just a robbery."

"You're as sharp as ever, Ames. I'm going to have to sit down with Mrs. Harold and find out everything I can about him. Maybe when we hear from April, we'll know more. If Ron Harold is related to William, someone is keeping secrets, and I sincerely hope the guy with the hole in his head wasn't the only one. Terrell, get on to Vancouver and then you can take notes. I've got Mrs. Harold coming in at one."

TERRELL GOT ON to the exchange and asked to be put through to the wholesaler in Vancouver. "Yes, good morning," he said to the woman who answered crisply at the other end. "I'm Sergeant Terrell of the Nelson Police. I'd like to speak to someone about connections between your wholesaler and Mr. Ron Harold, a jeweller here in Nelson."

"That would be Mr. Denchfield. One moment."

Terrell tapped his pencil on an unopened letter that sat before him on the desk. He tried not to think about it and focused instead on his list of questions. He knew that O'Brien was not ten feet away, pretending to take no interest in his affairs.

"This is Mr. Denchfield, how can I help?"

"Good morning, sir. Thank you. We are trying to find out how often a Mr. Ronald Harold, who ran a jewellery store here in Nelson, might have gone to Vancouver to renew his stock with you."

"Ron? Has something happened to him?"

Terrell was surprised by what he detected in the man's voice. Something he wouldn't call "businesslike." More personal.

"I'm not at liberty to say, sir. If you could just confirm his visits to the wholesaler?"

There was a shuffling of papers, and then an irritated-sounding Denchfield. "He came here last October, as usual. On the eighteenth. He usually comes around that time to get ready for the Christmas season."

"And no other time?"

"No. He comes once a year. What is this?"

"Would you happen to know where he stays? If he comes regularly, perhaps you socialized at times?"

"Has he done something wrong? I don't even know if you are who you say you are."

"Sir, I'm happy to contact the Vancouver Police Department if you're anxious about discussing this on the telephone."

"Yes, yes, all right. Yes, we do go out for a drink at the end of business. Usually to the Hotel Vancouver. He says he doesn't have any place that grand at home. Of course, I'm buying. He usually stays at a rooming house. Let's see. I dropped him off there one day. On Jervis. It had a funny number, 1010. And before you ask, I don't know the name

156

of his landlady. He came, he bought stuff, and we went for a drink. That's it. I'd be very sorry to learn he's in some kind of trouble. He doesn't seem the type. He served in the Great War."

"Thank you, Mr. Denchfield. You've been very helpful."

Terrell finished his notes and sat back. So, there was definitely something not quite right about the trips. If he was only at the wholesaler once a year, where was he the other times? And yet another testimonial that he wasn't the type to be in trouble. Who would want to kill such a nice guy?

Vancouver, October 1937

RON HAROLD GOT off the train and breathed in a great gust of air. Even blocks away from the water, he fancied he could smell the sea air. Though it definitely felt like fall here, it had a little less bite to it than it had in Nelson. While many people thought it was the feel of the year beginning to die, for him it was the feel of newness, a rush of some wonderful promise on the wind.

He felt stiff from the long train ride, and as the morning was fine, he took his satchel in one hand to walk across town to Mrs. Pendergast's lodgings. He loved the feel of the city. The traffic, the bustle of people as you got toward the busy centre with the old banks and Woolworth's, and the myriad of restaurants and tobacconists. It was the sheer anonymity. He felt he could be anyone here.

He lifted his hat when Mrs. Pendergast came to the door. She had a yellow flowered turban on and a housedress, and the smell of fresh floor wax wafted out when she opened the door.

He touched the brim of his hat. "Good morning, Mrs. P. Am I too early?"

She beamed. "You never are, Mr. Harold. Your room is ready. You go on up and get settled and then come down for a cup of tea and a sandwich. I'm about ready to down tools anyway." When they were seated at her little green kitchen table with bologna sandwiches and mugs of tea, she asked, "So, what are your plans this time? Will you be seeing your little brother?"

"Oh, I'll go see Bill, as usual, and I guess we'll go have a drink. He's just old enough now, if they let him at that university!"

Mrs. Pendergast had taken off her turban, and her red hair had been released to curl wildly around her face. He imagined complimenting her, but then thought better of it. He didn't want to risk ruining what he thought of as a comfortable friendship, though he had periodically thought about her in ways he ought not. Anyway, there was Bertha at home. He never quite ran to inquiring of himself why he loved being away from her quite so much.

"We might go have an Eastern meal. Not Chinese. We have a Chinese café just near the station in Nelson. Maybe Japanese."

"Oh," she said. "On Powell Street somewhere? I don't know. I don't go to those places. Good old Canadian food is plenty good enough for me."

He nodded genially. "Oh, you're right there. My Bertha puts out a great supper, don't get me wrong. You do too, for that matter. But, you know, a fellow has to experience different things."

His conscience barely rippled at the little lie about Bertha's meals. He hated them for their unrelenting sameness. Overcooked, tough meat, boiled potatoes, grey vegetables. It wasn't her fault. She had learned from her mother, no doubt, but her father's early demise from a heart attack had not surprised him.

"Thank you, Mrs. P. That hit the spot. I must be off. Bill will be expecting me."

Her meals were nothing to write home about either. His thoughts turned to his own mother. Now *she* could cook. She'd been out in China when she was a girl with her missionary parents, and she'd learned some lovely things from their cook in Shanghai. His father hadn't cared for it much, but he had loved it. It was funny, Billy had never known his mother the way he had, really, and they had experienced completely different versions of their family. When he was a young boy, long before Billy, they'd lived up a hill in a Cornish village in the old country. He could remember little about the house except the steep step up to the blue front door. According to his mother, his father hadn't wanted that blue door. It drew too much attention. Ron had tried to find that house when they'd gone to Lady Imelda's manor house during the war. In his later visit . . . but he batted away the guilt he felt at this memory and instead wondered why the business of the blue door stuck in his head. Their father hadn't been a bad person. Just a little predictable in his ways. But all his brother Bill had known was the Canadian family, the rugged open life of the lake and surrounding mountains and the serviceable meals their father had made after their mother had died when Billy was eleven.

He took the tram up Granville and got off at Broadway. Maybe he'd splurge and get a cab the rest of the way.

"HEY, LITTLE BROTHER. I told the taxi to wait. How about I take you to dinner?"

Bill had opened the door to his dormitory room, stared momentarily at his brother, and then looked at his watch and smiled. "Can't take another of Mrs. P's meals, eh? I guess so. I could use a break. Professor Hendricks just about killed me. He is possibly the most boring man in the country."

"Oh, yeah? What does he bore you about?"

"Economics," Bill said, taking his light jacket off the back of his chair. "How's Bertha?" he asked from where he'd sat on the bed to slip on his shoes and tie them.

"She's fine. Sends her love. What do you think about going across town to a Japanese restaurant?"

"If you've got a cab, I'll go anywhere. Three years here, and I don't think I've been three miles away from this campus!"

"I hope not! I'm not paying for you to gallivant around the city getting pie-eyed with your varsity chums."

"Yes, Ron," Bill said with exaggerated respect.

The cab, instructed to take them to Little Tokyo, turned east on Hastings Street and pulled up next to a baseball diamond and park. It was getting dark already, but there were children playing catch and practicing batting, shouting at each other in high-pitched voices. There was a group of older boys, closer to Bill's age, standing under a street lamp, talking and smoking. Some young women were walking briskly along the sidewalk, perhaps heading home from the shops or from work, their heads bent, or chatting together.

Ronald looked around and thought how little this East Hastings area resembled its namesake in England. He realized he could scarcely remember coming to Canada. He'd been four in '99. He ought to, but it was muddled by the whole new world they'd come to.

They walked along the edge of the park, looking at the shops and restaurants. Ron spotted a little jewellery store and smiled. He should go in, compare notes.

"Hey, that store's still open. Let's go in there and see how they do it. Maybe they could recommend someplace good to eat."

Bill rolled his eyes but put his hands in his trouser pockets and sauntered across the street after his brother. Ronald pushed open the door and they heard the bell tinkle above them. There was a middle-aged Japanese man bent over a watch, a loupe over one eye, the other squinting. A lamp loomed directly over him, throwing a circle of light on the watch he was studying. He looked up and then called out something in Japanese and went back to his work. They saw that he looked younger than he'd seemed at first.

A slender young woman in a dark skirt and a beige rayon blouse with a bow at the neck came out and placed her pale hands on the glass counter. "Good evening. May I help you, gentlemen?"

161

Bill had a sensation of light-headedness, but it was gone before he would even have been able to put a name to it. What he could name was the girl's dark hair, cut to just below the ears, one side held back with a gold barrette, revealing the curve of her cheek, and her pale skin and dark eyes. It was something about her chin, he would think later, something between gracefully delicate and steely.

"Howdy, miss. I run a little jewellery store in Nelson. I saw you were still open and thought I'd stop in for a look." Ron Harold felt he ought to buy something. "Your father?" he asked, nodding toward the watchmaker. She looked surprised and then shook her head. "My uncle. Do you have a watch that needs to be fixed?"

"No, no. Nothing like that. This is my little brother, Bill. We're just out looking for a restaurant where we could have Japanese food, but we saw your shop and I just wanted to have a look."

She smiled broadly at this and seemed to relax. "Do you have an uncle in the corner that fixes watches? It is a requirement here."

"I am that uncle, I guess. I fix watches myself. I'm just down here for my annual visit to the wholesaler. I go to Vancouver Wholesales. How about you?"

"I go there as well. It is a small world. I can recommend a place to eat if you want." Ron noticed that she looked at Bill as she said this.

"That would be grand. Say, I wouldn't mind buying a little gold chain for my wife." Ron peered into the glass cases.

The young woman laughed. "Hey, you don't have to do that! You can get it for half the price at the wholesaler."

"Now, little lady, you run a business. Don't go turning away custom! How about that one?"

Bill watched his brother, wondering whether he felt embarrassed or proud. Was Ron being patronizing or kind? He settled on kind, given his own experiences with his brother. The girl didn't seem to mind. In that moment, she flashed a smile at him, and a wink, and then turned and opened the case to get the chain and ring up Ron's purchase, chatting about local restaurants.

The girl leaned on the counter watching Ron head for the door with his little box in his pocket. Bill felt welded to the floor, unable to look at her, desperate to ask her name. "I . . ."

"Your brother is a nice man." She nodded toward the door, but then turned at the sound of her uncle's voice. She smiled again and said, "Good night. Enjoy your dinner."

CHAPTER THIRTEEN

LANE STOOD AT THE COUNTER and wondered what to do. She could hear some sort of machine whooshing quietly through the closed door, where she assumed the printer did his work. She wasn't sure how printing worked, really, but she assumed if he was mid-run, it might be difficult for him to stop. Well, nothing for it. He must have to deal with public, after all. She knocked loudly on the counter and called, "Hello?"

The sound stopped and in a few moments a man came through the door, wiping his hands. "Hello. Good"—he looked at his watch—"morning. Sorry about the wait. I'm the only one here. Lost my last assistant and haven't been able to find a new one."

She smiled. "I'm very sorry to disturb you, especially with such a small question." She reached into her purse and took out the scrap of paper she'd taken from the bomb scene. "I'm just wondering if you've ever seen anything like this."

The printer took the piece of paper and rubbed it carefully between thumb and forefinger, and then held it up to the light. He frowned and shook his head. "It's very probably *washi*, Japanese paper. This one is a little thicker than anything I'd use for printing. I do the odd vanity book for customers, poetry, that sort of thing, so I try to find *washi* suitable for those. It's not easy to get since the war. Nothing like this, though. This one has some sort of resin or something on it. Maybe to make it waterproof? It looks pretty strong. There's an overlap here where the sheets have been glued together." He pointed at the seam. "Where on earth did you get this?"

"I found it," Lane said noncommittally.

"It's been burned, I see."

Lane nodded and took the proffered remnant back. "You think it might be Japanese. Is it made from cloth?"

"Absolutely sure of it. This one is probably not cloth, though. Plant fibre of some sort, I'd say."

Smiling, Lane said, "Thank you very much for your help, Mister—"

"French," he supplied.

"Mr. French. I'm Lane Winslow."

"How do you do, Miss Winslow. Stop by any time if you have any more questions."

Lane thanked him, thinking that his information had indeed left her with more questions, if only she knew what they were.

"CURIOUS GEORGE HAS been very popular," Mrs. Treadwell at the bookstore told Lane, holding it up. "It's quite cute, really, with the antics of the little monkey."

Lane took the book and read through it quickly. "Another book about a hijacked jungle animal," she observed. "At least his mother hasn't been shot, like poor Babar's! But Sara is nine. I mean, this might be fun, but have you something a little more age appropriate?"

The bookseller smiled. "You don't hear that term that often, *hijacked*. But I suppose you're right. The children do love it, though, because George is curious like them. Now, let's see . . . oh, how about *Little House in the Big Woods*?" Mrs. Treadwell held up the book. "What's nice about this is that there are several books in the series. This is the first one. It's about a family homesteading."

Lane took it. The cover showed a cabin not unlike Sara's. "Nothing too dire happens? It's for a sick child."

"Well, it's all about the struggle of homesteading, but the little girl in the first story is five."

"Go on then, I'll have both."

Poor Sara had not evinced much curiosity about anything yet. Perhaps George would be just the thing.

Equipped with the new books, and feeling slightly guilty that she'd not told Robin Harris that she would be going to see the child, Lane collected her car and drove up to the hospital. She really wanted to see Darling, to tell him about the Japanese paper, but she had to catch the child just after her lunch and before her nap. Then she would have to make the long trek to New Denver to give Barisoff the note he needed to go to Prince George.

"She's awake, and I rather think she's hoping you might be coming," Sister Evans said, smiling.

"Has she spoken yet?" Lane asked.

The nurse shook her head. "Her broken bones and burns are still quite painful. I almost wonder if she isn't just putting all her energy into surviving. I will say she is eating better every day. But she must be quite lonely, poor thing. And, of course, she still doesn't know about her mother. She must wonder why she never comes to see her."

Sara looked up as Lane approached, and then looked past Lane, as if she was expecting someone else, and then back at Lane.

"Hello, Sara. It's lovely to see you again! Are you looking for Mr. Harris?" Could she be? That would be news to surprise everyone at King's Cove!

Sara looked toward the door, and then again at Lane. But of course, Lane thought with a pang, she could have been looking for her mother.

"I'll bring Mr. Harris tomorrow. He wasn't able to come today. But I have brought you some new books! Let's see what you think of them."

Pulling her teddy bear close, Sara looked at the books.

SHE WOULD HAVE to leave a message for Darling that she might be late coming home, but then, she realized, so might he. God bless the leftover ham, she thought, pushing open the door to the police station. You can never go wrong with a ham sandwich.

"Good afternoon, Mrs. Darling. Can I get his nibs for you?"

"No, no, Sergeant O'Brien, thank you. Don't disturb him. I just wanted to tell him I have to drive up to New Denver, so I'm not quite sure when I'll be back. Tell him not to worry, there's lots of ham left."

O'Brien, a man who could appreciate an abundance of ham like few others, smiled broadly. "I'll let him know, ma'am. Now, you drive carefully."

Lane thanked him. The thing about Sergeant O'Brien was that he was quite solicitous of her, and really meant it. With these warming thoughts, she made her way to the ferry.

GUILFOIL HAD FALLEN into a bad temper. He was not wrong, he knew. Those four men he'd sent to Prince George *were* guilty. They were known Freedomites, at least a couple of them were, explosives had been found, and there'd been a blast, and someone had died. And more importantly, if they were near Nelson, they were near the biggest potential target of all: the Corra Linn Dam just up the river near Castlegar. Damage to that would shut down power to the whole area. No. There was no question he'd done the right thing.

What niggled was that beastly woman and her suggestion that the bomb was something else. Alone, in his office, he would concede that she was right about one thing: that bomb was nothing like the explosives used by the Freedomites. But whatever it was, it might well be what they'd use next time.

LANE TOPPED THE hill and slowed down. Blackie, the Bales's Labrador, was lying in the road as he habitually did during the warmer weather, causing traffic to slow down and go around him. He lifted his head and watched her approach, his tail thumping a couple of times.

"Yes, you're right," Lane said when she'd pulled up in front of the gas pump. "I do need petrol." The dog got up, shook, and wandered over to sniff her knees. She scratched behind his ears and looked up as Bales himself came out. "That's a very good trick, having Blackie waylay passing motorists to bring custom. Can you fill it up?"

Bales smiled as he unscrewed Lane's gas cap and prepared to deliver gas. "You've found us out! Lovely afternoon. Doing anything special?"

"I'm off to New Denver to see a friend."

"Long drive. Now that I see you, there's something I wanted to tell you. What the heck was it? I'll forget my own name next. Want anything else? Something to nibble or a Coke to drink on the road?"

"That's a nice idea. I didn't really get any lunch. If you think of whatever it was, give me a call. I'll be home by early evening, I hope."

Armed with an open box of raisin bran, as being preferable to a chocolate bar, health-wise, and a bottle of Coke, Lane set off for New Denver. Though she was going to see Barisoff, her mind was on Sara. She could see that, at the moment, Sara's whole existence was the hospital. Lane had no idea whether the shock of the explosion had caused her to forget her previous existence. What she knew and remembered was locked in her silence.

It crossed Lane's mind that even if they found a relation, it might not be anyone the child had ever known, and that the transition from the hospital into the care of a stranger was bound to be traumatic for her. She shifted to low gear as she took the steep hill down to the wooden bridge at the hairpin turn at Coffee Creek and hurriedly finished her Coke to avoid spillage. As she reached the bottom of the hill, she saw that the bus that ran twice daily between Nelson and Kaslo was approaching from the other side. She pulled over and waited for the bus to clear the single-lane bridge. The roar of the creek in the shadowed cleft of the steep mountain almost obliterated the sound of the bus changing gears as it drove past her and prepared to tackle the uphill climb toward Nelson. Lane waved and continued on her way, breathing a sigh of relief that she hadn't met the bus higher up on the dangerous part of the road. Such a meeting would have required someone backing up a considerable distance, and it would certainly not have been the bus.

She would stop at the store and gas station in New Denver when she had finished with Barisoff. Hiro Wakada, who ran the place, had been interned at New Denver during the war and had elected to stay on in a little farmhouse. He might know something about the Sasaki family.

Her Austin bumped along the short, little-used driveway to Barisoff's cottage. She pulled up behind his battered white van and sat for a second with her engine off. She took a moment to settle in the sudden stillness. High in a nearby tree, a crow announced Lane's arrival.

The quiet was shattered by Barisoff hurrying outside, slamming the screen door he'd newly installed. "You have come, you have news!" he cried in Russian.

"Hello, Mr. Barisoff. Yes. Some news. It is not all that good." She got out of the car and opened her handbag, removing the note that Inspector Guilfoil had given her. "Andrei is being held with three other men in the jail in Prince George. The RCMP inspector said you could go and see him. He has sent you this note to show in case they try to

170

make it difficult for you." She shook her head as she handed it to him. "I'm afraid he doesn't hold out much hope. They believe the four of them were involved in the bomb, and because someone has died, they will face the maximum charges." She didn't like to use the word *murder*, thinking of the distress it would cause the already frantic Barisoff.

Tears sprang to his eyes as he took the note. Impulsively he took her hand and kissed it. "Thank you, dear Miss Lane. Thank you. Who else could I turn to at such a time? I will go tomorrow. There is a bus. I know this already. Please, come in. I will make tea. I don't know how I can thank you!"

Lane shook her head. "You don't have to thank me, but I will have tea. After that I must stop by the store and . . ." She hesitated. She realized that to tell Barisoff about searching for Sara's family would mean telling him that she had found the bomb site and the dead woman. Was it time for this? He was very focused on getting to his son, on his conviction that his son was innocent. Lane's suspicions about the bomb might give him unrealistic hope. After all, the RCMP might know something she did not that actually tied Andrei and his companions to the bomb. She knew that he would be terribly distressed about the dead woman. All he knew at the moment was that "someone" had died. "I must stop and pick up some milk to take home, and maybe some of that very nice bacon Mr. Wakada gets from around here."

The kettle was already hot. "I cannot believe this of Andrei," he said, pouring water over the tea leaves. "He is angry sometimes at me, or the government. He thinks many things are not fair, and he is not wrong about this.

171

But he would never burn down his house or plant a bomb somewhere. Never."

"I'm glad you will be able to see him," Lane said. "I think he will be happy to see you, as well. He will be worried about his wife and child, I expect."

Barisoff shook his head and put his hands around his cup, as if to anchor himself. "I don't know anymore what he would worry about," he said bitterly. "I don't recognize my own son anymore. He has gone so far from what I believe. It is all this disruption. When they broke up our communes and we sent our children to these schools . . . they learned not to respect the old teachings anymore. We do not believe in violence. It is the whole reason we came here. To get away from the violence of old Russia. To live in peace with our Saviour and our vegetables."

Lane could well see how the social disruption he was describing would create turbulence in a traditional society and divide the children from their elders. "Do you think it is because he went to school in English?"

"I don't know," Barisoff said, shaking his head. "This is probably my fault. I actually wanted him to be prepared to live like every Canadian, so I decided to send him. I saw, even as I hoped it would not be true, that one day our people would have to change how we lived. One day we will just be like everyone else, the children will be doctors, or farmers, or work in factories, and they will not remember or know what our lives were. That is why the Sons of Freedom refuse to send their children to school. They are resisting what they say the government is trying to do to them. Maybe they think about how our elders fought for their

172

way of life against the Imperial Russian state and want to be heroes." He shrugged with the air of a man unable to resist the pull of history or of his own son's behaviour. "Andrei was different right from the beginning. I am more realistic, but he was angry at me for moving away from the old ways. It is strange that a son should be more old-fashioned than his father, no?"

Lane thought about her own father. "I suppose it would be strange if a son did not differ from his father in his views. Is that not the way? If the father goes one way, the son must go the other?" Or daughter, she thought.

He promised he would telephone her when he returned from Prince George, and Lane drove thoughtfully back toward the general store.

She pulled up in front of the building with its one gas pump and was delighted with the changes. The last time she had been here she'd been dodging gunfire that had blown out the windows and punctured the greying clapboard. Now it was transformed. The windows were new, the place had been painted white, and Hiro Wakada had planted some boxes along the edge of the building with petunias and nasturtiums just coming into bud.

She pushed open the door and the bell summoned Mr. Wakada from the storage room at the back.

"Good afternoon. Oh, Miss Winslow! How very nice to see you again."

"You too. You've made the store really lovely. It wasn't like this the last time I was here! Are you enjoying running the place?"

"I am. It keeps me out of trouble. I was turning into a root vegetable out at my farm. Now my farm is neglected, and I plant flowers here. How is Mr. Barisoff? I'm guessing you went to see him."

"He's very upset. He doesn't believe his son could do what they've said."

"He told me. I don't know the boy that well, myself. I know they don't get along, but it's hard to believe anyone connected to Barisoff could do it. I'm sure he appreciates your help." Whether from respect for the other man's privacy or general reticence, Mr. Wakada said no more about his friend. "Do you need some gas?"

"No, I'm all right there. But I will take a bottle of milk if you have it, and Berenson used to carry some nice local bacon—do you still get it?"

"That I do."

Lane put her handbag on the counter and leaned forward a little. "But I really want something else, and I'm hoping you might be able to help."

She told him the bare bones of the story of Sara and her mother. "You see, we must find some family for her if there is any to be found. At the moment she has absolutely no one. Was there anyone here with you during the war called Sasaki?"

Mr. Wakada shook his head. "So that's the explosion Barisoff's boy is accused of setting off. I know I heard someone died. That poor little girl! But there was no one called Sasaki. Not here. It's funny, if she was married to an Anglo, they could have stayed on in Vancouver. But I do remember that name, Sasaki, from back home in Vancouver."

174

He stopped and shook his head with a rueful smile. "I don't know why I call it that. There is no home there anymore. Anyway, I seem to remember a Sasaki Jewellery store or something like that. There was an old guy who fixed watches. There wouldn't be anyone there now. We still aren't allowed to travel back yet."

Lane was puzzled. "Not allowed? Even now?"

He smiled grimly. "Even now. I don't know if the property was acquired by someone else, or what. I heard it was all sold off. We'll never see the money, that's for sure."

"But that's appalling! It is so unjust!" Lane exclaimed.

"That it is. What are you going to do? The might of the government and all that."

This, Lane thought, is exactly what the Doukhobors were resisting when they came to Canada, but they too had encountered the same thing here. It was chilling, she thought, how little someone like herself was inconvenienced by the might of the government, and how much people like Mr. Wakada and Mr. Barisoff were. And Mr. Simpson, the Sinixt man she'd come to know right here in New Denver, she noted to herself. His people had been inconvenienced right out of the country. "This woman, the child's mother, Ichiko Sasaki Harold, had been living up in the mountains behind King's Cove. I thought that might mean she'd been placed somewhere nearby."

Hiro Wakada thought for a moment. "I had friends in a couple of other camps. Maybe there were Sasakis where they were. I'll see what I can find. Where can I reach you?"

Lane gave her phone number and opened her purse to pay for the groceries.

175

"Now, milk and bacon."

They chatted about the weather while he held up the slab of bacon. Lane nodded. "And can you slice it?"

When she had paid, she said, "Thank you very much, Mr. Wakada. I'm so worried about Sara."

"It's the least I can do for a young child left alone like that."

Lane was just going out the door when he said, "You know, if you aren't able to find any relations, I feel certain there would be a Japanese family willing to foster or adopt her."

Lane turned. "That is an excellent suggestion, Mr. Wakada. I hope we do find her relations, but knowing there might be a good backup plan is very reassuring if we don't."

CHAPTER FOURTEEN

"POOR ROBIN. HE'LL BE CROSS when he finds out I've been up to town without him." Lane and Darling sat in front of the Franklin, slouched in their armchairs, happily full of ham sandwiches and a salad of lettuce and greens Lane had found in a paper bag on her front doorstep when she arrived home from New Denver. Kenny Armstrong, no doubt, she thought. They each had their usual nightcap of a short, neat whisky.

Darling cradled his on his chest, both hands around the glass. "Lillooet. That's where Dr. Miyazaki, the coroner we used, comes from. It's too bad we didn't know the family name before he left. He might have known if they were interned with him."

"*Interned.* I still can't get over that word being associated with this country. That's the sort of word you expect in a Soviet Union, or a Nazi Germany. Not in this peaceful, lovely place," Lane said.

"What's shocking is that it can happen so quickly, and the majority of people can be so completely convinced that it is the right thing to do."

"Is it true they aren't allowed to travel freely, to go back to the coast? It's 1948! It's been almost three years since the war was over. And they won't see a penny from their property."

Darling shook his head. "I confess, I learned that just today. I was as shocked as you. I feel like we are going to have a steady leakage of secrets and ghastly things coming out of the war in the next couple of years. Secrets, miscarriages of justice . . . the trouble is, this isn't going to feed the baby—and by baby, I mean that poor child. What I can't make out is why they were living, unknown to anyone apparently, in that cabin far from anyone. And how long had she been there? If she was interned somewhere, it can't have been that long."

Lane smiled suddenly. "Maybe your Woman on the Job in Vancouver will find something out about the family. Do you think she's having fun?"

"If she's even half as nosy as you, I'm sure she is. Bed?"

APRIL SAT IN the waiting room of Dr. Bowring's surgery. A man had come in after her and sat slouched in a way that suggested he was in pain. Had she better let him go first? But the decision was taken from her. The receptionist said, "Miss McAvity?" and ushered her through.

"Funnily enough, I do remember that birth because the circumstances were unusual. I remember being surprised to see she was Japanese, with a name like Harold. For another thing, it was a difficult birth because she was very slight, but I think what made it harder was the circumstance of the father. He'd enlisted and been killed only months before. I had the impression she was quite on her own, but I think she mentioned she lived with an uncle. No one came to see her while she was in hospital. I felt quite badly for her. But as so often happens, I think she was oblivious to being on her own because she was so in love with her baby. The power of motherhood, eh?"

LANE HAD ORGANIZED with Robin Harris that they should drive up to town in the afternoon, after he "got some work done." It occurred to her, as she hurried through the post-breakfast cleanup, that she really had little idea of what his work consisted of, besides driving around on his noisy, smoking tractor. Certainly, he was the King's Cove handyman, especially where the Hugheses were concerned, but what did one do in orchards?

Feeling a bit guilty that she had not made more of an effort in the two years she'd lived in King's Cove to find out, she set off in the car up the hill to the upper border of the Hugheses' top orchard. She stood outside her car for a moment, breathing in the cool fragrance of the morning air. The sun intensified the luminous gold remnants of winter grasses. As a child, she used to escape the house and her nanny and go up the hill behind their house and lie on the pine needles in the sun, relishing the warmth on her face, the dry-pine scent, imagining herself the only person who'd ever been there.

That hill, she thought, beginning her climb, had felt as steep to a child as this was, but looking back she realized it really was probably a very low hill, made enormous by her small size and big imagination.

At the bomb site, she stopped to catch her breath. The little fence the Mounties had put up was still there, but she saw that they had collected most of the debris. There were still scraps of paper caught among the surrounding brush. She sighed. Having learned that it was likely Japanese paper, she should really tell them, but she was reluctant to face any of them after being so roundly told off by that officious Sergeant Fryer. And it might make no difference; they might have found this out on their own. Now she continued on her way to her main object: the cabin.

Twenty minutes later she had reached the clearing where the cabin sat in the wash of morning sun. It had such an air of abandonment that she felt a bolt of sadness compress her chest. As she approached, she saw that the hose that had been connected to the outside tap had been removed. That would have been Hartis. He must have taken the hose right away to keep anyone else from tapping into the Hugheses' water supply. Who would now? Lane thought forlornly. Mrs. Ichika Harold was dead.

The front door hung open, and Lane pushed it and went inside. The RCMP had clearly been here as well. The boxes of clothes were pulled out from under the bed and emptied onto the floor, the dishes taken off the shelf above the counter where the basin had sat, everything removed from the high shelves. She wondered what, if anything, they had found. Indeed, what did she hope to find?

She would gather up the little girl's clothes. Sara would need these wherever she ended up. She knelt down and began to pick through the clothes that had been dumped on the floor, pulling out all the child-sized garments. She carefully folded and placed the woman's clothes to one side. She felt an infinite sadness as she folded a lovely flowered dress. She held it to her for a moment and thought about its wearer. She herself had had a dress not unlike this before the war. She remembered her own last days at Oxford before the war started as being carefree and full of optimism. Why had Sara's mother brought her here? To homestead? Or had she been hiding here with her child?

She put the dress down with the woman's clothes and sat back. Had they been hiding? From what or whom? Or had they spent the whole war here hiding from the authorities? She stood up and looked around the cabin with this new perspective in mind. Sara and her mother must have lived in Vancouver until the internments in 1942. How would a young woman with a child of three years end up here? If she'd come from Vancouver, she was unlikely to have known that such a cabin existed.

Not sure why, really, Lane put all of Sara's mother's clothing back into its box and pushed it back under the bed. She looked around, hoping to find a bag to carry Sara's clothing down the mountain. She would also see if she could find any sort of toy or stuffed animal she'd missed on her last visit.

There were no paper bags in the area where food had been stored. Perhaps they'd been used to light the fire. She turned to look at the small stove against the back wall and saw what she hadn't before: a basket filled with split wood for the fire. That would do. She lifted the basket to remove the wood and saw that it had straps, so that it could be carried like a rucksack. She piled the wood next to the stove and then took the basket outside to shake out the debris of wood chips and bark. It was ingenious. She'd never seen anything like it but thought how useful something like that would be for carting wood from her barn to the Franklin. The clothing packed into the basket, Lane put it outside and went back into the cabin.

With each pass, she saw things she hadn't seen before. There were coats hanging by the door on nails. She shook her head at her own lack of observation. There were coats and jackets hanging by the door in her own house. It seemed so ordinary that she hadn't even taken it in. With a slight feeling of guilt at trespassing at all into the tragic lives of the people who had lived here, Lane began to feel in the pockets of the winter coat and the lighter spring coat that hung there. Immediately she found a folded piece of paper in the spring coat.

Praying it was not in Japanese, she unfolded it.

> *Dearest I.,*
>
> *I am sorry. I spoke to the authorities. They are not hopeful. They don't even seem to know where most people are, now it's over. I will come as planned next Tuesday. Then I will drive to Vancouver to talk with them in person. At least we can find out if you will be safe. That would be a blessing.*
>
> *I am sorry you are alone. Maybe I will be lucky. I still hope we may find them. It must*

all end soon, and we will be able to make
plans. I know you don't want to leave, but I
think it is time.

Lane read the note again. It seemed, maddeningly, to conceal more than it revealed. Had there been a second page? Who had sent it? The writing was slanted almost backward. She imagined the writer as someone who leaned away from life somehow. Would that make it a woman? That idea of something being a blessing added to her sense that the writing was feminine. What was there no hope about? She had learned that the Japanese were still not allowed to travel back to whatever homes they might still find on the coast. Had she spoken to someone in government and been told that Sara and her mother could not return? Or that they could not find her husband? Or her other family members? If Mrs. Harold and Sara had been there for the last six years, Sara would have no memory of anyone she had known as a three-year-old. Certain that the writer could not have imagined the tragic end of this family that would never now go home, Lane re-folded the note and put it in her own trouser pocket. Most interesting of all to Lane was this comment that they knew Ichiko did not want to leave. Had she come to feel it was her home? That she would be safe here?

After confirming there was nothing to be found in the pocket of the other coat, she took down a sweater and a small, worn, pale blue coat to add to the basket of clothing for Sara.

She looked once more around the cabin and imagined it abandoned, falling into disrepair and becoming a relic that someone might find many years hence, with old cans of food on the counter and utensils from an earlier era still on the shelves, no memory left of the human story it had contained.

"I THOUGHT MRS. HAROLD would like to get in and start putting the store back together," Ames said, standing at the entry to Darling's office. "But she says she's reluctant to go back inside. She actually said she might never go in again."

Darling nodded, conceding the point. "That's fine. I'd rather she didn't go back in until we have gone through every inch of that office, just in case whoever tossed it didn't find what they were looking for. Whatever it was, it must have been important enough to kill for."

"Do you have an idea what sort of thing it could be?" Ames asked, and then immediately regretted it.

"No, Ames, I do not. If I did, would I be proposing we go search his files? No, I'd be out arresting the bastard who did this."

Ames grinned sheepishly. "Yes, sir. Sorry, sir."

"Yes, all right. Get your rubber boots. We might as well do this now so we can let Mrs. Harold back into the place when she's ready." With this Darling rose and waved Ames out of his doorway. "Terrell can hold the fort while we're spelunking."

Once in the murky office of the store, Darling looked around and sighed. He hadn't seen the office before it was ransacked, so he had no idea if it had been tidy and organized, or always a bit of a clutter.

"Light, sir?" Ames suggested, flicking the switch. There was a gratifying flood of light over the scene.

"That's a help," Darling said. "Now then, you can start over there in the corner file cabinet, and I'll go through the desk again and tackle this shelf. And before you ask, I'm not sure what we're looking for. Wills, love notes, threatening letters, anything unusual that you wouldn't expect to be kept in a jewellery store office. Or perhaps even travel receipts he'd been hiding from his wife."

"Sir." Ames took off his jacket and hung it on a nail, next to one that he thought Mr. Harold must have used in the same way. Rolling up his shirt sleeves, he reckoned he wouldn't even have to open the drawers to search, since the area around and on top of the cabinet was strewn with files and papers. He was right—when he pulled open the drawer, the cabinet was empty bar one slip of paper in the back corner. He pulled this out. A receipt from the dry cleaner from four years before. Sighing, he collected everything off the floor and piled the papers and files on top of the cabinet. It would be up to Mrs. Harold to put them all in order.

The entire contents of the cabinet proved, after a painfully long search, to be receipts and invoice copies. Nothing stood out in any way as unusual. Interestingly, there were very few travel receipts, only those from the October trips to Vancouver and two others in the last two years. Had he been destroying the rest for some reason? The records went back more than twenty years. Ames was just shoving the last paper into a file folder—he had no way of knowing if it was the right one—when he saw one more receipt on the floor, where it appeared to have been swept against the wall in the avalanche of paper the killer had precipitated in his search.

"Here's a receipt for a painting," he said, looking around the office as if he might see the actual item. "It's from England. He paid six shillings for *Scene of Boscastle* in 1918. It's from a gallery. Roskilly Gallery, Boscastle, Cornwall. It's not much, but it is different."

Darling turned from his perusal of the shelf next to the desk, where he'd carried out a similar process to Ames's: reviewing the contents of binders and then replacing them on the shelf from which they'd been swept.

"Keep it out. Maybe it has some chums somewhere in this mess." He returned to his work, and then looked back at Ames. "You all right?"

"It's just my back, sir, bending over like this, and my shoulder." Ames had been injured in the early spring, and it still gave him a good deal of trouble. "I just need to stretch."

"Yes. Why not go outside and walk up and down in the alley. That's what you get for getting shot." This he said kindly. "I could use a stretch myself."

Outside, they stood gratefully in the warmth of the sun, enjoying a slight breeze that wafted up the alley.

"Any luck in the desk, sir?"

"I haven't started it yet. I thought I'd scour the binders. Just wholesale catalogues. I've got them higgledy-piggledy back on the shelf. I guess she'll sort them out later. At least I can see the floor now."

"So, Cornwall. Isn't that where the missus said Mr. Harold had come from? Humphries said they visited during the

Great War. That's where they found out they were related. It would be interesting to see if his wife still has that painting."

"Your idea being?"

"Well, nothing really, sir. It's not as if something that happened thirty years ago killed him a few nights ago."

Darling nodded grudgingly. "It seems improbable, but we shouldn't discount it. Maybe Humphries can tell us more about that visit to Cornwall they were planning to make together."

ROBIN HARRIS WAS ready when Lane drove to the bottom of his driveway. She still was not used to seeing him in proper clothes. His faded denim shirt was buttoned up to his neck and tucked into dark trousers, and what there was of unruly white hair was slicked back, as if his mother had readied him for church. More interestingly, under his arm was a book.

"Good afternoon, Harris. What do you have there?"

"If you must know, it's a copy of *Winnie-the-Pooh*. I telephoned the bookstore, and they sent it up on the steamer." He made even this announcement sound rather spiteful, as if he believed she wouldn't think him capable of getting hold of a children's book.

"What a good idea! I don't know how I didn't think of that. It was quite a favourite when I was a child. I used to read it to my little sister."

That was the full extent of the conversation for some miles, and Lane thought uncomfortably about what sort of conversation she might offer that he'd respond to more agreeably. Filled with trepidation, she asked at last, "Did your friend like books?"

There was such a long period of silence that Lane wondered if she'd found the wrongest possible thing to say. Finally, in a very low voice, Robin said, "She didn't have any time for them, but she liked them, all right. Her mother must have brought some books in. She had some books with fairies in them. I remember she used to say as long as there were fairies in the trees and flowers, she could be happy. Tried to teach me to read." He barked a harsh laugh. "Fat lot of good it did me."

"But you read beautifully," Lane said, surprised.

"That'll be Kenny's mother, Lady Armstrong. She taught us all. Couldn't bear ignorant children, she said. She read to us too, and all. On a sunny day we'd gather outside that little schoolhouse, and she'd sit on the steps and read. Big grown-up books some of the time. Didn't know what was going on half the time, but she had a lovely voice. Used to say it was good for us to get things that were over our heads a little bit." He stopped and looked past Lane, out at the lake. "Never had any call for it in our way of life."

"Well, there's certainly a call for it now. I had to go into town yesterday and I stopped by to see Sara, and you could see she was just looking past me at the door, hoping you would come through it. She'll be very happy to see you." She wanted to glance over and see if this had made him smile, even a little, but it felt intrusive somehow.

He made a little noise that could have been satisfaction or skepticism.

At the hospital they were given the go-ahead to go into the room. There was a second child in the room now, who seemed to be asleep. Her head was wrapped in layers of bandages, and she lay with her hands outside the covers in two straight lines.

"Concussion," said the nurse. "Fell out of a tree at school onto a teeter-totter with a missing seat and a huge nail sticking out. Luckily the head of the nail. She'll be all right. Don't worry, you won't wake her with the reading. She's been sedated. I'd have that principal's head on a platter, leaving broken playground equipment like that!"

Lane went through first, but Sara had eyes only for Harris. She held up the bear, and he nodded and gave it a slightly abashed pat on the head. He held up the book. "I brought you a book about a bear. See what you think."

Lane thought, with enormous satisfaction, that she might just as well not have been there. Sara leaned forward, listening. Harris's voice was deep, and remarkably soft, Lane thought, as if he needed to be gentle even in his speech for this wounded child.

Sara pointed at the page suddenly, holding up her bear.

Harris stopped reading, and he and Lane both looked at her in astonishment. "Yes," said Lane smiling very happily. "He really does look just like Pooh."

Sara nodded confirmation and then looked back to Harris expectantly. Lane looked at him too. He was smiling and nodding his head, over and over. He reached into his pocket and took out a handkerchief and gave his nose a quick wipe, and then cleared his throat and continued with the story, as if the little miracle they'd both witnessed was just par for the course.

CHAPTER FIFTEEN

———

"**OH, YES. IT'S ON THE** wall in the living room. He said he got it during the war. I never thought much of it, and I've stopped noticing it. But then I don't know much about art," Mrs. Harold said with a slight measure of pride.

But I know what I like, Darling added mentally. "Do you mind if we go to your house to have a look at it?"

Mrs. Harold frowned. "Why?"

"That's a fair question, Mrs. Harold. I think, really, we're trying to understand why your husband might have been killed. Anything out of the ordinary, perhaps something from the past."

"You think he was killed for a painting?" She sounded almost scornful. They were meeting her at Mrs. Dee's house. She stood up and paced to the window and stared out. "You know, I did wonder sometimes . . ."

"About what?"

"I don't know. I always felt he was keeping things from me. It started right after his brother was killed. That was right at the beginning of the war—the secrecy, I mean. I always thought it was because he was grieving, and I didn't like to intrude. They were very close. But then—I know this sounds crazy—he began to tell me everything was all right, everything would be all right. As if we were suffering somehow but it was all going to get better."

"Were you suffering, aside from his own grief?" Darling asked. This was the first crack in what he had begun to see as her armour of the perfect marriage, the perfect household, the unassailable kindness of her husband.

"No. That's the thing. We never suffered. We have—*had*—a very comfortable life, but he always acted like it was going to get better. But then halfway through the war, he stopped talking about it and just seemed to work harder. Longer hours at the shop, more trips, that sort of thing."

"Did you have any sense the business might have been failing, or that it needed that sort of effort?"

"No. It seemed fine. I worked there a couple of hours in the morning, to look after the books, like I told you. I'd have seen. I mean, there was a bit of a letdown during the war, obviously. We both volunteered, and we were all watching our pennies for the war effort, helping our boys, that sort of thing."

Ames nodded. He remembered this very well. It had seemed as if the whole town had mobilized, collecting rags and metal and even bones, and absolutely everyone seemed to be in uniform—those who signed up, women in a multitude of auxiliaries—with posters everywhere encouraging frugality for the sake of the boys fighting Hitler.

"People still got married, though, and needed their watches repaired." She shook her head. "I don't know, maybe I was imagining it. You know how you imagine things in retrospect."

Darling nodded. "I do indeed, Mrs. Harold, but you mustn't sell yourself short. Someone did kill your husband, so any little detail might be very important."

She nodded miserably and then sighed. "The back door is open. You can go in. I still can't bear to go there. I know I should get back to work at the shop." But she said this without conviction.

"Did he have his own room?"

She was about to shake her head, they could see, and then she stopped. "Not his own room, exactly. We have a spare room, and he worked there, and did sometimes sleep in there if he came home late. I guess he didn't want to disturb me."

"May we look in there as well?"

"Oh. Yes. I see. I was going to say we have a wooden trunk there with the winter blankets and coats and things, but I never thought . . . he might have had things there as well. Yes. Yes, please search anything. I want to know why my husband is dead."

"Mrs. Harold, was your husband's younger brother married?"

Mrs. Harold looked at him, astonished. "Married? Certainly not. He was only twenty-one when he shipped out, and still at university."

So, Sara's father was a different William Harold.

MRS. HAROLD HAD not been in the house since her husband was killed, and though it was only a few days, the house felt abandoned and gloomy, as if it had given up on its people. Dust already appeared to be settling over everything. Ames started down the narrow hall to check the bedrooms while Darling stood in the sitting room.

Ames stopped and turned to Darling. "Do you believe her, sir, about wanting to get back to work at the shop? I don't think I do, if she can't even stand to come here, and this isn't even where he was killed," Ames said from the hall.

"You make a good point. Perhaps she's just trying to be strong, as if getting back to it would relieve some of the grief." Ames was right, he realized. Mrs. Harold was grasping for a sense of normalcy, perhaps believing that returning to old routines could wipe out the pain of what had happened to her husband.

There was an unpleasant smell, which Darling realized was caused by garbage in the kitchen that had been left when Mrs. Harold had not returned. He went into the small kitchen and opened up the cupboard under the sink and took out the metal garbage can. Holding his breath and averting his head, he placed it outside on the narrow back porch. He'd have to take it out to the metal bin in the alley.

"Sir, there are two bedrooms. The last one in the hall looks like it might be the spare room she talked about," Ames said, poking his head into the kitchen. "What's that smell?"

"Garbage. I've put it outside. Show me."

They walked through the sitting room and into the hall, passing the bathroom and what was clearly a shared bedroom, and went into the spare room. A narrow single bed with a brown bedspread, a bedside table with a lamp and several books, mostly detective fiction. There was a glass a quarter full of water and a bottle of Aspirin beside the books. A shirt was slung on the back of a chair by the window, and there was a pair of socks under it, on the floor. The entire room seemed dun coloured, as if it did not want to draw attention to itself.

"What do you think of this, Amesy?" Darling asked.

"I think this doesn't look like a spare room. I wonder if he slept here more than just some of the time?"

"My thoughts exactly."

Opposite the end of the bed was the closet door. This Darling opened.

Immediately evident was the wooden blanket trunk Mrs. Harold had mentioned, which took up the whole floor space. Above it were some coats and jackets, presumably put away for the summer, and above them a shelf with two shoeboxes. The musty smell of fabric left too long in enclosed spaces wafted out, which Darling found vaguely depressing. He moved some of the hangers to see what might be hidden in the darker ends of the closet. It looked like some of these had not been worn for many winters but were perhaps deemed too good to pass on to a jumble sale.

"Right," Ames said brightly, to offset the shadowy, stale atmosphere of the room. "What are we looking for?"

"A note saying, 'I'm going to kill you with a pointy object, please meet me at the store at ten.' Try the desk. I'll take the trunk."

There was nothing on the desk except a large blotter and a lamp. Ames pulled out the centre drawer and found two pencils and a fountain pen and some sheets of writing paper. Lifting these, he saw that someone had started a letter and then given it up. *Dear Auntie, I hope this letter finds you well. I don't know how to thank you for agreeing to this. As you know, circumstances have changed in a way I never imagined . . .* and it stopped there. The date at the top was August 15, 1942. He reached into the back of the drawer and found several envelopes, and, with a little cry of triumph, pulled out an airmail envelope addressed to Mrs. Imelda Cormysh, Glenn House, Boscastle, Cornwall, England.

"This is something, sir," Ames said, holding up the two items.

Darling had plunged further into gloom going through the contents of the blanket box, which contained two wool blankets of an indeterminate beige colour. Under these had been folded several dresses and a wool suit. Judging by the lapel size, this last was at least twenty years old. He stood up and surveyed Ames's catch.

"Cornwall again," he said.

"Exactly."

"Anything else? Overdue bills, threatening letters?"

Ames shook his head. "I haven't checked the side drawer yet. Let me do that now."

"Attaboy," Darling said, but he was pleased. He thought this might be important.

"Just some extra paper, envelopes, and a travel brochure."

"Let me guess. Cornwall?"

"That's right, sir," Ames said, smiling. "And recent enough, judging by the pictures."

They continued the search, finding nothing but what might be expected in a spare room: a bible in the bedside table drawer. Darling had pulled down the two shoeboxes, and found two pairs of shoes, both men's. On the floor, in the tiny amount of space left by the wooden trunk, there was a pair of lace-up boots. Hiking boots. He brought these out. "Interesting. Apparently, he was a hiker."

"Plenty of hiking to be had around here, I guess," Ames said, shuddering at the thought. His recreation consisted of fishing. "If he was sleeping here, it hadn't been for that long, I'd say, or he'd have moved more of his clothes in."

Ames nodded. "But something was not quite right between them."

Darling shrugged. "Or he'd taken up snoring recently and had been banned from the marital bed."

In the sitting room they put the three things they had taken from the desk on the dining table and made a cursory search through the magazines piled in a basket by the couch. It astonished Darling that there was no bookshelf, and indeed, no books on any surface besides those in the spare room, a fact that added to the sense of melancholy the house gave him. Taking a quick look around, he caught sight of the watercolour painting he was sure belonged to the receipt they'd found. It was magnificent, like nothing else in the room, the walls of which were otherwise occupied with smoke-stained reproductions of quaint nineteenth-century farm scenes.

"Look at that," he said.

Ames turned to look where Darling was pointing. "I don't know much about art . . ."

"Not you too!"

"No, I mean, I don't, but I wanted to say, that looks really beautiful. Like it's been painted by someone who knows what they're doing."

Darling, relieved that there might yet be hope for Ames, nodded. "That is correct, Amesy, it is indeed done by someone who knows what they're doing."

The frame was roughly eighteen by fourteen inches, and the paining within was about fourteen by eleven. It was a scene of a long narrow harbour with a stone jetty out to open water, and a pebble beach against which the water lapped gently. Opposite the jetty, a whitewashed building stood above the harbour on a stony hill covered with a soft green grass. The eye was drawn beyond this to the curving shoreline fading into the distance, and the sparkling sea. It was suffused with morning light. Two fishing boats almost seemed to undulate in the deeper water.

"Most cheerful thing in this place," Ames said.

Darling regarded it, feeling himself pulled into its sunny centre, and then on an impulse took the painting off the wall. A faded patch remained where it had hung. He turned it over to look at the back. It had been professionally, and rather nicely, he thought, framed by Harbour and Sons right in Nelson in 1922. He made a note of the name. Lane had had a couple of watercolours done of the house in King's Cove by, as it turned out, a lethal visitor she had had before they married. This would be the place to get them framed, though the corner of the backing was beginning to peel. He was about to put it back on the wall when he was overcome with an irresistible urge to peel the backing a little further. He overcame this destructive impulse with some effort.

Replacing the painting, repressing the urge to take it as "evidence" and just keep it, since Mrs. Harold didn't seem to have any idea how good it was, Darling said, "Well, let's go. You can go ask Mrs. Harold about these things."

On the way back down the street to the station, Ames said, "What do you think he was thanking his auntie for, I wonder?"

"You never fail to put your finger on the key point. A nice visit? Her kind letter? The soft woolly scarf she knit him? I expect Mrs. H will know. I don't know if any of it will have anything to do with why he was murdered."

Ames shot a sideways glance at him. "But you do think so, sir, don't you? I can tell by your expression."

"Oh, for God's sake, Ames!"

July 1916

"IT'S A BLOODY long way to go," Harold complained, looking out the train window. But then the sea suddenly came into view, and he felt his breath catch. It was a feeling of uplift that was more pronounced for the way it seemed to pierce the exhaustion and the gloom of his war. Like a sudden light in a dark, murky room, and it released something achingly familiar.

They had shared everything, he and Humphries, since they'd met. Every confidence, every physical humiliation from life in their separate trenches, every hope, every fear, but now suddenly he could not speak about this feeling of light. He stared at the sea, blue, grey, and sparkling in the gold of the afternoon, and locked it in his heart. And so familiar, like snatches of a dream he'd had long ago.

"You'll love the place, I'm sure of it. I haven't been there since I was sixteen."

Harold tried to hold on to the wisps of dream. "What makes you think she'll want a couple of muddy doughboys tramping all over her house?"

"She will. She loves me. You'll see."

In Penzance, they arranged for a bus to Boscastle. Harold could feel his weariness return, along with the dark memories of the trenches he tried constantly to stave off. "Now how far do we have to go?"

Where his mood descended, Humphries's seemed to rise, along with his chattiness. "It's only about sixty miles. We'll be there in no time. A short walk up the hill and Bob's your uncle."

"You're going to look a complete ass when she slams the door in our faces," Harold said, once they were in the bus. He was trying to crunch his body into a sleeping position with his head against the window. There was no sleep to be had. The road was winding and slow, and the roar of the omnibus changing gears prohibited any form of relaxation.

BUT NO DOOR was slammed. Indeed, the door was flung open wide at the sight of them by an ancient man in a faded and much worn nineteenth-century livery. "Is that you, young Martin?"

"It is, indeed, Biggs. How are you?" Humphries slung his kit bag onto the floor against the wall and was wringing

Biggs's hand. "This is my chum, Ron Harold. All the way out from Canada. Went there as a boy from here."

At this Biggs hesitated. Then, as if it cost him a struggle of will, he said, "You're welcome, sir. She'll be glad to see the both of you. Go on through, and I'll tell Mrs. Gantry to add to the pot." He turned to shuffle off and then turned back. "Leave your bags there. I'll get them later."

"You'll do no such thing. Directly I've seen Auntie we'll get them ourselves. My old room?"

"Certainly, sir. I'll make it ready."

"Come on, Ron, meet the old lady."

But the old lady was already standing in the door to the sitting room, one hand on the doorjamb as if for support, roused by the commotion. Harold had never seen anyone quite like her. She was small and slender and had a shock of white hair that stood out in a corona around her head. He'd never seen an old lady in Nelson who didn't pin her hair into tidy obedience. She had intense blue eyes and was smiling in evident delight. She wore a long blue dress with a loose cardigan of pale yellow, colours he associated with a younger woman, yet on her they seemed to add light in keeping with the scene outside. "Well, my boy. I didn't know if you were dead or alive."

"Very much alive, my dear old aunt." He enveloped her in an embrace that looked to crush her tiny frame.

"Oh, put me down! Who's this, then?"

"This, my dearest, is my very good chum Ron Harold. We met on leave in London and now take every leave together. Ron, my aunt Imelda Cormysh. Lady Imelda, if you please."

"How do you do, Lady Imelda?" Ron Harold said, offering his hand.

She took his hand, holding it for longer than he expected, and seemed to be searching his face. Then, surprisingly, she reached out and touched his cheek gently and withdrew her hand. "Where are you from, then?" she asked, in a tone that suggested he'd said, but she'd not heard properly.

"A little town in Western Canada, ma'am. British Columbia. It's called Nelson." He could still feel the soft flutter of her hand on his cheek. He was momentarily a child again, as if in the presence of his grandmother. But in the same breath of thought he realized he could not remember any grandmother. "I was born here, but of course I don't remember it. I was very young when we left. Canada is all I know."

"I see." She sighed. "Such a long way off. Well, you'd better come in. Have you come all the way from France?"

They followed her into the sitting room, and she waved at the array of seating available.

"That we have, Auntie. You don't look a day older, you know that?"

"And you are no less the charmer," she replied.

Their talk faded into the background as Harold sat gazing around the room. It was beautiful, like pictures he'd seen in the English magazines his mother sometimes got. A large window framed by silk drapes, a bleached pale blue colour, looked out toward the sea and the long slope of the garden. He felt a momentary rise of that spike of joy and familiarity he'd felt at the first sight of the sea. The room was frozen in time with its worn Turkish carpet and faded silk-covered chairs. It surprised him that it was not gloomy, but rather as if, along with the ancient furniture, the room still clung to the happiness of some bygone era when the place had been full of laughing people.

Ron got up and went to stand by the window. "I can't get over how familiar this view is to me. I thought I couldn't remember anything, but now I see I must, if it looks so familiar."

Directly opposite on the wall was a portrait of a woman in a long blue gown, holding a fan in one hand, her other hand resting on the back of a chair. He gave a little gasp. It looked just like his mother. Or rather, when he looked more closely, not exactly, but something in the face was his mother.

"Ah. You've seen," the old lady said. "What do you think of her, then?"

"She looks a bit like my mother," he said. "Isn't that odd? I suppose these old paintings all look the same."

"It's not odd," she said. "Your family came from Boscastle. Your mother was my second cousin."

She shook her head in wonderment. "I recognized your name, of course, but I knew it was you without a doubt the minute I saw your eyes. So like hers. I never thought I would see you again."

Ron moved back to the sofa and sat down quickly, feeling suddenly light-headed. "How . . . ?"

"Maybe that's why we get along so well," Martin Humphries said triumphantly. "We're related! How about that?" He pounded Ron on the back, and then turned back to his aunt. "How are we related again, Auntie?"

"Your grandmothers were sisters. There were three Rosvear girls; that's one of them up there, and one of them was your grandmother, Ron, the sister to that one. Her daughter married"—she paused—"well, your father. You two are second cousins, or first cousins once removed or whatever it is. I'm a sort of great-aunt to both of you because I was the third."

"I think Rosvear was my mother's middle name. I never really thought about who my grandparents or cousins might have been. It was always just us: Mother, Father, me."

"You know, I remember you as a tiny boy. Your father was a stonemason in the village. Is your mother still with us?" She had cocked her head and he could feel her kindness in this gesture.

"She is. She's going to have a baby. Bit of a surprise, that." He smiled. "It will be fun meeting a new brother or sister. I don't remember anything about living here but I wondered why it seems so familiar."

"You were a very sweet little boy. Of course, Martin, you were born in London, so you never would have crossed paths. Ah, Biggs, thank you." The butler had come in with a tray bearing glasses of sherry. "Dinner is in an hour, so I think we'd better not burden ourselves with tea, is that right, Biggs?"

"Yes, ma'am. Mrs. G has added some potatoes and carrots to the mutton stew."

"Tell me about your family, Ronald. You must miss them."

Considering the possibility of confronting mutton stew, a flavour he'd not encountered before, though anything that didn't have mud or rats in it was appealing enough,

Ron turned back to Lady Imelda. "Yes, ma'am. Especially now. I'd like to be there for my mother."

"I am sorry. Of course, it will be hard on her. I'm sure she's anxious to have you home."

ON THE TRAIN back to London, Ron Harold felt himself in a daze. He'd been looking out the window, tuning out the noise of other soldiers and crying babies. He finally turned to Martin, who'd been half dozing. "I can't get over it. We're related. I can't wait to tell my parents."

"Auntie sure took to you. When she dies and I get that place, we'll fix it up and come here for a holiday."

———

December 7, 1918

Dear Ronald,
I've learned from Martin that you are still in the country for another few months, so I am hopeful that I have caught you before you return home. I'm writing to ask if you will come out to see me. I know it is a long journey and a great deal to ask after all you have endured. I would not ask if I did not think it necessary. I would very much prefer you not mention this to him.

I remain yours faithfully,
Your Aunt Imelda

CHAPTER SIXTEEN

JOHNNY BALES KNEW HE COULDN'T say anything. He'd promised. He sat down on the trail and picked at the grass, letting it slide out of his hand. But this was different. He could feel his heart still beating hard from his run down from the cabin. He knew from listening to his dad and Miss Winslow that something bad had happened. It was that boom sound that they'd heard from the school. His teacher, Miss Keeling, had said it was probably miners, and they shouldn't worry. She'd said she'd try to find out and she'd tell them, but the next day she said there was nothing in the newspaper or on the radio, so it was okay.

He'd looked everywhere and called, but Sara hadn't been there anymore, and it looked like someone had gone in and made a big mess. Maybe he could say about that? When was it all right to tell? Who was it all right to tell? Maybe his dad would get really mad at him. He probably wouldn't even be allowed to go up there if he knew. Maybe Miss Winslow. She was really nice. She'd taught them last year and was always nice. I bet I could tell her, he thought. She'd know what to do.

APRIL STOOD AT the edge of the baseball diamond looking across the street to the row of shops. It looked like there were apartments over them: 421 Powell Street. That was it. It was a jewellery shop now. Who knew what had been here before the war? She'd asked Sergeant James about the Japanese in Vancouver and he'd shrugged his shoulders. "They were enemy aliens."

"I know, but what happened to them?" she'd persisted.

"They were sent away, east. I don't know. That was the end of it."

Whoever had this jewellery shop wouldn't know anything. Still, if they'd lived in the neighbourhood, they might have known the Sasakis before the war. She crossed the street and pushed open the door of the shop. At the ring of the bell on the door, a middle-aged woman came out from behind a curtain wearing an expression that suggested her whole life was one long story of being put upon by others.

"About time. We don't see too many lady policemen." She gave an exaggerated sigh. "Better than nothin', I guess. I told the first guy it was mainly watches. Have you found the bastard?"

"I'm sorry, Mrs. . . . ?"

"You people don't write stuff down? Peabody, I told him."

"Mrs. Peabody. It sounds like you must have reported a robbery. I'm not here about that, though, I'm sorry."

"Is it Larry? Because if it is, he can just take his lumps. I'm tired of bailing him out!"

206

"No, not Larry either." Whoever he was. She guessed from the age of the woman he could be either husband or son. "I'm trying to get some information about the people who owned this shop before the war."

"The Japs? Don't look at me. I don't have a clue. I bought this place fair and square. They were all gone by then, and good riddance. They were traitors, living right here. I hear they're sending them all back to where they came from."

Surprised by the vitriol so long after the war, April hesitated. "Is there anyone living in the neighbourhood who lived here before the war?"

The woman turned her mouth down and thought. "I guess old Reiner, kitty-corner across the park. He has the butcher shop. You could try him. He's old as the hills. I doubt he remembers to put his own teeth in in the morning." She said this with obvious distaste.

"Thank you, Mrs. Peabody." April put her cap on and turned to go.

"Tell those lazy bastards to find who stole my watches! We're good Christian people here."

Feeling stung by the woman's anger, though it was nothing to do with her, April stood in the middle of the park wondering why being a good Christian should speed up the work of the police. This is what it will be like, she thought. People always being angry at you about something. She'd heard it often enough in the café. The police were either harassing you or not paying attention to your concerns. The average person coming in to have a cup of coffee in the morning wondered why the police let people get away with crime, and they'd often have a good mind to go tell them a thing or two.

Constable Terrell must face snarly people like Mrs. Peabody pretty often, she thought. Anticipating another bristly encounter with a local merchant, April took a deep breath, squared her shoulders, and went across the street to Reiner and Sons Kosher Butcher.

Mr. Reiner senior nodded at her when she came through the door. "Hello, Officer. You looking for a nice piece of brisket?"

She smiled and shook her head. "No, but it looks good." She surveyed the meat laid out under the glass. She wouldn't know a good piece of brisket if it stepped up and shook her hand. She sensed he actually knew this. "I'm trying to find anyone who knew the Sasaki family from before the war. They lived where that jewellery shop is now, over there." She turned and pointed across the park. "I don't know if it was a jewellery shop then, actually, but it's the address I was given."

Reiner shook his head. "It's a shame, that's what it is, a real shame on this country. They were good people, good neighbours. All the people who lived here."

Hope igniting in her, she said, "So you knew them? Can I ask you some questions?"

He shrugged. "You can ask me questions. I won't be too good on answers. It won't bring them back." He took off his apron and came around the counter, pointing at a little table with two chairs. April wondered about the "sons" on the shop sign.

"Here, sit," he said, collapsing into the chair against the wall. For a moment his face was suffused with sadness. "I used to play chess with old Mr. Sasaki in the park. He pretended not to speak that much English, and he was a bit of a sourpuss, but he was pretty hard to beat. It's not the same. Everybody's gone. I got a letter from him just after the war, asking about his family. There was nothing I could tell him." He shrugged and looked at his hands. "Even my sons. One died with the Royal Canadian Engineers in '44; the other one moved away to the United States after the war. He said he could make more money there. There you go. That's life."

April sat, looking at her own hands, unsure what to say. "I'm really sorry, Mr. Reiner."

"Thank you, young lady. Nothing for you to be sorry about. It's not your fault." He patted her arm. "It's like the end of an era. There used to be great baseball in that park. I used to think about how lucky I was to have the shop right here. A home run once went right through this window. They came to try to pay to fix the window. I told them no. I said, 'Just let me keep the ball.' That's it over there." He pointed to the very end of the counter where a much-signed baseball sat in a wooden stand on its own little shelf. "Now? It's a desert. No point in lamentation, I guess." He gave a little sideways bob of his head. "Now then, that store across the street."

"There was a young woman who lived there?"

Another regretful shrug. "Very nice girl. Full of life. The old man was her uncle, and she never seemed to mind what an old grump he was. Except toward the end. It got bad then."

April had her little book out and was writing frantically. "When?"

"Just before the war started, maybe '38, '39? She fell for this college kid, and they used to go out whenever they could. A guy called Bill. One time I ran into them, he was bringing her home. They used to stop over there." He pointed toward the end of the park. "Down at the corner of Cordova and Dunlevy. They'd stand there and talk, and then she'd go home across the park on her own. They didn't want the uncle to see them. Anyway, she knew I knew her uncle and she asked me not to say anything. I figured her life was hard enough, stuck in the jewellery store because she couldn't go to university like she wanted to, with that old reprobate."

"Why couldn't she go to university?"

"She wanted to study medicine. If you were Japanese or Chinese, you couldn't get into those faculties. Once the war started, of course, even the students who'd made it in were kicked out. Probably some of the best students they had. Maybe it was money too. Maybe he didn't want her to go because there was no one else to put behind the counter."

"But her boyfriend was at school?"

"Oh, he wasn't Japanese. That was the problem. The old guy was very set in his ways. The boy went to the store several times to see her, and the old man finally kicked the kid out, told him not to come back. He told me that himself. Said he had to protect her till her parents got back."

"Where were they?"

"Oh, they had to go back to Japan, I'd say around '35? They had to deal with some business they still had there, and her grandfather was sick. Then with the war they couldn't come back." He shook his head. "I don't know if he was looking after her, or she was looking after him. I'm sure she had to do pretty well everything. She was a nice girl though—bright, spunky. She never seemed bothered by him. And she was brave, going around with that boy like that. Not everybody would have thought that was kosher."

April thought about Terrell, the man she'd most like to be "going around" with. "I guess she was pretty brave. She must have loved him."

"Oh, that she did. In '39, when the war started, that kid signed up. Wish I could remember his surname." Reiner stopped and looked up for a moment. "They got married before he shipped out. She must have been upset, but most of the young men were volunteering. He got killed right out of the gate when his ship was torpedoed on the way to Europe. Left her with a little one." He shook his head sadly.

"What did her uncle think of that?"

"He was mad, all right. Said he'd had enough of her. He said some rough things about her, but see, he didn't know she was married. They did it in secret. Asked me to be one of the witnesses. I didn't like going behind the old man's back, but she was expecting, and besides, I liked them. Hope for the future. That's how I saw it. You'd think I could remember that boy's last name. I think the war just wiped everything out. I had family . . ." He left whatever he was about to say unsaid. "Old man Sasaki left when the Japanese had to register; I guess that was 1942, right after Pearl Harbour. But now I think of it, I don't know what happened to her. She just seemed to sort of disappear with that little girl of hers."

"So, after she married and had the baby, she still stayed with her uncle?"

Reiner shook his head as if in disapproval. "She did. I don't think he was any too nice to her at first. He wasn't any too nice about her when he talked to me. Anyway. The war came right around the time the baby was born, and Bill was gone." He paused. "He was a hard man, old Sasaki, but he was soft on that baby. You couldn't help it. I'd see him outside when she was a little toddler, playing on the swings, or rolling a ball around with her."

"And you don't know what became of her? She didn't leave with him?"

"I don't think so. I think she left a little bit before. I think the order went out, you know, for them to leave, and she was gone right away." He sighed. "I went and stood outside and watched all those people walking away from everything, not knowing where they were going, not knowing they'd never see their places again. Told everyone they had to go to the PNE where they kept the animals. Made them wait for days, then started trucking them out. The world has seen that sort of thing before. That's how my family ended up here. It was just like Russia, watching that. Never thought I'd see it here in Canada. I always hoped she got away somehow."

"And you never heard anything from her, or about her?"

"Never did," he said sadly.

April rose, shaking her head with a smile to another offer of brisket. "Thank you so much, Mr. Reiner. You've really helped. If you remember Bill's last name, can you leave me a message at my rooming house?" She tore a piece of paper out of her notebook, wrote her own name and the phone number of Mrs. James, who owned the rooming house on

Howe Street. She'd been aching to ask if Bill's last name had been Harold, but she had an idea that a real police officer wouldn't feed someone a name in case it wasn't right and the witness was erroneously influenced.

"Do you remember where he was from, Mr. Reiner?"

"Now there you stump me. Small town somewhere in the interior. Said it was by a beautiful lake. Something with an M? No, Nelson! That was it. Nelson."

MAKING HER WAY back toward the central police station, April thought about William Harold and Ichiko Sasaki. They'd defied the "rules" because they loved each other and had married. A mixed marriage she knew was generally thought to be between, say, a Protestant and a Catholic, or any other two religious denominations. The Harolds were another level of "mixed." She sighed. How would they have been accepted if the war hadn't happened? She tried to imagine walking down Baker Street arm in arm with Terrell and longed for it.

She had quite a bit of information, in particular about the romance, but would it help the police in Nelson? She tried to think of what else she could find. But she'd spoken to the attending doctor, and what he had to say confirmed what Reiner had said. There probably wasn't much else to find out. April really hoped she wouldn't disappoint them.

September 1939

FROM THE OUTSIDE, the Vancouver courthouse on Hornby gleamed and seemed almost too grand for their tiny wedding party, on a magical day of sun before autumn set in. By contrast, the room they were ushered into was dark, with its heavy curtains and oak panelling. There were a few rows of chairs, but this wedding would have no guests. Mr. Reiner, standing by looking proud and avuncular, and one of Bill's friends from university made up the witnesses. While the official was organizing his book, Bill paced and then took his friend's arm and moved out of earshot, whispering, "I was sure my brother would be here. His wife, Bertha, doesn't know, or I could blame her."

"Hey, it's gonna be okay," his friend whispered back. "It's a long drive. He could have been held up a million ways. You know he's proud of you." He gave him a hearty bump on the shoulder. "You're still gonna get married to that mighty pretty girl, no matter what!"

"Gentlemen. We're on the clock here," the official said.

Bill and his friend organized themselves, and Mr. Reiner gave Ichiko's hand a little squeeze, smiling encouragingly.

After the usual preamble of "We are gathered here today," read in a slow and resonant manner, the official turned to Bill and cleared his throat. "Please repeat after me: I solemnly declare that I do not know of any lawful impediment why I . . . "

Ichiko looked sidelong toward the door of the room, her heart pounding from visions of her furious uncle suddenly breaking through, refusing to allow the wedding.

Bill held Ichiko's hand, the ring poised to slip on her finger, and repeated after the official, "With this ring, as the token and pledge of the vow and covenant of my word, I

214

call upon those present to witness that I, William Stephen Harold, take thee, Ichiko Sasaki . . ." He had been looking at her hand, but when he said her name, he looked up at her, saw the sweetness of her face under the fall of her dark hair, and felt himself stop, fighting back tears. "Both of you," he whispered.

The official repeated, impatient again, "To be my lawful wedded wife."

"To be my lawful wedded wife."

Mr. Reiner refused to entertain the idea of Bill paying the official, taking care of it himself, and then they were out on Hornby.

"Me, I gotta go back to my shop," Reiner said. "But you kids, you should go have a nice meal, celebrate." He reached into his pocket and pulled out a small, faded blue velvet bag with a drawstring. "Here, a little present. I wanted to get you one of those little carriage clocks, but this does the same thing and makes less noise. It belonged to my grandfather."

Ichiko took the bag and opened it, drawing out a gold watch and chain, and immediately saw its value and tried to thrust it back at Mr. Reiner. "We could never accept this, Mr. Reiner. It must go to your son. It is too much."

Billy looked at the watch and shook his head. "It sure is nice, Mr. Reiner, but I agree with Ichiko. We couldn't take that."

Mr. Reiner refused the watch, holding both his hands up. "My sons never wanted any of that stuff from the old world. You are like my daughter now. You don't know . . . maybe one day it can be useful in case you need something. Please, it's with all my heart." He gently closed her hand over the watch. "Please. Don't disappoint an old man."

With tears in her eyes, she impulsively threw her arms around Mr. Reiner. "I'll never, ever forget you."

THE SUN WARMED the bench where they sat by Lost Lagoon. The warm weather was a gift—poignant, like their meetings; beautiful, and too soon over.

"Don't worry so much. Women have babies all the time. Look at all these people." Ichiko waved at the many people taking advantage of the warmth. "They were all born to mothers."

"I want to come to the hospital and wait like any other father."

"You can't. No one can know, or my uncle will find out we're married. I promise I'll tell him soon. Right now, he thinks I'm just bad. Which is fine. He always thinks I'm being bad."

Bill gave a bitter laugh. "I can't believe he'd be more upset about you marrying me than about you having a baby! My brother doesn't care one bit that you're Japanese. He can't wait to see you again."

"Anyway, I don't want anything to disrupt your degree," she said. "When you have that, we can settle on our own. You'll see. Everything will be all right."

Bill turned away from her and put his arm around her shoulder, gazing at the water. "They say we'll be getting into the war any day now. The fellows are already talking about signing up." He turned to her. "If that happens, I'm going to too. You know I have to."

216

She nodded, feeling her heart constrict. "I know. Of course, I do. That's why it's better if I stay at the shop after the baby is born. If there's a war, I'll live there. Then when it's over . . ."

He took her shoulders and looked at her, his face earnest, almost pleading. "When that happens, we go back to Nelson. I'll have a degree in engineering, and there's all kinds of places I can work there. It's a growing concern. Nobody there is going to care. It's a beautiful place, you'll see. All mountains and lakes. We'll have our own cozy house. Why, I bet you could even work in my brother's store part-time when our baby is in school. You know the business. He'd be happy to have the help."

"Didn't you tell me his wife works there with him?" she said with raised eyebrows.

"Yeah, but then she can stay home . . ." He stopped. There was a long silence.

"What?"

"No, nothing. My sister-in-law is a lovely person. Really nice. She's always been kind to me."

"But?" Ichiko could feel her voice hardening a little and wished it hadn't. After all, the woman's prejudices were not Bill's fault.

"Well, you know. She might not be quite ready, that's all. But she'd come to accept it. She really would. If you met her, you'd see what I mean."

It wouldn't be just her, Ichiko thought. Small towns, small minds. Where had she heard that? But she could see Bill was all shiny eyed about going back to his hometown. Well, this, as imperfect as it was, was her hometown. "Why don't we just take it a step at a time? We don't know what's going to happen." She hadn't told him that the doctor she'd seen had worried that she was small, and the birth might be hard. "Anyway, we can live here for a while, just till we know what's what. I know some families that are mixed. Maybe people here accept this sort of thing more." She had a sudden thought of being the only Japanese woman in Nelson, and her child the only Japanese child at the school. She, too, gazed at the water now. Love is all well and good, she thought, but there are a lot of things that have to be sorted. We can be two against the world, but will the world's rejection start to take a toll on us?

CHAPTER SEVENTEEN

"YOU WERE VERY CONVINCING WITH that Winnie-the-Pooh. Even I wanted to curl up and hug a teddy bear." Lane and Robin were driving back up the lake.

"It's not right," was all he said.

"What's not, Robin?"

"That little girl, all on her own like that. What's gonna happen to her? I read the papers. You know how people are about the Japanese. No forgive and forget, I can tell you that."

"You seem to have," Lane pointed out. They were starting up the hill toward Bales's filling station and store.

"That's different. It's a little innocent girl we're dealing with here. Anyway, her people never did anything to me. War's not her fault."

"No indeed, it's not. I just have to run in and pick something up. Do you want anything?"

"Nah. You go ahead."

Lane pulled up in front of the shop, greeted Blackie, who seemed happy to see her, though not with the enthusiasm of Alexandra, the Armstrong's Westie, and went in.

"Need some gas?" Bales asked her. He'd been sitting behind the counter reading the paper.

"No. I'm all right. I just forgot to pick up some tins of chicken soup."

"And your usual Cadbury bar?" he said with a wink. "Oh, and you have a billy-do from Johnny. He asked me to make sure I gave it to you as soon as I saw you. I bet they're going to invite you to their little play they're doing." He pulled an envelope out from a shelf under the counter and handed it to her.

"Thank you. It's sealed and everything," Lane said, impressed with the carefully printed *Miss Lane Winslow, who is a Mrs.* She smiled at his rendering of *billet-doux.* "I will have that chocolate bar, now you mention it, oh, and a loaf," she added. "Thank Johnny for me."

When she had paid, she slipped Johnny's envelope into the bag with her soup and chocolate and went out to the car.

"Here's what I think," Robin began, as if she had never left the car. "I think if they don't find someone for her, you should take her."

"THANK YOU, MISS McAvity," Terrell said. He knew he sounded stiff, but it was official work, after all.

There was silence at the other end of the line. Finally, she said softly, "April."

"Yes," he said, lowering his own voice. "What's it been like?"

"Getting to actually investigate something has been fun. The old butcher was really a treat. I didn't think about how many different kinds of people you could meet. Snarly ones, and nice ones, different kinds of people from all over."

"You met a lot of different people at the café," he pointed out.

"That's true, I guess. It's just that if you're investigating something you get a deeper look into people's character, maybe. Whether they're kind, or don't care. The uniform is itchy though, and it's too big."

He laughed. "Welcome to policing. What should I tell the boss?"

"Just that the only thing I'm waiting to hear about is the marriage certificate." She hesitated. "And of course, the important thing: that William Harold was from Nelson. But I guess that's hearsay till we see the certificate."

"It is big news if it's true," Terrell said. He wanted to say "well done" but then thought it was too forward. He was about to hang up, and he hurriedly added, "Do you boat?" Again, a hesitation. He thought she'd gone and was about to put the receiver down.

"Of course I 'boat.' I'm a Nelson girl. Why?"

"I don't, too much. I think you'll have to teach me."

FEELING SOMEWHAT SATISFIED, and at the same time afraid he'd lost an opportunity of some sort, Terrell related the contents of April's phone call to Darling. "April called Vital Statistics to see if they could find the marriage licence. They told her it would take some work because it was so long ago. But if he is who we think he is, that will confirm it."

Darling nodded. "So, she was married to someone named William Harold, stayed over the shop while he went off and got himself killed, and then disappeared. Now that we know, or are almost certain, that William Harold was from Nelson, he pretty well must be Ron Harold's younger brother. I hope you're right that the marriage licence will confirm or negate this. All right, so I think we have to assume she was interned with everyone else, including her uncle, but Miss McAvity's source says she disappeared before her uncle left. It doesn't mean she wasn't interned somewhere. If the uncle had decided pro-Japanese sentiments about the war, he might have gone back to Japan. It sounds like Sara might have grandparents in Japan. It could be a job trying to track them down, if they survived the war. Did Miss McAvity say where in Japan they went?"

"Oh, no. She didn't. We could ask her to go check with the butcher again. He might remember."

Darling nodded. "You do that. She's done a good job. You can tell her that from me. In the meantime, I'll try to reach Dr. Miyazaki again and ask if he knew any Sasakis up where he was during the war. Trouble is, the Japanese from the coast who didn't end up here were sent clear across Alberta and even farther east, or even were allowed to go off on their own, I learned, as long as they left the coast. It will be hard to find complete records. We might have to put ads in the papers. Though the fact that she lived here with the child suggests that if she was interned, it was somewhere in BC. Thanks, Constable."

"Sir." Terrell rose and collected his notebook.

Darling watched him go with a slight smile. No doubt he was looking forward to April's next call. Well, it wasn't his business, though he admitted that since Lane, he viewed romance in general with more tolerance than he had in the past. He turned and looked out at Elephant Mountain, which displayed a variety of moods depending on time of day, how the sun slanted, or the clouds loomed. Today, in the flat light of the afternoon sun, it seemed to be napping.

So, Mrs. Ichiko Harold, widow and mother, leaves the place she's been interned, finds, somehow, a cabin slap bang in the middle of nowhere, and is not seen by anyone, he thought. Though, if she is married to Ron Harold's brother, she is near at least one family member: Ron himself. Her child is not in school, and she seems to magically have provisions, augmented by a large garden, but is never seen by anyone to be shopping. She does not appear to have a vehicle unless someone finds one squirrelled in the woods near the Balfour road at the bottom of the hill.

Darling remembered a few Japanese students at the university when he was there. It was his impression that their families were very big on education. He certainly didn't remember them being given to frivolity and varsity shenanigans like some of the other students. If that was the case, why would this mother choose to home-school her child? Was it because the child was mute?

Elephant Mountain, still snoozing, ventured no opinion. With a sigh, he fished around in his jacket pocket and found the card Dr. Miyazaki had given him and looked at it again with interest. "Osteopath," he said aloud, followed by, "Hmm." Hoping he was osteopathing right that minute

223

and could be reached at the number on the card, Darling asked to be put through. He was in luck.

"Dr. Miyazaki. How may I help?"

"Afternoon, Doctor. It's Inspector Darling in Nelson."

The doctor's voice cheered up. "Inspector. How are you? Not another body, I hope?"

"No, thank God. Just a question about the one I have on hand. This is about the Japanese woman who died in that explosion. We now know more. She was Mrs. William Harold, and her maiden name was Ichiko Sasaki. Her husband died very shortly after enlisting in '39. We are now working on the supposition that the dead jeweller might have been her husband's brother. We really need to find a next of kin to notify about her death, and more importantly, some relation for Sara, her child." Even as he said this, he realized that if the connection between William and Ronald Harold could be confirmed, Bertha Harold might now well be Sara's nearest relation. He found the thought disquieting.

"You know, I have compiled a considerable list of Japanese families in all the internment centres I am aware of. I will go through all the names and call you as soon as I can."

LANE, FILLED WITH an assortment of conflicting feelings, plunked her grocery bag on the kitchen table, and was immediately distracted by thoughts of Sara, imagining her living in their house. She pushed open the French doors and went to lean on the railing of the porch, looking down the garden and out to the lake. The steamboat that plied the distance between Nelson and the upper reaches of the lake was making its outward journey, its attractive paddlewheel stern just disappearing behind the point.

If they did take Sara until relations could be found, it would not be like her last outing with children, when she taught for a few weeks at the school until the missing teacher had been found. Then, she'd left a peaceful house and returned to a quiet evening with Darling. Having a child in the house would be a complete commitment. Especially if Sara were convalescing, both, Lane thought, physically and mentally. Would she even be capable of such care? And what would it be like when the inevitable relative was found and she had to say goodbye to her?

What was a child that age like? Not just at school, where she'd seen the local children in that unnatural habitat, but every day, all day? What had she herself been like at nine? She had a vague picture of herself crouching outside, hiding from Nanny, who wanted her to come in for her piano lesson or her bath. She shook her head, wondering if the trickcyclists would make anything of the fact that the first memory she could muster of her own childhood was of hiding. Really, she must have been the most appalling child! She turned to go into the kitchen, and then was drawn back outside. She closed her eyes and listened to the whispering silence of the wind in the tops of the trees. She had a sudden, vivid impression of being a child again in that forest above her childhood house. She had loved and feared that sound. The sound of trees talking. She had listened to it, eyes closed, sun warming her face.

The sensation was so powerful that she opened her eyes, but then it was gone; she reached for that feeling of being little, but it had evaporated as if it had never been. But it had.

It reminded her of the overwhelming way children absorbed their surroundings, laying in such powerful memories that though they might be buried, they were never lost.

Sitting down at her little desk in the kitchen, with its lonely, patient typewriter, she opened the drawer and pulled out some foolscap.

> *Nanny combs my hair, eternally*
> *Raking out the pine needles*
> *And shaking her head*
> *I see she's stumped, really*
> *For no scold or wheedle*
> *Stops my wandering tread*
> *But the sun has pierced me through*
> *And I've already sailed . . .*
> *There is no turning back for me*

How long had passed? She pushed the lines into the drawer with the others and tossed a pencil still on the table in after it, hoping it might take care of any necessary changes on its own. The clock said twenty minutes . . . for nine little lines? Really, at that rate she'd never have time to be a poet.

The grocery bag still sat on the kitchen table where she'd left it. She pulled the soup, the chocolate, and the loaf of inferior bread—she really must learn to make it—out of the bag and saw Johnny's letter.

She'd liked him when he had been one of her students. He was kind to the smaller children and had an easy laugh. The letter was painstakingly written in pencil with several erasures and many smudges of the lead across the paper.

Dear Miss Winslow,

*I wasn't supposed to say the secret, but now I
don't know what to do because I think something is wrong after the boom. Miss Keeling
said it was all right though the next day, so I
went to see Sara because it was close to where
she lives but there was nobody there, and I
think a robber came to their house and that's
wrong. And I can't find Sara anymore.*

*Do you think it would be all right if I told
the secret to you?*

Your student,
Johnny Bales

In moments Lane was in the car, dashing back to the
store. Blackie, perhaps sensing her urgency, got up from
the middle of the road and stood wagging expectantly as
she pulled up in front of the door.

"Forget something?" Bales asked when she burst in.

"No, I've actually come about Johnny's note. Is he
around somewhere?"

Bales looked at her with interest. "Is everything all right?"

"Yes, absolutely all right. I just should talk to him about
his nice note." She could see he thought it ridiculous that
she'd drive all the way back to Balfour on the strength of
a note from his son. He couldn't know how important it
was, and she could not really tell him. She'd let Johnny
know that it was quite all right to tell the secret in the
current circumstances.

"I think he's down by the water catching minnows. He

took a jar with him. You can drive. Back down and then around the north road by the lake. There's a dock there past that pond that freezes over in the winter."

"Thanks!" Lane said. She wanted to say she'd stop back and let him know what it was all about, but she was no idle keeper of secrets. She was a professional, after all.

She saw Johnny lying face down on the dock looking over the edge, his hands dangling into the lake, swirling it. The water under the dock was a luminous green from the shadows and sun. He was with two of the other children from her class, Samuel and Gabriella. "Hello, everyone, nice day for it."

They all flipped over at once and sat up, smiling. "Miss Winslow!" Samuel said. "We're looking for minnows."

"Find any?"

"Yup. But they don't want to swim in the jars we have."

Johnny watched her with wide eyes but said nothing, perhaps fearful that she would say something about his note.

"Hmm. Perhaps they don't like being in jars," Lane offered, kneeling down to have a look. "They are tiny!"

"I tried to keep one in a fishbowl once, but it died," Gabriella said.

"I suppose if you were able to get one into a jar, it would be a way to have a nice close look at it, and then you could put it back."

Samuel and Gabriella turned back onto their stomachs to look at the water. "Maybe that would be all right," Samuel said.

"I'm sure it would," Lane said. She looked at Johnny. "Johnny, I just came down from the store and I have a question for you. Can we talk over here, so it doesn't disturb the minnow catching?"

Johnny nodded and looked at his fellow ichthyologists, and then got up and followed her back to the path.

"Thank you so much for your note, Johnny. I think what you have to say might be very, very important. Do you think you feel all right telling me the secret?"

"I don't know what happened to Sara," he said. "I was scared."

"I can tell you that Sara is going to be fine. She got hurt in the explosion, but she is in the hospital, and they are looking after her very well indeed. Tell me about how you know her."

"What about her mother? Is her mother with her? She was really nice."

Lane, confronted with having to tell a child about someone dying, was silent for a moment. "Tell me about them. Here, sit down." She sat down on the grass beside the path and patted the ground next to her.

"They told me not to tell anything."

"I know, and I bet you have done a wonderful job of keeping their secret. It shows you are very loyal and a very good friend. But sometimes a friend needs help, and then your secret might be the only thing that can really help them."

Johnny looked down and plucked at the grass. "Sara got hurt, huh?"

"She did, yes. But she really is going to be all right. Can you tell me how you met?"

"I like to explore up in the woods. One day I went farther than ever up the mountain, and I found this cabin I didn't know was there. I saw the girl and she seemed happy to see me. She showed me all her books, and we would read and play, and her mother was scared at first because she said no one was supposed to know they were there. She made me promise not to tell anyone, not even my parents."

"And you visited her from time to time?"

He nodded. "She was really nice. I didn't know anyone got hurt in the boom. Miss Keeling told us not to worry because there wasn't anything in the paper."

"I know. I think the police were worried about the explosion as well, and I guess they are also keeping it a secret until they understand what happened. Tell me, how did you and Sara talk?"

He looked puzzled. "The regular way. She speaks English like I do. Her mother too."

So, her inability to speak was because of the shock, Lane thought. "Do you know something interesting, Johnny? I think Sara was so upset by the explosion that right now she isn't talking. It happens to people who have had a really bad accident sometimes. It's called shock. In fact, the people at the hospital thought she couldn't talk at all. It's very important to learn that she can talk. Thank you for telling me that."

"If she's hurt, can I go see her? Maybe she'll talk if I'm there."

Out of the mouths of babes. "You know, she just might. She might be very happy to see a friend. She really needs one right now. I will ask the hospital if it is all right for you to visit, and then we can go together."

Lane could see that Samuel and Gabriella were holding up their jars triumphantly, and about to approach. Lane tousled his hair gently. "You are such a kind person. It will be so important for Sara that you are her friend."

"Look! I caught one!" Samuel said, running up with his jar and sitting down with them. "Gabby, too."

"Well, shall we have a good look at them and see what we can learn?" Lane said.

Once home, Lane thought she ought to phone the hospital right away and give Dr. Edison the news, but almost unconsciously she pulled open the drawer to have a look at her poem. Pshaw! she thought. She could see that the pencil, left to its own devices, had effected no changes at all, nor had it added another stanza or two, and now, after time had passed, she could see how badly they were needed. This would need a lot of work. You can't expect to just dash poems off and have them be any good. She pushed the whole disappointing thing back into the drawer and went into the hall to the phone.

CHAPTER EIGHTEEN

"**SHOULD WE GO ON THE** supposition that he is Ron Harold's brother?" Terrell asked. They hadn't heard back about the marriage certificate yet, but it seemed clear to all of them.

He, Ames, and Darling were in the café for an afternoon break. Usually, Terrell and Ames took the break and brought something back for the boss, but today Darling felt the need of a break himself and hoped his underlings would not mind having their companionship intruded upon. Unfortunately, the waitress, Marge, did mind being intruded upon, and continued with her undiminished hostility to her customers.

"It's a comfort," Ames said, after a surly interaction in which they ordered their coffee, "that she doesn't just pick on us—she's like that with everybody."

"Yes, Terrell, I think we should go on that supposition, except Mrs. Harold is adamant that William never married," Darling said.

"But let's say he had, and for some reason it was kept a secret. It might explain why Mrs. Ichiko Harold ended up here," Ames said, turning away with difficulty from his fascination with Marge's malevolence.

"Unfortunately, so would the internment laws," Darling pointed out. "Let's say she's interned somewhere near here, Sandon, Kaslo, and Ron Harold tracks her down, and finds that cabin for her." He leaned back to accommodate the service of their cups of coffee, plunked on the table with ill grace. How does she not spill coffee doing that? Darling wondered. "Thank you." He was about to add "Marge" but worried she would think it a liberty.

Marge hovered, her hands on her hips. Puzzled, the three policemen watched for her next move. "You planning to be here all afternoon? Unless you're eating something, someone's gonna need that table."

Darling looked around the restaurant. They were the only customers, as it was the middle of the workday afternoon. He nodded and held up his mug. "Just till we're done," he said cheerfully.

"You done anything about that jewellery store robbery and murder? I'm surprised you have time to sit around drinking coffee when no one's life is safe around here."

It was hard to know what to say to a worried citizen about the complexities of an investigation, or indeed, what could be said about the progress of that investigation. Terrell and Ames appeared to be anxious to know as well. They were both looking at Darling expectantly.

"We do not," Darling said carefully at last, "think there is any danger to the public." He nearly added "at this time" but rejected it as making him sound like a politician.

"Ha!" was all she said, turning on her heel.

"Well played, sir," Ames said, sitting back and slurping down some coffee.

"Shut up, Ames. The question is, why keep it such a secret? And why tuck them up that mountain where no one can find them?"

"Maybe his wife wouldn't approve. I could see her being hard about that kind of thing," Ames suggested.

Darling nodded thoughtfully. "Now, I'm waiting to hear from Dr. Miyazaki about any Sasakis he might have on what he says are quite extensive lists he's made of the people who were interned in BC. And we still have not found a motive for the murder of Mr. Harold, or the weapon used to do it. We also have no idea why the office at the shop was ransacked. The trouble is, anyone who could help is dead: Ron Harold, his brother Bill, and Mrs. Sasaki Harold. But someone was certainly after Ron Harold, and maybe even Ichiko Harold."

LANE LOOKED AT her watch. It was very near King's Cove's tea time. She could use a cup of tea. She slipped on the plimsolls she'd kicked aside at the door and went out. It was a beautiful afternoon. She thought of the green lapping of the water under the wharf where the children had been catching minnows, knowing wistfully that for them the afternoon was endless. She could never decide if she missed her childhood with its expansive feeling of time or had made a lucky escape.

Nearly half a century older than she was, the Armstrongs might have some perspective on the fleeting qualities of time.

Alexandra did. For her it was always right now, and right now she was leaping about Lane and had added a new trick: excitedly chasing her own stubby tail.

"I can't decide if she's clever with that one, or as dim as a plank. She'll never catch the damn thing," Kenny said, approaching Lane from one of his garden sheds.

"I think it is terribly endearing, and very clever," Lane said. Alexandra had thrown herself on her back and Lane obliged with a tummy rub. "Taking a break?"

"I will if you have a clever and endearing story to tell," he said. "What's going on with that murder?"

"I don't know much about the murder, I'm afraid. You know how the police are with their reluctance to share with the mere public. I've learned something very interesting about the little girl, though."

"That will do. Come on. I think Eleanor has set us up at the back. I'll get her to toss on another cup."

"I love your walnut cake," Lane said, when she'd been served her tea and cake. She closed her eyes in delight. The little square table was covered in a white cloth with a corner of bright strawberries embroidered on it. Lane remembered seeing it on offer at the last vicarage tea in Balfour. "It's much better than the one I bought at the supermarket bakery."

"Never mind all that," Eleanor said impatiently. "Has Robin frightened that child to death yet?"

Lane put her cup down and wiped the crumbs off the corner of her mouth. "She seems to adore him. It's remarkable: he's a completely different person with her.

Soft spoken, kind, full of sympathy."

"That it is. It's never been done before."

"But I've learned something astonishing from young Johnny Bales. For who knows how long, he's been sneaking off to the cabin to play with her, and he says she could talk perfectly well. I've asked Bales if I can take him on the next visit to the hospital. Perhaps he can read to her as well, though I don't think Robin would like that privilege usurped. Or, with any luck, they will just chatter away. The doctor was thrilled to learn it."

Eleanor sat, holding her cup in both hands, looking out to the lake. Finally, she said, "She doesn't know yet about her mother, does she?"

Lane shook her head. "I don't think so, though she must wonder why she has never been in to visit."

"I wonder if when she starts talking it will break the spell for her. It's a sort of magical never-never land right now, isn't it? She'll have to come back to earth with a horrible crash, and then what?"

Lane nodded. "Children can be quite resilient. Remember Samuel, whose father died and mother disappeared? He seems quite grounded and happy now, and that's after spending so much of his last year or two being almost completely neglected."

"But now he lives with that nice family. What's the name of that little girl he lives with now?"

"Gabriella. Yes, of course. You're right. It will matter what happens to Sara after this. Robin has offered to have her live with him if no one can be found for her. It's extraordinarily kind of him."

"Ha!" barked Kenny. "That should just about do for her."

"You might be underestimating him," Eleanor said.

"Not bloody likely! An old scoundrel like that. No, no. You're the one. She needs a kind womanly face to greet her every day."

Lane gave a twisted smile. "Robin did suggest that as well."

"So, he's not a complete halfwit, after all. What about it?"

"I dare say it won't be up to me," Lane said evasively. "And with any luck we'll find a relation soon."

They sat companionably until the return of the stern-wheeler out on the lake heading back toward Nelson seemed to signal the rest was over.

"I'd better go telephone the inspector. I don't know if it will matter, but he ought to know she can talk."

Back in her hallway, she kicked off her shoes and was preparing to call Darling when the ringing of the telephone startled her. Two longs and a short. She picked up the earpiece and spoke into the trumpet. "KC 431, Lane Winslow speaking."

"Miss Winslow, it's Mr. Bales."

"Oh, hello, Mr. Bales. You've not changed your mind about Johnny coming into town with me tomorrow?"

"No. It's not that. I just saw that they published a photo of that Mr. Harold who got killed in town. Well, I recognize that face. He used to come in pretty often and buy groceries. I was a bit surprised, because he doesn't, er, didn't, live around here. I figured he must work at the construction site and was just picking things up to take home. But if he lived in town and had his business there, that doesn't make too much sense."

"IT'S GOOD NEWS that that little girl can talk," Terrell said to Ames. "That's going to make whatever comes next a lot easier for her. I was hoping April would find something there in Vancouver. I was pretty shocked to learn the Japanese still can't go back. I thought things were bad for us back home. I came out here to start a new life, but at least I can still go home if I want to." They were on their way to see Mrs. Harold. They had something else to ask her now that Lane had called in with the news from Mr. Bales.

Mrs. Harold was helping Mrs. Dee pack her mail-order cosmetic products when they arrived. She looked almost normal, Ames thought, working at the kitchen table in the late afternoon light. Happy. As if her life hadn't been blown up.

She looked up when she saw the officers, ushered in by Mrs. Dee. "Do you have news?"

"I'm just going out to the post office. I'll leave you to it," Mrs. Dee said, scooping up a pile of parcels.

"I'm afraid not really, Mrs. Harold. It will require a painstaking collection of information for us to understand how your husband died," Ames said. "We do have a couple of questions, though. May we sit down?"

She nodded, weary now, and sat down herself, her hands tightly folded in front of her on the table as if bracing herself.

Terrell had his book out and put it on the table. Ames cleared his throat. "We are just following up on every angle. Can you tell us if your husband made a weekly trip up the lake to Balfour to shop for groceries?"

Now she just shook her head, as if she were dealing with imbeciles. "Obviously my husband did *not* go up the lake to buy groceries. He was a jeweller and watchmaker right here in town. I took care of all that sort of thing. Whoever told you such nonsense?"

"The man who runs the filling station out in Balfour. It's a small grocery store as well. He said he recognized Mr. Harold's face in yesterday's paper. You know we published a request for information."

"Balderdash! You wouldn't recognize Gary Cooper from a photo in the *Nelson Daily News*!" She stood up, pushing her chair back angrily, causing it to tilt and then fall back onto its four feet with a bang on the floor. "Are you going to find out who killed my husband, or not? Until you do, I'm in limbo. I can't bury him. I can't deal with the will. I can't do anything."

"Have you been to see his solicitor?" Terrell asked suddenly.

"No, I have not. I don't see what business it is of yours . . . of the police."

"I know what you mean, ma'am," Terrell said with a mollifying tone. "Sometimes, though, the will might reveal something that could be relevant. Who things are left to and that sort of thing."

"Hmm," she said, conceding slightly. "Not this time, though. Whatever he had, we had, is left entirely to me. There is no one else. We never had children. That's why I haven't bothered. There's plenty of time for that."

Terrell nodded. "So, you have seen the will?"

She hesitated fractionally, then said with a slight air of defensiveness, "No. Not since he sent Padgett that note. But it's obvious, isn't it? Bill is dead, and we didn't have anyone."

She turned and looked out the window, her arms crossed. "I'll sell up. Everything, the shop, the house. Maybe move somewhere else where I don't have to be reminded. Barbara says I can stay here as long as I like. We get along, and I can help with her business." What she didn't say was that the fears she harboured about her husband's secretiveness were beginning to mount.

"ARE WE SURE about the guy in Balfour? She's right about newspaper photos. They aren't all that clear," Terrell said when they were heading back to the station.

"For one thing, I think I *would* recognize Gary Cooper from a newspaper photo, and for another, Miss Winslow said he was very sure it was the same guy," Ames retorted. "No, she's either covering up something she does know about, or she has no idea. According to the boss, she was sure Ron's brother Bill wasn't married, but we're pretty sure it's the same Bill, so she could be covering that up or didn't know. That would be something!"

Terrell nodded. "I wonder if Bill kept it secret from his brother Ron, or Ron did know but didn't tell his wife."

"Yes," agreed Terrell. "What we've got here is a wife who didn't know her brother-in-law was married and had a baby—and didn't know her husband had something to do with looking after them. The big question is, why didn't she know?"

CHAPTER NINETEEN

MRS. DODI CARTWRIGHT, HER VACUUMING and bed-making done, had stepped outside to fish the newspaper out of the grass. In his hurried exit to his office, her husband hadn't brought it in. The boy had slammed it against the door, and it had bounced off and fallen down beside the steps. She smiled. He was getting quite good with that right arm.

She spooned some coffee into the basket of the coffee pot, filled it, and put it on the burner. She'd just have time to clean the bathroom while the coffee burbled.

Coffee poured, she took her mug, her two cookies on a little plate, and the newspaper to the side table by her chair. Adjusting the ottoman, she propped her feet up, unfolded the paper, and took up her coffee with a sigh of something near momentary contentment. Usually there was not much more to read about than marriages, church bazaars, and interviews with boys who saved dogs from drain ditches. Lately, though, it had all been a lot more interesting. She took a cookie—she did make the most delicious oatmeal raisin cookies, and she certainly wanted more of them nowadays—and perused the day's headlines.

Still no progress on the murder of poor Mr. Harold, the jeweller. Jerry had bought her wedding and engagement rings from him. Somehow that brought the whole thing closer to home. She held out her hand and looked at her rings, the facets of the small diamond engagement ring catching the morning light. Shaking her head, she returned to the paper. She knew it was fashionable to blame the police for taking so long to get to the bottom of things, but she also knew, no one better, that life was full of puzzles. And his wasn't the only death. Some poor woman had died in an explosion up a mountain, where? She read forward to see if they said. Ah. Between Balfour and King's Cove. There had been arrests of several Freedomites by the Mounties. It was funny that they didn't say who and had said almost nothing about the explosion except that it had happened. And they'd taken long enough to report even that.

She let the paper fall to her lap and took her cup from the side table, holding it with two hands and staring at the wall opposite, where the wireless sat in solitary splendour. Now, that didn't seem quite right. Not at all.

She'd followed the trajectory of the Doukhobor splinter group who called themselves Sons of Freedom for the last year. It was, she thought, an interesting problem for democracy. She had always believed that the Canadian democracy was founded on everyone getting the same education, understanding the institutions in more or less the same way. On the other hand, the whole point of it was that people had freedoms. Isn't that what she had fought for, day after day, night after night, half freezing to death on the wild Pacific coast of Vancouver Island? So, this particular group of Doukhobors didn't want their children educated in provincial schools. Didn't they have that right? Not according to the government. Who knew, perhaps she herself might take against something being taught and want to take a child out of school. Should she not have that right? On the other hand, where would be the common understanding of what might be expected of citizens if everyone did that?

She frowned at the paper and put her cup back. She wanted to refill it, but something was nagging at her. She reread the very sparse article about the explosion. Clearly the RCMP hadn't released much information to the reporter from the *Nelson Daily News*—who the woman was, where exactly the explosion was. She was familiar with that area between Balfour and King's Cove. She'd driven past it often enough on her way to the hot springs at Adderly. There was nothing there except mountains and thick forest. The thing that was nagging at her came into focus: No Son of Freedom would put a bomb out in the middle of nowhere halfway up a steep mountain. There would be no strategic or publicity value to it.

She got up and began to pace. No matter how she turned the thing around, there was no one she could talk to. And she might be wrong. But if she wasn't, several men were in jail for no reason. Her friend, Susan Edison, suddenly sprang to mind. She'd been in charge of an Air Force medical unit. The first woman to be given that assignment. Susan, at least, would take her seriously. She folded the paper and drank down her coffee. She wouldn't be able to say anything, really, except "I think they're wrong."

She slipped on her shoes and took her cardigan off the bedpost. She found her hat and pinned it on, tucking in a loose strand of dark hair. She stood by the door, feeling a moment of irrational rebellion, as if some internal force said she ought not to leave the house for unconventional reasons. She wondered what Jerry thought she did all day, and then knew in the next instant that he would give no thought to the matter at all. His life was full of insurance brokering, a subject he could wax on about the whole evening. *His* life was important. Well, it was soon to be more important. And a whole lot less important.

She shook her head. He was a lovely man. Kind, considerate, puzzled. He was better than many. She set off down the street toward the hospital. The slight melancholy she sometimes felt about how little her husband knew about her, or would understand, was alleviated by the sunshine. Cool air rose from the lake with what she thought of as "that lovely lakey smell" and she could feel her mood lift. There was a gulf between her and Jerry filled with silence and secrecy that could never be bridged. Her attempts to bridge it by falling in obligingly with the way of life for which women were apparently destined somehow made it worse. Still, on a beautiful day, she could almost feel normal, and she *did* love him.

She arrived at the hospital just behind a very beautiful woman with a little boy who'd clearly been dressed and scrubbed up for the occasion. She was certain she'd never seen them before. She nodded and smiled at the woman in the elevator.

"One ought to take the stairs," the woman said with a smile and a shrug. She had an English accent and a lovely low melodious voice. The boy was resting his behind on the wall of the elevator and watching the lights as it climbed.

Dodi would have answered, but the doors slid open and she just had time for "Excuse me," only to discover they were all getting out on the same floor. Furthermore, the woman made directly for Dr. Edison, as she herself was doing.

"Good afternoon, Miss Winslow. Who have you here?"

"This is Johnny Bales. He'd like to see Sara because"—she paused here—"he used to play with her sometimes."

Dr. Edison looked down at the boy and nodded. "Ah. Very good. I was so pleased to get your call!" But before an answer was offered, she looked past the Englishwoman. "Oh, good heavens, here's my friend Dodi Cartwright!" Dr. Edison exclaimed. "Now, if there were ever two people who ought to know each other it's the two of you." She turned to Lane. "Miss Winslow, meet Dodi Cartwright; Dodi, meet Miss Lane Winslow."

Dodi smiled and took Lane's hand. "How do you do?"

"Very well, thank you. Certainly better than the little girl we've come to see. Would it be all right if we just barged in?" she said, turning to Dr. Edison. "It's not bath time or anything, is it? I wonder if I should send Johnny in on his own, so she's not overwhelmed."

Dodi watched her friend consider this. "Does he know about her mother?" Susan whispered after a few moments, and Miss Winslow shook her head. "Go on, then."

Dr. Edison turned back to her friend. "What brings you here?"

Pulling her eyes away from Miss Winslow talking quietly to the boy, Dodi looked at Dr. Edison. "I need to talk to you, if you have a moment."

"Yes, all right. Let me just make sure this is all settled. Why don't you go into my office," she said, pointing down the hall.

"Who is the little girl?" Dodi asked, nodding toward the door the boy had gone through.

"It's a dreadful thing," Edison said, shaking her head. "I'll be right in and will tell you what I can about it."

Dodi nodded and went into the office. Sitting with her hands on her handbag, she thought about the little girl, whoever she was. There are always people worse off than oneself, she thought.

LANE AND THE doctor stood at the door and watched Johnny approach Sara, who turned to look at him, her face momentarily blank.

"Sara?" Johnny said. He put his hands on the covers. "It looks like you got really hurt."

Sara watched him, her eyebrows pulled together, and then she nodded and said very quietly, "Something happened to me."

Edison turned to Lane, astounded. "She *can* talk!" she whispered.

Lane nodded, smiling. "Yes. Johnny was most perplexed

to discover we thought she couldn't."

The doctor turned back to look at the children. Johnny had sat down and was looking at Sara's books. "We heard a big boom when we were at school," he said.

"Gosh, I'd love to hear the rest of this, but I must go speak with Mrs. Cartwright," Dr. Edison said.

"Yes, of course. I'll give this a few more minutes and then join them. All right if I steal a chair from the empty bed?" The little girl with the playground concussion seemed to have gone home.

"Absolutely. Goodness, I feel quite fizzy! What a treat to hear her voice."

"I'M SORRY TO take you away from your work. I . . . I just couldn't think who else to talk with."

"Yes, of course. It's not Jerry, is it?" Dr. Edison had shut the door and was leaning forward at her desk.

"No, no. Nothing like that. In fact, well, I'm expecting. It might be what's making me jumpy."

"Oh, brava! I'm thrilled to hear it, and heartiest congratulations! But you are not and never have been a woman who gets jumpy without good reason. You don't think there's something wrong with the pregnancy? Have you told Jerry about the baby yet?"

Dodi shook her head. "No. I haven't. I will, though. Tonight, I think. No, what I'm here about is that I think there's something wrong about that explosion, you know, out by Balfour."

"Oh," Dr. Edison said, sitting back. "I'm not sure what I have to offer on the subject." Anything she said would violate her patient's confidentiality. On the other hand, Dodi knew things, and she thought there was something wrong about the explosion. Maybe she could help. "Actually, that little girl in there was injured in that explosion. In fact, it was Miss Winslow who found the little girl. She lives up that way. What do you think is wrong?"

"I just don't think it was done by the Freedomites. It doesn't make sense. Was someone killed? Because if that happened, they could face the death penalty."

"I really can't say."

Dodi sighed and looked through the glass window in the door to the ward. "I understand. Is the little girl Japanese, do you think? That would be extraordinary." It was a rhetorical question. She had a sudden sweeping vision of long cold nights, the sound of the ocean crashing against the rocks, the exhaustion of straining to hear with those earphones.

"Listen," Dr. Edison said, "why don't you hang about and speak to Miss Winslow? If she saw the bomb site, she might be able to tell you something. I have a feeling, though I wouldn't swear to it, that she might know a bit about what she saw." She stood up. "I'm sorry, I've got to dash. It's lovely to see you. We must have dinner. One night when Jerry's off at the Legion."

Dodi watched her friend go into the ward. She *could* go to dinner when Jerry was out. Susan was right. Even a married woman need not be home for supper if her husband was out. She stood up and went into the hall. Dr. Edison was leaning over and whispering to Miss Winslow, who nodded and said something to the little boy, handing him a book.

"It's a lovely day," Lane said without preamble to Dodi, as she came into the hall. "Why don't we go outside? I think there's a bench overlooking town and the lake. I expect Johnny and Sara have a good deal to catch up. If not, he can read to her. I used to teach him, and frankly, he could use the practice reading aloud."

Nodding, Dodi followed her into the elevator, and they went down without speaking, as though they'd agreed on silence. Once on the bench outside, she said, "So, you're a teacher?"

Lane laughed and shook her head. "Not even remotely. I stood in for the real teacher during a crisis this last winter. It was good fun, and the children were lovely and very, very tolerant."

Smiling, Dodi said, "Children are lovely generally, I'm told." She put her hand on her tummy.

"Then I'm to congratulate you!"

"Thank you." Dodi became serious. "I understand you might know something about that explosion up at King's Cove."

Lane appraised her companion. The question was unexpected. Whatever the reason for the question, she knew little enough. "I'm not entirely sure about what I saw, but I do think there is something wrong about the men they've arrested."

"You think it was a bomb?" Dodi Cartwright asked.

"I saw the site when my neighbours and I climbed up the mountain. We found Sara there and I rushed her here, but I went back later. There was clear evidence of a bomb, including the tail. Twenty or thirty pounder. I don't know enough about what the Freedomites use, but if it wasn't them . . . well . . . I suppose I can't bear a miscarriage of justice."

Dodi was quiet for a moment. What she would say next was unreasonable, she knew. The woman was clearly intelligent and seemed to know something about what she'd seen. She herself knew next to nothing about bombs. "It must have been dreadful finding the little girl. What did you see, exactly?"

Lane looked at her and considered. That way of asking. It had a military quality to it. Dr. Edison was no fool. She intended something from this meeting. "Well, it was dreadful to find Sara. If we hadn't, she'd have died. I also found her mother's body the next day. She'd been buried under a tree that had been knocked down. I would think she died almost instantly." She paused. "I was troubled about the explosion because it is in the middle of nowhere. When I tried to tell the odious Mountie what some of the ingredients of the bomb probably were—you could smell them—he told me to go boil my head. There were some peculiar aspects of it. Will it mean anything to you if I tell you?"

"It's hard to say. I also didn't think it was the work of the Freedomites when I read about it. They wouldn't bomb anything in the middle of nowhere. It would have no practical or political value to them."

Lane considered. "I think that too. The trouble is, I don't know what they usually use. This bomb was unfamiliar to me. It had sand and some sort of white cotton sacking, and this very unusual heavy paper. The Mounties worried that the Freedomites might have a new source for their explosives. They could even, I suppose, have set this one off in the middle of nowhere as a trial run, but that doesn't seem like the little I know of their methods. Poor Sara and her mother might even have been the target."

"I wonder."

Lane looked up. There was a sudden withdrawal in that "I wonder." A closing up, as if she'd heard something she could not talk about. Lane carried on. "There must have been a good deal more of that paper, as there was quite a pile of ash not accounted for by the undergrowth being burned. In fact, it had rained heavily the night before, so that really kept the surrounding forest from catching on fire, thank God. The paper was thick and sort of beige and had a coating on it, like one of those Chinese umbrellas that are made of paper. In fact, if it was some kind of resin, it might have made it quite flammable."

"And the Mounties?"

"Well, I don't know about them." Lane stopped. She hardly knew this woman. But she looked at her intelligent, practical face. She knew something that might help. She was sure of it. "They certainly didn't talk to me. I got my husband to talk to his counterpart—oh, I should have said, I'm married to Inspector Darling, at the Nelson Police. Anyway, I got him to talk to an Inspector Guilfoil to at least have the police do the work of trying to find a next of kin for the child. The Mounties, thinking of security, I suppose, wanted to keep the whole thing to themselves, but they did relent on that. The girl and her mother had been living in a cabin about 500 yards from the bomb site, and I found the papers that identified them. Good job I did, or we'd still have no idea who the girl is."

"I see." Dodi looked out toward the lake far below. She would have to talk to someone. She wasn't even sure who anymore. Frank might know. She turned back to Lane.

"You know, I took a piece of that paper from the site," Lane was saying, "before the Mounties got there, and I took it to the print shop on Baker. The printer, a man called French, told me that it was almost certainly Japanese paper. Something called *washi*. I haven't told the Mounties yet, because they've been pretty clear with me that I'm to stay away. They've rather threatened to put me in the clink."

"They'd never! The inspector's wife?" Dodi smiled. "They wouldn't hesitate with me, though. And they wouldn't listen to me, either."

"One of the men that's been arrested is the son of a friend of mine up in New Denver. Poor man's very upset and doesn't believe for a moment that his son would be involved in the bombing. He's dashed up to Prince George where they have them in prison. The son is quite surly with his father and may even have pals in the splinter group. But"—she shrugged—"a father's faith, don't you know." Lane turned to look at her companion. "But tell me about your own special interest. I'm sure the average Nelsonite is quite happy to accept the newspaper reports. Why not you?"

"It's nothing, really. It's interesting, that's all. I've been watching this Doukhobor 'problem' since they broke up the communes they lived in. It's an interesting social problem, don't you think? How immigrants are integrated. Apparently, you can only integrate if you behave exactly like us."

"Yes, I suppose you're right. I'm an immigrant myself, but I have experienced no difficulty because I do behave exactly like us." She sighed. "I've certainly seen the problem. My friend Mr. Barisoff has talked to me about it. The trouble is, he does want to be just like us. It is the path of least resistance. It is his son who is angry about their treatment."

"You speak Russian?"

Lane felt a moment of embarrassment, worried that she might come across as showing off. "I do. Just an accident of my upbringing, I'm afraid."

"They must have given you something interesting to do in the war," Dodi said.

"Not very, I'm afraid. Translating, that sort of thing. Lots of time in the typing pool. What about you?"

"Oh, we were all in uniform in Nelson. I organized a lot of fundraising efforts. It was all hands to the pumps here." She stood up, smiling. "It's been lovely meeting you, Miss . . . oh, should I say Mrs.?"

Lane smiled. "I go by Miss Winslow, except by my husband's very correct desk sergeant who insists on Mrs. Darling. I'd love to give you a lift, but I'd better go see how Johnny is getting on."

Dodi shook her head. "I enjoy the walk, thanks. It's such a lovely day."

There goes a very dark horse indeed, Lane thought, watching her walk down the steep hill to the street below. She felt a sense of relief, almost, and a little defiance. The woman was a complete stranger, to be sure, but she somehow felt talking to her had been the right thing to do. If the Mounties were going to be barking up the wrong tree, and Darling's hands were tied, she might as well put a few feelers out.

"HA!" SAID SERGEANT O'Brien, slamming the receiver home with a flourish. "We've got him!" Terrell looked up to listen as O'Brien called upstairs.

"Sir, just had a call from Reynolds, the pawnbroker in Castlegar. Someone tried to unload some watches and a couple of rings. They'd seen the alert, so he put the guy off, told him to come back later because he didn't have time to do a proper valuation."

"Hot dog!" Darling said with uncharacteristic glee. "Did he say who?"

"Guy called himself Slim. Wouldn't give a last name. Expects him back around three."

"Won't Slim have a surprise. Ames!"

CHAPTER TWENTY

August 1939

PUSHING THE BACK DOOR OPEN slowly, cursing that squeak that seemed like a thousand decibels in the quiet of the night, Ichiko Sasaki stepped into the kitchen and then removed her shoes. She was happier than she could ever remember being. And frightened. Bill had signed up. She wondered at happiness and fear seizing her at the same time. She clutched her shoes under her arm and turned to close the door when the light came on. She gasped and whirled around. Her uncle stood in the hall doorway, his hand still on the light switch, glaring at her.

"Is this what you do behind my back? Go around like an alley cat?"

Her heart pounding at the sudden flood of light, and her uncle's palpable rage, Ichiko tried for her usual teasing tone that had always worked to keep his constant fury at life at bay.

"I'm not behind your back, Uncle. I'm right in front of you. Anyway, I went to a dance with my friends. Miku was there." It was true as far as it went.

"I talked to her father. She came back three hours ago. You've been with that boy! I made them tell me, so she confessed to her parents, so don't try to lie! I told you, you aren't to see him!"

"Uncle," she said, trying to sound calm. The trouble was, he didn't know the half of it.

He advanced suddenly, his hand up. "Don't 'Uncle' me! You have disobeyed me." He swung his hand as if to strike her across the cheek.

She gasped and put her hand up to protect herself and stared at him, frightened now, angry. "My own father never hit me!" she finally managed, backing away toward the door. She imagined herself going back out into the night and stopped. Where would she go? Tears sprang into her eyes, burning, blurring her vision. She could not go anywhere. Not now.

Sasaki stood aghast, his arms now hanging down, as if he didn't know what to do with them. He had never imagined he might hit her. "Maybe he should have," he finally said, trying to fight back the shame. Shame for himself, shame for his brother, shame for her behaviour. He turned away and began trudging down the dark hallway.

"Uncle!" she called, following him. "Stop." She realized she still had her shoes under her arm and put them down. He had turned, his hand on the stair railing. She reached for the light switch and turned it on. A single bulb hung above him, casting his shadow on the stairs. He looked defeated.

She approached him. "Uncle. I married him today. Bill."

His face crumpled, rage replaced by sorrow. "No, no! You can't marry without my permission, without your father." He was shaking his head, his face registering incomprehension. "He is not Japanese. You can't marry him."

"I don't need your permission, Uncle. It's Canada. I'm nineteen. I'm an adult," she said quietly.

He turned and began his ascent, his tired steps shuffling up each stair. "Then you can pack up your things and go live with him. He is in charge of you now. I don't know how I will tell my brother. First thing, you should go. I don't want to see you again." But there was little conviction in his words.

"Uncle, I can't." She moved to the bottom of the stairs, looking up at his back. "He is signing up, and . . . and . . ." She paused. "I'm going to have a baby in three months," she finished.

January 13, 1942

ICHIKO STOOD SHIVERING at the train station, holding Sara close. She'd muffled her in a blanket so that only her face showed. It amazed her that Sara could sleep while she herself was in a state of utter turmoil. Was she doing the right thing? All she knew was that she had to get away, and she'd been offered the way out. Ever since Pearl Harbor, anti-Japanese feeling had escalated—no one even bothered to hide it anymore. She'd even been spit at on her way into Woodward's one afternoon. She knew the provincial government would make a move against the Japanese soon. Uncle Akio was already preparing, thinking how to hide things in the yard. She could not bear to think that anything might happen to her daughter.

She thought of her uncle. He loved Sara; who would not? She glanced again at her daughter's sweet face. But his anger at Ichiko had never really diminished. Her chest was compressed with anxiety. Maybe he was calling angrily for her even now. She felt a wash of hot fear that he might have guessed, that he would turn up here, enraged, and drag them back. Watching the people coming into the station, she tried to breathe, to calm herself. Someone walked past her and muttered an ugly slur at her. She could hear the train whistle behind the station, but she wouldn't be taking the train today. With a gush of relief, she saw Ron's car pull up in front of the station.

January 15, 1942

AKIO SASAKI SWEPT the contents of the safe into a leather satchel. All the money for this was borrowed, he thought bitterly—stock he would never be able to sell unless the war ended. He closed the clasp and sat back. He would have to weigh it. They had weight restrictions for what they could take. He had buried what he could and would carry the rest. He could hear the activity outside, loud, panicked shouting, people unable to believe what was happening, now that it was here. They would have to go to the exhibition grounds where the trucks were rumbling, waiting. But in the shop, it was as if silence filled the space like a balloon, pushing all the air out. The police must be there to move them. He put his hand on his heart. He was having trouble breathing. It was anger that suffocated him. Anger at the Canadians, anger at Imperial Japan, anger at his niece, anger that he'd been left in charge, and she'd gone and done that. Anger and pain at the loss of little Sara.

He had registered like they'd been told to, but he had not told them everything. Not about the safe, not that he didn't know where Ichiko and Sara were. They'd gone, disappeared two days before. He wondered if she'd run into some police, and they'd already taken her somewhere. He'd tried to track down the family of that boy, but he'd never learned anything about him. Well, Ichiko wasn't going to get out of this, because no one would. She'd end up somewhere and he'd find them. There had been only one letter from his brother, a few months back, asking about his daughter, and he hadn't answered. He hadn't known what to say. Never mind, he thought, furiously throwing his tools into a bag. When this was over, he'd track her down all right.

ONCE HOME, DODI took off her hat and cardigan and went to stand at the window in the living room. She would have to do this before Jerry got home. She went into the hall, turned on a light, and reached up for the looped rope to the retractable stairs to the attic. She'd been in the attic only once since after they married when she had stashed a small khaki bag behind a box of his mother's kitchen things. The beams of the ceiling were visible under the boards they'd set across them as walkways, and she made her way along one of these, ducking as the roof slanted sharply down. She knelt and pulled the bag from behind the wooden box, releasing a cloud of dust that caused her to turn away, coughing.

Hastily she unclasped the bag, pulled out her uniform jacket, and ran her fingers along the underside of the collar. There it was, the small opening she was looking for. She reached in with her index finger and hooked out the small piece of paper that she had wedged there almost three years before and shoved it into her pocket. She had just latched the clasp on the bag when she heard her husband's voice.

"Honey? I came home early. There's—" and she didn't hear the rest because of the startled pounding of her heart.

She shoved the bag behind the box of dishes and table-cloths, and then frantically pulled a folded tablecloth out of the box, and stood up, banging her head. "Damn!" she muttered, teetering on a beam to the centre of the room.

"What are you doing up there?" Jerry's good-natured inquiry reached her. He was standing at the bottom of the steps, looking up.

She leaned over and smiled. "It's as dusty as all get-out up here! I thought I'd get one of your mother's nice tablecloths just for a change. I'm afraid I'm going to have to give it a good wash before we use it. Here. Catch." She dropped the tablecloth down to her husband and started down the stairs. When she reached the bottom, he handed back the tablecloth and pushed the stairs back into place.

"I remember this one. Mother only used it for special occasions." He kissed her. "Do we have a special occasion coming up? It's not our anniversary."

"It's good to know you remember when our anniversary is. What are you doing home so early? Playing hooky?"

"No, Ed and them thought it would be fun if we all went and ate at the Dade tonight, get you girls out of the kitchen for a change."

"That's a wonderful idea, dear." She paused, and then took his hand. "Come and sit down for a moment."

"I was thinking of having a bath, getting into that blue suit you like so much."

"After. There's something I have to say."

Puzzled, he followed her and sat nervously next to her on the couch. "You're not thinking of going back to work, are you? I thought we'd talked about that. I mean, I wouldn't stop you. Something light, like a few hours at the Hudson's Bay or something, but you know I prefer to have you at home."

She smiled and shook her head. "No, honey, I'm not going back to work." She took both his hands in hers. "We're going to have a baby. Now, what do you think of that?" She would have to wait until the next day to make the call.

"A baby! That's swell! Oh, boy!" He put his arms around her and kissed her softly, and then pushed her away gently to look at her. "Clever girl! Oh, is it all right if we tell the others tonight? What does the doctor say?"

"It's after three months, so he said we could tell people," she said hesitantly. She was not fond of being the centre of attention.

"Three months?" He looked at her, his brow furrowed. "Why didn't you tell me before?"

"It's perfectly normal, darling. They like to wait. Anything could happen before three months, and I didn't want you to be disappointed." She put her hand on his cheek. "I'm really happy, aren't you?"

"I am over the moon, as my granny used to say. It's the best news in the world! I'm going to spoil you to death!"

"No need for that. Why, there are countries where women don't even take half a day off work in the fields. Just have the baby, strap it on, and go back to work."

"Not my gal!" Jerry declared.

"WHAT A RELIEF, sir," Ames said as he sped along the road to Castlegar. "With the guy behind bars, maybe Marge will give us a sandwich without the lecture."

"Your boyish optimism has always been your failing, Ames. You will live your life encountering disappointments at every turn. Though I must say, it is a relief. Whoever 'Slim' is, he has a lot of explaining to do."

The pawnbroker's was a cramped space stuck at the end of a row of shops on the main street, as if it had been an afterthought. It was crammed with musical instruments, radios, blankets, and a glass case full of odds and sods of jewellery, all tossed in together, with no thought of sorting real from costume, gold from silver, cufflinks from earrings.

Reynolds looked up when the two policemen came through the door and nodded. "Gentlemen, Nelson Police, I assume. He's still not here, but I've no doubt he will be. I kind of hinted it would be worth his while, looking at the value of the stuff. A malodorous sort of fellow." He pulled a wooden tray out from a cupboard below him. "Here it is. A couple of diamond rings, some gold earrings, and these four watches. Quite valuable, all new. I asked him if he had more, and he just told me it was his business to know and mine to find out, and to just hurry up and give him the money."

Darling and Ames peered at the collection. "Where'd he say he got them?" Ames asked.

"Said he found them behind a bin, if you can believe that. They were in a jeweller's bag all right. Hey, that's him coming now. You'll spook him. Go pretend to look at stuff."

Darling and Ames receded to separate corners with their backs to the pawnbroker and listened as the door opened and the bell above it tinkled. Darling looked surreptitiously at their mark, and then frowned. Oh, for God's sake, not him! Was that why he was lurking around the day they moved the body? He waited.

"So. You got my money?" The voice was the voice of a man who drank and smoked. The odour was that of a man who lived primarily out of doors.

"Well, Mr. Tom Booker, or 'Slim,' if you prefer," Darling said, coming up behind him. Ames went to block the door. He knew this man well. He was one of several indigent men who lived on the fringes of town. Most were vets of the Great War who had never found a footing when they got back. Their lives were rounded about by drinking and scrounging to survive, their families and prospects long gone. Booker had been living with a couple of other fellows in an abandoned house along the water by the ferry. They'd escorted them out after complaints from the owner and found a rooming house that would take them. None of them stayed there.

At this, the man wheeled around and saw the two police-men. "What do you want? I ain't done nothing!"

"Trying to pawn off stolen goods isn't nothing, I'm afraid, and neither is killing the person you took them from."

"Killing?" Booker reeled backward, stumbling against the counter. "I didn't kill nobody. Like I told this guy, I found the stuff. Finders keepers. I have a right to it."

"You're going to have to come with us, Mr. Booker. Reynolds, could you bag that lot for us?" Ames cuffed the protesting Booker and walked him out to the car while Darling picked up the stash.

"Thanks for calling, Reynolds. This has been a big help."

"No trouble. I sure don't want to expand my business to fencing!"

NOW, THEN, HOW about you start at the beginning," Darling said. They were in the interview room, a move he instantly regretted because even with the door open, there was not sufficient air to shift the smell of their suspect. When they'd come into the station, he'd asked Terrell to go to the charity shop and find the man some clean clothes. When they were done with him, they'd have to make sure he bathed before they put him in a cell.

"How did you come by that jewellery and those watches?"

"Found 'em, I told you." He'd become sullen, and his eyes swung from Darling to Ames with hostile anxiety. Ames had brought him a glass of water, which he took in his hand from time to time but did not drink.

"Where exactly?"

"Behind a bin. There's them big bins behind the station. I sleep under the platform on warm nights, at the back there. I woke up in the middle of the night a few days ago because some guy was walking around back there. That bag was behind the bin in the morning, so I went to see what was in it. I figured he dropped it and didn't want it anymore."

"Where exactly? How far from the bin do you sleep?"

"I don't know. Ten feet, maybe. Bin's at this end of the platform."

"Was this on June 12?"

"June what? You think I know what day it is?"

Darling conceded he well might not. "Five days ago."

"Maybe. I want to go now."

"Did you get a look at the man?"

"I was lying under the platform, and it was dark. All I saw was feet. I want to go. You can't keep me here."

"Stolen goods and a murder charge, Mr. Booker. I think you'll find we can," Darling said. He stood up and made a motion to Ames.

"You gonna leave me here?" he shouted as they went out and closed the door. "I'm hungry. How about some food?"

"Whew. Even with the door open it's hard to take," Ames said. "What are you going to do, sir?"

"I think I just need some air. I suggest we book him. Stolen property alone is enough; get O'Brien to get him cleaned up and fed and find him some legal representation. I don't think he realizes how much trouble he's in." Darling considered. "When Terrell gets back, the two of you go to the station and look around under the back end of that platform. See if there's signs of him rough sleeping, and, if by some miracle his story is true and he found the stuff tossed away behind the bin, look for any sign of anything else. I'm going to take this lot to Mrs. Harold and verify it's from her store."

Relieved that any further interrogation would continue after the bath, Ames said, "You don't like him for this, do you, sir."

"Not particularly, Amesy. He's always been a nuisance and a sad sort of case, but I can't imagine him killing someone. But that's the point. You can't imagine someone killing someone until they do. And someone hitting the end of their rope might well be enough."

Ames went outside to wait for Terrell and see if the supposed medicinal qualities of fresh air would clean off what he now believed was a permanent reek. He thought he'd better clean up before he went to see Tina. He smiled at the thought of her, feeling a slight buoyancy because they had caught their man, and he'd have time to think about her and what he should do, and then immediately fell into a funk. He'd bought the ring, and then he had been seized by, he had to admit it, fear. It all suddenly seemed too big, too permanent. Maybe Violet, his previous girlfriend who'd left in a huff because he didn't ever seem likely to "pop the question," was right. Maybe he was a coward. The difference was he really wanted to marry Tina.

Seeing Terrell coming along the street holding a paper bag was a relief. "We've got to go to the train station. Get those clothes in, and then let's go. The boss seems pretty sure that he might be our guy."

"'Pretty sure' he 'might' be?" Terrell asked when he came out. "That doesn't sound that sure. But Sergeant O'Brien looks unhappy, so whatever we have to do at the train station is better than that."

JOHNNY BALES TALKED most of the way home. "I tried to tell her," he was saying, as they reached the bottom of the hill on top of which his father's filling station and store sat, their house just behind it. "I said she ought to come to our school, because she was really close to the school, and Miss Keeling is so nice, don't you think so, Miss Winslow?" He didn't wait for her answer. "But Sara always said her mother taught her at home and they weren't allowed to go anywhere else. She always made me promise never to tell anyone. It was hard sometimes, but then I got used to the idea that I had a secret no one else did, and that made it easier."

"You did a wonderful job of keeping their secret," Lane said.

"I never saw anybody else up there," Johnny said, shaking his head. "I guess she didn't want anyone to know."

"You said there was a sort of path through the forest and up the hill?"

"Uh-huh." He nodded. "It must be how her mom came down to get food and stuff."

"Did her mom go down to get food? Did you ever see her?" Lane was pulling the car to the front of the store. She stopped it just short of where Blackie was lumbering to his feet and turned to look at Johnny.

"Yeah. I mean, one time. She told us to behave and then she went down the path. She was gone for a while, and then she came back with a box with some grocery bags in it. She seemed happy. She made peanut butter and jam sandwiches for us."

267

"And you never told anyone they were there?"

"Uh-uh!" he declared fervently. "I promised."

"Your parents never asked where you were?"

"Nah. In the summer we go everywhere. As long as I came home in time for dinner. I wanted to bring a friend there, you know, Randy or Samuel, but Sara's mom made me promise never to bring anyone."

They got out of the car and Johnny ran inside. Lane followed more slowly, trying to put together the whole extraordinary business.

Bales came outside holding out a Popsicle. "Johnny made a beeline for the freezer and has already disappeared down the hill to his pals. How did it go?"

"Thanks. I love the red ones," Lane said, leaning against the car. "It went extraordinarily well. As soon as Johnny talked to her, she began to talk herself. He was so kind." She shook her head. "I don't really know who will tell her about her mother or when, or what she will be able to tell us about that day, or indeed, about her life. Perhaps now that she is talking, she will finally be able to ask. But she certainly remembered Johnny was her friend and seemed genuinely happy to see him."

Bales shook his head. "It's awful. I can't believe that wily little monster never told a soul about the whole thing. He normally never stops talking. I'm gonna have to give him more credit."

"He's a lovely boy," Lane said, smiling. "And there really is something magical about the children on their own. I hope I can take him again to see her?"

"You say nice things like that about my boy, you can take

him anywhere! Did he tell you anything else?"

"Well, funnily, he told me that one time he was there, the girl's mother told them to behave and disappeared into the forest, down the path he'd followed to their cabin, and came back with a box of groceries. Apparently, someone was leaving them on the path somewhere for her to pick up."

"Now, then. You know that guy I told you about, the one who got killed? When he came in for groceries, he always asked me to put them in a box. I had some cardboard boxes from wholesale deliveries of this and that, so that's what I'd do. You think it coulda been him?"

"It could certainly have been him." Lane looked at her watch. "I'd better dash. Thanks for the Popsicle and the loan of your son!"

"I sure hope you find out what's going on," Bales said. "I'm putting money on you finding out before your husband!" He laughed and waved as she started up her engine.

At home, at sixes and sevens, Lane contemplated some domestic chores. She'd left a pair of trousers hanging over the back of the chair in the bedroom. That would be a start. She picked them up and, seeing they'd suffered no ill effects from her last hike up to the cabin, was about to fold them to put them back in the drawer, when she heard the slight crinkling of paper in one of the pockets. She reached in and took out the note she'd found in the woman's jacket at the cabin. She slapped her forehead and thought how very wrong Bales was. She'd never discover anything if she was capable of this sort of thing! She hurried into the hall and put a call through to the police station.

CHAPTER TWENTY-ONE

HER HEART FLUTTERING, DODI WATCHED her husband down the steps, finally. He'd been in a terribly jovial mood and wanted to draw breakfast out as long as possible just to "look at his beautiful girl." She waited impatiently another fifteen minutes, trying to still her anxiety while she was clearing the table, carrying the plates through to the kitchen. She'd hardly been able to eat anything but had forced herself in order not to raise fond concerns, which would simply have delayed her husband's leaving.

Finally, she went to sit on the sofa beside the telephone. She took a few deep breaths and dialled the number on the paper she had hidden in her apron pocket. She closed her eyes as she listened to the ringing, taking a few more deep breaths.

"Yes?" A curt male voice.

"Frank, it's Dodi."

"HE'S DEFINITELY BEEN sleeping there," Ames said to Darling. Terrell had stayed down at the train station to tidy up after a shouting match had broken out between a couple of drivers evidently contesting a parking space in front of the train station, so Ames and Darling were in Darling's office before the growing file of Harold's murder. "Old blanket, garbage, whisky bottles, cigarette butts. And I did look around the bin—it's right against the edge of the platform, so I had to jiggle it away to see the back, and I found this." He pulled a gold chain out of his pocket like a conjurer and held it up triumphantly.

"Damn," said Darling, taking it. "The rest of that stuff was from the jewellery store, according to Mrs. Harold. But the big stuff is still missing, the expensive watches and rings. You didn't find anything else?"

"Nope."

"So, he's taken this much to try to sell. What's he done with the rest of it? Wouldn't you try to sell your best stuff first? We're going to have to ask him about the rest of it."

"I'm still not sure he's our man," Ames said, a little sadly. "I mean, you know him better than I do, but he doesn't seem strong enough to drive anything into someone's skull."

"Well, if that's the case, and maybe we can verify it when we question him later, we're going to have to go back to our other thread. What about all the secrets Harold was keeping from people? Are they the sort of secrets that would get him killed? Perhaps the robbery and the murder are completely separate. Harold's killed, the door's left open, and Booker takes advantage of it to scoop up the loot."

THEY'D HAD A call first thing from April, who'd asked to be put through to Darling himself. She'd finally had a response from the department of statistics: Indeed, William Harold, of Nelson, British Columbia, had been married to Ichiko Sasaki on September 4, 1939. They had a special file of records for Japanese people married to non-Japanese citizens because people in mixed marriages had been allowed to stay on at the coast, but the Harolds had never applied to stay.

"That poor little girl is well and truly an orphan," Darling said, shaking his head. "But I think we have our William. His place of birth is listed as Nelson, BC. He is almost certainly Ronald Harold's brother."

"The question is, did Ron know about his brother Bill being married? According to his wife, Bill would never have kept a secret like that from his brother because they were so close. But"—he shrugged—"I guess he could have."

Darling shook his head. "I don't see it. I think she's right. I'm guessing he wouldn't have kept it a secret from his brother. He's signed up and is leaving behind his pregnant wife. In a pinch he might have hoped her uncle would look after her, but, of course, he wasn't to know he'd die, or what would happen to Japanese Canadians in '42. My guess is that Ron was probably keeping an eye on Bill's wife, especially as the political situation became difficult. And now we know from what Bales told my wife that, indeed, Ron Harold was most likely the man supplying her with groceries. And she—my wife, I mean—called earlier to tell me about a note she found at the cabin." Darling recited the contents of the note.

"I think we can surmise that Ron Harold not only knew about his brother's wife and child, but perhaps had even arranged for her living situation."

Ames smiled for a moment. "She's done it again, sir."

"Yes, thank you, Ames. Your regard for my wife is legendary. Now, why don't you run along and figure out how Mrs. Sasaki Harold, if you will, ended up in a cabin in the mountains being supplied by Mr. Harold the elder with groceries, and how he wound up dead."

"Well, I actually had an idea, sir. Mr. Humphries, the locksmith, was Harold's best buddy. I wonder if he's got stuff he's been keeping from us. Wouldn't Harold have told Humphries at least about his brother, if not the woman on the hill?"

Darling nodded. "It's worth a try. But if he was protecting them, he might not tell anyone." The desk phone rang, making them both jump. Darling picked up the receiver. "Darling." He listened for a moment and waved the curious Ames off with an impatient hand. "Yes, all right. Send her up." He waved at Ames. "Find out how O'Brien is getting on with Booker."

Ames disappeared and Darling went to stand in the hall. He could hear someone slowly making her way up the stairs and wondered if he should have gone down. From the sound of the footsteps, she sounded old.

She *was* old. Or at least not very mobile. Darling leaped forward. "I'm sorry, Mrs. Fellowes, I should have come down," he said, taking her arm and leading her into his office.

"Oh, that's quite all right, Inspector." Mrs. Fellowes,

a plump woman clearly in her seventies, wearing a straw hat and a very ancient cardigan, dropped into the chair she was offered and yarded her handbag onto her lap. "The nice sergeant offered that, but if I gave up on stairs at my age, where would I be?"

Not sure where, Darling said, "Very good advice. How can I help?"

"Well, I just only now saw, you see, and I came right away, though I'm sure it is much too late. I was surprised to learn that it was several days ago. I don't know where the time goes, but of course I was driving by at the time. Oh, I don't mean I was driving, my grandson was driving, but he had to be back at work, and he didn't see, but I was quite astonished. And then I saw the paper, so I've had him drive me in. I live out past Ymir, you see."

Darling, who'd been wondering how to extract a coherent narrative, nodded encouragingly. "Which day was it, Mrs. Fellowes, that you saw something?"

"Why, the day of the murder, I suppose it was. Well, the evening, really. I just read the papers about it today. I mean, I only expected it to be about the jewellery store, because I saw that, you see, so I was very surprised about the murder. Poor Mr. Harold! Poor Mrs. Harold. I've met them often at church. Such a nice couple. Such a very kind man! Always helping everyone up and down stairs."

Relieved at the rope she'd thrown in the ocean of chatter, he lunged at it. "You saw something about the jewellery store robbery?"

"Yes, I did. I mean, I didn't see the robbery as such, you know, but we drove into the alley because Rog wanted to drop something off at the repair shop. It was after hours, but they said they'd stay open for us. Not the alley behind the jeweller, the other one, and while I waited, I saw a man in a hat and trench coat coming out of the door of a store that I'm sure was Mr. Harold's shop. He was in a hurry and was carrying a bag. He came in my direction and turned down the street toward the train station. My grandson came out just about then, and I asked if he'd seen what I just saw, but he said he hadn't and that he wanted to get back. Of course, I knew the police would be right onto it if the man had been up to anything, so I didn't give it another thought. Then today I was talking to my neighbour, and she asked hadn't I seen the newspapers? I don't read them as a rule. I'm much too busy. But my grandson keeps them for the fire, but it's been so warm, you know, that they were still there."

"What time was this again?"

"Well, I think it was right around eight, because it was still sort of light out. But then it was sort of dark because it was raining."

"Did you get a look at his face?" This might be nothing. On the other hand, it was near the time when Harold had met his end.

"Well, yes, you see, that's the point. I did. He was an Oriental man, you know, Chinese or Japanese. Maybe Japanese, I suppose. Those poor people have been shunted around so. Even so, I don't think that's any reason to rob poor Mr. Harold. I thought at the time how tall he was."

"A BREAKTHROUGH LEADING where exactly?" Darling grumbled to his underlings. "Tall Asian man coming out of what she thought might be the jeweller's back door. But she was in the next alley, and it could have been any business along there. He might have had a perfectly legitimate reason for being there. Though, eight at night is after most businesses are closed."

"Hmm," said Ames, not very helpfully. "How tall?"

Darling shifted in his seat and was about to deliver a scathing reply.

Seeing the expression on his face, Ames said, "We can ask all the other shopkeepers on that street if they had a tall Asian visitor."

"Well, aren't you a shining light today? Go ask, then, and then I want the two of you to go back to the locksmith, find out if he's keeping anything back."

"The combination of events is what I find interesting: a murder, a robbery, and a desperate search. What is the motivation?" Terrell mused.

"The desire to take possession of some expensive jewellery?" Darling asked, with a slight air of sarcasm.

"Well, yes, sir, but is that the main thing, or is the search the main thing? And if it is, was the tall man involved? Did he use stealing jewellery as a cover for what was a desperate search? We already have Mr. Harold involved with the Japanese family of his brother, so I'm guessing the tall man is himself Japanese."

Darling stood up. "What if we stop speculating and start investigating?" He pushed the papers into his file folder.

"But thanks for the ideas," he added, as Ames and Terrell left his office. "Oh, Constable."

"Sir?" Terrell asked, stepping back in.

"What was the fuss at the train station?"

"A delivery truck backed into an expensive roadster. Broadside. It didn't come to blows, and the insurance people will have a good time sorting it out. I've taken everyone's name and issued a ticket to the roadster for parking in a no-parking zone. He'll be filing a complaint to you."

"I look forward to it. Thanks, Constable."

"I'M VERY CURIOUS to see if she'll speak when Johnny is not there. I'm sure children trust other children in ways they wouldn't trust adults," Lane said to Harris. They were on their way into town to visit Sara. Harris had hurried his morning's work in order to make the trip.

He was about to contradict her when he suddenly had a memory of his childhood self, sitting in the tree with Betty, talking about their mothers. He had trusted no one so much as her, and he had never really trusted again in his whole life.

Lane glanced at him. Perhaps he was not in the mood to talk. She was not surprised. He often wasn't, in her experience. In the mood to scold, usually, or complain about the incompetence of others. But what she saw surprised her. He was sitting looking down at his hands, far away. She left him there and reminded herself not to fill the air with her own chatter to make up for his silence.

HE SHIVERED AT the warmth of her hands as she took his. They had sat cross-legged facing each other under a blanket. As if they could hide from what was coming.

"Promise me," she said, "you'll never forget me. And when I need you, you'll come for me like King Arthur."

Robin nodded, clutched her hands tighter, and willed himself not to cry. Fear and sorrow gripped him. He could not have given name to the feelings, except to recognize he was afraid of whoever would come.

"Promise!"

"I promise," he finally managed, terrified that when the moment came, he would not be able to.

He was the first to hear the rumble outside, someone saying "Whoa, there."

"I'm not going to cry," she said, suddenly the adult.

"Me either." It cost him everything to stop.

"Get a move on!" Her father whipped the blanket off their heads. "He's waitin' for ya. No time for nonsense."

Father and daughter watched as he climbed up next to the driver. The horse snapped his head up and snorted, making the bridle clank. The morning was cold still, and the steam from the horse's breath faded into the mist that lay across the fields.

Betty's father suddenly approached the cart and put his hand on the rail. "You'll be all right, lad." His voice was gruff, almost apologetic.

Robin knew he was supposed to say something, but he could not imagine what. He finally nodded, and then felt his head jerk back as the cart lurched suddenly, the driver snapping the reins to get the horse moving. He wanted to look back, but he'd promised he wouldn't cry.

HAD SHE CALLED out after him? "Don't forget me?" Or was that something he invented? He lifted his head to look out at the passing forest, so familiar after all these years. But he had forgotten her, hadn't he? Except once when he was at war. Now his memory was like a bruise that still hurt when he touched it.

"You're right about that," he said suddenly.

Lane looked at him in surprise.

"They do trust each other, more than anyone. When you grow up, you never trust like that again. I don't think people understand that."

"You had a friend like that?" Lane asked.

"I told you about her."

"Yes, of course. I remember. Betty."

"It isn't right that little kiddies should be separated from people they love."

"No," Lane said. "It will be hard when we have to tell her."

"I meant from their friends, but yes. Her mother too. Maybe now she can talk, she'll ask for her. Then you're gonna have to say something."

Robin didn't look at Dr. Edison, who was explaining about Sara's condition. He was watching Sara's patient face, in her bed in the little ward, as she was having the dressing changed on her arm.

"We've had a busy day today. We put her in a wheelchair

and wheeled her up and down the hall. All the nurses and doctors smiled and waved. She's such an endearing little thing. I am hopeful that in a few days we can begin to try her on crutches, but that arm needs to heal a bit more first. It was a lot of excitement, so she might be a bit more tired than usual."

Sara looked up and saw Robin and after a moment smiled. He lifted his hand in a little wave and turned back to the two women.

"When's she gonna be able to get out?" He'd barely heard what Edison had been saying.

"If she were a child that had a responsible home to go to, then it wouldn't be long, and she could recover at home. She has been doing better than we hoped," she said. "But under the circumstances we can take our time. If we can begin her on crutches in a few days, maybe another week after that for practice. Her leg was badly broken in two places, and we frankly don't know how much her ability to walk will be affected."

Robin grunted and turned back to look through the door to the ward. The nurse was moving away, the soiled bandages in an enamel dish. He went in and pulled up a chair.

"Hello, Sara. Shall we read *Winnie-the-Pooh*?"

Sara pulled her bear out from under her pillow and sat him on her lap. She made him nod.

Robin nodded several times and then he reached into the cupboard in the bedside table and pulled out the book. "You know, I never did learn your name." He said this to the bear.

"Mr. Harris," Sara said.

"So he's a mister, is he?" He felt an unaccustomed warmth in his chest.

Sara nodded.

"That's very formal. I like that. He's a dignified bear. Would he like to hear about Winnie-the-Pooh and the rainy day?"

The bear nodded.

Lane watched from the doorway. She didn't want to interrupt what was happening. "I feel like I've picked up the wrong Robin Harris," she said quietly to Dr. Edison.

"Oh, I know just what you mean. One of my colleagues was astounded to see him the other day. He said he'd been brought in with a bad gash from an accident with an axe in '43 sometime and he was absolutely the worst patient they'd ever had. They couldn't wait to get him patched up and on his way."

"She's certainly got him wrapped around her finger. In the nicest possible way. Has she spoken at all since young Johnny Bales was here?"

"Only a very little, according to Sister Evans. She did say 'ouch' when she was carried to her bath yesterday."

"She still hasn't asked about her mother?"

Dr. Edison shook her head. "She may be in a kind of altered state, completely separated from her old life by the shock. Children tend to completely inhabit the present moment, if you will, so all her life revolves around what is happening to her here. I'm not saying she's forgotten her mother. More that she imagines her mother will be there when this is over, perhaps."

"I wonder," Lane said. "Perhaps she does think about her mother but knows something is wrong and is afraid to ask."

Dr. Edison nodded. "You could be right. I think it will be difficult, her transition. She'll have so much to cope with. I do hope she'll have someone to help her." She looked directly at Lane. "It would take someone like you." She turned back to the scene at the bedside. "Or him."

CHAPTER TWENTY-TWO

THE SENSE OF BEING FOLLOWED was so powerful that Lane looked into the rear-view mirror. Instead of the silence that had been his refuge on the way into town, Harris was now coming close to chattering.

"Doesn't that beat all get-out?" he was saying.

"It's lovely," Lane said. He'd been talking about Sara's bear being called Mr. Harris. Lane was barely attending now. On a straight, rising stretch of road that passed the Harrop ferry turnoff she glanced again at the mirror. It was a blue sedan, keeping a discreet and very controlled distance behind them.

It was nonsense, of course. She really had to shake off all this leftover wartime paranoia. It was high time. It had been almost three years since she'd been demobbed. She tried to bring her mind back to Harris and Sara.

"I don't know why she can't come and stay with us in King's Cove," he was saying. "It'd be a nice change from those Bertolli barbarians."

She'd wondered the same thing herself—not about the Bertolli boys, of course, whose wild energy she rather enjoyed.

"I know the police are looking for relations, so you mustn't get your hopes up."

"I don't have my 'hopes up,'" he said crossly as if he'd been found out in a weakness. "But she has to go somewhere. I know they wouldn't stick her with me, though why not, I don't know. Do they think I can't look after a child? But they would stick her with you."

She smiled, then looked up and caught sight of the blue sedan, still keeping pace on the long uphill to the Bales store. "You know a lot more about children than I do, Robin. You've completely won her heart. She doesn't even want me to read anymore."

He humphed modestly. "She says my voice is more like Mr. Harris's."

"There you are, you see. Anyway. I think we should just wait and see how it all goes."

She pulled off the road into the dirt patch in front of his house. Harris got out and nodded at her.

"Bye, Robin. Thank you."

She eased back into the road and took the turn up to King's Cove proper. The blue sedan must have stopped because she could no longer see it on the road. She waited a few moments to see if it appeared and passed her, but it didn't, and then drove pensively up the road and into her own yard.

Standing by her car with her arms crossed, she waited, listening to the sedan climb the hill and then crunch down on her turnoff and pull up in front of her gate.

"Who are you, again?" she asked the expensively suited man who stepped out of the car.

"Frank Smith. How do you do?" He lifted his hat briefly, then shoved his hand back into his jacket pocket. "It's nice out here."

"Thank you. You've been trailing me since town. What do you want?" She kept her voice light, skeptical though she was about the "Smith."

"I'm with the Canadian government," he began.

"That covers a multitude of sins. Are you coming in or are we talking out here?"

"Out here is fine for the moment. I'm here because I understand you recently came across the remnants of a bomb. I'd like you to tell me about it."

"That's a surprise," Lane said. "No one else seems interested in what I have to say. Do you have any sort of identification? I should mention the Mounties have ordered me to stay strictly away from the site and have nothing to do with it. You really should talk to a Sergeant Fryer at the Nelson detachment. He might be able to help you."

Smith reached into the inner pocket of his jacket and pulled out a card. "Canadian intelligence services. I outrank Sergeant Fryer by a large margin."

Lane laughed. "Your name really is Smith?"

He made no answer. "I'd like you to tell me exactly what you saw, and I want you to take me to the site."

She sighed. "You'd better come in, then. I'll have to change my shoes."

"THERE IT IS." She waved her hand in the direction of the blackened circle where the bomb had gone off. He had taken copious notes while they had sat in the kitchen, and she had led him by car up the hill to the path, which, though well worn by now, was still long and steep. She'd been able to hear Smith wheezing behind her on the way up. His jacket was off and in his hand by the time they arrived.

"A woman was killed. I found her body on the far side, and a little girl was lying over there, badly injured. She's in the hospital now."

"Yes. I know about that." He started to circle the site, and said, almost to himself, "We've been afraid of something like this."

Lane frowned and began to follow him. "You've been 'afraid of something like this'? You know what this is, don't you? Is it anything to do with the Sons of Freedom? Because I never thought so."

He ignored her outburst. "Show me where you found the sand."

She walked around him and farther along the curve of the site. "Here. You can still see it. There were bits of white cotton, from the bag, I guess, that held the sand, and of course the paper I told you about. Except for that paper, I'd ask if it was some bizarre secret experiment by the Canadian intelligence people that imperils citizens. But I suppose you could use Japanese paper." She thought for a moment. "Was it meant to be a parachute of some kind? Or a balloon? The ashes show a large amount of paper burned." She watched him picking up a scrap of the sacking. "Oh.

Of course! It was a balloon. Those were sandbags used as ballast." She looked up, as if another such might sail into sight. "What an extraordinary way to deliver explosives. Is it Japanese?"

Standing up from where he'd been stooping, running his fingers through a little pile of the sand, he turned to her, not responding to her question. "I've had you looked into, you know."

"And that is supposed to alarm me? Who gave you my name in the first place? Certainly not Fryer."

"No. Not Fryer. As you can imagine, Miss Winslow, I cannot say."

She had not told him her name. "It's evident to me that you know perfectly well what this is and have been keeping back the information from the public—and as a result, a woman is dead and a child maimed and orphaned. And some probably blameless men are sitting in jail about to go on trial for sedition and murder."

He smiled briefly and looked up at her from where he'd been focusing on the ashes. "I wouldn't be so sure about those men being blameless." He took out a very small camera from his jacket pocket and snapped a couple of pictures, then held it up. "War was useful for some things. You could hide this thing in the palm of your hand. But you're right. Perhaps they are blameless for this, at least."

"Are you going to do something about that?"

He gave a tight-lipped nod. "In good time. There is still a possibility that they were involved. You have an impressive knowledge of explosives. We could use a girl like you." He had pocketed his camera and was dusting his hands on the back of his trousers.

Lane was about to respond that no one who called her a "girl" was likely to procure her services for anything when it came to her. "Dodi Cartwright. She's one of yours. Or was."

He turned and had started back down the hill toward the cars. "I'm sorry about the little girl. I understand you have been visiting her. How is she doing?"

"Not very well. She has no relations and doesn't yet know that her mother is dead. She is in shock and may never walk normally again. Since this is likely your fault, maybe you could turn the considerable resources of your agency into finding her people."

He stopped and turned back to where she was following him down the hill. "I understand your bitterness, Miss Winslow, and I have set something in motion. We are not completely heartless."

"Set what in motion? What does that mean?"

He remained silent until they'd arrived at where the cars were parked at the edge of the orchard.

"Our considerable resources, Miss Winslow. Here is my card. I meant what I said. We could use someone like you." He opened his car door. "Lovely orchard. Too bad about the DDT. I can smell it. Another product of the war. It was very useful for malaria and so on, but now farmers have it to hand. There's some work that suggests it's not just dangerous to pests. I saw that little stand of apple trees by your house. If you take my advice, you'll not use the stuff."

SHE'D WATCHED HIM drive off with mixed feelings. He was arrogant in a smooth "I have all the cards" sort of way, but on the other hand she felt some relief that someone that high up had become involved. She had no faith in the abilities of Sergeant Fryer to discover anything of use. Perhaps that wasn't fair. If the intelligence people had created a blackout about whatever this was, he was operating in the blackout as much as she was. Perhaps he was entitled to assume the Freedomites had found some new source for their bombs.

Rather than drive home, she turned back up the hill and made the long hike toward the cabin. These hikes were certainly helping her stamina, she thought with satisfaction. Any breeze off the lake had stilled, and though it was nearly four in the afternoon, the day felt at its hottest. Not sure what she expected to find but feeling drawn to it, she stopped above the little homestead and sat down. From this vantage she could see the cabin, the garden, the stretch of meadow, and the path that she now knew Ichiko Sasaki had gone down to pick up groceries, and Johnny Bales had come up to play with Sara. They were laid out below her like a cipher she could not understand.

"What were you doing here?" she asked aloud. She could not shake her thoughts of that last day. She imagined Ichiko pulling clothes out of the laundry tub, wringing them out with strong hands, hanging them on the line, Sara perhaps playing, running across the meadow with Johnny, laughing, unaware of whatever dire circumstances had brought them there. No. Johnny would not have been there that day. It had been a school day. Perhaps Sara had been sitting outside reading or doing some writing exercises in her scribbler. Her mother had finished with the clothes and said, "We've both worked hard. Let's go for a walk. We can bring some cookies."

Lane closed her eyes, felt them coming up the hill, then passing her, Sara running ahead, her mother telling her to be careful. In that moment, had Ichiko Sasaki been able to forget her constant worries about their life in this remote cabin?

"Why were you here?" she asked again of the ghostly figures receding up the hill behind her to their final fate. Lane's eyes flew open, and she looked quickly around, but the afternoon continued still and hot, no sound, not even of birds that had settled in trees out of the heat of the afternoon. She knew then that the voice of the woman had come from deep inside her, and she knew she'd been right.

"Hiding. Waiting till it's safe."

DARLING HAD TELEPHONED Mrs. Dee and learned that Mrs. Harold was there and would be willing to talk to him. Did he want to come up or just talk on the telephone?

"I'll come up there, if I may. I have one or two errands to run." Nosing the car out of the parking place, he drove along Baker and saw the jewellery store, still boarded up. Would she ever be able to go back there? She couldn't even stand to be in her own home, let alone the place where her husband's body was actually found. It was an agonizing stage for the surviving victims of crime, this limbo while the police tried to find the killer, the relatives unable to find what solace there was to be had from a funeral and a final goodbye. The inability to look forward and imagine a future, this endless burden of waiting where normalcy was suspended.

THE CLOSED-UP SHOP was a kind of suspension as well, evidence to the whole town that the police had not found the killer. Shop girls were being walked home by their brothers and boyfriends and fathers. Wives who'd been happy working alone in the back of the tobacconist and pharmacy closed and locked the back door even on the warmest day.

Usually, he knew, a murder was committed by people known to the victim, for reasons that lay in the history of the relationship between killer and victim, but until that reason was uncovered, townsfolk could not know if the undiscovered killer was a menace to all. Then there was Mrs. Fellowes's bumbling assertion that the man who broke into the shop was Asian; if that got about, it would only increase people's anxieties and anti-Asian feeling. But he felt certain that Ron Harold had Japanese connections. His brother had married a Japanese girl, and he had a Japanese niece. Was this mysterious Asian man some connection to them?

Mrs. Dee opened the door dressed for outdoors, hat on, handbag on wrist. "Come on in, Inspector. I'm just off. I have to go to the dentist, worse luck. There's fresh tea." She leaned forward conspiratorially and whispered, "See if you can get her to have something. She's becoming an absolute wraith. She's no appetite at all."

Wondering how he could possibly persuade someone to eat while asking difficult questions about her dead husband,

Darling removed his hat and walked to the dining table where Mrs. Harold sat. She made a move to get up, but he put up his hand.

"No, no. Don't get up. May I sit?"

She nodded, her expression opaque. "Have you found something out?"

Only that your husband's activities appear increasingly mysterious, he wanted to say. "Any investigation consists of the slow gathering of information. It's putting it all together to make sense of it that is the trick." He shifted in his chair, considering his next words. "Can you tell me about any association your husband had with Japanese people?"

If he'd wanted to stun, he achieved his aim. Mrs. Harold looked up at him, dumbfounded. "Japanese people? No. Never. Where would you get an idea like that?" She looked away, shaking her head. "Japanese people. Ridiculous."

"We have discovered that his brother, William Harold—"

She interrupted. "His little brother, yes. Died in '39."

"William James Harold, of Nelson, BC, was, in fact, married to a Japanese woman in Vancouver just prior to shipping out. She was called Ichiko Sasaki. Were you aware of this?"

She looked directly at him, almost defiantly. "No, he most decidedly was not. William never married. It's absurd. He never would have married without his brother being there. They were as close as any two brothers could be. Ron was like a father to him. Married to a Japanese? The notion is monstrous! We were at war with them!"

"Not in 1939. I'm afraid there is no mistake. The bureau of statistics has the paperwork."

She shook her head violently. "No. It's just not possible. He would never have married without telling Ron. Never! There is a mistake. It is someone else. I'm sure the name William Harold is as common as ditch water."

Thinking with sympathy about the chasm that opens up when a wife learns her husband has utterly deceived her in something monumental in his life, Darling wondered how she would take the next revelation. "We think that your husband did know and took measures to protect his brother's wife and child during the war."

TERRELL AND AMES were once again at the locksmith's shop. A man in his twenties, built like a linebacker, was at the counter reaching into his pocket for some coins, which he slapped down noisily.

"Thanks. She better not lose this one!" He took the brass key, flipped it like a silver dollar and pocketed it. Nodding in a friendly fashion at the policemen, he went out the door, slamming it.

Humphries looked at them and took a moment to say, "Gentlemen. How's the investigation going?"

"Still working on it. Do you mind if we ask you a couple of questions about Mr. Harold?"

"Ask away! I have to go out on a call in a few minutes." He leaned back, crossing his arms, nodding encouragement.

"This won't take long," Ames said, folding his arms as if in imitation. He waited, as he was thinking about how to word the questions.

"Did Ron Harold ever tell you much about his younger brother?"

Humphries looked genuinely surprised and uncrossed his arms, slipping his hands into his pockets. "Certainly. He never shut up about him. He loved the kid. It was a blow to him when he died. I know he felt guilty. I always told him, 'You didn't make him sign up; he wanted to. He's a hero.' But he wouldn't listen. He said it felt wrong that he should have survived the Great War, but Bill should die right out of the gate. He used to talk about leaving Bill the shop. I don't know what Bertha thought of that idea. Bit of a dreamer, Ron. From what I knew, Bill was planning to study engineering or something, so he'd never have come back here."

"So would he have told you if Bill had married, for example?"

Humphries chewed his upper lip and looked down at the counter. "He sure would have. I always thought it was sad that the poor kid never got the chance. But what's that got to do with anything?"

"Just exploring every possibility."

Humphries redoubled the head shaking. "No. Heck, if the kid got a haircut, I'd hear about it. He sure as hell would have said if he'd got married."

"Did you know of any association Mr. Harold might have had with Japanese people?" Ames asked.

Humphries looked out the window, his brows pulled together in thought, and after a moment shook his head. "I know every single person he would have associated with, believe you me. You wouldn't be able to hold your head up at the Legion if you 'associated' with them. Anyway, Bertha hated them. Never shut up about it after Pearl Harbor."

Ames nodded and said, "Thank you, Mr. Humphries. I think that will be all for now."

"He hesitated several times, sir. I wonder if he was telling the truth?" Terrell said as they made their way back up the hill to the station.

Ames looked surprised. "You think he did know?"

"I wonder, sir. Maybe Harold never told him, because he really wanted to keep it secret and protect the family. But he could have kept secrets from his wife he'd be prepared to tell his friend."

"But he wants us to think he doesn't know. That's possible. I think what it depends on is how important the secret is. If there was strong anti-Japanese feeling, and the mother and her daughter were supposed to be somewhere else by law, he might keep it secret from everyone."

"War's over, though. Why still?" Terrell said.

CHAPTER TWENTY-THREE

"WE KNOW THAT HAROLD'S BROTHER** Bill married Miss Sasaki before shipping out and, given the comparisons of the dates of the wedding with the birth of their child, Sara, she was already pregnant. Bill dies that same year, and then what? According to the information we got from April McAvity, she lived with a bad-tempered uncle above a jewellery shop in Little Tokyo in Vancouver. We can also surmise that the uncle did not approve of the liaison because early on she was hiding her relationship from him. So, from 1939, when Sara is born, to 1942, when war is declared against Japan, is she living with her uncle? Where do they all go during the internment? We know nothing until now, when we find Miss Sasaki, or Mrs. Harold, living in an isolated cabin with her daughter. She is killed a short time ago by a bomb of some sort." Darling stopped. They were clustered once again around Darling's desk.

"It's clear Mr. Harold was in some way looking after or protecting his brother's wife and child, apparently keeping them hidden. Right from the beginning of the order, or did he collect her from an internment camp? And why still, after the war?"

"If he kept her hidden and she didn't go to any camp, I can see he might worry that she'd face consequences, even now after the war, if the authorities found out," Terrell suggested. "The sad irony is that it appears Mrs. Harold might have been able to stay put in Vancouver because some Japanese in mixed marriages were able to stay on."

Darling nodded. "That's a possibility. The trouble is, both William Harold and his wife have taken the whole business to their graves. I think the protection, or hiding, theory is as good as any, but I don't think we'll ever know the full truth of the matter."

"And," Ames said, "since neither Ronald's wife nor his best friend knew anything about any of it, he kept a bunch of pretty big secrets. And I bet that's what killed him. That Japanese man who broke into his store could be our murderer. Maybe he learned that Harold had taken her and hidden her here, and he wanted to take revenge."

"That is, if Booker, who as far as we know also broke into the store, isn't the killer. And if so, the killing is much more likely to have been just the consequence of the break-in, as opposed to some revenge motive. By the way, Booker is still adamant he hasn't got any other jewellery. Mrs. Fellowes is pretty doddery, and we don't know if the man she saw is Japanese, or that he broke into the store. If she's wrong, and it gets about town that the killer might be Japanese, it's going to get very ugly."

"If she's right, it'll get ugly," Ames said.

"He's the second suspect we have at the moment," Terrell said. "Or rather, don't have."

"Good point, Constable. All hands on deck finding the tall Asian man. Because we don't actually know if he's Japanese or not, though it is suggested by Harold's brother's marriage. Let's start with any Chinese or Japanese businesses."

"I don't know of any Japanese businesses, but we can check with the Chinese ones," Ames said.

"Mrs. Harold was so vehemently denying the possibility of Harold's brother's marriage that, though I'd gone there with plans to tell her she had a little niece by marriage who would need a home, I just couldn't, even though she might be the only relation we'll find. I have a feeling she would absolutely refuse to have anything to do with her," Darling said.

Booker had by this time been cleaned up and had enjoyed a sandwich and cup of coffee from the café. He was sitting in the interview room where O'Brien had deposited him, jiggling his right leg up and down convulsively. "Finally!" he said when Ames and Darling came in. "Thought I was gonna just be left here all day and all night."

"Mr. Booker—" began Darling.

Booker threw himself back in his chair with exaggerated impatience. "Here we go! I told you guys, I haven't done nothin' and I don't know nothing about a dead jeweller. I never hurt anyone in my life . . ." Here he stopped. "If you don't count the Somme, I guess. I told you. I was sleeping under the platform, and someone dropped that bag and I took it. The way I see it, it's mine now."

"Unfortunately," Darling said, "the way Mrs. Harold sees it, it's hers. Those pieces were all stolen from her shop. And we're still looking for some more, so we'd love you to tell us where it is. Tell me, have you ever gone in for prospecting?"

"What's that got to do with the price of tea in China? No, I did not. When I got out of the army, I went out logging and got a little too familiar with the drink. Wife and I weren't getting along, and she packed up and left. Come on, Inspector, you know me. You ever had me in here for hurtin' someone? I've swiped a few things along the way, I don't mind saying. Times has been hard. But I never hurt no one." He settled back with his arms across his chest as if it was all he was prepared to say on the subject.

Up in his office Darling looked out the window. Ames was waiting to hear the outcomes of Darling's ruminations.

"Do you have to breathe down the back of my neck, Sergeant?" Darling said impatiently.

Ames took it for the rhetorical question it was. "Sir."

"What do you think?"

Ames opened his mouth to speak.

"Exactly, Sergeant. I don't think he did it either. We better keep him in, however. Go find me the missing Asian man. Maybe we'll have better luck with him."

DARLING DROVE HOME feeling both anxious to be in the peaceful silence of King's Cove—something he had taken to almost at once as an antidote to his work in town—and anxious about the unresolved nature of the murder. It was strange to know so much and so little at the same time. Harold had certainly led a double life. Is that what had killed him? As he turned up the hill and drove past the little church, his window open so he could hear the babble of the creek that ran along just below the church, he wondered at married life. Could he keep such a massive secret from Lane? Not bloody likely, he decided. She'd have it out of him in no time. This fantastical contemplation was wiped from his mind by the sound of angry chopping coming from the barn. He knew it was angry because each blow of the axe was accompanied by a loud "Damn!"

He walked around to the opening of the barn to see what was going on. There was a very respectable pile of split wood next to where Lane swung the axe and was hurling the results onto the pile. Seeing Darling, she swung the axe one more time to lodge it in the block and turned to him, her hands on her hips, breathing heavily.

"Oh, it's you."

Darling nodded at the pile. "Has the wood been misbehaving?"

"I'm absolutely furious," Lane said. "Good day?"

"Better than yours, evidently. I hope you are never that furious at me."

At this Lane flashed a momentary smile and relaxed fractionally. She looked at the wheelbarrow and then shook her head. "I'll bring it in later. Shall we go in and think about supper?"

"Let's have a strong slug of sherry and sit on the porch, and you can tell me what's going on."

On the porch, Lane flung herself into one of the chairs by the wrought-iron French table and stared out at the lake. She could hear Darling inside collecting sherry glasses.

She looked up when he came through the door. He had the bottle as well as the glasses.

"I didn't know how bad it would be," he said. He filled the glasses and re-corked the bottle lightly and sat down opposite her. "Now then. Chin-chin."

Clinking her glass against his, she said, "Look at that lake. You wouldn't think anything could disturb beauty and serenity like that."

"Never mind the lake. Who's disturbed your serenity?"

"Do you know, I was followed all the way home from Nelson by a beastly member of Canadian intelligence. A smooth, pompous, brilliantined bastard who knew my name and knew all about me. He claims to be called 'Smith,' if you can believe it."

Darling began to speak, but Lane put down her glass, interrupting him.

"And that's not all. They *knew* about whatever that was up there, and because of their secrecy that poor little girl is maimed and motherless."

Darling frowned. "I really think you'd better start at the beginning." He refilled the glass she'd bolted back.

Lane told him about tracking Smith's car behind her all the way from Nelson, and their conversation when he pulled up, free as you please. "I felt really rattled having him say my name like that. That ghastly feeling that one lives in a glass bowl like a goldfish with not a single frond of privacy. But that was nothing to my fury at learning he knew all about that sort of bomb. Oh, he didn't say so in so many words, but he had a glib manner that did not seem to allow for any sympathy for that poor child."

Darling sat back. He'd had experience with the intelligence branch before. He was not at all surprised by what Lane said. "What's next, I wonder? Do the Mounties know?"

"He intimated he'd have a word with my chum, Sergeant Fryer. The only ray of light about this whole thing is that Andrei Barisoff might get out of prison. Otherwise, I feel like we are all absolutely powerless against this sort of dangerous bureaucratic secrecy. I had enough of it during the war. It's why I came out here, for God's sake, but there's nowhere far enough, evidently."

Darling reached out and took her hand where it rested on the table. "My poor darling. It's beastly."

"It's not your fault," she exclaimed. "Unless the Nelson Police are also a bulwark of secrecy that you and Ames cackle over together in your office."

He smiled. "I'm sure the Canadian intelligence service doesn't cackle."

"Ha!" She stood up. "Our stand of chives is looking very good. Why don't you tell me about your day, and we'll attempt a chive and cheese omelette. Eleanor has provided a lovely afters in the way of a chunk of Madeira cake."

Later, brushing crumbs of cake off the front of her sweater, Lane stood at the window with Darling, looking at the moon reflecting on the lake.

"Someone should paint that," he said. "Though, of course, why would one? It's right here to hand."

"I suppose if one were moving to another part of the world, it would be nice to have as a memory," Lane said. "Something on the wall of a place one could never go back to."

"It's funny. This whole case of the murdered jeweller has been ugly and tragic, especially if he indeed was helping to look after Sara and her mother in that peculiar but very kindly way. Which, by the way, fits in with his friend's assessment of him as kind, in fact, overly kind, if one can be such a thing. We've been to his house, you know, and everything is slightly down at heel. The chairs threadbare, the walls in want of painting, an assortment of really ghastly reproductions all in varying depressing shades of brown, but on one wall is this exquisite watercolour of a village in Cornwall. You know, one of those perfect English watercolours you see."

She turned to him. "A village in Cornwall? Had they holidayed there? There are villages in Cornwall that are quite remote."

"No. Not as far as I know. I should ask Mrs. Harold that, actually. No. It's a village where both Harold and Humphries had, at least during the Great War, an elderly relation. It was during that visit they ascertained that they were actually related." Thinking about Harold led Darling to consider the man they currently had locked up for his murder. "I hope Booker is having a sound sleep. He sleeps rough most of the time. He won't stay put. Bad time during the Great War. I remember he told me once when we had him up for some petty theft that he felt like he had to keep on the move, or he felt he was constantly in danger. He could have run mad, I suppose, and killed Harold, but I'm not too bullish on him for this."

"He must have been one of those optimistic young patriotic men when he signed up, thinking only of glory, no doubt, and now his whole life is reduced to this. It's appalling, when you think about it."

"Well, it didn't happen to everyone. Look at Harold and Humphries. They were able to adjust, and there are millions of others."

"If you gentlemen could stop arranging wars, we wouldn't have to talk about these things at all."

LANE WATCHED DARLING drive off and stood by the blue spruce that guarded the door, enjoying the quiet of the morning. They had talked long into the night, and she felt the pleasant, heavy-limbed languor of being slightly tired. It was too early to go to the post office, so she went back into the house, leaving the front door open, and opened the French doors to let the morning sweep through the house. She stood at the bottom of the steps into the attic and called up, "You might as well open those windows, Lady Armstrong. It's a lovely day for it."

She paused for a moment, listening to the silence, but hearing nothing from the resident ghost, Kenny Armstrong's deceased and fresh-air-loving mother, she went about the breakfast cleanup. Finished, she thought about turning on the wireless, and then realized there was nothing she wanted to know or hear that would be worth the interruption of the delicious morning silence. She opened her desk drawer and, ignoring her recalcitrant poem, pulled out some paper and a couple of pencils, and spread six sheets of paper across the kitchen table so they made one large surface.

She stood over it with one hand on her chin, and then smiled once again at the distant sound of Harris's tractor belching to life. Starting at one side, she wrote *Ichiko and Sara Harold*. A short distance to the left, she wrote *Bomb, Japanese UXB?* She added Bales's store and drew a more or less direct path across the road and up the hill.

Leaving space, she labelled a section *Nelson* and wrote in *Ron Harold*. Then she stood back for a moment and added *Murdered. Tall Asian? Mr. Booker?* Darling had updated her on these developments. For good measure she added the hospital and wrote *Sara Sasaki Harold dob Nov 10, 1939*.

Realizing she needed to move the sheets of paper, she took the two from far right and moved them to the left and added *Vancouver* and then wrote in *Bill Harold, married Ichiko Sasaki 1939, died 1939*, and *Ichiko's uncle jewellery and watch repair*. Upon consideration, she added a big question mark next to Ron Harold in Nelson. His wife and best friend knew nothing about Bill's wife or child, or indeed that Ron had likely been supporting the child. This might be important, so she wrote in *Mrs. Harold* and *Martin Humphries* with a little question mark after each. Were they hiding anything? From the police? Each other? Had they been hiding something from Ron, or only the other way around? She found a place for Mr. Booker around Nelson, resisting the urge to show him behind bars, and then sat back.

This process of locating people on a sort of distorted geographical layout helped her think and make connections in a way that listing things didn't. She knew it was a bit like the very clever London Underground map—not a true representation of the geography but an extremely useful way to see connections. She wondered for a moment if she ought to get a packet of coloured pencils in imitation of the tube map, and then decided that when she went into town this afternoon with Harris, she'd do just that. She'd leave him reading to Sara and pop down to the stationer's.

She would draw the connections in different colours. Should she make room for Andrei and his possible Freedomite friends? Or for Dodi Cartwright? This thought caused her to put down her pencil and walk out onto the porch. The sun was almost hot, reflecting off the white of the house. She'd liked Dodi Cartwright, though cautiously, she realized. She was certain now that Dodi had deliberately pressed on the matter of the bomb. For a wild moment, she wondered if Cartwright had known she'd be at the hospital, had known somehow that she'd been first to the bomb site, but she drew back from this bit of paranoia. Their meeting at the hospital had been a genuine surprise. She suspected Cartwright, perhaps troubled by reports of the bomb, or something else—what?—had sought out the advice of her friend, Dr. Edison, a former military officer, and had met Lane completely by chance.

She was certain Dodi Cartwright had told Frank Smith about her, which suggested she too had something to do with intelligence. What? It was unlikely she'd ever find out, though it didn't surprise her in the least. Lane wandered into the bedroom, smiling at the meticulously made bed, and pulled various garments off the chairs where they'd been slung and folded or hung. She wondered what, if anything, Mr. Cartwright knew about his wife. She was lucky, she thought, that though he could never know the full extent of what she'd done in the war, Darling knew enough that she felt less absolutely alone with her past.

And he withdrew respectfully from any prodding or prying.

She took one last look at her map as she taped it down, wondering if there ought to be something else on it, and then slipped on some shoes to walk across to the post office.

DARLING WENT INTO the police station, greeted O'Brien with a cheery good morning, and then, spotting Terrell in the corner at his desk, called out, "Constable."

Leaping up, Terrell approached Darling. "Sir?"

"Can you get in touch with your friend April in Vancouver?"

"I can leave a message at the police station to have her telephone me."

Darling nodded. Something Lane had wondered about last evening had prompted this request. "Do that. And when you get her, ask her to go back to visit the butcher and ask him how tall the uncle is."

"Sir." Terrell turned back to his desk just as the phone rang at the front. Darling paused, looking at O'Brien, who said something into the receiver and then put his hand over it and said, "It's that Dr. Miyazaki."

"Oh, good. Send it up, thanks," Darling said, taking the stairs two at a time.

"Inspector Darling. I am happy I find you in. How are you?"

"Excellent, thank you. You've not had second thoughts on one of our bodies?"

Miyazaki gave a light laugh. "No, Inspector. I have been consulting my lists about the Sasakis. I could not find any Ichiko Sasaki or Ichiko Sasaki Harold on my lists, nor had any of my contacts who'd been at the other camps heard of her. There is another family of that name who have moved to Quebec, but they are intact. No one missing. However, I was able to locate one other person of that family name. Akio Sasaki was in a sort of single men's farm camp in Alberta where they could go for the duration of the war on their own recognizance. Because he was older, they did not bother shipping him back to Japan."

Darling made a note. "'Akio,' just the way it sounds?"

"That's right, with a *k*."

"Is he still alive, do you know?"

"I was able to contact someone who had a grandfather in the same place. He said Akio survived the war and disappeared last year. He's not sure where because no one has been able to return to their former properties. He was a watchmaker."

Darling sat up. "A watchmaker. Might he have worked in a jeweller's shop? Is the name terribly common?"

"I don't have information on the former, but the latter, I would say it is not like 'Smith' among the English, but common enough. I'm sorry I could not, as you English say, 'beard him in his lair.' But if you are looking for a relation to that little girl, he might be a place to start, if you can find him."

"You've certainly done more than I could have done in the time. Does he speak English?"

"I asked that. Apparently he spoke reasonably well, but he didn't like to. I don't know what that says about his proficiency, I'm sorry."

"That's fine. I'd like to thank you . . ." Darling stopped.

It was worth a try. "One more question, Dr. Miyazaki: Did anyone say anything about Akio Sasaki's height?"

"Now, isn't that funny? The old man I spoke with who lived with Sasaki in Alberta actually mentioned that he was very tall for a Japanese. Why? Do you have someone of that description?"

"We may," Darling said.

CHAPTER TWENTY-FOUR

"**O**H, GOD," HUMPHRIES MUTTERED, LOOKING through the curtain at his front walk. "She's coming. Too late to pretend we aren't home."

"I don't see what you have against her, and she's having a terrible time, I'm sure," his wife said.

"The only reason we were ever friends was because of Ron. Now he's dead, I don't see the point. She's small-minded and mean. I never knew what he saw in her." He dropped the curtain and looked toward the kitchen, as if he might bolt out the back door.

"Well, I don't know what's got into you. Try to be nice."

"I don't know where to turn," Bertha said, walking through the front door. "This is a nightmare I just can't wake up from. First, he gets murdered. Murdered! My Ronny! A man who wouldn't hurt a fly. Of course, that was his . . . what's that thing with the heel?" Bertha Harold had been talking without cessation as if she'd been silent for a month and had just found her voice.

"Achilles heel?" suggested Martin Humphries. He remembered *something* from his classical education.

They were sitting on the porch overlooking the water, with glasses of lemonade.

"That sounds right. His weakness, anyway. And now, as if all that wasn't bad enough, I just learned from that Inspector Darling, who is nowhere near finding the killer, that Ronny's brother married some Japanese girl and she had a baby! It's—I don't even know what to say! He kept it from me! All those years he never told me anything except that his brother died on an outbound ship. And not only that. Ron apparently was protecting the mother and baby. They should have gone to those camps with all the rest of them. It's where they belonged. He hid them somewhere! Without telling me! He's been lying to me for ten years! It shows you can never really know someone, no matter how long you've been married."

Susie leaned forward, her eyes wide with surprise. "Goodness! How astonishing! You mean, you have a niece or nephew?"

"A niece. It's disgusting. I hope I never lay eyes on her! A Jap girl, in my own family!"

"The war *is* over. I'm sure she's perfectly lovely," Susie said. "Where do she and her mother live? I mean, I'm sure you don't have to be involved, but it might be nice to have a child around."

"The war may be over, but mixing like that just isn't right. It shouldn't be allowed. And now the girl is an orphan because her mother died in some sort of explosion. The girl was hurt and she's in the hospital now, apparently. I just know they are going to expect *me* to look after her, but I won't do it." She clamped her mouth hard over this declaration. "She can go to a home or something. It's nothing to do with me." She took an angry sip of lemonade and glared out at the lake.

THE LOCKED-UP STORE with the No Trespassing sign and the boarded-up window had become a familiar eyesore on Baker Street. People had stopped really seeing it, but at the same time it was a daily reminder that the case was not nearly solved. While most people believed it was what it appeared to be—a break-in gone terribly wrong— nevertheless there was a slightly heightened feeling that their world was not quite secure. Something like this could happen to anyone, after all. This feeling took on a practical air for businesses all over town, the owners of which had become more attentive to making double sure doors were locked when they left for the day. And fewer stayed on after the shop was closed to finish up paperwork at night.

Darling was just driving past the jewellery shop on the way home—late, as had become usual recently—when he thought he saw a quick flash of light through the edges of the plywood on the front window of Harold's shop, and he stopped, pulling up to the curb to watch. He looked behind him to see if it was simply the reflection of another light on the street, but it was not. Someone appeared to be in the shop with a flashlight. Blast! Someone was taking advantage of the shop being vulnerable. Fat lot of good their sign and boarding up was! Someone must have gotten in the back door.

Sighing with annoyance at this delay, he got out and put his hands against the edge of the window to peer through. There it was again. Someone was at the back, in the office. He felt the inside pocket of his jacket. He still had the key to the back. Alert now, he opened his passenger-side door and took his flashlight out of the glovebox. He made his way back up the street, turned the corner, and trotted down the alley. It was fully dark now and the alley did not enjoy the benefits of the street light near the corner of the shop, but he was reluctant to turn on his flashlight in case he alerted whoever it was.

The door was ajar, and he could hear someone moving around inside, opening things, dropping things, slamming things. He stood just behind the door and considered his next move. Should he forewarn the intruder, or just go in and catch him red-handed? If he snuck up on him and the man was armed with anything, he'd risk getting hurt. On the other hand, if he called out . . . at that moment he walked straight into the metal garbage can that had been placed behind the door, and it fell over with the sound, to him, of a thousand metal trash cans falling on concrete all at once from a great height.

He stood, his heart beating, listening. There was absolute silence. The flashlight that the intruder carried was extinguished, and there was a moment of stillness. Then the door was slammed violently outward, and Darling, who'd been leaning slightly forward, took the full brunt of the blow on his forehead. He felt an explosion of light and pain and he toppled backward, smashing the back of his head on a low concrete parapet. He had a momentary sensation of seeing something moving fast, and then he slipped into oblivion.

LANE, WHO KNEW Darling would be home later than usual, had decided it would be a perfect time to try a tomato and hamburger soup recipe Gwen had told her about, for which she had supplied Lane with a jar of green beans. The benefit of such a soup was that it was inexpensive to make, it could serve for a couple of days of suppers, and it could be kept warm on the stove till a late-returning husband got home.

Having fried the hamburger, she added two cans of tomato soup and the beans, declared it surprisingly good, though certainly not haute cuisine, and went back to her map, this time with her coloured pencils, acquired in her trip up to town in the afternoon with young Johnny Bales, who had been anxious to visit Sara again.

It was not, she realized, so easy to determine which colours to use where. Should she differentiate locations? Green for the local area, blue or red for connections outside of Nelson, yellow perhaps for that connection to Vancouver? Or use colours for individuals—green for every connection of Ron Harold, blue for every connection of Sara, another for Sara's mother, and so on?

Realizing it was going to take some thought, she stared out into the night where the lake far below was made just visible by its reflection of the stars. Water, she thought, was always dynamic, always beautiful. How we humans gather around it, living along lakes and rivers and oceans. She wondered about the watercolour Darling had described as being the only beautiful thing about the Harolds' otherwise rather tired house.

"Cornwall," she said aloud, and looked down at the map again. It was ridiculous, of course. Cornwall only connected Humphries and Harold, and long ago during the Great War. She was about to turn away to check she hadn't left the soup on too high a heat when she took up a blue pencil and, at the farthest right-hand corner of her map, wrote *Cornwall*. Blue, she thought, for the blueness of the Cornish sea.

In the kitchen, satisfied the soup was not burning, though it was palpably reducing, she turned off the heat and looked up at the clock, dismayed to see it was well after ten. Darling had said he would be home by nine at the very latest. She looked at her own watch and frowned. Something must have kept him longer. A break in the case? Only that would have been engaging enough to prevent his calling to say he'd be later than he planned.

She was not of a nervous disposition, but she felt the compression of worry in her chest. She shouldn't be a ninny and telephone the station. That would only be a distraction if they were digging into something, or responding to yet another crime, or . . . but then her mind turned to other perils. Had he had an accident on the way home? It was hard to imagine how. The weather had been fine; no storms or rain to slick up the roads. But her ever-active mind moved with lightning speed to drunk drivers and a logging truck losing its brakes.

Taking a deep breath, she resolved to give it another half hour, and then perhaps telephone. She turned on the reading

315

lamp in the sitting room and settled into a chair with a book, and then tossed it aside, and fetched the atlas out of the shelf. Running her finger down the index, she found the page for the map of England and opened it. There was Cornwall, poking out into the Atlantic. She'd only been once, when she was at Oxford. She'd been invited by a classmate who had been reading history, as she had been. It had been Christmas. St. Ives. She remembered the whitewashed buildings and narrow streets working their way down to the water. It had been cold and grey most of the time. She smiled and ran her finger along the coastline. Why would she have chosen blue? It had been so unremittingly cloudy there.

It was 10:35 now, and she was moving inexorably from unease to outright worry. She got up and went into the hall, and, before she could talk herself out of it, put a call through to the station. After only a couple of rings it was answered. "Nelson Police, Constable Keating."

"Good evening, Constable. This is Mrs. Darling. I just wonder if my husband is still about?" No need to say she was worried.

"Why, no, Mrs. Darling. He left a good while ago. Maybe around 8:45? He mentioned he'd promised to be home by nine, so he was running a little late."

"Oh. I see. Yes. Thank you," Lane said. She paused.

"Maybe he stopped off somewhere?" the constable suggested vaguely.

"Yes, of course. The others have all gone, I guess."

"Yes, ma'am. It's just me. I don't think there was anything on when I got in. The boss, er, Inspector Darling, was in his office with his paperwork, and that was it."

She didn't want to raise an alarm. Perhaps he had stopped off somewhere. She'd look a right goose making a fuss for nothing. Thanking Keating, she rang off and hung up the earpiece, and turned to lean against the wall, her arms folded, looking at the floor.

It was no use. It was a kind of worry she had come to trust, as much as she'd like to talk herself out of it. Darling, she knew, would never have left it this long without telephoning. She'd left the front door open, and the night had turned decidedly cool. She was about to close it, but went instead to the kitchen, double-checked that she'd turned off the soup, and then returned to the hall. She took up her plaid jacket and car keys and went out to the car. If he'd had an accident along the road, she'd see it.

Grateful that people in the countryside went to bed early and did not clutter up the roads, Lane drove slowly, trying to peer into the darkness on either side of the road. The need to crawl so she'd not miss him if he was in trouble somewhere conflicted with a sense of desperate urgency to hurry. By the time she reached the ferry into town her eyes were exhausted from searching the murky darkness, but she felt reasonably sure he'd not had an accident on the road. She sat waiting for the ferry, halfway to the north shore when she arrived, drumming her fingers on the steering wheel. What now?

The man running the ferry on this late shift nodded at her as she drove on, clunking noisily up the steel ramp.

"Good evening," she said, leaning out her window. "Did you see Inspector Darling drive on this evening? Do you know him?"

"Yes, ma'am, I do, and I ain't seen him. Mind you, I come on at seven, so if he was on the road before that I wouldn'ta seen him."

Lane nodded and thanked him. Having exhausted one theory, she now began to imagine others, some benign—he'd gone to his house in town and the phones were down—some terrifying—he'd been kidnapped by Ron Harold's killer, or even some criminal he'd put away before who was back for revenge. She wanted to shake off the lunacy of this kind of worry, but she really couldn't imagine another explanation.

She drove off the ferry and made her way toward the police station—it was the only logical place to start retracing what might have happened. She was two blocks away when she saw his car parked in front of the jeweller's. She pulled off to the side and darted across the road, waving apologetically to a lone driver who'd had to slam on his brakes at her sudden appearance in the middle of the street.

The door was unlocked and his hat and briefcase were on the passenger seat. She looked up and down the street, puzzled and trying to still her anxiety. Clearly, he'd hopped out of the car, expecting to be back in a moment. The intermittent waves of light and shadow offered by the street lights revealed that not a single business was open. She peered into the darkness of the jewellery store. It must have been something to do with the shop. Why else stop here? Had he seen something? There was certainly nothing to see now.

Pulling her jacket close around her to still her pounding heart as much as for the cold night air, Lane stood momentarily undecided. A man and woman arm in arm, perhaps returning home from the cinema at the Civic Centre, were making their way up the hill at the corner and she watched them disappear into the darkness. The alley! She ran toward the intersection and then around and up toward the alley behind the shop. It was nearly pitch dark at first as she moved forward. Becoming accustomed to the blackness, she began counting back doors, estimating the shop should be three doors from the end, but she stopped counting when she saw a wide-open door ahead.

She ran forward and stood outside the open door, listening. Why hadn't she brought her flashlight from the car? If there was someone inside, she'd be at a distinct disadvantage, but there was nothing but silence. She felt her way into the dark back office and began to run her hand along the wall near the door into the showroom until she found the switch.

The flood of light revealed a sight that made her gasp. The office was completely torn apart. Paper everywhere, things knocked over, drawers hanging open and pulled out and upended. Darling had told her that someone had searched the office and left it a mess, but she hadn't imagined anything on this scale.

"Frederick?" she called. He certainly wasn't in this shambles. She pushed open the door into the rest of the shop, found the light switch, and, now desperate, looked everywhere a crumpled body might be behind counters and the watchmaker's work area. Defeated, she leaned forward on a display case, the top glass still smashed, but obviously swept up at some point. She could feel herself in the grip of a now tearful alarm. If he wasn't here, where was he? She was sure he'd been drawn to something going on at the shop; the flung-open door was proof enough.

She gulped a big breath of air and tried to think. She must go to the station. Possibly she and Keating could think of something together; perhaps Ames and Terrell could be brought back in to help with the search. The idea of having them involved steadied her. She turned out the lights and went back into the alley, closing the back door.

Almost back at the street, something made her turn and look back toward the shop. As if propelled by an inner demon she rushed back, her heart pounding, and saw the dark shape of the figure slumped on the ground where it had been behind the door. "Oh my God! Frederick!" she cried. She was rewarded by a low groan.

"BOSS IS AT home today," O'Brien said without preamble when Terrell arrived, closely followed by Ames. "Got beaned on the head last night in pursuit of his duties and his lady wife is keeping him at home. Possible concussion."

"What the hell happened?" Ames asked, taking off his hat and running his hand through his blond hair.

"According to his missus, he saw a light in the back of Harold's shop and went around the back to investigate. He could hear someone in the office crashing around, and that's all he remembers. He's got a bruise on his forehead and a good-sized golf ball on the back of his head. Refused to stay at the hospital."

Terrell frowned. "Front and back? That's odd. I wonder if whoever it was heard him, or saw his flashlight—did he have his flashlight?"

320

"Dunno," said O'Brien.

"I see what you're saying," Ames said. "Whoever it is sees him, or knows someone's out there, and he slams out the door and hightails it, stopping only to hit the boss on the head, or the door hits the boss and he's fallen backward and hit his head on something. Come on, Constable, let's go look at the scene."

"We've had a call from Padgett at his law office, if either of you cares. He thinks someone broke in."

"He can wait," Ames said, making for the door, and then stopping. "Tell him we'll be there in half an hour." He stopped again. "How's the prisoner?"

"Remarkably content and full of breakfast. Can't guarantee how he'll be later. He doesn't like the clothes you chose for him, though, Constable. Cheeky beggar!"

THE ALLEY WAS already abuzz with people sweeping out storerooms, and a white van was making a delivery toward the end of the block. "Look," Terrell said, pointing about five feet beyond the jeweller's door. "That'll be his flashlight."

"And this blood drying on this block of cement will be his too, I guess." Ames stood up from where he'd been crouched and tried the back door. It opened.

"Wow," Terrell said. "This is several degrees worse than the last time we saw it. The killer must be absolutely desperate if he came back to continue the search."

"It's hard to imagine what would make him come back. I was going to say it was a real risk, but maybe not. You know what this town is like. Deader than a doornail after eight, except for the few watering holes and the cinema. But anywhere here on Baker, you could definitely do quite a bit of damage and not be seen. Except by our intrepid boss. Very bad luck."

"I'm just happy he's all right," Terrell said.

"You and me both," Ames said with feeling. "I don't know what we can do here. Let's go back and see what's what with the law office."

CHAPTER TWENTY-FIVE

MR. PADGETT WAS WAITING IN the tiny reception area of his law office when Ames and Terrell arrived. "Thank God. I've been frantic. Please come through." He turned to his puzzled secretary, who had not been asked to make the call to the station and had not been told what the matter was. "No one is to be admitted," he said sternly.

She turned to watch them go into the inner office. No one to be admitted into the building? No one to be admitted into his office? She had never seen the staid and portly lawyer ruffled by anything like this before. It seemed as if, for once, the almighty dictates of the law could not be counted on to smooth all paths and explain all disturbances.

Once in his office, Mr. Padgett went to stand in front of his two oak file cabinets and appeared to suddenly lose the power of speech. Terrell, notebook in hand, gave a quick look around the room. Immediately obvious was the somber seriousness of the place: the heavy leather chairs, the bookcases stuffed with volumes of books that looked like they never left their shelves. The desk that fairly shouted reliability and discretion. The second thing to notice was that whoever broke in was the tidiest house-breaker imaginable. Absolutely nothing looked disturbed. He was just noticing the dark Persian carpet when he looked back toward the books. There was a blank space on a shelf to the right of the desk. He scanned the room to see if the missing volume was elsewhere and located it on the lawyer's desk. He'd seen rooms like this before, and had wondered if lawyers really ever consulted the vast libraries of leather-bound books they all seemed to have. Evidently, they did.

Ames broke the silence. "What's happened, Mr. Padgett?"

"The enormity of this is incalculable. My reputation . . . I inherited this firm from my father . . . the disgrace." He waved at the file cabinets, which looked orderly enough. "Someone broke in during the night and has been going through the files."

"I see," Ames said, looking at what appeared to be undisturbed file cabinets. "Let's start at the beginning. How do you know someone was looking at the files?"

"This drawer was hanging open, maybe an inch." He pointed at the top drawer of one of the cabinets.

Struggling not to suggest that Padgett himself could have left the drawer open—he did not think one inch constituted a drawer "hanging" open—Ames cleared his throat. "What is kept in that drawer?"

"Files *A* through *I*."

"And are any missing, or is anything missing from them?"

"No. No, I checked very carefully. In fact, I went through all the files." The lawyer wrung his hands and then pulled a handkerchief from his pocket and wiped his brow.

"And how did they get in, do you think? A window, was the back door forced?"

Padgett took a deep breath, as if Ames's methodical approach had calmed him a bit. "Yes. I see. I didn't think of that. I was just so distressed to come in and find the mess."

Ames looked around. "Mess?" He was beginning to think annoyed thoughts about people who called in crimes that weren't crimes.

"Well, what I said. Look, I know you think I'm making it up, but I put everything exactly to rights when I leave at the end of the day. I would never leave a cabinet open. I close them and lock them and put the keys back in the drawer, here." He pulled open the middle drawer of his desk to show where a ring of small keys sat.

"I don't think you're making it up, Mr. Padgett. I'm just trying to understand. It would appear that someone came in but took nothing. The cabinet keys were in there as they should be?"

"Yes."

Sighing, Ames looked around the office. "Could your secretary have left a drawer open?"

Padgett pulled open the office door. "Mrs. Fraser, could you come in here please?"

The secretary came in warily, looking from one man to the other, her eyes settling anxiously on Terrell with his notepad.

"Yes, sir?"

"Mrs. Fraser, is it possible you came in last evening and did some work, and perhaps left a drawer ajar?" Padgett was talking as though to a child whom he didn't want to frighten.

Mrs. Fraser's expression turned to one of outrage, her cheeks reddening. "I most certainly did not! I'm surprised, Mr. Padgett, that you could ask me such a thing! Have you ever known me to leave a file drawer open?"

"No, no. Quite." Padgett was obviously finding the task of doubting Mrs. Fraser daunting.

"Mrs. Fraser," said Terrell, "you haven't got a set of keys to the office? Ones you keep at home?"

"No, I do not. There is one set of keys for the office and Mr. Padgett keeps them at all times."

Ames didn't want to add to her distress. "Thank you, Mrs. Fraser. Constable, could you go check both doors and the windows for any sign of a break-in?"

Terrell nodded and went out.

Trying hard to still his own doubts, Ames asked, "Have you ever had a break-in before?"

"Not in thirty years. I'm extremely distressed. And the expense! I shall have to get Humphries to come and change the locks. It's too bad, it really is!"

At that moment Terrell returned. "There is no evidence to suggest a break-in, sir. Is it possible the door was unlocked?"

The lawyer's face clouded. "Impossible. No, no! I am always the last to leave, and I always lock up. Not to would be more than my life is worth."

"WELL, WHAT DO you think of that?" Terrell asked as they made their way back up the hill. "There really was no sign of any kind of break-in, not even of someone using any sort of lock-picking tool."

"I think he's off his rocker. Maybe he's just gotten all worried because of the jewellery store break-in. I'm sure he's not the only merchant who's extra vigilant now."

Terrell nodded. "You could be right, sir."

December 1918

IT HAD BEEN difficult, not telling Marty. They were supposed to go to Canada together. He made up the excuse of a girl, one he thought would be absolutely transparent, as his diffidence with the opposite sex had become a joke in their unit. But Martin had bought it, gleefully even.

"You dog! What's her name? You never told me about this."

"Rosie," Ron had said, clutching at the first name he could think of. "She lives in Oxford." This name he grasped at also, as being one of the only place names he knew in England.

He'd been welcomed, been called "young sir" by Biggs when he'd arrived. He sat now, looking at the portrait of Lady Imelda's mother, thinking of his own, and then of his father. He'd been astonished to learn his father had been a stonemason. It was true his father had begun a small construction company in Nelson. It had never occurred to him that he himself was not Canadian in every way, but of course, if he'd been born in England . . .

Everything in his life had been upended by the war. What he'd understood about life, about the notion of kindness, about "do unto others," all had been tumbled and broken into splinters by the trenches. He scarcely felt he knew himself anymore, except, he thought in wonderment, in this room. Here there was another version of him, already formed by a life he'd never known had been his, a version he could walk into, reclaim some lost part of himself. He turned at the sound of footsteps on the wood floor.

"Ah, dear boy. Thank you for coming." Lady Imelda came forward, her arms out, reaching for his hands, kissing him on the cheek, leaving a powdery scent of rose. "Come and sit." She pulled him to the settee, keeping a grip on his hand.

"Lady Imelda," he began.

"Please call me Aunt Imelda," she said. "I should like that so very much. I want to tell you a story, and you must listen, and you must not object. And then we will go down to the village, and I will show you everything you knew as a tiny boy."

CHAPTER TWENTY-SIX

"DARLING, THERE'S REALLY NO NEED for you to go in today. I thought when the doctor said you should take the day off, we could understand that to mean a whole day. Besides, you look like something the cat dragged in."

Darling had indeed dragged himself into the kitchen at eleven in the morning, clutching a bottle of Aspirin and looking for a glass of water. "Thank you very much. Not a thing wrong with me. Where are the glasses?"

"Where we always keep them, in the cupboard over there. The fact that you can't quite recall this means that bump on the head is still rendering you useless to man or beast." Tempted to let him continue his desperate search, Lane relented and opened the cupboard and waved her hand at the contents. "See? Now go back to bed, and I will bring you a glass of water."

"I know where the damn glasses are. I was looking for the one I had last night."

"Mm-hmm," Lane agreed, instilling in it a pronounced skepticism. She filled a glass with water and held it out to him. "Here, let me open that."

"And I can open a damn bottle of Aspirin," he added, relinquishing it.

"I know, dear. Now go back to bed. You can't expose your poor men to either the golf ball you are sporting on your forehead or your especially charming temper."

"My poor men have put up with worse."

"That's too bad. I feel sorrier for them than ever." She watched Darling disappear down the hallway to the bedroom and, with a sigh of relief, set about doing the washing up. She'd only just dried and put away the last plate when her husband appeared again, fully dressed.

"I'm off," he announced.

Lane shook her head disapprovingly. "No one wants you there. What everyone wants is for you to stay in bed and rest. You've had a concussion, I'm sure of it."

"There is absolutely nothing wrong with me, and I have to go in to work. We've a murder case on, and whoever hit me over the head is doubtless roaming around town looking for his next victim."

"You're not driving in that condition. I'll take you."

"Oh? And what are you going to do all day?"

"It won't be all day, I assure you. I'll just have time to visit Sara and pick up groceries, and then it will be time for you to come home."

BERTHA HAROLD SAT staring out the window. She felt numb, as if she were turning to basalt. Her hands had been folded on her lap, and she finally pulled them apart and rubbed her cheek with her right hand. It was no good. She'd been keeping a tidal wave away. How long ago had she begun to wonder? Ron had been so sweet, it was impossible to disbelieve him. He was the kindest person she knew. Of course, that had its drawbacks. He was always feeling sorry for somebody. One of the only arguments they'd ever had was about the Japanese. The newspaper headline about the Japanese being enemy aliens back in '42 had started it. She hadn't been able to make him see sense—that they were enemies, and dangerous, that they didn't belong in Canada in the first place. They'd agreed to disagree on that one.

But things had changed then. She knew it. There was no way back from that moment. Most people wouldn't have noticed. He was still his same old self around everyone, but there was a distance growing between them. He was polite and attentive as always, but . . . she sighed. It didn't matter now. He was dead, and someone had killed him. Someone from that secret life he led. All that rubbish about his brother being married before he died. She couldn't believe he wouldn't have told her. And that there'd been a baby. A *Japanese* baby. But she knew it was true. All that secrecy! It made sense now. When she'd told Susie and Marty about the baby they'd been surprised, so they hadn't known either. She shook her head. She wasn't sure if she believed that. Humphries was Ron's best friend. He knew. He knew all along, of course he did! She felt hot with anger at his betrayal. He, or Susie . . . she must have known too, deliberately kept it hidden from her. Covered up her husband's secret. When this was over, she'd take everything and leave. Sell the store and the house, take what was hers, and go somewhere far away from all of them.

She stood up and laid her hands flat on the table for a second. It was time, she knew. Time to go back to the house. Not to stay. Just to look around, to get used to it. She wouldn't tell Barbara she was going. She'd only make a fuss and want to come with her. It was a first step. And then she'd have to decide what to do. Her visit to the Humphrieses' had been a mistake. That friendship, like so much of her life, was irrevocably changed because of Ron's murder. She'd thought she wasn't yet ready to go back to the way things were, but the truth was she could never go back. Eventually she'd have to plan a funeral. She sighed and went to find her cardigan in the spare bedroom. This is what people meant when they said they were in limbo. A murder had to be solved before the family could have the body. Everything in her life seemed to be on hold. On her way down the hill, she realized she'd hardly left the house in days.

The last time she'd left Barbara's house to go to the grocery store for milk, she'd been fearful of meeting anyone, having to respond to condolences, or worse, questions. But people she knew slightly had only glanced at her and looked away, as if having a murdered husband was some dreaded plague. Maybe it was. Maybe they were afraid for their own husbands. Until the police found whoever it was, they had a right to be, she supposed.

Now here she was on the sidewalk again. She had a sensation of not quite knowing who she was. She was someone whose husband had been murdered. She tried to recognize herself but couldn't. She'd talk to Padgett. Maybe, just maybe, there would be something in the house that would tell her, that would answer questions, that would explain what the police had been telling her. Maybe something there would help her knit herself back together.

DARLING PICKED UP the phone receiver. "Darling." O'Brien had told him it was Mrs. Harold and he tried to keep the weariness—or was it wariness?—out of his voice.

"What have you done to my house?" Her anger came stabbing down the line. "When I allowed you to search the house, I did not expect you to turn the place inside out and slash up the furniture. It's ruined! Who's going pay for it?"

Darling sat up. "Where are you phoning from?" he asked urgently.

"The house, where do you think? Are you going to do anything about it or not?"

"Mrs. Harold, listen. Don't touch anything, and leave the house. Wait for us outside. Do you understand?"

"Yes, but why—"

"We'll be there in ten minutes. Please do as I say."

He slammed the receiver into place and was on his feet, his hat ripped off the coat rack. "Ames!" he shouted.

Ames was in the hallway in an instant at the dire sound of his boss's voice. "Sir?"

"Stop 'Sir-ing.' Get your hat. Someone's tipped the Harold house!"

THEY FOUND MRS. HAROLD standing at the front of the house, her arms wrapped tightly around her waist, pacing.

The minute she caught sight of them, she approached. "What's going on?" Her anger and now fear were palpable.

"I don't know, Mrs. Harold. What time did you arrive here?" Darling asked her.

"Just before I telephoned you. I never saw anything like it. I thought it was you people."

"It wasn't. What did you touch?"

"Nothing. I mean, the phone. I went to put a cushion back on the couch, but it was such a disaster, and I was so angry—"

"Good, good. Do you by any chance have a safe in the house? We didn't see one, but it might be hidden."

"No. We use the safe at the shop. What's going on?"

Darling debated. If he told her, it would increase her anxiety, but he was now sure that someone had been searching the office of the shop and the legal offices; Ames and Terrell had briefed him on their strange encounter with Padgett. "Someone is looking for something. Perhaps some sort of legal document. Is there anywhere at all you or your husband might have kept any sort of legal documents?"

Mrs. Harold looked nervously back up the stairs toward the house, where Ames stood by the door, waiting, and shook her head. "No. No, I told you, we kept things at the shop, and obviously anything legal with Padgett." She hovered between anger and tearfulness, and she sat down on the steps, as if her legs would no longer hold her up. "What was he up to?" she asked, almost to herself.

Knowing Mrs. Harold meant her husband, Darling was relieved that she seemed finally to have accepted that he had been up to something. Darling signalled Ames to go into the house, and having instructed Mrs. Harold to wait, with an offer to drive her back to Mrs. Dee's when they were done, he followed.

"I don't know what the point is, sir. We come into a place that's already been searched and do what? If whoever it was didn't find whatever it is, we certainly aren't going to find anything." Ames stood in the middle of the topsy-turvy mess in the living room, one foot under a cushion that had been slashed and tossed on the floor. The couch itself had been pulled away from the wall about three feet and they could see the back fabric had been cut as well.

"You're probably right, Amesy. And I don't think he found what he wants this time either. Which means either whatever it is doesn't exist, or it's hidden in the world's most unobvious place."

"You think it might be that Japanese guy?"

Darling had begun to walk carefully among the wreckage. He knew already this was a cleanup operation. He'd wondered the same thing himself. "He's the one anomaly, to quote Terrell. But I can't believe, if he's been going all over town ransacking places, that he wouldn't have been spotted by someone. The neighbours here"—he waved his hand in the direction of the house next door—"would surely have noticed someone going in who didn't look like he ought to be there."

"Unless it happened in the middle of the night. If it's him, maybe he knows that Ron Harold was looking after his niece and he's trying to find her. He thinks there must be something somewhere that will tell him where she is."

"Not a bad theory. Let's check the front and back doors and windows. How did he get in?" Darling said.

The kitchen was relatively untouched, except that all the cupboards and drawers were hanging open. The back door was locked. The bedroom and spare room had been sacked: drawers pulled out, clothing dumped, cupboards open with things pulled off the top shelf. The large blanket box they'd encountered during their own search had had its contents emptied, filling the room and the hallway with the strong smell of mothballs.

But the doors and windows had not been interfered with.

"It's like Padgett's law office, sir. No evidence of forced entry anywhere. Do you think anything a jeweller uses could be used to pick locks? What kind of things do watch fixers use? Whoever robbed the store could have taken them."

"I've no idea. But whoever is doing it is pretty good. They leave no trace. Go and look at what sorts of tools Ron Harold had on hand."

"And who's going to clean up this mess?" Ames lifted his arms almost helplessly before the disaster.

"I'm afraid it will have to be the householder, poor woman." He started toward the door and tripped over a turned-up carpet corner.

"Sir, you still look a little shaky. Should you be at work?"

"Thank you, Ames. I can always look to you for support and encouragement. I'm perfectly fine, thank you very much. Anyway, my wife is picking me up after she visits the child, so I'll be leaving early."

"I'm glad to hear it, sir," Ames said, relieved. "We'll hold the fort."

"Oh, goody. I'd better look to my job, had I?"

DARLING, WHO WOULD not be talked out of going to work next morning, was relieved that Dr. Miyazaki was at home when he phoned. "I don't suppose you've had any luck yet?" he asked.

"Nothing yet, I'm afraid. I was able to trace one Sasaki family, but they are not related to the people who owned the jewellery store in Vancouver."

"You mentioned that the uncle went to a place where single men were sent. Can you remind me where that was?"

"He was with other men at a sugar beet farm in Alberta, near Lethbridge. They worked there replacing the labour that would have been provided by the men who signed up. It wasn't just single men. Men who had families as well. They were separated, and their wives and children were sent elsewhere. I imagine they've all dispersed by now."

"Thank you. I'll put in a call to the police there."

WHEN HE HUNG up, he knew that the police in Lethbridge would not be able to help. Akio Sasaki had most probably come to Nelson, at the very least rummaged around in the jewellery shop, perhaps stolen some watches, and maybe even killed Harold. And now it was possible he'd been searching Harold's house and files, and he seemed to have vanished without a trace. April had said that Reiner had told her that Akio Sasaki was virulently against his niece marrying Bill Harold. Had he come looking for her? How angry had Sasaki been? Perhaps the explosion Lane had found had nothing to do with the Sons of Freedom but had been set by Sasaki. He had to find Akio Sasaki, and right quickly. With a sigh he knew he might have to do

337

something he dreaded: make some sort of public appeal for information about the missing man. He shuddered to think what the result would be—at the very least, a revival of wartime fears that might affect Asians in the area.

CHAPTER TWENTY-SEVEN

"WHAT'S GOING ON WITH THAT bomb of ours?" Gwen asked Lane as they stood outside the post office holding their day's cache of mail and packets of shortbread. "It's never the wrong time of year for shortbread," Eleanor had said almost apologetically. No one had disagreed.

"I have no idea," Lane said truthfully. "They cleared everything more or less away and put string around the site to keep people out." She didn't tell Gwen about being followed home by a Canadian intelligence agent.

"It's funny, not much has been in the papers about it. Just that a woman died in an explosion. They don't even say it was a bomb," Gwen said a little sadly. She'd imagined a photo of the three of them standing by the site, along with the story of the daring rescue of Sara.

"I suppose until they can notify next of kin," suggested Lane. She was sure the bomb experts, and whoever Frank Smith really represented, would like to keep it all to themselves. She wondered about Dodi Cartwright. She was used to secrets, that much was clear. It was a good question, she thought: Why the secrecy?

"And what about that little tyke?" Gwen asked.

Lane smiled. "She's progressing nicely. She has Robin wound around her little finger. It's a stroke of luck that we discovered that Johnny Bales had been sneaking up the mountain to see her. Without that we'd still be thinking she was unable to speak."

"Robin told Mabel he ought to take care of her! He's really not himself. I hope he's not headed for some sort of breakdown."

Lane shook her head. "I guess he has a soft underbelly after all," she said, smiling.

At home, Lane had only just put down her mail and shortbread, stopping to break one in half just for a taste, when the telephone trilled in the hall. Hers. "KC 431, Lane Winslow speaking."

"Ah. Miss Winslow. It's Dodi Cartwright in Nelson."

"Yes, good morning, Mrs. Cartwright. What can I do for you?"

"I was wondering if you'd be coming into town any time?"

"I'm coming in later today to visit Sara." What was this in aid of? Lane wondered.

"I wonder if you'd like to have a cup of coffee? We could meet at the café. What time are you finished with your visit?"

Lane looked at her Waltham. "I'd like that. Two thirty or so?"

"Good. I'll see you then."

LANE WAS IN for a second surprise when she arrived at the hospital. The nurse on the floor of the children's wing said, "Sara's had another visitor. There was something odd about him, and we weren't really convinced he knew her. We didn't let him in, of course, but he brought her a doll. I hope we did the right thing." She shrugged. "We have it behind the counter. He claimed he knew her father and he'd only just heard about her being in hospital."

"Goodness," Lane said. "I'm absolutely sure you've done the right thing." She felt a stab of anxiety. "Did he give his name?"

"Dave somebody, let me check." The nurse went around the counter and picked up a paper. "Blackstone. He wasn't pushy or anything, but I don't know . . ."

"You've done the right thing, Sister. You've trusted your own feelings. Did he leave any address or telephone number?"

"No. Maybe that's what alerted me. You see, I asked him to leave a number so that we could . . . well, I didn't want to say 'check his bona fides,' so I said we keep a record of visitors. He just said, 'Never mind,' and left. And now that I think of it, I don't think he even knew the girl's name." She slammed her forehead. "Of course, he just said, 'I'd like to see the little girl you have here.' Then claimed to know her father."

"Can you tell me what he looked like?" She wasn't sure what it meant, but Lane would have to tell Darling.

The nurse compressed her lips. "Isn't it odd? In books, the police always ask what people looked like and the person always knows and can even tell them what kind of shoes they were wearing. I don't know that I can. Brown

341

hair, average height. He was wearing a hat pulled low over his forehead, so I couldn't get a good look at his face." She chuckled. "Sorry, can't tell you about the shoes. Oh, wait! He handed me that doll and I noticed his hands were rough . . . something with his fingers, like there was something dark embedded in the ends of them. I think I had this momentary idea he worked delivering coal or something. Other than that, I'd say he was about as average as a man could get."

"From here, accent-wise?"

"Yes, no. Yes, but there was something a little funny about the way he spoke. I wondered if he'd spoken another language when he was little."

Lane smiled. "Well, you might not have remembered his shoes, but those details are excellent."

The nurse smiled and looked down shyly. "Oh, thank you." She began to walk toward the ward. "She's in good shape today. We've been for a ride in the wheelchair, and we might try a few more steps tomorrow. She's a little bit small for the training bars in the therapy room, but we'll come up with something. I haven't said anything about the visitor," she added.

"Thank you, Sister. Best not, I think, just now. Has she asked about her mother at all?"

Shaking her head sadly, the nurse said, "No. In fact, I'm a bit worried. I think that for the moment the whole world is in this hospital. She's what I might call institutionalized. I don't know what the answer is, but she will have to leave one day soon, and it will be a dreadful shock to her. I don't know much about the subject, but your visits, and that dear sweet man you bring sometimes, and her little friend are very important because they keep her somewhat in touch with her other life."

Dear sweet man, Lane thought. Ha! "If there is another attempt by this man, or anyone else trying to see her, could you call the Nelson Police? I'll pass this on, and they may telephone for more details."

"Absolutely, yes. No one will get past us!"

Musing on what a thoughtful and intelligent woman Nursing Sister Evans was, Lane made her way back down the hill. She could go far, Lane thought. But a keen observer herself, she'd seen the engagement ring on the young woman's finger and wondered if setting up a household would be as far as she ever got. What a loss that would be.

SHE HAD JUST enough time to stop in and see Darling to tell him about Sara's mysterious and unsettling visitor.

"I've already got two mysterious men to deal with," he said. "Was it absolutely necessary to bring me another? And what does it mean?"

"I thought I'd leave you to sort that out," Lane said, smiling sweetly. Serious again, she said, "You can contact Sister Evans if you want to wring a few more details out of her. I must say it puts a new wrinkle on things. How did he come to know about her? What does she have that he might want? I'm just happy they are like guard dogs up at the hospital, protecting her. I had a word with Dr. Edison, and she is going to make sure no one comes but Harris, Johnny, and me, unless we vet the person."

"It's absolutely maddening, because the only people who could really tell us anything about her are both dead. Mrs. Harold expressed complete and, I must say, outraged ignorance of her brother-in-law's marriage and the existence of a little girl, though I suspect she knows it's true, so she's no help. You're right with your question of what does Sara Sasaki Harold have that anyone would want? If we could catch up with one of my mysterious men—who might be a relative, in fact—maybe he would know."

"Really? A relation of Sara's? But that's wonderful!"

"We think. Same last name, and he's possibly been here. Alas, we might want him for murder." Darling closed his notebook and dropped his pencil, lead end up, into the cup he kept writing implements in and folded his hands. "Where are you taking your pestilential and interfering self to now?"

"It's funny you should say that—not the pestilential part, obviously, because there are people out there who might not find me interfering and just want to see me for my scintillating company. I've had a call from that woman I told you about who seemed so interested in my description of the bomb, and who, I think, may have sent that Canadian government man. She has asked to have coffee with me in the café"—she checked her watch—"in three minutes' time. I must be off. Will you be late?"

Darling shook his head. "I don't think so. We are well and truly in the doldrums here with this. At the moment, I'm fervently hoping someone will just stroll into the station and say, 'Hello, I'm the guy who hit Harold over the head.' I'm not holding my breath."

344

"Speaking of being hit on the head, how's yours?"

"It was fine until you reminded me of it. Don't you have someplace to be?"

She smiled demurely and gave him a wave.

"THERE USED TO be such a nice young woman working here," Mrs. Cartwright said when Lane had settled in. They were in the last booth against the wall, which Lane realized her companion had picked to keep them from being overheard. "I don't think I've ever been so gracelessly welcomed in a public place in my life." She nodded at the retreating Marge.

Lane smiled. "That lovely young woman is April McAvity. Daughter of the fire chief. She's in Vancouver at a police course to see if she likes it."

"Is she indeed! That's what I like to see. Yes, good afternoon. I'll have a coffee, and do you have a scone or a muffin?"

"Pie," Marge said in her best take-it-or-leave-it voice.

"Good. All right. What about you, Miss Winslow?"

"Tea, thank you very much, and . . ." She had been on the point of asking what sort of pie, but something in Marge's expression militated against any inquiry. "Pie as well. Thank you." She offered a broad smile, which was unrequited, and turned back to Mrs. Cartwright. "It will be a mystery pie," she said.

"How is the little girl today?" Mrs. Cartwright asked.

"She's making very good progress. I believe they are beginning some sort of physical therapy to help her walk soon." She hesitated. The more she thought about

Sara's mysterious visitor, the more anxious it made her. But she knew that the inquiry was only polite, and that Mrs. Cartwright had some other business.

"What will happen to her?"

Lane sighed. "That's my worry. I have a rather curmudgeonly old neighbour who has quite taken to her—he helped us get her off the mountain the day we found her—who says he's quite prepared to take her or have me take her."

"Would you mind?"

"Not at all. I'd quite like it, and we have some nice if rambunctious children in King's Cove who would be happy to have her as a playmate. And she could go to our excellent little school. But I don't know what the procedure is, exactly, and in truth I've not really discussed it with my husband. He'd have to agree, but I think he would. Which all brings to mind that I don't understand what happened in the first place. Why was there a bomb in the middle of nowhere like that?"

"Ah," Mrs. Cartwright began, and then stopped as Marge was approaching with their orders, which she managed somehow to plunk down petulantly, yet without any spillage. When she'd gone off, with their unacknowledged thanks ringing in her ears, Mrs. Cartwright continued. "That is what I wanted to talk about. I know what it is."

Lane nodded. She was not surprised. "Are you able to tell me?"

"Well, that's the thing, isn't it? Not really, is the answer, but I'm so mad about it all that I'm rather inclined to. I feel I can trust you. Well, in fact, I know I can."

"Smith?"

"Yes, I'm sorry about that, but the minute I heard about the bomb from you that day and saw that smidgy little bit in the paper, I had to contact him. Was he awful?"

"Not particularly. I was a bit cross about being followed home in so obvious a manner. And the fact that he seemed to know who I am. Did you tell him?"

"I told him your name, and that you are English. And that you seemed to know about explosives. I am sorry. I wanted him to see the bomb site and I didn't know what else to do. It's just like him to take the thing too far and actually dig into your background." She shook her head and stabbed her pie, blueberry today. "I'm hungry all the time these days."

Lane stirred a couple of heaping teaspoons of sugar into her tea. She felt cross that she'd been told by the Secret Service to hold her tongue until she was languishing in her death bed, and yet information about her could be passed to all and sundry. But she smiled at the thought of Mrs. Cartwright's pregnancy. "How lovely. How far along are you?"

"Three or so months. The doctor told me to be careful about eating too much, and I suppose he's right." She sighed. "I suppose he means for me to eat more fruit and less pie." She smiled and dug into her pie as if she had no intention of following the doctor's orders. "The point is," she continued, getting back to it, "that there are people who know what that thing is and are just not saying. I know perfectly well but was told to keep quiet when we began to learn about them."

"I know just what you mean," Lane said. "Can you tell me about them?"

"I can't, but I will. I had . . . an opportunity . . . to learn of them during the war. They are Japanese balloon bombs, at least, that's what we called them. They are a rather quixotic effort by someone in the Japanese military to use prevailing winds and the jet stream to carry bombs from Japan over to the United States, mostly, under giant paper balloons. I think they were intended to disrupt things, more than bomb towns or hurt people, though they carried anti-personnel equipment, small bombs, as well as incendiary devices. More like set forest fires to pull services away from the war effort. They're quite clever in their construction, really, with a ballast they could automatically shed when they got too low and so on. But they were a colossal failure, overall. We don't really know how many were sent, in the thousands perhaps. They began sending them over in '44 and we detected at least 300."

"I've never heard of them," Lane said, fascinated. "So effectively, any undiscovered ones are UXBS."

"That's exactly right—they are unexploded bombs, right here in Canada. The Japanese military had no real control over where they'd land, and they've been found as far north as Alaska. Our side kept them a secret, of course, because that's what they do, claiming they didn't want to alarm people. After the war, in '45, most of a family were killed in Oregon when one was found by some picnickers. After that the authorities decided they'd better tell people so they'd know to stay away. There was one found in Saskatchewan that year, but luckily no one was hurt. In fact, there was a bomb disposal expert here in Canada during early winter of '45, who went around finding them in the bush and detonating them. I knew him, Captain East. He was very intrepid, crashing around in the back country in the snow. I think he thought the whole thing was a bit of a lark. But he knew the work was important. In fact, he didn't agree that they were a failure. He believes they were responsible for a number of forest fires."

"But obviously they didn't find them all?"

"And they never will. They are no doubt sprinkled all over the forests and mountains from Oregon to Alaska, and obviously that one made it as far east as Saskatchewan, pretty far across the country. The point is, people have to know about them. The war is over, it's long past the time of secrecy, and now look—a woman has been killed and her little girl orphaned. And it doesn't help that the Mounties, in full tilt against the Freedomites, are hanging on to this one because they want it to be something to do with the Doukhobors."

"Do you have an idea about what to do?"

"I'm not at all sure, except I know it can't be a secret, or more people will get hurt, not the least those men they've arrested."

"I understood Smith might do something about it," Lane said. "He seemed to imply he would tell the Mounties what that device really was."

"Smith would say anything. He's a perfect cog in the intelligence machine. I just don't trust him to do this." She sighed and drank some coffee. "The pie is always very good here. I suppose I could buy it from the same bakery they do, but I'd just eat it all myself. I think I'm hoping you could tell your husband. I understand the police work quite amicably with the Mounties."

"I could at that," Lane said. She would stop back at the station on her way home. It occurred to her that she had not heard from Peter Barisoff about whether his son was still being held. Perhaps Mrs. Cartwright was right: Smith had information and might be sitting on it for reasons entirely unfathomable and all his own.

"You know," Dodi Cartwright said, "that fascinating paper they used was made by young Japanese girls who had no idea what it would be used for. When that family died in Oregon they were horrified, and a delegation came over to apologize."

"I wasn't here yet in '45, so I never heard about any of this. Wouldn't it have made quite a splash after a family died?"

"It was news for a moment, I expect, after the government finally agreed people ought to know. And it was three years ago, and it was far away in Oregon. I guarantee that no one around here knows anything, and the Mounties would like to keep it that way, it seems."

CHAPTER TWENTY-EIGHT

"INSPECTOR, YOU'RE GOING TO WANT to take this!" O'Brien shouted up the stairs. "It's the hospital."

Now what? Darling thought anxiously.

"Inspector Darling? It's Dr. Edison."

"Good afternoon. Is everything all right?"

"Yes, no trouble with Sara, but we have a visitor here whom we can't let in, but he won't leave. He's sitting here like a smouldering volcano. I've snuck upstairs to call you."

Darling frowned. "Is it the same man who was there before?"

"No. In fact, this man appears to be Japanese. He approached the front desk, and before he could say anything, unfortunately, Lisa, Miss Cathcart, asked if he was here about the little Japanese girl. He asked, 'What little Japanese girl?' and she, very unfortunately, gave the man her first name. Then he said, 'What about Mr. Harold?' And she said she didn't know anything about any Mr. Harold, and he said, 'Where's the girl?' and she sent him upstairs. He came in here claiming to be a relative of the little girl, and he knows her name. Her full name, I mean. I was surprised because I called Miss Cathcart downstairs and she said she didn't tell him Sara's last name. I told him we are not letting anyone in to see her as yet, so he's set up camp."

Out of his seat now, Darling said, "I'll be right up. Is he in the lobby downstairs? I'll need to speak with him, and I don't want to create a disturbance on the ward."

"Yes. I told him we were just checking with another doctor about the visit. Should I say anything to him?"

"No. I'll be up momentarily. We don't want to spook him."

"Ames!" No answer. "Where the bloody hell is Ames?" Darling asked when he was halfway down the stairs.

"Gone back to the Harold house, sir, to figure out how an intruder got in. I can offer you Terrell." O'Brien indicated with his hand where Terrell was already on his feet, putting on his cap.

Nodding, Darling hurried out, tossing the car keys to Terrell. "Hospital, quick as. A Japanese man has turned up asking for Mr. Harold, and, thanks to the indiscretion of the girl at the front desk, demanding to see little Sara. They are keeping him, hopefully, in the foyer till we get there."

"Our tall Japanese party, sir?" Terrell said, hopping into the car.

"Forgot to ask. He knows the name of the child, says he's her relative. Chances are he's the same man."

"Bit of luck, sir."

"We'll see. If he turns out to be our murderer, then yes, but not for little Sara if he is also her great-uncle. Though it is surprising he was asking for Mr. Harold. Why? What does he know, or think he knows?"

They arrived at the foyer of the hospital to find their man leaning back in a chair with his arms folded, glowering at Miss Cathcart at the front desk. He was looking very much the worse for wear, as if he'd been sleeping rough. His face was haggard, and his clothing was unwashed and pungent.

Miss Cathcart spoke up the minute she saw them. "Are you here to get him? Because he's giving me the creeps. He's been staring at me the whole time." Then she added, "I didn't mean anything."

Darling had started toward the seated man, but Terrell stopped and looked at her. "What do you mean? Didn't mean what?"

"Well, he came in here and I thought he was here for that little girl upstairs. I only said her first name. I don't think this is my fault. I'm down here on my own, you know."

Terrell sighed. "I see. So you sent him up to the ward?"

"Don't look at me. What was I supposed to do?"

"Follow hospital protocol, and don't give away patient information," Terrell said, and then joined Darling, who had sat down next to the angry man.

"Are you Mr. Akio Sasaki?" Darling asked quietly.

"Who are you?" the man said angrily.

"Inspector Darling of the Nelson Police, and this is Constable Terrell." He held out his warrant card. "I wonder if you'd come with us? We need to speak with you rather urgently."

"No. I want to see my niece. I have a right!"

Darling was relieved that he appeared to speak good English. He had been worried about the time involved in finding a translator. "All in good time. We will sort all that out, I promise, and if the hospital allows it, we will make sure you see your great-niece. If you would be so good, we have a car outside." Darling held his hand toward the door.

Sasaki, his arms still crossed, made a dismissive noise and looked away. Darling stood silently, wondering what might have to take place now to get this man quietly to the station.

"Mr. Sasaki," he began, but then to his surprise Sasaki got up, and with a curt nod began to walk toward the door.

Terrell opened the back door of the car and Sasaki got in and sat in the middle of the seat, his arms crossed again, a picture of defiance.

"Would you like a glass of water?" Darling asked when they were settled in the interview room. Sasaki shook his head.

"Constable Terrell is here to take notes. Can you give us your full name, and where you live?"

"You know my name. I don't live anywhere, thanks to the Canadian authorities. I want to know why my great-niece is in that hospital. I'm her mother's uncle."

"What can you tell us about her mother?"

"I haven't seen her since '42, so I can't tell you anything. Why? What's going on?"

Darling switched tactics. "I believe you were in Alberta during the war. When did you come back here?"

"I don't know," he said angrily. "A few days ago? What business is it of yours?"

"Where were you before you arrived here in Nelson?"

"Here and there." He was becoming sullen.

"Looking for your niece?"

"Obviously looking for my niece!"

"Did you find her?" Darling suddenly wondered if he had somehow found her in the cabin.

"What is this? I obviously didn't find her, or I wouldn't still be looking for her." He suddenly looked alarmed and leaned forward. "Where is she? You aren't telling me something."

Darling's heart sank. "That is what we would like to talk to you about. One of the things."

"Why? What's happened?"

Darling cleared his throat. The moment he hated above all the moments that comprised being a policeman. "Then you don't know your niece is dead?"

Akio leaped up, knocking the table, and then seeing Terrell begin to stand, sat down again quickly. "What do you mean she's dead?"

"I'm very sorry to say that your niece, Ichiko Sasaki Harold, has been killed. There was an explosion near where your niece and her little girl were living. She was killed outright." He stopped, and then after another breath that was almost a sigh, he said, "I'm very sorry to bring you this news."

Sasaki's eyes blurred and reddened. He looked determined not to cry. He was looking straight ahead, past Darling, at some vision only he could see. Finally, he turned back to Darling. "And Sara?"

"Sara is very lucky, at least in this regard. Her injuries,

while severe, have been healing nicely. She is otherwise, I think, a healthy and sturdy nine-year-old. The worst were two severe breaks in her leg that may cause a limp. I am told she will be able to leave hospital soon."

"Nine years old." Sasaki shook his head. "Last time I saw her she was three." He shook his head again, swinging it as if it was too heavy for him. "I hope you are not asking me to take her. I can't look after a child. I don't even have any place to live myself."

"I understand. Usually under these circumstances the city welfare worker will try to find a home that will foster her. My wife, who found her, has been visiting every day. We are going to do our best to make sure she won't have a rough adjustment. There is a child Sara used to play with who lives quite near to us, so perhaps they will be able to find a family somewhere nearby. Just until you, or someone else in her family perhaps, is settled and able to take her. That is, if you agree to this arrangement."

"I don't understand. Why would Ichiko be killed by a bomb? Where was she that a bomb could kill her?" Sasaki had moved from belligerence to utter confusion and sorrow.

Darling explained what he knew. "The important thing now is Sara."

"When can I see her?"

"We'll try to arrange it, of course." Darling set his lips in a grim line. "There are still a couple of questions we have to ask you."

Sasaki grunted and composed himself. Darling was sure he already knew what was coming. "Mr. Sasaki, we have

356

reason to believe you broke into the jewellery store on Baker Street six days ago. We have a witness who described someone who matches your description."

"I'm not surprised. I'm sure all Japanese look alike to the so-called witness."

Darling shrugged acknowledgement and waited. Terrell was interested in Darling's long silences. He had seen more than once that patience was rewarded when the person being questioned became anxious to fill the void.

After seeing that Mr. Sasaki would not be shaken by silence, Darling continued. "When we went in after the break-in, we found the shop vandalized, some expensive watches and jewellery taken, and the owner dead. As you may imagine, we are anxious to find out anything we can about this."

Sasaki started. "What? Dead? I didn't kill anybody! You can't blame me for that!"

"Why don't you tell me what happened?"

Slumping back, Sasaki shook his head, muttering, "I knew this would happen."

Conscious of how difficult the day had already been for Mr. Sasaki, but certain now that they did have their break-in artist and very possibly their murderer, Darling said, "You knew what would happen?"

"That I'd get the blame. I was looking for that Ron Harold and it was the only place I knew he might be. He didn't answer when I banged on the back door around eight, so I left."

"I see. And why were you looking for him?"

"He's the reason I never saw my niece or the baby all

this time! I finally figured out after the war, when I tried to find them, that he was the one who took them. I wanted him to tell me where they were! I wouldn't kill him."

"Mr. Sasaki, I have no intention of blaming anyone but the person responsible. If it was not you, I will be the first to be happy. You can understand, however, that we want to know what went on that day. Can you explain why you thought he might be in the hospital?"

Sasaki sat sullenly silent and folded his arms across his chest, looking away from Darling at the wall.

"Mr. Sasaki? Why did you imagine he'd be in the hospital? If you knocked on the back door of the shop at eight at night, why didn't you assume he'd be at home? You're not telling me everything."

Resting his arms on the table and clasping his hands, Sasaki looked down. "Okay. I did go back. Much later, around midnight. I thought I could break in and wait inside the shop. I got nowhere to sleep anyway. When I got there, the back door was open, so I went in. The place was a real mess. Display cases broken, glass everywhere. I ran back to the office and even in the dark I could see that someone opened everything and threw paper and everything around. I didn't even stop to look. I knew if I didn't get out of there, I'd get the blame. It was clear he'd been robbed. He wasn't there, or if he was, I sure didn't see him." Sasaki hesitated. Terrell was writing notes and looked up expectantly after writing "witness didn't see deceased." Another long silence from Darling.

This time Darling was silent because he was flummoxed. "You didn't see him?"

358

Sasaki glowered. "No, I didn't. I ran out into the alley, and down the next alley and down the hill until I got to the water, and then I went away from the town. I found some sort of fishing shack or something and went in there. I figured I could stay the night and start looking for Mr. Harold after all the panic over the break-in had calmed down and you guys found who had done that to the store. A couple of nights later I went by the store again, but it was all boarded up. Then I thought maybe he'd been in the store and been hurt. That's when I figured he might be at the hospital, but I didn't want to go looking for him in case they blamed me for the break-in."

Darling rubbed his eyes and sighed. On the one hand, Sasaki was telling the truth about when he was there, according to the witness who'd seen him. He might have been responsible for Harold's death. He might have searched the place. But if all he wanted was to find his niece, he could have forced Harold to tell him and then killed him, but he wouldn't then need to search the place.

"And why were you trying to contact Ronald Harold only now? You said you've not seen your great-niece since she was three. That's six years."

"By the time we were allowed to leave the farm, I still didn't know where they had gone, so I sent a letter to my old neighbour who ran a butcher shop. A guy I used to play chess with. I knew he'd know something because my niece used to talk to him. He told me Ichiko's husband had a brother from Nelson, and I remembered he'd come to our store on Powell Street and was a jeweller too."

"I'm wondering, you see, if you searched the shop looking for any information about where your niece was because Harold refused to tell you and you killed him."

"I told you, I never saw that man!"

Darling contemplated him for a moment, then rose. It might be true that he'd not seen Mr. Harold, but if he had seen him and they'd argued . . . he could have hit Harold and thought he wasn't dead and might be in hospital. "Mr. Sasaki, I'm going to detain you for breaking in and for the possible murder of Mr. Harold, and I will be holding you here. I can see that you are tired, and I don't know when you last ate, but I can have some food brought in from the café up the street. Coffee, a sandwich. We can continue the interview later."

Sasaki slumped and shook his head. Of course, he thought. What did he expect? Ichiko dead, Sara badly hurt, and now a charge of murder. "So that's it. You have me. You can wipe your hands and close the case. What an amazing country!"

"We are still investigating, Mr. Sasaki. If you are innocent, we will discover it. However, I cannot let you go until I am sure. Let's get you some food, and we will continue later."

In the cell, the empty plate and cup beside him, Sasaki lay down and closed his eyes. There was a man in the next-door cell who'd tried to start up a conversation, but he ignored him. His body felt burdened by sorrow, and here, with the afternoon light coming in through the tiny window, he thought of Ichiko. By the time the order came in '42 for the Japanese to clear out, the two of them had been getting along. Even with the passage of time since they had been separated, he felt her loss like a heavy blow. He squeezed his eyes shut, trying to remember her. He couldn't quite bring her into focus, but he remembered admiring her, the way she stood up to him. She'd been like his mother that way. Why had she and Sara even been here? Had they not been interned? Why had she ever met that damn Harold boy who ruined everything, his whole family, everything? And with this unanswerable question and his broken heart, he drifted off to sleep.

"THEY DIDN'T SEND just me. I was with a whole bunch of other men I didn't know." The interview had been picked up, and Akio was telling Darling about what happened when war broke out.

"We had to close our store, and the old man told me they finally gave it away to someone white. No, I bet they sold it. Extra cash for the government. I used to have a nice store and a life in Vancouver, and thanks to them, I spent the last six years forced to work in Alberta for nothing. Terrible winters there! And now? Store gone. Nice life gone. Family gone."

Darling nodded. "So you thought Harold might have been hurt and asked for him at the hospital. But of course, he was not there because he'd been killed."

Sasaki leaned on the table with both elbows and put his hands on his head. "This is my fault. All my fault. If I . . . if we had never been separated, she would be alive."

"Mr. Sasaki, that was in no way your fault. It was a tragic accident. It really looks like your niece and her daughter accidentally tripped an unexploded bomb."

"A bomb," Sasaki said, shaking his head. "Was it one of those Freedomite bombs? I can't believe that. I heard those Doukhobors here were always helping out our people."

Darling shook his head. "It may not have been the Doukhobors. We aren't sure yet how she got where she was, but we believe Mr. Harold protected her during the war, perhaps finding her that place to hide. She was his younger brother's wife. But, of course, you know this."

Sasaki leaned back. "I was so mad about that. My niece going off with that boy. Then he died, and she was left with the baby." He didn't talk about how close he came to throwing her out, or how attached he became to that baby.

"Mr. Sasaki, I am very sorry for your loss. I'll hold you here, take fingerprints and so on, and we are following all our leads. But I will arrange for you to see Sara. Do you know if she has any other relatives besides you?"

"My brother's wife," Sasaki said. "Sara's grandmother. She and my brother couldn't get back from Japan, then he died. But she wants to come back. She's a Canadian citizen and she has papers to prove it. I don't even know where we would go. Our home is gone . . . everything we had, gone."

"If you can give us all the information about the child's grandmother, we can see what we can do with the authorities to speed her return to Canada. In the meantime, we are going to do our best to make sure Sara goes to someone she knows until such time as your family can make arrangements. In the meantime, we can arrange for a bath and a change of clothes for you." He was beginning to feel like their little jail was the Ritz Hotel and Spa.

"IT'S REMARKABLE, SIR. There is definitely no sign of forced entry. Is it possible Mrs. Harold did this herself?"

"To what end?" Darling said. Ames had returned from his second exploration of the Harold house.

"To throw us off the scent?"

"What scent would that be, Ames? And did she also get into the lawyer's office and have a poke around, because she has that key as well?"

"Point taken, sir. Two break-ins."

Darling drummed his fingers grumpily on the desk and stared out at Elephant Mountain. "Three if you count the jeweller's."

"Three searches. Someone is really desperate to find something."

"Do you think so, Ames?"

Ames sighed. His day almost wouldn't be complete without these little doses of sarcasm. "Sir. The question is, what?"

"Yes, it is Ames. Well spotted. I personally don't think either of the two men we have downstairs killed Ron Harold. Though Sasaki at least had a reason to."

Terrell moved on his seat. "Does he strike you as a particularly vengeful person, sir?"

"You're saying you believe him?"

Terrell made a noncommittal nod.

"Yes, all right, Terrell," Darling said moodily. "I see your point. Unless he was the one who secreted a bag of jewels and watches behind the bin for Booker to find. But why would he? He'd keep them, try to fence them somewhere. No. The searches and the murder seem all of a piece. Neither

363

Sasaki nor Booker quite fit the bill. Well, until you two can get off your hind ends and find me another killer, I'm going to have to hold them, and Booker is already getting restive so it's going to be no fun. Oh, and check at the station to see that Sasaki indeed was on the train the day of the murder."

"I'M GLAD ABOUT Mr. Sasaki. If he's cleared, of course. I feel better for Sara." Lane had gone to the station to tell Darling about her conversation with Dodi Cartwright.

"I'll make sure you're the first to know when he's cleared and we find the real murderer," Darling said. "Probably," he added with a touch of mock sadness, "if you don't find him first. Now, if you're not here to interfere, how can I be of help?"

"I spoke with Dodi Cartwright. I told you about her. She knows exactly what that bomb was, and where it came from, and she knows it has nothing to do with the Doukhobors. At this point the Mounties are clinging to their pet theory—and, according to her, endangering the lives of others, because, she says, there may be, and very likely are, other bombs out in the bush where anyone can trip them without knowing what they are."

"What are they exactly?"

Lane told Darling everything she learned about the balloon bombs. "I mean, strictly speaking, it's probably the military who have been covering up. That buffoon Smith claimed he would sort it out, but he hasn't. There have been a couple of incidents with the things—one in Oregon and one in Saskatchewan. The instinct there was to cover up as well, but they finally did put something in the papers to prevent any more mishaps. That was back in '45. Of course, no one even remembers that far back, now that the war is well and truly behind us and everyone is squirrelling away building new lives. I suspect Smith hasn't because he answers to someone somewhere who is telling him to hold off. Mrs. Cartwright thinks that it is simply that they don't want to raise the public's alarm, but if the public's alarm ever needed a good raising, this would be the time."

"You're right there. How does she know so much?"

"I didn't ask, and neither should you. Can you talk to Inspector Guilfoil, your Mountie pal?"

"Poor Mr. Cartwright probably doesn't know a thing about what his wife gets up to," Darling said. "If you're anything to go by," he added. "All right. I will go see Guilfoil. Again. Neither force has any influence over the military, however, I should remind you. You're off to see Sara?"

She nodded and got to her feet. "She's doing very well. They were going to try her at walking the last time I was there. I'm anxious to see how that's going."

Darling reached for his telephone. "I'd better see if Guilfoil is there." Then he withdrew his hand. "The other thing is that now that we've found the girl's great-uncle, he says he can't look after her, even if he weren't in jail. We've learned there's a possible grandmother in the offing, but she's stuck in Japan. His sister-in-law. But it's something."

"Now that I think of it, that ass Smith said he might help with finding her relations. Maybe he has pull." She shrugged. Maybe he only said that to appear agreeable.

Darling cleared his throat. "I was thinking that perhaps it would be a good idea—I can't believe I'm saying this—to bring the child to King's Cove. Should we think about it?"

"To Robin Harris?" Lane asked, smiling. "But of course, you mean to us. Are you sure? It's just what I have been thinking. I was going to bring it up over dinner." She was surprised. She had thought all along that she would be the one trying to persuade him. "Two minds but with a single thought," she said.

"I sincerely hope not, or I'll never have another thought of my very own. I'm glad you agree. It's somewhere safe, at least until her grandmother can come. In the meantime, as soon as the uncle is cleaned up, I'll take him up to see Sara. She won't know him, of course, because she was three when they last met. And I'd better go along and see Guilfoil now." He leaned over and kissed her, and she kissed him back.

CHAPTER TWENTY-NINE

❝ I T HAD BETTER BE SOON, though I must admit I'm afraid to say it. That man that came before—not the Japanese man, the other one—was seen by Miss Cathcart at reception, hanging around outside. He didn't come in, but I don't know who he is, and it worries me. Though in normal circumstances, it would be good news that Sara is nearly able to go home." Dr. Edison stood outside the door of the room where Sara was just trying to get into bed on her own, a nurse standing behind her to help. "She did very well with the crutches today. I don't know why we didn't put her on them sooner. I'll have to have child services in because they'll have to find a place for her. I just don't know if we can protect her adequately anymore."

"Oh," said Lane. If Dr. Edison was worried, then it was a serious matter indeed. "My husband and I were thinking of having her at ours. There is a grandmother who is working to get back to Canada from Japan who might be the relative we want, but until then . . . of course, one can't just waltz in and take a child like that. If you think Sara could be discharged soon, perhaps I'd better meet with the child services people. Is it something you could help organize?"

Dr. Edison smiled. "Are you sure? It would be a wonderful thing to do because she knows you. It will be some work yet, as she gets better movement and so on. But you live out in the country, so it would be very good for her. Does that lovely little boy live near you?"

"Johnny. Yes, only three miles away, and we have three boys living right in King's Cove who are a bit rowdy, but very kind."

"I'm due to meet with someone tomorrow morning. They'd asked me to alert them as the time for her to leave the hospital approached. I'm going to recommend you, if I may. They will probably want to meet with you, of course, and perhaps see your home and so on. In fact, I'll telephone today and ask if you can sit in on our meetings right from the beginning. Will you be free tomorrow morning, nine thirty?"

"Yes, of course." Lane could feel a combination of anxiety and anticipation. She always had difficulty distinguishing between the two. Would they accept the proposal? And what would it mean to her? Would she be up to it? Well, she'd jolly well have to be. One thing she was absolutely certain of: King's Cove would take the little girl into its bosom wholly and completely. But the one thing she was left with was a good dose of Dr. Edison's worry about the strange man.

LATER, AFTER READING *The House at Pooh Corner* to Sara and Mr. Harris the bear, Lane closed the book and took Sara's hand. "Dr. Edison tells me you have been doing very, very well. That you are walking beautifully with your crutches."

Sara nodded solemnly.

"It means you will be able to leave the hospital soon."

Sara tilted her head a little, like an inquisitive bird. "Will my mother come for me then?"

Lane felt her heart seize in her chest. Breaking. This was what it felt like to have your heart break. She took a breath in and exhaled, taking Sara's other hand, holding them both, folded into the warmth of her own hands.

"No, my little angel." She stopped and looked down. How could she tell her this? "You know that explosion that hurt you? Your mother was very badly hurt." She hesitated. "She died." She wanted to say "and went straight to heaven," but she didn't know if the little girl even had a concept of heaven, any more than she had herself.

"She is with my father? He died too," Sara asked very quietly after a moment.

"Yes," Lane said. "Yes, that's right. She is with your father. But do you know what I know? She loved you very, very much. Better than anything, and I'm sure she is watching over you right now." For some reason Lane found herself being quite certain that this was true. She understood Sara's subdued reaction to such a huge loss. It would take time for her to fully comprehend.

LANE ARRIVED HOME much later than she had anticipated and stood at the window watching the drawn shadows of the dying day. She had sat with Sara long after she had finally gone to sleep, her little face composed and somehow knowing. She had told Dr. Edison, who said she would alert the morning staff to be extra kind, and the night staff to be on the lookout in case Sara woke. "I hardly need to remind them," she'd said. "Everybody loves her here. They'll miss her when she leaves." She'd put her hand on Lane's arm. "But how are you?"

Lane had shaken her head. "My mother died when I was very young. I think it is such a big thing that one hardly knows how to be inside a loss like that. I hope so very much that the grandmother can come, that she is kind, that she will have the strength to care for her. I almost wonder if Sara somehow knew all along. We'd assumed the shock had caused a sort of amnesia, but I now think she always hoped her mother would come for her, and yet somehow knew she wouldn't."

With a sigh she went into the spare room and looked critically at its sparse furnishings. The narrow closet was full of clothes they stored during the changing seasons, and the counterpane was one that had been left by Lady Armstrong. It was a sort of dusty, fading beige. From the point of view of a child living here, it lacked nearly anything that was warm, playful, or comforting. The last person to occupy the room had been a flinty Russian spy, who, she reflected now, probably loved its punishing meagreness.

If it transpired that they would be permitted to have Sara until such time as her grandmother was able to come, she would go into Hudson's Bay and buy some cheer for this room. It would make the room more attractive in any case, even if Sara were not allowed to come.

"INSPECTOR DARLING! GOOD to see you. Come in." Guilfoil showed Darling into the inner offices of the RCMP with a certain largesse. "What can I get you? We don't often have you down in this neck of the woods. I feel it ought to be celebrated."

"Thank you, nothing at all, and thanks for seeing me on short notice. I come under slightly false pretences, I'm afraid. I am representing my wife and a friend of hers."

"Oh, dear," Guilfoil said, smiling, "an invidious position. And what can we do for the ladies today?"

"Well, I hope not invidious. Both of them have very good reasons to believe that the bomb from King's Cove is in fact of Japanese manufacture and has nothing to do with the Doukhobors. I cannot tell you precisely how they know this, as they were unable to share much with me. However, I do believe it to be the case. My wife, mindful of the request from your officers not to interfere in your part of the investigation, has asked me to come along and talk with you."

"I see." Guilfoil sighed and picked up a glass paperweight, rolling it in his hand. After a long moment he said, "Isn't your wife friends with the father of one of the Sons of Freedom we arrested?"

Darling noted he reeled out the full title of the organization, as if to make absolutely clear they were likely all criminals. "Yes, that's right. Old Mr. Barisoff. And you're also right if you are going to mention that no doubt she feels they ought to be let go if they are not responsible for this particular explosion. But even that is not the point of this visit. The second woman, a Mrs. Cartwright, is extremely concerned that there has been no publicity or warning to the public about this bomb, or other bombs like it. According to her, they were sent over in quite large numbers from Japan during the war and landed all up and down the coastal mountains from Oregon to Alaska. Most did not go off, but it turns out they are in effect unexploded bombs and can be set off very easily, as was the case with our bomb. There was a family somewhere in Oregon that were all killed when they ran across one of these things. Mrs. Cartwright would like to see some sort of notification to the public to stay away from them to prevent any further deaths. It is my understanding that the military and the RCMP have not been entirely forthcoming about them."

Guilfoil went in for another long bout of silence. "Of course, if that is the case, I imagine they are wanting to prevent any sort of panic among the public. And when all is said and done, I imagine that if such bombs were sent over with balloons, they would be widely scattered across forest and mountain. The chances of running into one in the wild would be very slim."

"Not in the case of Mrs. Sasaki Harold." He'd not mentioned balloons. Obviously Guilfoil was perfectly well aware of them, and knew, without a doubt, that the bomb his men had scraped off the ground in the clearing at King's Cove was indeed just such a one. He'd said enough, he decided. Guilfoil would not commit himself to any particular course of action, he knew, but he might well act in a way appropriate to the circumstances the minute Darling was gone. He stood up. "Incidentally, the uncle of the dead woman has turned up. He was looking for her and is understandably distraught

372

to learn she has died. I thank you for letting me show Dr. Miyazaki her remains, but as they are still officially in your custody, I wanted to mention that her uncle, Mr. Sasaki, may want at some point to see her and bury her."

"Quite right, Darling," Guilfoil said. He'd spent the better part of Darling's speech filling his pipe, and he held it clamped between his teeth, emitting a fragrant stream of smoke ceiling-ward. He stood up to join Darling, took the pipe from his mouth, and rested it in the large glass ashtray on his desk. "Let me know, then, when that looks likely to happen. I don't think she's got too much more to tell us."

It was difficult, Darling thought, as he made his way up along Front Street back to the station, to feel entirely satisfied with this interaction. Did Guilfoil already know the bomb was Japanese? It was likely, he realized now, that even among the fragmentary remains, there might have been Japanese script. And if so, why were they still holding the four Doukhobor men? With a sinking heart he wondered if Guilfoil might want to cover up the origin of the bomb so it could be pinned on the Russians. He shook his head. Guilfoil might be Victorian in his views, but he surely was honest. Had Darling done enough to convince him? He wasn't quite certain, and he imagined that he might be rightfully called a coward by his wife.

Back in his office, pipe back in his mouth, Guilfoil was feeling the same way. It irked him that Darling was right, though he gave a mental lift of his hat to his not having pressed the point, and not only was he more than likely going to have to have his four Freedomites released, but he might have to craft some sort of warning to the public about something no one might run into again for another fifty years. In both cases he was bound to feel, and, what was worse, look, foolish. It further irked him that he'd had a very similar conversation with some blighter from the federal government about the same thing a day ago. He'd have liked to tell the man to go jump off the top of Elephant Mountain, but out of respect did not. It had seemed to him that Mr. Smith—who could believe that name?—might, in some way he would never fathom, outrank him.

He thought about Darling's wife, Lane Winslow, and again, for the third time since Darling had left him, shook his head. It never did to have the ladies involved in this sort of thing. This irked him as well. That they knew what they were talking about was obvious, just as it was unseemly. Well, he wasn't accountable to a rabble of women, that was for sure. He'd act as he felt the circumstances warranted when he jolly well felt like it, he thought defiantly. But suddenly imagining a headline that said, "RCMP Gets Wrong End of Stick, Fails to Warn Public of Bomb," he picked up his phone.

"Fryer? Get in here."

CHAPTER THIRTY

"HE'S NOT OUR MAN, I think," Darling said with a sigh, his whisky resting on his chest, his feet next to Lane's on the grate of the Franklin. "I mean, he is for a break-in, I suppose, but realistically the jeweller had been dead for hours and the back door had been open."

"Why didn't he steal anything?"

"It was never his intention. He was looking for Harold and didn't find him. The minute he saw the state of the place he legged it, sure that he'd be blamed for the mess. I'm keeping him in the clink because I still haven't got a murderer, and he really has nowhere else to go. I don't know if it is cruel and unnecessary to keep him there when he's just found out his niece is dead, or a kindness just at the moment. Terrell's a marvel, by the way. He said that when we do let him out, his landlady has agreed to have him in a room that's just freed up. I can't think how he persuaded her." He lifted his glass. "Constable Terrell!"

They clinked and Lane said, "His landlady must be one in a thousand. Not only was she willing to take Terrell in the first place—I wouldn't like to think how that first meeting went, though perhaps she was fine about it from the start—but being willing to put up a bad-tempered old man who has been under arrest is stellar on her part."

"Terrell might have omitted that bit about the arrest. She's a remarkable sort of landlady, to be sure, but don't underestimate Terrell's charm. And I'm sure he drew on his status as a policeman to reassure her that he would keep her safe if need be."

They sat amicably for some minutes, listening to the gentle whoop of the fire.

"What about the other fellow? You didn't seem too convinced about him either."

"We'll let him go. He's promised to go back to the rooming house we found for him last time, but I doubt he will stay long. He did have some of the stolen jewellery, and tried to sell it on, but I just can't see him as the killer. The mystery there is that Mrs. Harold said what he had was only a portion of the jewellery. The expensive watches and rings were not found when we turned him upside down and emptied his pockets. Figuratively, of course, before you think we are brutes. He finally confessed to having seen the door open when he was scouring for things in the bins in the back alley and went in to help himself."

"It's looking like you might have two thieves? One murderous, one opportunistic?"

"Yes, well, possibly," Darling said, staring into the fire. "The peculiar thing is that neither of them saw the body, according to what they are saying. I'm not surprised, I suppose. I was in there during the day and nearly didn't see him. In the dark with the lights out it would be impossible. I imagine Booker went straight to the front of the shop without looking at anything because it was somewhat illuminated by the street lights, but you couldn't see a thing in that office." He sighed and took another drink. "I see you've done a map," he said at last, looking at the map where Lane had laid it unfolded over the sofa back.

"I'm afraid it's offered no insight." She put her drink down and got up to fetch the map. "Do you like my new innovation with the coloured pencils? I got the idea from the London Underground map, of which I am very fond for its completely inaccurate accurateness. It hasn't helped me solve this for you, I'm sorry, darling. I think you'll have to muddle through on your own with your men, but look at how the lines link people and places. It's as if we all have threads linking us with people and places all over the world. If you look at it carefully, even Sara has a thread that goes all the way to Cornwall, and another that goes all the way to Japan. Oh! I must add her great-uncle and grandmother in tomorrow morning before I go into town. I'm meeting with the welfare person at nine thirty." She put the map down on the window seat and came back to sit with him. "I mean, when I think of the threads, I might draw across the world from my own life and travels . . ."

"Hmm. When I think of mine it would be a solid line between here and Vancouver. Nothing too ethereal, I'm afraid."

"Nonsense. There is the war and England and bombing raids over Germany. There's occupied France where you crashed, and that French farmer who hid you. And don't forget, you are connected to me. There are all my threads you'd be linked to, as well."

"I never forget I am connected to you." He reached out and took her hand and kissed it.

"And think," she said, "somewhere in all the maze of threads lies the reason for the murder of Mr. Harold. That much I'm sure about, though I cannot begin to see what it is."

Darling groaned. "Do you never stop?" He sat up. "Time to down tools and go to bed. I have a long day tomorrow of trying to find who the man was who visited Sara but was not allowed in. And let us not forget there is an actual murderer to be found as well. I expect an impatient summons from Dalton any minute." Dalton was the mayor, whose chief delight seemed to be harrying his underlings for not fixing things right smartish.

"Look who never stops," Lane said, smiling, and kissing his hand in return. "But I am worried about that unknown man as well. Dr. Edison said he'd been seen outside the hospital again. The business about his hands is interesting. The nurse said he had hands like someone who delivered coal."

"That's right. She said something black was sort of embedded in his fingers. Coal, but what else might do that?"

"A railway man? A miner? A metalworker of some sort? What sort of tools do metalworkers use? They must all use tools that would fit the bill. I'm worried about Sara."

"She'll be perfectly safe in the hospital," Darling said. "Now let's get some sleep."

But Darling did not sleep. It was as if the sound of deep breathing from his wife next to him freed him to begin thinking. What were the peculiarities of this case? Akio Sasaki, certainly, entering the shop but taking nothing, if that was true. Mr. X getting into the shop, breaking it up, perhaps taking watches and jewellery—Mrs. Harold had said the most expensive they had on hand—killing Mr. Harold and ransacking the place. Booker taking advantage of the chaos of the evening to pop in and help himself. The same, or a different, Mr. X, trying to visit Sara. Why? In what way was Sara's fate tied to the break-in, besides the fact that her uncle had been killed? Then the break-ins at the law office and the Harolds' now empty house. Only not break-ins. No sign of break-ins at all. Missing papers, a deed? A note from the dead man? This ever-present theme of searching, searching.

After some time, his breathing began to slow, and he could feel himself entering that pre-sleep state of muddled thinking. He saw himself by the sea, watching the sun glinting off the water, a storm coming on in the distance. He felt the warmth of the water and sun, the premonition of darkness only just grazing his consciousness, and streams of coloured lines growing up on the shore behind him, climbing, up, up.

When he woke in the morning, he would know this for a dream.

THE MEETING WITH Mrs. Harkness, from the city welfare office, took place at the hospital. She was an uncomfortable mixture of tense and fluttery, wanting somehow to lay down the law, but in a constant flap of worry. She had a tired beige hat that lay flat, as if it were a hand on her head, holding her in place.

"It's unusual," she said. "I don't know . . ."

"How do you normally find foster homes?" Dr. Edison asked.

"People offer. There's a little money in it, you see. We don't have very much call for it, though sometimes for some Indian children. I don't know who'd be willing to take a Japanese child, though."

"There you are, then. Here is a woman who is willing. And she has the added benefit of knowing the child. She visits nearly every day and has even found a little boy who was her playmate, who lives nearby."

"We would have to vet you," she said, addressing Lane, "in the normal way."

"Of course," said Lane. "Any way you like. My husband is the chief of police here. And I have wonderful neighbours. And there would be no question of money."

"But you say you live over thirty miles out of town. It will be very difficult to monitor a placement that far away." Flutter, flutter.

"Why don't you come out and have a look at the house? We've a very nice school nearby as well. I taught there briefly." Lane crossed her fingers that she would not be asked for how long. Two weeks was hardly a teaching career.

"Of course, you *are* English," Mrs. Harkness said with anxious hesitation. Apropos of what, Lane wasn't sure. "Well, when can I come out? I do have a little time this afternoon, since time is of the essence, I understand."

"It is indeed," said Dr. Edison with a note of satisfaction. They had secured the ground.

"That will be lovely. You can follow me out if you'd like to go soon," Lane said, relieved as well. "If I am approved, I would like to buy some things for the room." They weren't completely out of the woods, but she could tell from Mrs. Harkness's demeanour that it was—she rather liked this expression—in the bag.

"SIR, THE MAYOR," O'Brien called up the stairs.

"Of course! That's all we need. Put him through."

"Right you are, sir, I'll send him up."

Bother! Had Dalton heard him? Darling got up at the sound of the mayor clumping up the stairs, and prepared to welcome him, experimenting once or twice with smiling convincingly. It made his cheeks hurt.

"Sir, good afternoon. Come in. It's unusual for you to stop by. Shall I get some tea sent up?"

Dalton dropped tiredly into the passenger-side chair. "Why can't you have a downstairs office?" He grumbled. "I don't suppose you have something a little stronger in your desk drawer?"

Darling shook his head with genuine regret. Something stronger would be helpful to them all. "I'm sorry, sir."

"Every fictional inspector keeps a bottle of whisky on hand."

"Yes, sir. What can I do for you, besides that?"

"Where are you on the murder of that fellow, Harold? The shop is still closed up with that sign on it. It makes an unsightly blot in the middle of Baker Street."

"I'm afraid the state of the shop is not in my purview, sir. That would be up to Mrs. Harold, and she has not found herself able to cope just yet." He hesitated. Should he explain about Akio Sasaki having gone into the shop about the time of the murder, or, he realized, a little after? The shop had already been ransacked by the time Sasaki had gone in the second time. He thought Dalton might be the kind of man to leap on this in an unhelpful way. "We are making some progress in amassing our facts. There have been several more break-ins that we believe may be associated with the murder itself. They have an unusual flavour to them."

"'Unusual flavour'? What the devil is that supposed to mean? Are the townspeople in danger? Can't have that."

Crossing two fingers ever so subtly, Darling said, "No, sir. I don't believe they are. The break-ins have all involved searching. Whoever did kill Harold searched thoroughly in the store office, and, possibly, has gone through the lawyer's files, and has gone into Harold's house and searched it very thoroughly as well. This, we believe, indicates it has very specifically to do with Harold himself, and is someone who wanted something from him." Besides, he thought, the whereabouts of Sasaki's niece.

Something about the little girl, Sara, floated into Darling's head. Something not right. A blue line connecting her to something. It had connected her to Harold, but now it

382

was floating, severed, looking to attach itself to something else . . .

"Well?" Dalton's voice pierced his thoughts.

"Sir?"

"What are you doing about it? You're a detective. Detect! This sort of thing unsettles the place, and sooner or later people start thinking it's my fault."

Ah, Darling thought. That's where the dog lies buried. One of Lane's expressions, and apt. And in the next moment he realized people would blame Dalton, and he, the head of the Nelson Police, was Dalton's man, and it was his job to solve the case as quick as. "Yes, sir. I do appreciate the urgency and the unsettled town." He wanted to add, "We're working as fast as we can," but that would edge into whining, which was undignified. But the thing was, he believed they were. "We believe it might have something to do with his will and are following this thread." They weren't, but he saw quite clearly, suddenly, that that was exactly what they had to do. Look much more closely at the will.

When Dalton had been ushered out, Darling called Ames and Terrell to his office.

"The will. We should look more closely at that will. There might be something there."

PADGETT OPENED THE file and pulled out several sheets to show Darling and Ames when they arrived at his office a short time later. "There are two parts of the will. Everything in one of the documents goes to the missus. And then there's another part, which Harold wanted kept secret from his wife. It's for the proceeds of an English property, and half of that was to go to Harold's brother, and half to Humphries."

"Secret from his wife? What does she think of that?" Darling asked.

"That's the strange thing. She hasn't been in to ask about the will at all. I did call her, but of course I understand she is not living at home just now. I think she just expects it's all coming to her."

"Ron Harold's younger brother has been dead for some time. Did he not alter this part of it?"

"No. I think at first it was because he couldn't face it, and then I suppose he thought, as we all do, I guess, that he would have plenty of time to change it. And, in fact, his wife dropped off a note to me, in a sealed envelope, oh, gosh, it must have been the day Ron died. I was surprised to read that he now wished all of the English property to go to his niece, Sara Sasaki Harold, in trust with her mother Ichiko Sasaki Harold until her twenty-first birthday. You could have knocked me over with a leaf! I had no idea he even had a niece."

"Can I see that?" Darling asked, looking expectantly at the pile of papers in the file.

Padgett looked uncomfortable and cleared his throat nervously. "Well, that's just it, you see. I can't find the note. I should have put it in the file, but I didn't. I suppose it's not grave, but if anyone wanted to contest the will, I would need to have the paperwork."

"Is that what someone could have been after when someone came into your office?"

Padgett shook his head. "Oh, dear. I hadn't thought of

that. I don't see how, though. No one would have known about it. I don't think Mrs. Harold did because she would have had something to say about the whole thing, believe you me. I'm presuming, as the envelope was still sealed when she dropped it off, she just thought it was some ordinary communication about something else."

"Did Martin Humphries know he was to get half the English property?"

Padgett shrugged. "That I couldn't tell you. It was property from a relation of both of theirs, so it stands to reason, though why he wasn't left his portion independently, I don't know. Ron told me he sold the property and left the proceeds in England many years ago."

Darling frowned. "Why not bring it over then, divide it up, put it to use?"

"I seem to recall it was something about a rainy day. If his death teaches us one thing, Inspector, it is surely to do things now because the future is not guaranteed."

"I assume under the provisions of that note, the entire proceeds would go to the child when she is twenty-one?"

"Yes, that's right. I'm afraid poor Humphries would be out of his half."

"Can you look for the note and let me know the minute you find it?" Darling still had trouble believing completely in the "break-in" at Padgett's office.

"WHAT ARE WE to make of the note arriving at the law office the same day that Ron Harold is murdered?" Darling asked Ames and Terrell. All three were back in his office.

"Well, I'm not completely sure, but whoever it is kills Harold because he has a reason to," Terrell said. "He's searched the office, and perhaps he's found what he is looking for, and kills Harold. Or, he searches the office and doesn't find it, but for some reason he already knows something that makes it advantageous to get rid of Harold. The only one who fits the bill, I'm afraid, is his good friend Humphries. I think it's possible Ron Harold said something to Humphries that night about it."

"Brilliant," Darling said. "Well, that takes care of everything. We make our arrest and Dalton is off my back." But something in Terrell's speculation reminded Darling of that floating blue line. "Proof, Constable, proof. You can't just pull names, however likely, out of a hat."

Ames glanced at Terrell and winked a "You're one of us now!" wink, and Terrell's lips twitched at the corners.

"Yes, sir," he said.

"You know what I'm wondering, sir? What if it is Mrs. Harold? She gets everything if he dies," Ames said.

"Let's look at that," Darling said. "She bashes him in the head with whatever it was so she can collect the lot and run off with her lover." But then he thought, when his men had left, it was a consideration. Though Humphries suddenly did seem more obvious, Mrs. Harold perhaps had reason to kill her husband. But would she have struck him a blow like that? She would have to be stronger than he thought she was. It would be much easier to put a drop of strychnine in his morning coffee. That property in Cornwall. Had Humphries expected to get it all? Had he only just discovered he might only get half? Or worse, had he somehow discovered he wouldn't get any of it? Is that what Harold told him that night? He sat up and ran his hand feverishly through his hair. "Oh, saints preserve us! How did I not think of that?"

MRS. HARKNESS PULLED her car up behind Lane's and looked at the surroundings through the windscreen for a moment and then got out. She'd picked up her handbag and was positioning it over her wrist when she appeared to think better of this, and she tossed it back onto her passenger seat.

The weather had decided to be helpful, and the garden was flooded with sunlight, showing the gleaming white house and its blue spruce by the front door to its best advantage.

"Please, come in," Lane said. She'd been about to make some apologetic noise about what sort of state the house might be in, but, she thought, it was in rather a good state since Darling always tidied up the bedroom and she didn't like to leave unwashed dishes sitting around.

"It's very beautiful out here," Mrs. Harkness observed cautiously.

"Thank you, yes. The minute I saw this place two years ago when I first arrived, I knew I could live nowhere else. And I've been proven right. Can I put the kettle on?"

Shaking her head, Mrs. Harkness said, "No, thank you. It's a long way out and I have to get back. Can you just show me what would be her room, the bathroom, the kitchen facilities, and so on, and then I'll just take a wander around to see about safety, if you don't mind."

Lane took her first to the spare room, suddenly worrying about what would be unsafe. Here she did apologize. "It's very bare just now, but I'm going to buy a new counterpane and I think a little bookshelf for her books—she loves books—and do something about the curtains."

"These watercolours are rather lovely," Mrs. Harkness said unexpectedly. She had stopped before a pair showing the view of the lake from the porch, and the view of the house from the lawn.

"Oh. Thank you. They were done by an elderly friend." She hesitated marginally before saying *friend*. The painter, a Russian, had not been, strictly speaking, a friend, but she thought it best to keep this to herself. A woman with Mrs. Harkness's sense of responsibility would hardly place a child in the care of someone who hobnobbed with spies. And there was Mr. Smith. Really, she thought with irritation, she'd like to get out of the business of having anything to do with spies completely.

"Lovely." Mrs. Harkness looked around the room. "Does this window open?"

"Yes, indeed."

"Good. Children need fresh air."

Lane smiled and nodded. As if there wasn't a plenitude of the stuff all around them in King's Cove!

"The bathroom, then."

When the whole thing was over, Lane watched Mrs. Harkness drive off in a whirl of dust and then collapsed onto her deck chair to gaze at the lake for a restoring minute. The woman had said she was inclined to approve and she would write a report saying so.

Having breathed in a sufficiency of cleansing, fresh, King's Cove air, she went to the telephone and called the hospital, asking to speak to Dr. Edison.

"I think it went well," she told her. "When might Sara be ready to leave?"

"I think as soon as possible. She's much, much too used to the place. She needs to get out and be among children her own age before she completely forgets how to be a child. Could we arrange something for as soon as tomorrow?"

"Yes, of course," Lane said. She looked at her watch. That seemed hurried. Something in Dr. Edison's voice said her worry was increasing.

"Inspector Darling is bringing the uncle this afternoon, soon, in fact, to visit her. I'll send Sister Evans in with him. She is very fond of her. And, of course, your husband will be there as well."

"Sounds like a bit of a delegation," Lane said. "I hope she's up for it."

"Will you be picking her up tomorrow?" Dr. Edison seemed anxious to establish this as a certainty.

"Yes. I'm thinking of asking Johnny to come with me. It will mean having him out of school, but I'm sure Miss Keeling and his father will agree to it. They can explore the place together," Lane said.

"I'm not sure how much exploring she'll be up to. She's still mostly wheelchair bound. She is improving, but slowly, with the crutches. Her burns are healing nicely, so I'll send along some dressings, but I'm worried about the pain. And of course, she's quite subdued, I think because of her mother. Oh, dear. Now I think of it, it's rather a lot of care she might need. Are you sure about this?"

"I certainly am. It's just an hour away if we need anything."

Dr. Edison sighed. "I'm so relieved. I don't mind telling you, I was a little alarmed about that strange man who came, trying to get in to see her. I don't think we've had anything quite like this happen before, and it makes me very uneasy."

"Yes, I see. Has he made another attempt?"

"No, thank God, just that he was seen outside yesterday. I'll be happy to have her far from here. What if we arrange to have a visiting nurse come out a few times just at the beginning?"

"Yes, that's a splendid idea. It'll give me some reassurance as well, that I'm not completely botching things."

Dr. Edison laughed. "I'm sure you are quite incapable of botching things."

Dr. Edison was not wrong. While things were most definitely botched, it could not, in fairness, have been laid at Lane's door.

CHAPTER THIRTY-ONE

August 1910

❝ I T'S JOLLY NICE OF YOU, Auntie. Mother sends her regards."

"I thought a little break from the city might do you well."

Martin Humphries put his leather bag down and looked in amazement at the great, bright open foyer of this house he'd only heard about but never been in. He had grown up hearing that Aunt Imelda was eccentric. And rich. In his family she was referred to as "mad as a March hare."

"How is your mother?"

"Oh, you know."

"I don't, or I wouldn't ask. Ah, Biggs, can you get young Martin up to his room. Tidy up; we'll have tea and then walk down to the village. There's a fisherman there I want you to meet. He's agreed to take you out with him, provided you do a bit of work."

Martin smiled in surprise. "I've never been on a boat out at sea. What sort of work?"

"Don't get excited—you won't be sailing around the Cape of Good Hope, just going out to open waters to fish. It'll be hard work, I expect. I don't know if you'll be up to it."

Martin snorted in amusement. "Oh, I'm up to it, don't you worry."

Imelda watched him up the stairs and shook her head slightly at how easily he'd taken the challenge. It spoke to her of a sixteen-year-old boy who had no self-confidence. Or too much. She'd agreed to this experiment because her niece had begged her. He'd been sent down from school after several incidents, she'd said.

"What sort of incidents?" Imelda had asked.

"Well, I mean, nothing dire. He struggles a bit with school. If we were working class he'd be apprenticed to some trade or other, but, well, you know."

He was such a charming boy. Lady Imelda supposed they were the worst kind. Charm without much in the way of brains or morals. The world was full of people like that. When the butler had returned, he hesitated and then said very quietly, "We'll need to keep an eye on him."

Imelda looked at him in surprise. "For what reason?"

"Perhaps I misspoke," Biggs said, turning to leave.

"You never misspeak. What worries you?"

He hesitated. "He seems rudderless, madam. Under the circumstances, the fishing boat seems a good idea."

Laughing, Imelda said, "That's rather good. Tea in, say, twenty minutes?"

"Madam."

TERRELL SMILED. "**SO** far, not very much. I don't get out that often because of work." This was in answer to a question from Williams the bank teller about how expensive it was to keep a bike.

"I envy you. My girlfriend has put her foot down. Her cousin was killed jackassing around on a gravel road, so no bike for me."

Terrell wanted to say, "My girlfriend likes my bike," but of course he had no real right to call her that, so instead he said, "They can be dangerous, that's for sure. I was lucky; the teaching in the military was pretty good."

"That's it as well," Williams said ruefully. "She's just glad I came home in one piece from Europe. Now then, you want to open a savings account?"

His mouth open to reply, Terrell stopped at the sound of a door slamming so hard it reverberated in the vast space of the marble foyer, causing everyone to jump and look.

What everyone saw was an angry man storming out of the manager's office and making for the exit, where he tried to slam the glass door onto the street. What Terrell saw was Martin Humphries, his face contorted and red with rage. What he thought was, Now then, what's going on here?

The teller was shaking his head when Terrell turned back and then he shrugged. "Sheffield, that's the manager, *can* be pretty firm."

"You think he was trying to get a loan?" Terrell said, as casually and offhandedly as he could manage.

"It's not for me to say, of course. How much would you like to put in?" Then Williams leaned forward. "He could probably use a loan," he said sotto voce.

Terrell noted the lift of the chin toward the front door. "Fifty dollars for just now, thanks."

At the café, where he'd agreed to meet Ames for a quick cup of coffee, Terrell described the scene.

"I'm surprised Humphries could get that mad. He seems pretty mild-mannered to me. Well, you know, unless he . . ." He looked up at the approach of Marge with their coffee. "She doesn't even ask us anymore. Just brings it. What if I wanted tea?"

"She'd throw you out," Terrell said.

"You got time to sit around here drinking coffee?" Marge asked, having delivered the coffee with a force that a lesser hand would have caused to slop over onto the table.

It was hard to know what to say to this. She had a point. Ames just smiled and thanked her.

"With you two on the job it's surprising we're not all dead," she said, turning to make sure everyone else in the café could hear her.

"That's it. I'm buying a Thermos like O'Brien's," Ames said. "What are you thinking?"

Knowing he didn't mean about Marge or a Thermos, Terrell said, "It's just interesting that he was in such a rage about, I'm guessing, not getting a loan. It makes me think he's desperate. Didn't he say he was doing very well?"

"Yes, now I think of it. Very well. So how did he get into the bank manager's crosshairs? Maybe he's lied about how well he's doing."

OF COURSE, THE whole of King's Cove was atwitter about the arrival of Sara. Lane spent the morning organizing

Sara's room. She was especially pleased about the eider-down coverlet with the beautiful red roses on it, and as she still had a couple of hours before picking Harris up for the trip to town, she went over to the post office. She arrived to find nearly everyone in King's Cove. Mabel and Gwen had both elected to come down to collect the mail, Angela was there and Reg Mather, holding forth much as usual. They all turned expectantly when Lane arrived.

"Do you have everything you need?" Mabel asked first. Practical as always. Clearly everyone knew Sara was arriving that day.

"Heard you're taking Robin Harris with you. Is that wise?" Reg Mather and Harris had an antagonism that went right back to the Great War. Not three years before, this had culminated in Harris breaking every window in Reg's Morris with a tire iron.

"Mabel made a very nice cake with coconut icing. I'll bring it down later," Gwen said. Everyone ignored Reg as a matter of course.

"I've got a nice pile of the boys' books they seem to have lost interest in. Do you think she'd like some of their Dinky toys?" Angela asked.

"Thank you so much. You're all so kind! Once she's settled, why not send the boys down tomorrow? I'm not sure how exhausting the whole thing will be for her. She's been practically bedridden, and it may be hard for her to leave the hospital. She might be anxious about it. Though I'm sure cake with coconut icing will help!" she said, turning to Mabel and Gwen.

"It'll be nice having a little girl here." Mabel looked ready to add something perhaps a little disparaging about boys, but she stopped herself because of Angela.

"The boys are over the moon. I think they are preparing some sort of welcome card at school today. I heard Johnny is getting the afternoon off to go with you?" Angela said.

"Yes," Lane said. Angela looked radiant, she thought, perhaps at the thought of having someone else to mother. "She knows him, and I thought it might ease the transition."

"Sounds like a bloody circus to me!" Reg grumbled. "Girl doesn't need all that to-do. Harris alone is enough to take ten years' growth off her. Mark my words, she'll get airs with all the fuss being made of her."

This from the man who gave himself airs to an exorbitant extent. Lane bit back an irritated riposte and said instead, "I'd best collect my mail and be off. Still one or two things to do."

Balancing a tin of brownies, a bouquet of sweet peas, and her mail in her right hand, Lane turned the handle on her door and went to the kitchen to deposit her cache. Then she stopped. Something on the periphery of her thinking, something to do with Darling's case. She made several attempts to capture it but shook her head at last. It was gone.

She put the flowers in her favourite blue glass vase and carried it to Sara's room, and then, back in the kitchen, with only a moment's unexamined hesitation, popped the lid off the tin. It was a George VI coronation tin, much loved and transported back and forth between Lane and Eleanor, who had an infinite capacity to bake wonderful things to put into it. The brownies looked—Lane checked the clock—delicious. Yes, time for a cup of tea, and only half a brownie. That couldn't hurt. She put the kettle on and settled down to look at her bills. The winter bill from the coal man and the electric bill. These would be better once the warmer weather took a firm hold. The month's bank statement. Ah! A letter from her grandmother.

The kettle whistled and she sloshed some water into the teapot, and there was that slight nudge again. It had happened when she'd come through the door. She put the lid on the teapot and walked back into the hall, staring out the now open door, but nothing came.

"Maddening!" she muttered and went back to prepare her cup. Then, while the tea steeped, she went into the sitting room and took down her map. She'd added the great-uncle and the hoped-for grandmother from Japan. But whatever she sought to explain, her lost thought was not to be found on the map. While she poured her tea, she wondered how the visit with the great-uncle was going, and again she looked at her watch. Darling had said they'd arranged to go at around eleven, after Sara had done some exercises and before her lunch.

Honestly, she thought, biting appreciatively into the brownie, the girl had been so worldly-wise about her mother, she wondered if she might also perhaps have a memory of her great-uncle. After six years it seemed unlikely, but she hoped there might be enough there that she wouldn't be afraid to meet him. Lane had understood from Darling that he was a bit growly and gruff. It was even possible he could be dangerous. Maybe therein lay the secret of why Sara had taken so readily to Harris.

It was only when she was in the car, waiting for Harris to come down the stairs, watching him close the door behind him, that she realized it had something to do with doors.

"You don't lock your door," she said after the good mornings.

"Don't be ridiculous. No one does. You don't, do you? I mean, maybe Eleanor locks the post office, because of the mail. We're safe as houses here."

"No. You're right. I don't either. Are you all ready?"

"What's to be ready for? She's not coming to live in *my* house, after all." He still was a bit sniffy about not being considered, though in his heart he understood why he wouldn't even get a look-in.

But Lane was only half listening. One break-in and two "walk-ins." No one in town kept their doors unlocked. Certainly not a house you intended to stay out of for a period of time, and certainly not a lawyer's office. Should she phone Darling when they got to the hospital? It was ridiculous. He'd only laugh. But . . .

"COME IN, MR. SASAKI, Inspector. She's a bit at sixes and sevens today because she will be leaving this afternoon," Dr. Edison said.

Akio Sasaki looked past Dr. Edison to the room where he could see a nurse talking with Sara, holding several books. His thoughts were in a turmoil and his chest clamped with anxiety. "Can I go in?"

"Let me just have a word with Sister Evans. She is very much Sara's favourite. Just in case, I'd like to ask her to introduce you to your great-niece."

Sasaki shrugged agreement, feeling his mouth suddenly dry and unable to work.

Darling, standing next to Sasaki, could sense his anxiety, and gave him a nod of encouragement.

Sister Evans came out of the room, and though a momentary look of concern crossed her face at the sight of Sasaki, who looked to her to be as curmudgeonly as an old man could get, she gave a friendly enough smile. "Mr. Sasaki, it is nice to meet you. It is wonderful that Sara can meet a member of her own family. I've told her you are here. I'm not sure she understands the concept of 'great' uncle, so I've said you are her uncle. Do you mind if I stay while you visit, just to make sure she is all right?"

Sasaki did not take his eyes off Sara, who was tucking her bear into the covers beside her. He nodded.

"Come along, then," she said, leading the way back into the room. "Sara, here is your uncle, come to see you."

Sasaki stood, holding his hat in his hands, gazing at Sara, drinking her in. She looked so like her mother! Memories flooded, threatening to overwhelm him. Little Ichiko laughing at the kitchen table, begging him to show her how he fixed a watch, how to play chess with the old man across the park. Ichiko, a young girl of fifteen, in tears when her parents left. Ichiko, who could always bring him round when he was mad.

He took a step forward, almost saying "Ichiko" and then saying instead, as if the word were foreign in his mouth, "Sara."

"Are you my uncle?" Sara had pulled the bear out from under the covers and now held him, pressed against her body with her right arm.

He nodded. "I am your mother's uncle. To you I am a great-uncle. Great-Uncle Akio, you can call me."

"That sounds even more important than a regular uncle."

He smiled, feeling his chest unclamp a little. Pulling the chair by the bed, he sat down, nodding, as if his head had taken a life of its own. "What is he called?" He pointed at the bear.

"His name is Mr. Harris. Are you his uncle too?"

"I guess so. Does he want an uncle?"

Sara nodded. "I think so. He only has me."

He wanted to say, "You would be enough for anybody," but he only continued nodding. "I hear you are leaving today." He regarded her still-bandaged arm and the lump of the cast on her leg under the covers. "I hear you are getting very good at walking. I would really like to see that!"

"I can show you! Is it all right, Sister Evans?"

"Yes, it's a very good idea. We've been a bit busy today, so we only practiced our exercises and how to get around in the wheelchair."

"That seems to be going all right," Dr. Edison observed to Darling where the two of them stood in the hall. "It's very generous, what you're doing. Are you sure?"

He shrugged and nodded. "The burden, if you could call it that, will fall on my wife, and she is quite determined."

Smiling, Dr. Edison said, "I should think once she is determined about something, there's no getting her off it. I must say, she's been a godsend. I think her visits have done more than anything to help Sara's progress. And of course, that nice young fellow, Johnny."

"And not Mr. Harris?" Darling asked, smiling.

She laughed again and nodded. "I think she's done more for him than he has for her."

"You're right about that. I don't think anyone in King's Cove knows what to make of him just now."

Sasaki had stood up to give room for Sara to be helped to her crutches. "That's good," he said. "That's very good. Soon you will walk better than me."

"Well," Dr. Edison said, watching them make slow progress down the hall to the patient lounge, "she is transforming more than one old man."

WHEN LANE ARRIVED at the hospital later that afternoon with Robin Harris and Johnny Bales, she sent them upstairs and asked if there was a phone she could use. Miss Cathcart at the desk hastily dropped her gum into the wastepaper basket under her counter and pointed to a glassed-in, closet-sized room.

"Darling," she said when she'd been put through to her husband. "It's me."

"I guessed as much. The voice rang a bell. I was finally able to place it. Are you at the hospital?"

"Yes, I sent Harris and Johnny up, but I wanted to tell you something I thought about. How did the visit go with the uncle this morning, by the way?"

"Swimmingly. Another cranky old man for her collection. What is it you thought about? I suppose you are about to tell me I've neglected an important clue."

"Don't be silly. It was just about the doors. It came to me when I was coming home with the mail and the brownies. I only had a half by the way. I'd like my virtue recognized."

"The day is young. I may still return home and find them all gone. What about the doors?"

"Eleanor did make them for Sara, you know. Well, I opened the door and walked in, and it came to me in bits and pieces. You've had a break-in. The jeweller's. Only it's not really. And then the shop, though I don't know if that was a break-in. But then you have two more where there is no evidence of break-in. I know you think the culprit is a pro and used a slim jim to pick the lock. But what if he had a key?"

"A well-bred woman should not even know a word like that. Are you suggesting the lawyer walked into his own office to upset his files, and then called us to say he'd been broken into? To what end? And then, perhaps, strolled into the Harolds' house with the key entrusted to him by his client and mussed that up as well?"

"Don't laugh. You know what they say about lawyers. Look, I have to go. I just thought, you know, that someone *might* have the keys. See you at home."

"Thanks ever so much. Do call again sometime. And save me a brownie. I'll need it after accusing a perfectly respectable lawyer of wasting police time."

Damn, he thought. It's been right in front of our eyes.

CHAPTER THIRTY-TWO

"THOUGHTS?" DARLING ASKED. HE WAS still in the grip of Lane's suggestion about keys. It seemed to him to be so obvious it could not be right. The three of them were in Darling's office.

"I still think it's something to do with the will," Ames said. "The will was made ten years ago, before William died. Now suddenly, just when that note with the change goes to Padgett, poof! He's done for."

"Very articulate," Darling said.

"When I was in the bank earlier, Humphries slammed out of there in a temper, and though he shouldn't have, the teller implied he needed money," Terrell said. "What if Humphries goes to the shop that night to tell Harold he's broke, and he wants his half of the money?"

Ames said excitedly, "Yes, and Harold tells him, 'No dice. Sorry, I'm doing something else with all the money. I'll be sending instructions to my lawyer.' So, let's say he kills Harold, thinking he should kill him now before he sends those instructions, only to find out Bill had a niece that no one knew about!"

"If," said Darling, "Humphries killed Harold and then finds out about Sara, it would make him extremely dangerous. If he did kill Harold, he has nothing to lose. The question is, does he know about Sara?" The watercolour came suddenly back into Darling's head for some reason. Why? Was there something there?

"Mrs. Harold is friends with the Humphries. She might have told them," Terrell suggested.

Darling smote his forehead. "Of course she did! She's upset about it herself and she's gone off to complain to them. And something my wife said—"

"Ha!" said Ames with satisfaction. "Miss Winslow!"

"Shut up, Ames," Darling said imperturbably. "She suggested that a professional with tools might not be the only person to get into the Harold house and the lawyer's office. Anyone with a key could do it. We had supposed it was a professional with a slim jim, but what if it is that he simply has keys? Humphries may have everybody's keys. He's the main locksmith in town, unless you want to just get a key duplicated at the hardware store. What if he's been quietly keeping copies of people's keys?"

"We should double check that Humphries needs money, but I bet we'll find he has got keys, while we've been stumbling over ourselves trying to figure out how the break-ins happened," said Ames.

"And, sir, remember Dr. Edison was worried about a man who tried to see Sara Harold? It might have been Humphries," Terrell said.

"It might indeed." Darling stood up. "And maybe this renewed desperate searching is because he's learned about Sara. Ames, you and I to Humphries, with a brief stop at Harold's house. Damn!" Darling smote his head again. "His hands! A key cutter's hands! All that metallic powder. Terrell, you to the hospital at once to make sure Sara gets away safely." He looked at his watch. "I expect my wife will be leaving just about now. If she's already left, make your way to King's Cove to make sure no one is following. Chance for you to take that machine on the road. It had better be as fast as it looks."

"It is, sir," Terrell said.

SARA SAT SIDEWAYS with her legs stretched out on the seat with a blanket over them. Johnny was on what remained of the seat, holding her hand. Both children were very quiet. And for that matter Harris wasn't saying much either, leaving Lane free to think about dinner. She hadn't shopped for any proper food for all she had cake and brownies at the ready. She tried to think about what might be provided by Bales. Certainly, cans of Spam or frozen fish sticks. She was sure she'd seen them in one of his frozen food cases. Perfect! She glanced back to look at the children, who seemed suddenly shy and quiet. She was about to speak to Harris when something caught her eye on the road behind them.

Not again! She clutched her steering wheel with both hands, and then looked again, this time in the side mirror. It was a brown car, a good way behind but keeping an unnervingly steady pace behind her. Not Smith, she thought. He drove a much later model blue car. She relaxed, wondering at her own fears, and went back to contemplating what sort of vegetables might go with fish sticks. In the back of her mind, though, there still was something about the car . . . no. Not the car. The man driving it. She glanced again. No. He wasn't doing what she thought. She'd had an impression that he'd been leaning forward over the steering wheel as if he had trouble seeing ahead of him.

Pulling up in front of Bales's store, Lane stopped and looked in the back seat. Sara had fallen asleep, her hand in Johnny's. Sara's eyes fluttered open, and she let Johnny's hand go. "Are we here?"

"No, not quite," Lane said, smiling. "We're just dropping Johnny at home, and we'll pick up some nice fish sticks for supper."

"Oh," Sara said, sitting more upright, her eyebrows drawn together in worry. She seized Johnny's hand again.

"Don't worry," Lane said. "He can come over to visit tomorrow because it's Saturday and there's no school for him. Would you like that?" She suddenly realized it was a good deal to ask of Mrs. Bales, who was busy with her other children, and Lane couldn't be the one to drive him over, as she could not leave Sara. Perhaps Angela would.

"I'll bring Snakes and Ladders," Johnny said, "and my best cars. When you're better we can go to the lake and catch minnows!"

Sara nodded, seeming to relax. Lane got out of the car and went into the shop, stopping at the door. The brown car must have turned off somewhere. She shook her head at her own uneasiness.

"Sara is most anxious to have Johnny visit tomorrow, if that would be all right," she said to Bales as she paid for her fish sticks and a bag of peas. She had a couple of potatoes still that she could boil and mash.

"Sure thing. Is the afternoon all right? He's got a few chores he does on Saturdays for me. Can someone pick him up?"

"I think Angela might do it," Lane said. "If it's nice we can have tea on the porch. The bakers at King's Cove have provided lots of sweets as a welcome to Sara."

Bales went to stand by the window. He saw his son leaning in the open car window talking to Sara. "It's unbelievable that she and her mother were up that hill the whole time and no one knew. Well, except my intrepid son." He turned back, sighing. "Kids, eh?"

A loud motor noise penetrated even through the closed door, and they both looked over to see a motorcycle arriving in a cloud of dust.

"Good gracious, that's Constable Terrell!" Lane said, taking up her bag of groceries. "Now, what's he doing here? Come meet him," she said to Bales.

Terrell had pulled off his goggles and was waving at Sara.

"Constable, you're a long way from base," Lane said.

"The boss. Just wanted to make sure you got home all right."

"Had he reason to think I might not?" Lane asked, frowning slightly. But why not, she thought, she herself had.

"You know the boss."

Johnny was now devoting all his attention to the motor-cycle, which absolutely dwarfed him. He walked around it, gingerly reaching out to touch parts of it, muttering "Wow!" under his breath.

Harris was sitting in the front seat of Lane's car, scowling and shaking his head. He wanted to say, "Bloody noisy machine," but there was Sara, sitting wide-eyed in the back. "You think Mr. Harris the bear would like a ride on that thing?" he asked instead and was gratified to see Sara nod and almost smile.

"Mr. Bales, meet Constable Terrell. Newest member of the Nelson Police Department," Lane said.

"How do you do." Terrell offered his hand.

Bales took it and said, "A fine machine; '35 or so?"

"That's right. Good catch. I bought it before I shipped out. I was in a motorcycle MP corps while I was in Europe."

"I think I'd better get Sara and these melting fish sticks home," Lane said. "We'll see you tomorrow, Johnny. You coming all the way?" she asked Terrell.

"I'd like to see you all the way home, if I might," the constable answered.

"There's a story there, I imagine. Right you are. We'll all need a cup of tea, I think."

In the car she said, "Why don't you join us, Robin?"

"Nah. I'll help you get her in and then I'd better get home."

"Mabel's made a cake with coconut icing." But in the back of her mind, Lane still wondered about that man, leaning so far forward in his brown car.

One of the many things she learned during the war was to know when to pay attention to her instincts. Something one thought was a threat might just as easily not be. When

408

she ascertained something wasn't a threat, her fear would dissipate. She took a moment, slowing as she turned up the sharp turn into King's Cove, to look back in the mirror. She could see the whole great curve of the road that ran along the lake, and the only thing visible was Terrell, kicking up dust on his bike. She could shelve this particular fear, she decided. Perhaps it was having a child she was responsible for that made her jumpier. This must be what it was like to be a mother. Alert to everything.

"Here we are!" Lane said as she pulled as close to the house as possible. Happily, King's Cove and her house were looking their very best in the afternoon sun.

Harris held out his arms to pick up Sara, who, rubbing sleep from her eyes, lifted her bear toward him and then allowed herself to be picked up. Lane brought the bag and crutches, and opened the door, leading them to the newly refurbished bedroom.

"There, what do you think?" Lane said as Harris set Sara on the bed.

"I can see outside!" the girl said.

Thinking of how dreary the hospital must have been for her, with one window far from her bed, Lane said, "You can indeed, and on warm days we can open the window. Shall we do that now?" At Sara's nod, Lane lifted the sash and a waft of fragrant air came in. "Why don't you two look through the books in your bookshelf? I just have to go have a quick word with Constable Terrell and then we'll have something to eat."

"I have something else for you at home," Harris was saying to Sara as Lane left in search of Terrell.

She found him standing with his hands in his pockets on the porch, looking out at the lake.

"This is something," he said. "You are truly blessed with this view to look out at, Miss Winslow." He had wavered, almost saying Mrs. Darling like O'Brien did, but Ames always called her Miss Winslow. "Do you ever just stop seeing it?"

She shook her head. "I don't. It's different almost every minute. When I was away last month, I missed it all the time." She stood beside him, silent for a moment. "Constable, did you notice a brown car, male driver, as you were following?"

He nodded. "I did, ma'am. He was going pretty slowly so I passed him. I couldn't tell if he was looking for an address or just worried about the gravel road. I kept an eye out in my mirror and saw him turn off about a mile that side of that gas station we stopped at. What is it that worries you?"

"It'll sound silly, but I think I was worried he was following me. Did you get a look at him?"

Terrell shook his head. "He was wearing a hat and was turned away from me. That's what made me think he was looking for an address."

Lane took in a breath. "He was keeping pace with me all the way from the Harrop ferry. I don't know why I'm worried. The responsibility of a child, I suppose. I was followed before by a Canadian government agent who had got wind of the bomb."

Terrell wanted to be able to say she shouldn't worry, but he respected her instincts, and the strange man who had tried to visit Sara was not yet explained. Now he wondered again if that strange man was Humphries.

"I'll keep my eye out on my way back. It is hard to imagine why anyone would want anything with a child like that . . ." Terrell stopped. Humphries might, if he thought she'd inherit. "Unless it is you yourself that is eliciting the interest. Did you get a feeling from the government man that they were going to keep you in their sights? Or this place, perhaps, because of the bomb?"

"Of course, I don't know why I didn't think of that, though again, if the man turned off somewhere, it was nothing to do with me anyway. I'll feel better knowing you'll be keeping an eye out for him, though! If the truth be told," she added, dropping her voice, "I'm a bit worried about how I'll entertain a child, and make sure I've done the dressings right."

Terrell smiled broadly. "You'll be fine, ma'am."

"I'll make us all a cup of tea, then. I have cake and brownies thanks to the lovely people of King's Cove. They bake up a storm here."

"I don't think I can say no to that."

Cornwall, 1910

"MADAM." BIGGS STOOD just inside the doorway, clearing his throat.

Lady Imelda looked up from the letter she was writing. "Yes, Biggs. You look worried."

"I am, madam. I found the lad going through your things."

"My things? Whatever can you mean?" For a wild moment

she imagined him rummaging through her small clothes.

"Your jewels, madam. He claimed to be looking for a safety pin."

Lady Imelda nodded thoughtfully. "How interesting. Did he say why?"

"He said it was for his trousers. I directed him to the kitchen. Mrs. Gantry has a box in the sewing drawer."

"Thank you, Biggs."

Biggs inclined his head and removed himself.

Lady Imelda put down her pen and got up and began to pace. She stopped and looked out at the sea below. He would be out there now, with Roskilly the fisherman, who, in fairness, said the boy worked hard, though he wasn't well accepted by the other boys he worked with. She suspected he behaved arrogantly because he was from London. Well, it would only be for ten more days. His mother had called for him to come home to help his father on the docks in London. She was not deceived about the safety pin. He had, she knew, already pilfered several things: a small silver box, one of her silver napkin rings. This last was especially irritating because it was one of a set of eight with the family initials. She'd inherited them from her father.

The trouble was, she knew he had them but could not bring herself to subject him to the indignity of a room search; he was, after all, a relation. And indeed, she scarcely begrudged him these small items. She could well imagine coming from a tiny, crowded, dark house in what was close to being a slum, watching your mother scrimp and your father bring home what little he had left after the pub. You would come into a house like this, so full of sunlight and peace and silver, and think, She won't miss this one little thing. Doubtless his inventory of her jewels was to determine what item she might miss the least. In any case, she was still optimistic about the possibility of his reclamation. He seemed to be less impulsive, though his stealing might have been the result of his impulsiveness. But he had not got into any fights since he'd come to stay with her. His mother hadn't been entirely honest at first about the troubles at school but had finally confessed that his misdemeanours had included fighting. It had become clear that his fighting was not over particular conflicts that might be resolved, but as a result of an unthinking recklessness. The school officials had not felt he would be able to change.

At dinner that evening, when Martin had cleaned up and was digging into supper, she said, "I have made up my mind, Martin. In a few years, when you are a little older, and a little more certain of the path you wish to take in life, I will make sure that you have all that you need to start you out." Perhaps if he felt more certain of his own future, he would not resort to stealing.

Putting down his fork, Martin looked at her, at first frowning and then smiling; there was this brief moment when the frown and smile were still together on his face, making him, she thought, look slightly disingenuous. "Aunt Imelda, that is very good of you. I don't know what to say. I've been so afraid of ending up like my father, down the docks and nothing to show for it."

"That's good honest work, Martin, what your father does. It doesn't do to disdain it."

"No, of course not. I didn't mean anything by it. Perhaps I could go into the army or own my own shop."

"What sort of shop? Thank you, Biggs." She took up her refilled wineglass.

"I don't know. Something steady. I'd have something everybody needs. Shoes, gloves, hats."

That wasn't a bad thought. His public-school stint, albeit short, had given him good manners, and wiped the slovenly London East End speech out of him a bit. He could quite successfully run a little hat shop, if only he proved to be a good businessman. So far, he'd not demonstrated an ability to plan ahead, to take the long view, to save his pocket money, but he was young. There was, she hoped, time. "A little game after dinner? I believe it is your turn to deal."

"YOU MARK MY words, Mr. Biggs. He's a bad 'un. He'll rob her blind before she knows where she is. I don't care that he's family. The way he makes free around here, as charming as he is, it'll all end in tears," said the cook.

"I suppose you are right," Biggs said, blowing on the soup in his spoon. "But I don't think it'll be her tears. She seems to know exactly what he is. I think she thinks that kindness and overlooking will fix him up. Make up for his mess of a family. I think she feels guilty because her one niece copped the lot, and the other was sent off in disgrace because she was in the family way and was going to marry an unsuitable man."

"You can't blame her for her relations' sins. Make your bed and lie in it, I say!"

"I suppose madam feels the children shouldn't have to suffer for the sins of their fathers, but he may go a step too far one day."

"More fool her."

There were only four days left before Martin was to leave. That's when it happened.

CHAPTER THIRTY-THREE

"DON'T MAKE A RUCKUS. SHE doesn't need you all running around yelling." Angela stood at the door with her three boys—Rafe, Philip, and Rolfie—and Johnny Bales straining to see down the hall, jostling each other out of the way. Each of them carried a small gift. She, with a large glass jar of lemonade cradled in one arm, rapped on the door frame and called, "Helloo! The Bertolli visiting committee is here!"

"Hang on!" Lane called. She appeared in the hall with a tray of glasses. "We're around the back." She led them around the house, past the unfinished pond and the weeping willow, to the front lawn. There they found Sara sitting in her wheelchair with a blanket over her knees and Mr. Harris the bear on her lap. She had a book open but closed it when the children crowded around her.

Angela's boys all became shy at once and stood for a moment fidgeting and looking at Sara, and then they all said "Hi" at once. Lane and Angela filled glasses with lemonade and the children settled on the ground at Sara's feet. Lane gave a quick inclination of her head to Angela, and the two went to the bottom of the garden to look out at the lake.

"It doesn't do to interfere with the introductions, I don't think," Lane said. "You've outdone yourself with this lemonade. It's delicious. Thank you for bringing it."

"Lots of sugar. Works wonders. My word, what a view you have. We can't see the lake, even in winter." Angela turned to look at the scene unfolding behind them. "How is she doing?"

"She's very quiet. We tend to think a home will be better than a hospital, but the hospital is all she's known since the accident. It was quite noisy and busy there, when you think about it, and of course it's terribly quiet here. I sat with her until she went to sleep and kept an ear open through the night. The move exhausted her, but she looked quite perky this morning. Excited and nervous to meet your lot. The children will be very good for her. Thanks for bringing them."

"They've been very excited. Johnny, of course, freed from his pledge of secrecy, has told everyone at school about how he met her by accident and she lived at a secret house and all that. It's made Johnny quite a celebrity, the way I hear it."

The chatter behind them made them turn and the scene was, barring the presence of the wheelchair, as ordinary and delightful as any group of children could engineer. Toys were being shown, questions asked about the cast and her bandages and when she might be able to start school,

417

promises made about all the secret places they would go when she got better.

"Look at that. If children ran the world, we might all be better off," Lane said.

"You wouldn't say that if you saw my house at the end of the day! Still, it's lovely to see them getting along. They each thought very hard about what toy they'd want to bring her, and I must say, they've each made a bit of a sacrifice with a favourite. It's been fun seeing them be so generous for a change."

"I am certain this will hasten her recovery. Tomorrow Eleanor and Kenny are going to bring Alexandra, and of course, Harris has popped in several times today to keep an eye on her. She's learned that the racket of his tractor means he's nearby and she gets quite excited. I hope she'll sleep like a log tonight after all this commotion."

Angela shook her head. "It's completely weird to see him smiling. It's against nature."

"WE APPRECIATE YOU stopping by," Darling said. Humphries was in the interview room with his hands folded on the table, looking, Darling thought, amazingly non-chalant. Most people would have exhibited some nerves if they were called into the station for a chat. Ames sat nearby.

"Sergeant Ames will be taking notes. We are trying to amass as complete a picture of the activities of the victim, Mr. Harold, as we can, and as his close friend, we are hopeful you can fill in a few gaps in the days or hours leading up to his death."

Humphries nodded solemnly. "Yes, yes. Anything I can do to help. Poor Bertha! All this being unresolved must be very painful for her. Thank you for offering the station for this, by the way. I mean, I haven't done anything, obviously," he laughed, "but my customers might get nervous seeing the police at the shop."

"Quite. Now, can I take you back to June 10? That is the day before we found him. Can you recall seeing him that day?"

"Will this get back to his missus?" Humphries became suddenly conspiratorial. "See, he wasn't even supposed to be in town."

Darling remembered Mrs. Harold being so shocked because her husband was supposed to be making a trip to Vancouver. "I see. But he was with you?"

Ames looked up in surprise, watching the side of Humphries's head from his vantage point slightly behind him.

"Well, yes. He wanted to discuss something, and then he was going to go to Vancouver. He liked to drive at night."

Darling watched Humphries as he talked. He had a vague sensation that all of them were beginning to slide slightly on a slick surface. Why did Humphries bring up Harold's wife? She knew he liked to drive at night. "What did he want to talk about?"

Humphries made an almost imperceptible swallow. "It was just some business between us about a will. We had an aunt in common, I think you know, in the old country, and she died at quite an advanced age back at the start of the recent war. She left her estate to him. Of course, I didn't mind at all. She'd given me money to start my business and had helped me when I was a kid and left school. He felt he didn't deserve the legacy, so he'd made half out to me." He had to stop and clear his throat. "We had a very amicable discussion, shared a few memories of her. He met her once when I brought him there on leave in '16 or '17. It was the darnedest thing to find out we were actually cousins, well, second cousins of a sort." He tipped his head sideways and then straightened it. "At least, I thought they met only the once. Funniest thing, he told me she'd invited him out there in '18, after the armistice. At the time he told me he'd gone to visit a girl, but he was off seeing Aunt Imelda. Apparently, that's when she told him she was leaving everything to him. Of course, he was shocked, and tried to talk her out of it. Anyway, that's what he said. I know he was embarrassed about it because he didn't have the nerve to tell me until a couple of years before she died. That's when he made out half to me anyway. I told you, we were close. I made up my mind to emigrate after meeting him. It was hard to make a living in Blighty after the war. He made it sound grand over here. So, I decided to take what my aunt had given me and start up over here." He shook his head and smiled. "I think she felt some sort of responsibility for me because her side of the family had done so well, and my mother married, well . . . let's just say she married for love and repented at leisure.

"My parents spent what money they had to send me to a good school, but I'm not a school sort of person, really. I got sent down and so my aunt said she'd be happy to have me, maybe find something I could be good at. Apprentice me to someone. She never minded me not being good at school. She said it took all sorts."

"Did he say why she had proposed leaving him her estate?" Darling asked. He was curious now about how voluble Humphries was being.

Humphries shook his head. "No. I suppose she didn't trust me with it. But it didn't matter. She'd already given me a good portion to start up my business. He said he was unhappy about it and would give me half. That's why I wanted to talk to him. I understand with the war and all, not cashing in, but the war's been over for a couple of years now."

"You could use the money?"

There was the slightest flush of red in Humphries's face. "Oh, yes. I see what you mean. I could actually. The mine . . . I borrowed a bit more money than I could pay back with the mine as collateral. It's . . ."

"You led us to believe it was doing very well. Was it not?"

Humphries flushed again but said nothing.

"So, you went to see Harold and asked for your half."

"Yes," Humphries said at last. "Of course he agreed right away. He said that's what he'd always intended." Humphries leaned back, more relaxed now. "He said he was going up to Vancouver and as soon as he got back, we could visit Padgett and sort it out."

Ames looked up again and put a question mark next to this.

"And he never mentioned another disposition for the property?"

421

"Well, no. Obviously his half, the half he'd originally left to his brother, would go to Bertha if he died. I mean, it must go to her now."

"Are you aware that his brother had a wife and child that survived him?"

Another flush. "Yes. We just learned that. Extraordinary he could keep a secret like that."

"And you weren't concerned he'd change his will to make sure they were included?"

"No. He didn't mention them at all. I just said I needed my half of the money, and he . . ."

"He what?"

"Well, he just said that when he got back, we'd go to Padgett to arrange things."

"You had this conversation with him on the day he was supposed to be going to Vancouver?"

"Yes, that's right. He told me that he was going to drive overnight so that he could arrive and get his business done and get back."

"So, you met him at the store?"

"Yes, that's right. He was finishing up some things he needed for his trip."

"What time did you leave him?"

Humphries looked at the ceiling. "A little after nine, maybe? Gosh. I must have been the last person to see him alive! I left him finishing up his paperwork. It's bloody awful to think of someone breaking in and stealing everything and killing him when we just assumed he was happily on his way to Vancouver!"

Darling let this sit, and then started on a new tack.

"Were you responsible for any work on the locks at Padgett's law office, or at Harold's home? You see, both places were broken into, but there's so little evidence of any break-in that we wondered if there is something faulty about the locks that makes them easier to open."

Humphries looked startled and then put on an ingratiating smile. "Oh, dear. Well, I'm the main locksmith in this town, so yes to those questions. I'd be sorry to learn my locks would be easy to get into. They're the latest model. I'm certainly not aware of any flaws in them. But the tools for breaking into locks are pretty sophisticated nowadays, I expect. I could take a look at them for you. I might see some sign of damage you wouldn't have known to look for."

He's talking too much again, Darling thought. He'll get himself into a real muddle soon. "We might take you up on it," Darling said. "Do you keep a copy of the keys you've made?"

Humphries paused as if to think. "I do, as a matter of fact, yes. In case the householder loses the keys, they can always get one from me."

"Is that usual?"

"That's a good question, Inspector. Maybe it's not, I don't know. But I've always done it here as a favour. It's saved the bacon of more than one person over the years, I can tell you, and saved them the cost of installing a whole new lock."

"Quite. Do you still have those particular keys?"

Humphries nodded and then coughed and reached for the glass of water Ames had got him. "Sorry. Very dry in here. I have a touch of asthma. Yes, I'm pretty sure I do. I tie a label on them and drop them in an envelope and throw them in a drawer till they're needed. I haven't checked lately, but I expect they're there."

"I can't remember if I mentioned, but there was likely a break-in at the lawyer's office. Could someone have got hold of your key?"

Humphries raised his eyebrows. "Definitely not. I keep them very safe."

"You mentioned you were thinking of going back to England. Why is that?" Darling asked, infusing the question with friendly curiosity and a tone that suggested the interview was at an end. Ames closed his notebook at a barely perceptible sign from Darling and made as if to get up.

Relaxing now, Humphries said, "Well, we were going to go on a holiday with Ron and Bertha, but now with him gone, I'm thinking of moving back when I get my half. You don't want to let money go to waste, do you? With the setbacks here, frankly that half of the inheritance gets me out of a bit of a financial bind." He stood up. "Don't invest in gold mines is my advice." He winked.

"I'm sorry to hear that. I guess they are always a risky proposition. A tip from a friend?" Darling asked, standing.

"You could say that. More of a snake oil salesman, as it turns out. I was a little . . . well, it looked attractive. I was getting in on the ground floor and would realize significant profits once it got up and running. More fool me! I even tried to get Ron to put his money in, but he said he didn't have a taste for gambling. I should have listened. Gold mine turned out to run out of gold." He sighed and nodded. "I could have thrown all my money in the lake and got the same result. The missus wasn't happy, I can tell you. At least that's one problem I don't have to worry about. She's actually looking forward to the move. She's never really been out of Nelson, and she is dying to go somewhere else." He stopped and looked at each of them in turn, smiling. "I'm a bit pressed at the shop, actually. Is there anything else you'd like to know?"

"So when you left Harold that evening, the question of the money you needed was resolved?"

Humphries leaned back, relaxed, smiling. "Yes, indeed. I was relieved, I can tell you! I'd got myself into such a mess and I hadn't told the wife. Harold has always been the best of friends."

"And you left him at what time?" Would he change his answer?

Looking at the ceiling, Humphries considered. "Nine thirty? Before ten, anyway. He put his coat on and we left together. He was going to start his drive out to the coast."

"Together?" Darling asked in surprise. "Harold was at his desk when we found him."

Frowning, Humphries glanced at the door and back. "Oh. He must have gone back. I left him, anyway. I was tired. Had an early morning next day."

Darling clamped his lips together and nodded. "All right, Mr. Humphries. I'll ask you not to leave town until this is resolved. We may have to ask more questions as we clarify this matter."

"Right you are. Thanks, Officers. You know where to find me if you need me!"

Darling nodded, and just as Humphries was going out the door of the interview room, he asked, "What will you do now that he's dead? Are you certain about your half of the money? I understood there was to be a change in his will."

"Oh, I'm not worried about that. I'm sure Bertha will understand and honour what he said. She'd be getting it all now, I suppose. I don't reckon she'll give any to that kid if she can help it. She is very anti-Japanese."

AMES AND DARLING sat in Darling's office. "What do you think, sir?"

"What I think is that he is in this up to his neck, but I want to be careful not to jump to conclusions based on my growing prejudice about him. He seems so eager to help."

"I thought the same thing. It was interesting that he was having financial problems. The opposite of what he said before. That inheritance would have come just in time. But you can see he was making it up as he went along. He said Harold agreed right away to give him the money and then scrambled and said Bertha would give it to him. Which we know could not possibly be true, given the note changing the will."

Darling nodded. "I don't believe he's not worried. If he did kill Harold, he was killing the goose. There's no guarantee Mrs. Harold would share the estate if she even got it all, and we know the note is a change to leave all the English money to Sara. I've wondered if the note is missing because Humphries did go into the office with his key and take it out of the file, but I'm not so sure. If he'd found the

426

note, he'd have destroyed it, and to me he looks like a man who's waiting for the other shoe to drop."

"You're right, sir. I think Harold told him he was out of luck and all that searching was because Harold told him he was going to change his will."

"At a guess, you're right, Amesy, and what he was looking for was anything that showed who the estate was going to. It's certainly true that Harold intended at one time to leave half to his friend, but maybe he changed it because he thought the girl would have greater need of it. It was his to do with as he liked, I suppose. Though again, it is a mystery why Ron Harold got left *all* the money by this aunt."

"But would Harold have told Humphries about any change in his will? As far as we can tell, Harold kept the whole business of Sara and her mother from absolutely everyone."

"What if he said, 'Sorry, but I have to change everything about the will. I'm not going to be able to give you the money after all. I've written it all up, and I'm going to meet Padgett when I get back.' Now, if Humphries kills Harold, he's thinking he can prevent that from happening. All he has to do is kill him and recover the note Harold sent to Padgett."

"Yes, except Padgett said he'd already received it. It was too late. And what was all that business of Harold putting on his coat and their leaving together?"

"He sort of almost talks too much, sir."

"He sort of almost does, Amesy. I wish to God we had something to hold him on." It was at that moment that Darling decided he'd stop by Mrs. Harold's house to have just one more look at the damn picture.

CHAPTER THIRTY-FOUR

"YES?" THE BUSINESSLIKE VOICE SAID when Darling asked if he'd reached the offices of the BC Security Commission.

"I need to speak to someone about an orphaned girl here in Nelson who has a living relative, a Canadian citizen, currently residing in Japan." He wondered if there were one person designated for so specific a problem.

"Is the child being repatriated to Japan?"

Ah. Perhaps there was one department or person that dealt solely with *that*. "No. She was born here. I am hoping to have her grandmother come here to care for her."

"I see. I'll put you through to Mr. Taylor."

Darling explained his problem all over again and in much greater detail to Mr. Taylor.

Mr. Taylor sighed, sounding tired, as if this was but one more special request he was going to have to refuse. "Was the grandmother repatriated at the end of the war?"

"No. She and her husband returned to Japan in the mid-'30s to look after business, leaving a teenaged daughter in the care of the husband's brother. Because of the war the girl's parents were not able to return. I understand that the grandmother has applied to return to Canada. She is a widow and has learned she has a grandchild."

"The Japanese aren't allowed back here to the west coast, you know. Until recently there was a policy of sending them back to Japan. *That* went by the wayside." Darling couldn't tell if Mr. Taylor approved or disapproved of the cancelled policy. "But they aren't welcome back. There are a few Japanese who have Canadian passports who have managed to return, but they have gone on to Ontario. They are taking them there."

"I'm sure this woman has a passport. She is a Canadian citizen and thus a British subject. What I want is for her application to return to be looked at and hurried along. There is a nine-year-old girl who is recovering from dreadful injuries and is without either parent. Her father died in the war; he was not Japanese, by the way."

"A Canadian?"

"If by that you mean someone of English descent, then yes. The Sasakis are, after all, themselves Canadian."

Taylor ignored the jibe. "Did you say Sasaki? Just a moment. I think I had a note about someone of that name." Darling could hear the receiver being put down with a clunk, and then the sound of drawers being opened and paper being moved about. "Yes, here it is. I've already had a request on this matter. It's in hand. I don't understand why that mother and child just didn't stay on in Vancouver.

She could have persuaded the authorities she was entitled to." He sounded slightly petulant as if their failure to "stay on" was occasioning him a lot of trouble now.

"Her husband's ship was sunk by Germans at the beginning of the war. It's possible that in the confusion, and without him, she didn't know that. I don't know all the ins and outs, but I do know I have a nine-year-old here who needs her grandmother and right quickly."

"As I said, it's all in hand. I do need to remind you they would not be able to settle here on the coast. In any case there is still quite high anti-Japanese feeling, so it wouldn't be any fun for them either."

"I understand. The idea is to get her here to Nelson as soon as possible. How long will this take?" He understood, but he deplored it. And he was relieved to learn someone had already made the same request. Perhaps Lane's Canadian government agent.

"We're dealing with a bureaucracy here, and it's a shambles out there with everyone trying to get back, Inspector Darling. Just give me all the details again. I'll put this record together with the extant request just to have on file. Who knows. It might help."

Darling supplied all the information he'd gotten from Akio Sasaki, including the last known address of his sister-in-law, and for good measure gave Mr. Taylor Sara's full official name, Sara Himari Sasaki Harold. It was ridiculous, he considered, that he actually believed that if the child were half English, action would more likely be taken on her case. Had he imagined that Mr. Taylor's tone had shifted slightly upon discovering the child's father was not Japanese?

"It's going to take some time. She's not the only one trying to get back here, you know." Mr. Taylor sounded peevish.

"Thank you for anything you're able to do to expedite this matter," Darling said, hoping a spot of sucking up would help.

"I FOUND IT!" It was Padgett on the line.

Ames knew at once what he meant: the note from Harold with the changes to the will. "Harold's note? Where was it? Never mind! I'll be right down. Don't let it out of your sight!"

"I should have put it in his file," Padgett explained when Ames had arrived, almost out of breath, "but I didn't, because I expected him back within a day or two. He told me that these were his intentions, but he wanted to find a way to tell Mr. Humphries. It's a good thing I found the darn thing. I'd slipped it under my blotter. It's a silly habit." He lifted the blotter and pulled out several notes and held them up. "This will teach me."

"So you knew before he sent the change that he intended a change?"

"Here it is in my notes. June 8, he came to see me to inquire about what would be necessary to again change his will. Mind you, I think he knew. He'd done it before. But he seemed to be struggling with the decision. He didn't tell me what he was thinking then. When I got the note, I saw that he intended to leave all the property in trust for this little girl. I was extremely surprised as I had no idea his brother had a daughter. I guess he didn't want to give me the note until he could square it with Humphries."

"So now that you have the note, you will change the will?"

"I'll be doing it immediately. I have the details of the niece's name, etc. It is in fact left to her mother in trust. If she is underaged, it will be hers when she is twenty-one."

"Unfortunately, her mother is now deceased. She is the woman who died in that explosion up near King's Cove," Ames said.

"Oh. Oh, dear!" Padgett sat with a thump in his chair, as if the whole thing had become too much. "That is a tragedy. Who will be her guardian?"

"We're not sure as yet. There is a grandmother whom we are trying to trace."

"I see. How dreadful for the child. Nevertheless, the money will be hers when she turns twenty-one. That's a blessing, anyway."

"So, it is possible Martin Humphries knew about this change? Harold told you he was going to talk to him about it?"

"He said he was. He and Humphries were very old friends. But on the other hand, Humphries stood to lose. Perhaps he didn't tell him. It won't affect the final outcome. His intentions were clear."

"We know Humphries installed the locks in your office. We believe he may have kept a copy of the keys," Ames said.

"But surely that would be illegal?" Padgett almost squeaked. "You're not saying *he* broke into the office?" Ames was about to respond, but Padgett burst out, "It makes sense! He was looking for the will . . . no . . . he was looking for anything that would change the will. He must have known. Harold must have told him! Does this mean . . ."

"Can I see the note, Mr. Padgett?" Ames said.

> *I'd like added to my will that both my portion*
> *and that which I previously left to Martin*
> *Humphries be left instead to Mrs. Ichiko*
> *Harold in trust for her child, Sara Himari*
> *Sasaki Harold.*

It was the same backward-slanting handwriting as that in the note Darling had shown him.

Padgett shook his head. "I think it's entirely possible that even Ron's wife knew nothing of his brother's marriage and child. I'm not sure why exactly, except this name, Sasaki. The brother's wife must have been Japanese. Perhaps Ron Harold's wife is anti-Japanese. A good few people were, leading up to the war, I can tell you."

DARLING CONTEMPLATED THIS news from the lawyer. The window of his office was open, letting in a soft breeze. "Well, for starters, Padgett thinks that it's only recently that Harold was going to square the whole thing with Humphries. What, exactly, did Harold tell Humphries?"

Terrell, who'd joined Ames and Darling, said, "I wonder if he told him that night that he was changing the will, told him he'd be sending something to the lawyer, but had been waiting, out of fairness, to tell Humphries. He might not have told him about the child because he was still hiding the information."

Ames snapped his fingers. "I wonder if that was why Harold was going to Vancouver in the first place. He

433

wanted to meet some sort of government official to make sure Mrs. Harold and her daughter would be all right, and not charged with anything because they hadn't complied with the detention laws. That certainly squares with the note Miss Winslow found at the cabin."

"It's as good an explanation as any, I suppose. Aren't you two clever? Both writer and recipient are dead now. Unfortunately, we'll never know. He didn't confide in his wife, and whatever he confided in Humphries, we can bet Humphries is lying about it. I think Humphries is as guilty as sin. I think he learned he was to be cut out, killed Harold in the hopes of getting it all, and then set about seeing if he could find this note Harold must have told him about so he could destroy it. Then there would be no change to the will, and his financial troubles would be fixed. According to what Padgett told you, Harold was going to send the note directly once he'd told Humphries about the change. Something he said led Humphries to believe the note was still not sent." He sighed. "What we don't have is proof." He thought about what he had found. It wasn't proof. But it was interesting. "And more importantly, I'm guessing he knows about Sara now. If he does know about her, it will be from Harold's wife, who learned it from us. Let's keep a close eye on him. I went back to look at that painting again, and on a hunch took the backing off. I found this." Darling held up a tightly folded piece of paper and read the contents out loud. "Let's keep a very, very close eye on him."

LANE STOOD AT the bedroom door watching the sleeping Sara. Darling had left early, and Lane prepared anxiously

434

for another day of caring for her. Eleanor had told her to call and that she'd come over to help with the dressings on the arm after Sara had had breakfast. As Lane watched, Sara stirred, and then woke with a cry, her eyes wide and staring. Lane, seeing what looked like fear and disorientation, rushed over and sat next to her and put her arm around the child, pulling her close.

"It's all right. You're here in King's Cove with me, and Mr. Harris." She found the bear where he'd fallen to the floor in the night and included him in the embrace.

Sara relaxed marginally but then began to cry, clutching the bear against her chest. Lane, her heart compressing, held her gently, whispering, "There, there." She wanted to say, "It'll be all right," but of course she'd always thought that a silly thing to say when something awful had happened, and yet people invariably said it. "Did you have a bad dream?"

Sara did not respond at first, but continued crying, sobbing into Lane's shoulder. Then she nodded.

"Can you remember it?"

Sara only clutched Mr. Harris tighter. After another interval, Lane said, "Was it about your mother?"

This time Sara nodded right away and pulled away from Lane a little. "She was by a tree, waving. She was saying something, but I couldn't hear her. I was so happy to see her. I tried to go to her, but I couldn't move. I was really scared." She seemed on the verge of bursting into tears again.

"That would be very scary," Lane said, stroking Sara's hair away from her eyes.

"I won't ever see her again, will I?" Sara asked in a small voice.

"No, darling. But it's lovely she could come to you in a dream. You know what that tells me? That she is still in your heart. My mother died when I was a little girl, too. And she is still in my heart."

"Is she?" Sara said. "I wish Mama was here."

"I know. I wish she were as well because she could see how brave and wonderful you are. She would be so very proud of you." Lane held Sara's good hand. "Would you like to get up and have something to eat? It's a lovely day. We could sit outside."

At this Sara turned to look out the window, where morning sun had shot a shaft of light across the floor and was beginning to illuminate the trees outside.

"We used to eat outside sometimes, when it was nice."

"Did you?" said Lane, standing up and laying out Sara's clothes. "How lovely! We'll have a breakfast picnic on the porch. We can have scrambled eggs and toast. What do you think of that?"

"Can't I have cake with white icing on it?" Now there was a twinkle, as Sara raised her arm so that Lane could slip her T-shirt on.

"Not till you've had something proper to eat. Do you want to go out in your wheelchair, or shall I carry you out? Or would you like to try the crutches?"

Later, while Lane and Sara were reading on the porch, there was a knock and a cheerful "Hallooo" from the front door. Angela.

"Come on in, we're on the porch," Lane called. "My friend Angela is here."

"Are the boys here too?" Sara said, looking toward the kitchen door.

"They're in school today, but I think they'll come after to see you."

Angela swept through the door with her usual exuberant energy. "Goodness, what a day! My word, look at you, Sara! You look wonderful!"

Fetching a chair from the kitchen, Lane called, "Cup of tea?"

"You people and your tea. How about coffee? I brought your mail, and of course, Eleanor has been baking again. Nice little vanilla cookies."

Leaving Sara with her books on the porch, Angela joined Lane in the kitchen. "How is it going? Are you coping? Of course you are! You could cope with anything."

"I don't," Lane said quietly, "know how you handle three children. You're an absolute wonder!"

"Oh, you get used to it. I imagine the time comes when they are all handling themselves. Philip is already handling himself and making inroads on the other two. I expect to retire soon! But I had time to build up to it—I didn't go overnight from nothing to a nine-year-old. An injured one, at that."

"She's a lovely little thing. She had a dream about her mother this morning, though. She was absolutely broken up. One is powerless in the face of such a loss." Lane heaved a great sigh. "But it's a lovely day. We'll read, and Eleanor will come over and help with the dressings, and we'll practice

437

walking, and then it will be lunch time, there'll be a nap, and then your boys will come visit?"

"Absolutely. It's sounds like you'll be the one needing the nap! How sad about her mother. Are they making any progress with finding her a relative?"

This was complicated. Lane didn't really feel she had the right to talk about Sara's great-uncle, currently under arrest. "I think so. There is a grandmother still in Japan, trying to get back here. I think Frederick is trying to push the thing along with whatever department is overseeing the whole mess. Honestly, she's a British subject—the grandmother, I mean. It's ages after the war. There's no excuse for it. There was never any excuse for it. Not that we were any better. Masses of British citizens were shipped out of England under a similar 'Enemy Aliens' sort of act. Absolutely blameless people, Jews and second- and third-generation Germans waking up in Australia wondering what happened. It's rather a shame to arrive in Canada and find the same sort of thing going on."

"War," Angela said, shaking her head. "And an excuse to try to get rid of people the government thinks it doesn't want. They did the same thing to the Japanese in the States, according to my sister." The coffee by this time was beginning to perk, and Lane took two cups and put out the milk and sugar.

"I'll just see what Sara would like to drink. She doesn't seem to like milk much, though apparently the sisters at the hospital encouraged her to drink it because it would help her grow. I bought some apple juice instead, and she seems to like that. She has an awful sweet tooth, and all this sort of thing just adds to it!" She pointed at the packet of cookies Eleanor had sent in greaseproof paper.

"Oh, don't be like that! I'm fully intending to have one with my coffee. After what she's been through, a cookie after breakfast is the least she deserves!"

The day unfolded much as Lane had thought it might, and by nap time, a necessity, Lane was finding, a sleepy Sara settled under her blanket and tucked Mr. Harris in beside her.

"When can I go to school?" she asked, as Lane was just closing the door of her room.

"Do you feel ready?" Lane asked in surprise.

"I never went to school before."

"Of course. It's a lovely school with a very nice teacher. She's called Miss Keeling. I'm sure she'd be happy to have you. Shall we talk about it after your nap?"

Sara nodded and closed her eyes. Lane watched for a few moments as Sara's face settled and relaxed into sleep. Lane thought about the loss of her own mother. There was a pale layer of sadness that had never quite left her, she realized. She wondered if it would be the same for Sara.

"I THINK WE should look into his financial affairs, though he admitted things were bad," Darling said.

"It's a good idea, sir. Williams, a teller at the bank, hinted that Humphries had need of money. Absolutely talking out of school, but it may be worse than what Humphries is letting on," Terrell said.

"Good. You're chums with that bank manager after our last case. Why don't you go insinuate yourself into the judge's good graces and see if you can scare up a warrant and find out what you can. Tell the judge we suspect Humphries of murder. That might do it. Ames, you and I are going back to that damn house to see if we can find anything else. And yes, we'd better get a warrant for that as well. I don't think Mrs. Harold will give permission this time."

When his men had gone, a restful silence fell in the office, and Darling turned to contemplate his old friend Elephant Mountain. How was Lane getting on? he wondered. He'd found it strange, going home to a house with a child. It had been a disruption to their comfortable routine, but a pleasant one. He'd been commissioned to read to Sara and was gratified to see her eyes closing before they'd even finished the Heffalump story. He'd been obliged to read it through to the end on his own, to see what happened. He'd felt rather the conquering hero, that his reading had had such good results.

On the other hand, he knew it would tie Lane down. She'd not be able to roam about visiting neighbours and finding dead bodies, and generally saving the world the way she normally did. These musings led to thinking about her map of this case, and once again, that dangling blue line nudged at some corner of his brain. He closed his eyes and imagined it waving about, trying to reach something, like an inchworm, finding its next landing place. What was it after? But of course. The English money. Bypassing everyone and landing on Sara.

He was jolted back to the present by the phone ringing. "Darling," he barked.

It was O'Brien downstairs. "Just had a call from Mrs. Humphries. Her husband didn't come home last night. She's in a dither about it."

CHAPTER THIRTY-FIVE

NOW WHAT, DARLING THOUGHT. WAS Humphries doing a bunk? O'Brien had told him that Mrs. Humphries wanted him to come to her house, so Darling bellowed for Ames, leaving Terrell to the delicate business of handling the bank manager, and the two of them set out. The Humphries house was a little farther than a comfortable walk, as it was in a new home in the north part of town. And, he thought, looking up, a storm was brewing over the mountains. Darling got out of the car and looked up and down the street. There had been a drop in temperature, and it felt momentarily ominous, but he shook it off as nonsense. The houses in this little quadrant, at least, were farther apart and had bigger gardens. He'd had very few calls over the years to this part of town.

"Funny old place for a man short of money to be living," he said under his breath, as if Mrs. Humphries might hear.

"Sir." Ames walked down the sidewalk to the house and knocked on the door and then stood back. Seemingly out of a clear sky, the first drop of rain hit the sidewalk behind them. The door opened and Mrs. Humphries looked out at them, clearly distraught.

Ames stepped back to allow Darling in first and reached into his pocket for his notebook.

"Thank God! I've been frantic."

How long, Darling wondered, had she been frantic? It was almost ten in the morning now. "Can you tell us what happened?" he asked. They'd been ushered into the sitting room where they now stood, as if they were waiting for drinks to be brought at a party.

"Well, just what I said to the policeman who answered the phone. He didn't come home." She looked at Darling's skeptical expression and said, "Oh, I see. But you see, he sometimes goes off early to work. I haven't been sleeping well since Ron . . . you know . . . so I didn't hear him leave. But when I called the shop, he wasn't there."

"You didn't see him last night?" Ames asked.

She turned to look at him. "Yes. Yes, that's right. He didn't come home, and I fell asleep waiting for him. But I know he wasn't even at the shop yesterday afternoon, because my friend Kathleen called me saying she was supposed to pick up a key—only he wasn't at the shop when he told her it would be ready. She was very put out about it."

Darling paused, giving a surreptitious glance around. There were new furnishings. They certainly lived as if they had a substantial income. Had he told his wife he'd been interviewed at the station?

"Have you lived here long, ma'am? I haven't been up here for a while, and these are very nice homes."

"About three years," she said. She tried a small smile. "Marty had been doing well at the shop, and he put some money into a little gold mine he got a tip about, and it's been doing pretty well, so we thought, why not? Our kids are gone. We can spend a little on ourselves for a change. Anyway, he has an elderly relative—well, he *had* an elderly relative back in the old country—and she's left him a pile."

"That's lucky," Darling said. "Lucky about the mine too. Often, they aren't quite what people hoped. Speculative business, I suppose. What's it called? I might look into it myself."

"Oh, yes. Of course. A policeman's salary can't be all that good, I suppose. It's the Little River Gold Mine. It's up in the Mackenzie. Here, in this photo, he went up to see the mine himself about ten years ago." She handed Darling a photograph in a white frame.

Darling looked at it. It showed Humphries, a decade younger, standing in the rocky mouth of what looked like a mine, leaning with one arm on the rock face and the other hand on his hip, smiling for the photographer. He could hear Ames writing. He was about to put it down when he saw it. Hoping the sudden pounding of his heart could not be heard outside his own head, he fought back his nausea and quietly handed the photo to Ames. "Here," was all he said.

Ames put his pencil down, looked closely at the picture and then handed it back. "Yes, sir," he said very clearly. He'd seen what Darling was showing him.

Ames spoke up. "Did he perhaps say he was off somewhere to another town?"

She shook her head. "No. It's not like it was with Ronny. He was always having to go somewhere. Marty never had to."

"And he's taken the car?"

"Oh, dear. I didn't think of that! Let me check. He usually walks down to the shop. He says it does him good. It's an awful long way, and he's not getting any younger!" She got up and disappeared up the hall, and then they could hear footsteps going down to a basement, or a garage under the back of the house.

Ames turned quickly to Darling. "The tool," he said.

"The murder weapon," Darling said at a near whisper, all his fears collecting in one place. They heard her coming back.

"Yes," she called out from the end of the hall, moving swiftly back toward them. "He did take it. Now, I'm just trying to remember if he took it to work yesterday? I'm thinking now he must have."

"What colour and make is the car?" Ames asked. He was already on his feet.

"Oh. It's 1937, I think, when we bought it. It's a Ford, brown. Um, four door."

"May I use your telephone, Mrs. Humphries?" Darling asked, also on his feet.

"Yes, yes. It's in the hall." She pointed distractedly to one side where he found the telephone perched on a little spindly table that must have been a considerable obstruction in the already narrow space. The clouds Darling had seen were already darkening the day outside, and the hall was in near obscurity with only a dim light filtering in from a window in the bedroom on the right. He thought of the

445

paper he'd found. He felt a terrible, terrible foreboding. He barked at the operator, because really, they hadn't much time.

"CONSTABLE," O'BRIEN SAID, as Terrell came into the station brushing off his jacket. The rain was not yet in earnest, but the sky had darkened and the raindrops were big and very wet.

"Boss is up the hill at the Humphries place. Apparently, mister took the car sometime in the night and disappeared. Can we alert our colleagues down the hill to be on the lookout for it?"

Stopping in his tracks, Terrell asked, "Humphries?"

"Yes, Constable, I said," O'Brien said patiently, though he read something in Terrell's thunderstruck expression that raised an alarm. "It's a 1937, brown, four-door sedan."

"You call the colleagues! Tell Darling I've gone to King's Cove! Humphries will be after her!" He wheeled out the door and then stopped. "Call Mrs. Darling first, right now, and tell her not to let anyone in and to lock all the doors." The next thing O'Brien heard was Terrell's bike revving into action.

"In this weather?" O'Brien said aloud to no one. But anxiety clamped in his chest. Was the "her" Humphries was after Mrs. Darling, or worse, her young charge?

He put the receiver down, his mouth set in a grim line. There had been no answer.

BY A MIRACLE that almost made Terrell whimper a prayer of gratitude, the ferry was on the Nelson side for a change, and he managed to roar on just ahead of the chain being clanked across and hooked.

The ferryman looked at Terrell and gave something that could have been a shake or a nod and said, "It's really going to be coming down in a minute." As if in support of this prediction, there was a distant crack of thunder.

"Yes, sir. How long have you been on shift?"

"I come on at five." The ferryman pulled down his hat after an accusatory glance at the sky.

"Did you take a brown Ford, maybe '37, single male driver, over since you came on?"

"Nope. Just the usual lot. Mostly coming into town that time of day. Something up?"

Damn, thought Terrell. The man has had a massive head start. Even with the best will in the world it would still take him forty minutes to get to King's Cove. In this weather, who knew? Seeing the man still waiting for an answer, Terrell pulled himself back. "Yup."

"Good luck with it, then."

The ferry ride across the lake, being a matter of fifteen minutes, seemed interminable to him. Somehow riding in the rain made him feel, entirely ridiculously, he knew, like he was somehow evading it, but it was beginning to come down steadily, and he was wishing he had his slicker. When they finally arrived at the other side, he was surprised to see himself being ushered forward, and the other drivers being told to wait. He just had room to manoeuvre down the side of the row of vehicles, and with a wave he burst down the ramp and onto the road. Another distant roll of thunder rumbled toward him from the direction he was going. Another quick prayer of gratitude that he had gotten Tina to put new tires on for him. "All weather, all service, heavy-duty" the Dunlop ad had said. Good for our dirt roads, she'd said. She'd better be right.

The wind was not strong, but it was coming at him and driving the rain directly into his face, blurring what he could see through his goggles. He recited the formula he'd memorized for bad-weather riding: smooth, no braking, relaxed hold, eyes focused on the road ahead. And try not to think about what might be happening in King's Cove.

HE ARRIVED AT the sharp turnoff up to King's Cove soaking and nearly blinded by the downpour, took the hill a little too fast and careened on the gravel. Righting himself, he pulled back onto the road, his heart racing at the near accident. Miss Winslow's Austin was still there in the driveway. The noise of the downpour filled the silence when he turned off the bike, and he thought nothing could look bleaker and more abandoned than the house. The day had darkened to the level of twilight, and not a single light shone through the windows. He kicked the stand into place and hurried to the front door. It was ajar. Not a good sign.

Pushing it open, he called out, "Miss Winslow?" Hearing no answer, he started down the hallway, regretting the water he was dripping in his wake. On his left he saw what he thought was the little girl's bedroom. Ominously, the coverlet had been pulled off and lay half draped on the floor. A teddy bear looked as though it had been flung against the wall, and one child's shoe lay beside it. He turned and continued down the hall, his heart pounding with anxiety. A little wheelchair was parked awkwardly, blocking the door to the kitchen, and a glass of milk had been knocked over, the milk pooling underneath the table.

Clearly some sort of violence had gone on here. If it was Humphries, where in God's name would he take them out in this wilderness? As he opened the front door, the sky lit up with a lightning strike that felt like it was right behind the barn somewhere. Immediately a crash of thunder followed that made him flinch.

"WHAT A BEASTLY day," Kenny observed. "The damn thing is right over us." He'd come in from the garden, and now shook the rain off his sweater. Alexandra, wisely, had chosen not to go out with him. Kenny turned his head toward the door. "That sounds like a motorcycle just pulling into Lane's place. Do you think something is wrong? That young policeman rides one."

Eleanor had been giving the sink an extra scrub, and she wiped her hands on her apron, peering through the little window over the sink. Rain was lashing against it, making it hard to really see anything outside. "Ought we to go and see if anyone needs anything? Angela did telephone just before I came out to say that someone was going along up the road toward the old house at a fearful speed. She couldn't find one of the dogs and worried it might be hit."

Kenny put on his hat and rain slicker and made his way along the path toward Lane's house and crossed the boards that forded the little gully that lay between their properties.

449

He was in time to see Constable Terrell rushing out of the house and running to the barn.

Alarmed, Kenny hurried after him. "What's the trouble, Constable?"

Terrell threw open the double doors at the far side of the barn and looked into its dark interior. The noise of the rain echoed loudly inside its empty space.

"Have you seen Miss Winslow and the little girl today?" he asked.

"No. She's not come over. But with the little girl there, it's Angela, one of our neighbours, who usually picks up her mail, so I wouldn't have expected her. Especially not in this."

"Look, I'm afraid she may have been abducted. Can you call around your neighbours and see if anyone has seen anything unusual?" Terrell was in a panic. He had no idea which way Humphries would go with them.

"Good God!" Kenny cried. "My wife just told me that Angela called to say someone was driving much too fast up past their place. She was afraid for the dogs."

"When was this?" Terrell felt himself latch hopefully on to this news.

"I'm not sure. I was in the garden. But not more than half an hour, I'd say, maybe twenty minutes. Just before it really started coming down. That's about when I went out and she hadn't called by then yet."

"Where is this place?" Terrell was pulling on his gloves and moving quickly toward his bike.

Kenny explained how to get to Angela's and that instead of turning down the hill at the end of the road, he should turn up. There was an abandoned house at the end of that bit of road. "I'll be right behind you!" he called as Terrell turned his bike and roared back up the road.

Moving as quickly as he could, Kenny went back to the post office in time to see Harris lumbering up on his tractor, swathed in a sou'wester and a thick waxed raincoat.

"What the devil is going on? I just saw that motorbike racing hell bent up the road."

"It's Constable Terrell. He thinks Lane and the little girl have been kidnapped. I'm taking the truck and going after them. Angela said a car drove up past her place toward the old Anscomb house." Another bolt of lightning illuminated the sky, much too near, and thunder drowned out whatever Kenny was going to say.

Harris was off his tractor with a swiftness not normal for him and had clambered into Kenny's passenger seat before Kenny had finished talking to Eleanor, who had hurried out to find out what was happening.

"I told her to phone Angela and tell her we're on our way with the police and to phone the Hugheses and let them know to keep an eye out in case anything turns up their way," Kenny shouted as he put the truck into gear and swung around and onto the road.

"Who the blazes is trying to kidnap them?" Harris growled, clinging on to the frame of the open window. Kenny had taken the road at such a speed that the truck momentarily skidded sideways until he righted it. "And watch what you're bloody doing! How will our being killed help the situation?"

THE BROWN CAR had slid to a halt in front of the house because the road had ended right there.

"Who lives here?" the man snapped at Lane, who sat in the back holding Sara. The little girl had her arms around Lane's neck and had buried her head in Lane's shoulder. She was sitting across Lane's lap, the leg with the cast awkwardly pressed against the door. Lane was glad she'd managed to seize the blanket folded at the bottom of Sara's bed as they were being hustled out. There was another blanket already in the car. Had this man slept in the car somewhere nearby, waiting to snatch Sara?

Desperately wishing she could say someone did live there, she finally said, "No one. There's really nowhere to go from here." She stopped. Her heart was thudding against her ribs. She could not make out who this was in her panic, and part of her mind was running through the possible people who populated Darling's latest case. The other part was trying to work out how she could talk him out of whatever he planned. She looked anxiously at the storm outside. Surely he wasn't planning some sort of trek in this?

"Listen, why don't we just go back down the hill to my place. It'll be warm and dry, and I'll put the kettle on, and we can talk about this . . ." She wanted to add "whatever it is that's troubling you," but she didn't know what might aggravate him. A peal of thunder cracked so near that all three of them recoiled. Sara's hands dug into Lane's neck, and she whimpered.

"Don't!" he snapped, and turned toward her, pointing the revolver that had persuaded her it would be the better part of valour to do what he had asked in the first place.

Then it came to her. That trace of an East London accent. This was the locksmith, the one who had been friends with the dead jeweller. What was his name? Had Darling told her? Of course he had. Damn.

"Look, Mr. Humphries . . ." The name had appeared out of nowhere; the blue thread from Cornwall floated and settled. "If you're in some sort of trouble, maybe I can help you. Why don't we get Sara home? This is usually her nap time. We can talk about this. If you need to get away, I know the area, maybe I can help—I can show you an escape. Even from here, I know some paths, a way out." She'd blurted this and immediately regretted it, but she'd been thinking about her trip the winter before last when she'd snowshoed to a cabin hidden above the road to Kaslo. It wouldn't do now to encourage him to drag them out to find it!

"How do you know my name?" he snarled.

"The thing is, Mr. Humphries, it's a very small place and everyone knows everyone else, you know what that can be like, and it won't be long before someone sees something's wrong. My friend will be picking up my mail, and she'll see there's been a bit of a struggle, and she'll phone the police and come looking for me." She could feel Sara's fingers digging into her. She was terrified, Lane knew. Who wasn't?

Running a calculation of what she might be able to say that would calm him or offer him some sort of escape, Lane wondered if what she said was true. Would the alarm be raised in King's Cove? Not if Angela didn't go and get the mail. No one in their right mind would go anywhere in this storm. No one might know until . . . she thought the words "too late" but quickly changed them to "Frederick got home."

She wasn't to be given time to do any useful thinking. The man had got out of the car and pulled open the back door. "Get out. Show me."

"Show you?" she asked, trying not to hold Sara tighter in her alarm.

"The paths."

She started to put Sara down and he snapped, "She comes too."

"Mr. Humphries, we can't lug a wounded child through this storm. Let me leave her here. She can sleep on the back seat. I'll show you where to go and then get her home. She needs—"

"Shut up and get out!" He waved his revolver in a convincing manner.

Whispering "I'm sorry, sweetheart," Lane pulled the blanket over Sara's head and hoisted her so that her one good leg was around her waist and she was carrying her as one might a tired four-year-old. She was nearly as light as a toddler, Lane reflected, trying to position her, and keep the blanket over her to protect her from the worst of the downpour.

It was the moment of indecision that struck Lane. He had got them out and waved them ahead of him and then had stopped and looked into the driver's side of the car for just a split second. In that same second, Lane had turned around because she was going to tell him the lightning was much too close. She'd seen that pause, seen him momentarily distracted by something. The keys. He'd left the keys in the ignition and couldn't decide if he should bring them.

She quickly looked away, and patted Sara on the back, murmuring, "It's going to be all right," in a manner that didn't even remotely convince her. Perhaps the child was more trusting. But what she'd seen was like a tiny scraping of hope. He was muddled. Like a swimmer who'd swum too far from shore and suddenly didn't know if he could get back.

But in the next minute that tiny scrap of hope was dashed. If he had killed the jeweller, then he had done it precisely because he *was* muddled. Because in that moment he'd seen no another way out. If he felt trapped or uncertain now, he could kill them as well. She had thought his uncertainty meant she might somehow be able to talk him away from whatever cliff he was taking them all to the edge of, but she saw at once that it may represent the greatest danger of all. Rain was pouring down her face, and she turned back toward the path that ran past the side of the house.

His moment of indecision had passed, and he'd turned away from the car and was close behind Lane. "Move."

Still clinging to the hope that talking reasonably might help, Lane said, "There's a path that goes down the hill just along the way. There's a cabin about halfway down toward the Nelson road. But let's just wait out the rain, can't we?"

"Who lives there?"

"No one. It's an abandoned miner's cabin, I think. But we could just sit here, under this porch roof. I'm really worried about how close that last bolt of lightning was."

He looked back toward the porch of the house, and then through the woods, as if he were trying to decide. "The cabin, now!"

Crestfallen, she led him around the side of the house. She began to search for a more active solution. The trouble was, Sara, as small and light as she was, was becoming heavy and her arm was beginning to tire. Even if she saw a handy axe handle or heavy stick, she'd be unable to wield it. She stopped suddenly and turned to him. Sara's head lifted at the change, and she looked up.

"Mr. Humphries, what exactly are you planning to do?" She was going to add "with us," but worried it would provide some sort of incentive.

Humphries, who'd been close behind her, was forced to take a step back.

There was that uncertainty again. If only she could do something with it!

"That"—he raised his chin toward Sara—"has taken everything that's mine. Now turn around and keep moving."

CHAPTER THIRTY-SIX

"HE'S BARKING MAD!" DARLING CRIED at O'Brien's news. O'Brien knew he meant Humphries and not Terrell. Ames was already at the door, holding it open, giving them a full and depressing view of the rain washing down in sheets.

O'Brien handed over the revolver he kept in the drawer, and Darling seized it and raced to the car.

"Keep trying to reach her on the telephone!" Darling commanded.

"He's had a thirty-five-minute head start, sir. He'll get there in time. Not to worry," Ames said.

"Shut up, Ames! And give me the damn keys!"

Well understanding his boss's mood, Ames did as he was told. The weather had driven almost everyone for cover, so there was very little traffic and they made good time to the ferry, which was about halfway across, heading in their direction.

It was barely visible in the downpour. Another bolt of lightning momentarily lit up the sky toward the north, followed by a roll of thunder.

"It's about twenty miles away, sir," Ames said, who'd been counting.

"Thank you. Right over King's Cove no doubt! That'll help." Darling clutched the steering wheel and bent his head forward, trying to see the road ahead. He'd still not recovered from the wash of horror he'd felt at seeing the photograph of Humphries, the murder weapon in his hand. He was terrified they'd be too late.

THERE WAS NOTHING for it. She knew more or less where the cabin lay, through the trees and across a meadow, but if there'd ever been a path, it was certainly not visible now. They'd have to trample through the grass and bracken, but at least the strip of forest ahead might provide some respite from the rain.

"There's no path here," Humphries said behind her. "What are you up to?"

She could hear the growing anger, or panic perhaps, in his voice. "I'm not up to anything, Mr. Humphries." Lane had had to turn again to look at him. She kept her tone reasonable. "The cabin is down there. I've been there myself." She had been trying to understand why he wanted so badly to go to the cabin when there was shelter right here in this abandoned house. Then she thought it must be because he was fearful someone would follow the road up and find them. No, worse. He could kill them and leave them there and no one would find them till God knew when.

"In fact, it's a good thing the path isn't visible. No one can find us. In this rain, even our way down won't be found." She felt like she was absolutely mad herself, talking like this, as if she and Sara were part of some scheme to hide from . . . whatever he feared.

She adjusted Sara in her arms, which now were really beginning to ache, and saying loudly "This way!" she lowered her hand, found Sara's good foot and pulled off her little white sock, praying he wouldn't see it fall at the edge of the path she was hoping they would create in their trample down the hill. She waited, pushing her feet through the grass, but he said nothing. He'd not seen it. Now she had only the mess she could make in their walk through the forest because she had nothing more to drop.

The effects of the rain were lessened by the thick forest of lodgepole pine, and Lane was desperate to push back her soaking hair, which was delivering a steady stream of rain into her eyes. She longed to stop, or to hand the child to Humphries to carry, or to just wake up and find herself snuggled in bed next to Darling, enjoying the sound of rain coming down outside, anticipating a nice fire and tea and some scrambled eggs and toast with some of Mabel's jam. Perhaps sitting on the window seat with Sara, reading and watching the storm on the lake below.

And then she began to get angry. What the blazes was he playing at? He clearly had no plan. No real plan. He just wanted to get rid of Sara, apparently. With a sinking heart she realized she had no plan either.

She tried to drag her feet through the bracken in a way that would leave as visible a trail as possible. She thought

459

about what had happened: the knock on the door, seeing Humphries with the revolver demanding the little girl. His frustrated declaration that if Lane wouldn't let her go, she'd have to come too. His own confusion and lack of any solid plan was evident right from the beginning. If push came to shove, would he really be able to bring himself to kill a child? She wanted desperately to believe he wouldn't.

They were in the strip of forest now, and though the trees broke up the sheets of rain, it was dark and ominous. A crack of lightning struck so nearby that she herself gave a little cry and stopped, clutching Sara closer. She turned to see Humphries looking up, his gun hand brought down beside his leg. When he saw her turn his arm shot up.

"Why are you stopping?"

"Mr. Humphries, we really can't go on. It's not safe. We'll be exposed when we come to the meadow just along here, and the storm is right overhead." She could feel water pouring over her lips as she talked. They were beginning to feel numb. "It's not perfect, but at least here we're a bit protected. We can crouch down near some of these smaller trees."

"No. Keep moving."

"Mr. Humph—" she began, but he brought his revolver perilously close to Sara, so she turned and continued pushing through the undergrowth, hoping he would not see her efforts to leave some trace of their passage.

At the edge of the forest, they could see the meadow sloping down toward the now visible distant cabin. All Lane could think about was whether they'd even be able to make it there. She tried to remember what was in the

460

cabin. Another desperate man had used it a couple of years before as a place to hide. Had there been blankets? She remembered a rustic stone fireplace, but she couldn't, try as she might, remember if there was any wood still piled by it. She looked with extreme misgivings at the distance they had to travel over open meadow, and now, pausing as they were, she became aware again of Sara's weight, and the ache in her right arm, and more alarmingly, Sara was beginning to shiver.

"This is quite far enough, Mr. Humphries. Sara is cold and is likely to become ill, and I'm tired. She's been injured. She can't afford a bout of pneumonia. There is the cabin. Go if you want. I'm stopping. By the time I've rested and made my way back up that beastly hill, you can collect yourself and be away to safety before I can bring anyone back." With that she sat down on an outcrop just under the edge-most tree. "Unless you're planning to shoot me and take the child, and I don't really see how you can get away with it. Whereas now, unburdened by her, or my, death, you can get clean away."

To her amazement, Humphries actually seemed undecided. He looked down the hill at the cabin. The rain continued to bucket down from the heavy blackness of the clouds above them. Perhaps the centre of the storm had begun to move away. There had been no lightning for some minutes.

He turned back to look at them. Lane couldn't read his face. Rain plastered his hair down and seemed to distort his features. "She's Ron's kid brother's kid, you know that?" He nodded as if it had been a shock to him. "He lied to me. I was supposed to get the money, but he told me it wasn't going to be like that, that he couldn't tell me why, but he'd changed his will. How could he change something that was supposed to be? He was prepared to ruin me!" He turned away and said, as if to the sky, "I got so mad." His head dropped, he shook it and turned his gaze back toward them.

"I can understand that, Mr. Humphries," Lane said. He had killed Ron Harold. She knew now. He got so mad . . . Perhaps she could keep him talking. She used her most soothing voice, trying to still the chattering of her teeth.

But this only seemed to make him angrier. "No, you can't! No one can! It was supposed to be mine. She was *my* aunt. I sank everything into that mine, and I lost the lot, but it didn't matter, you see? Because I knew I'd get what was mine. And without her"—he waved his gun at Sara—"it would be mine, you see?"

So, was he planning to have her die of pneumonia? Lane thought angrily. She said very softly, "I'm going to put you down for a moment, Sara. I know it's wet and you're cold, but I'll put my jacket over you."

"What are you saying to her?" Humphries barked, taking a step forward and turning his gun on them.

"I just have to put her down for a moment, Mr. Humphries. My arm really aches, and if we wait out the storm here, I'm going to have to rest it before we move on."

"Don't try anything!"

"I'm hardly in a position to, Mr. Humphries." Lane was sliding Sara to the ground when the child whispered to her.

"He's mean."

She almost wanted to laugh. "He sure is," she whispered back. She took off her own sodden jacket and was happy to feel there were still dry patches inside and that it was warm from her own body. She quickly tucked it around Sara, who was leaning against the rock. The blanket she'd been in was soaked through, but at least it provided a bit of a cushion from the ground. "I'm going to stand up now, Mr. Humphries, and just jump around a bit to warm up and get some feeling back in my arm."

As she pushed herself up, she could see something she'd missed. Humphries himself was beginning to shiver. "You came from London?" she asked conversationally, rubbing her arm, and stamping her feet a bit. Trying hard to reduce the dangerous tension.

"Shut up!" he said, angry now. "Just shut up!" He took a step toward her and then away again, walking in the direction of the meadow, as if he were trying to decide what to do next.

She watched him, saw his growing confusion, and feared it. He was a tall man, considerably older than her, but stronger. She might be able to outrun him, but she could never best him in a wrestling match. Her only hope was that she might in some way be able to surprise him, get behind him and push. Perhaps he'd drop the gun.

He obligingly had his back to her at that moment, and she began to move slowly in his direction, but in what almost seemed like an animal state, he sensed it and whirled back, the gun pointing straight at the middle of her body. He opened his mouth to speak, and in that instant the sky lit up and seemed to explode. Something struck him and he fell backward, the gun flying out of his hand. Thunder rolled and cracked with the sound of boulders sliding down a mountain toward them.

Lane had been knocked over by the force of the explosion and was momentarily stunned. She scrambled onto her hands and knees, looking first for Sara, who sat, curled inward, with eyes wide, but unhurt. How close had the lightning come? Humphries lay on his side and was just beginning to move. He'd been stunned by something. She saw a branch of considerable size lying beside him. The tree he was standing by must have been struck. Where was the gun?

On her feet now, her heart pounding, she went closer to him, hoping the gun had dropped somewhere nearby. Her ears were ringing, and she felt disoriented. Humphries was trying to push himself up. Budgeting that he was in a more confused state than she was, she searched frantically in the soaking tangle of long grasses and ferns. She saw it on the other side of him, much too near his hand. Just as he seemed to have got a grip on himself, she tried to lunge past him. He was half sitting up now, alert to her sudden movement, realizing what she was doing. He lifted his leg, catching her on the shin, sending her sprawling.

Her arms flew forward to break her fall, but the blow as she hit the ground was hard. She could feel her left arm jam into its shoulder socket. Her legs sprawled over his, and she could sense him struggling to move. The gun, she knew, was close to his hand somewhere. Did he know that? She'd seen his face, blood pouring from a cut somewhere above his eye. Was he dazed? She pushed herself upright, and turned, just as his hand was reaching. With a flash she moved her foot toward him and stepped on his hand, leaning down to seize the weapon.

The moment she lifted her foot off him to get away, his hand was up, grasping at her ankle. Later she would try to piece together how she'd slipped her foot away, how she'd kept herself from falling or letting go of the gun, but in a moment, she was standing in front of Sara, pointing the revolver at him.

By this time, he'd managed to stagger to his feet; the cut on his head appeared to be gushing blood, but of course she realized that was the effect of the rain, still bucketing down, mixing with the blood from the wound, pouring down his face. He stood, looking at her, then at Sara.

"Don't come any closer, Mr. Humphries," Lane said, still trying to keep her voice reasonable. She was wet, and angry, and her shoulder hurt like blazes. How long would this standoff go on? She wanted nothing more than to get Sara back and into dry warm clothes, clutching a mug of cocoa, telling Mr. Harris the bear about her adventure. Could she order him to go to the cabin? It would take time to watch him put distance between them, but once he was there, she could get back to the car and home before he could get back up the hill. Where was the blasted cavalry?

"You won't shoot me," Humphries said. His words were muffled, whether by rain or shock she wasn't sure.

"I wouldn't count on it. I want you to go down to that cabin." She held the gun in both hands and gestured with it toward the long sloping meadow he'd have to traverse.

465

She felt her hands might begin to shake any moment. "Go on. I'm a very good shot. This is a Webley and I've used one before. I might not kill you, Mr. Humphries, but I'll be quite happy to shatter your knees."

All the fight seemed to go out of him. He wiped the blood and rain from his eyes and turned toward the open meadow.

When his back was turned, and he'd walked a few yards forward, Lane felt relief flooding through her, and it was then that her hands began to shake. She wanted to lower them, to take Sara in her arms, but she dared not in case he turned.

"Miss Winslow!"

She'd not even heard him approach, and her name sounded muffled in her still stunned ears, but there was Terrell, large as life. She dropped her hands as he rushed forward and took her shoulders carefully. "Are you all right?"

"Just," she said, wincing at the shoulder pain. "He thinks I have the revolver trained on him." She held the gun out to him.

Humphries evidently hadn't heard Terrell arrive and was still walking slowly toward the cabin.

"That car out there still has the keys in it. Get her home and I'll take care of him. Can you manage?"

She mustered up a nod, mouthed a thanks, and turned to collect Sara. "Come on, sweetheart. It's all over." She stooped and picked up the girl, who already had her arms up. "We'll have a real story to tell Mr. Harris, won't we?"

The little girl nodded, her first tears beginning to fall. Lane held her tightly with her good arm and made her way back to the deserted house and the car.

She met the maroon police car halfway down the hill to the Bertolli house. They stopped beside each other, and Darling rolled down the window. "Lane . . ." he said, just as Ames was making a move to get out.

"We're fine. Poor Terrell is up there on his own with Humphries. You might go help him."

CHAPTER THIRTY-SEVEN

━━━━━━━━━━

"**A** **MUSTARD PLASTER, IT'S THE ONLY** thing!"

"Don't be ridiculous. Much too strong for a child. An old-fashioned hot-water bottle and sips of lemon tea with apple vinegar."

"That wouldn't help a juvenile mouse with a sniffle! You want to get in with something strong, prevent the worst from happening. Garlic and milk. My grandmother gave us that."

"Don't be ridiculous! We're English! No one has garlic around here."

This animated medical discussion was taking place in Lane's kitchen, where she was trying to at least get the tea poured for all of them.

She and Sara had arrived back at the house to find Eleanor and Kenny Armstrong, and all the Hughes ladies, in possession of her kitchen. Robin Harris and Kenny, who had been sent back by Terrell and asked to keep an eye out for Darling and Ames, were watching hopefully from the sidelines, their job done. The kettle had boiled, tea was in the pot, cups and saucers at the ready. And they had not come empty-handed. Eleanor had brought a jar of honey and a bottle of cider vinegar, her medical bag, and, Lane was delighted to note, a tin of cake. Gladys had brought various things from her medicine chest: Aspirin, Mercurochrome, and the ingredients for a homemade mustard plaster.

The child had been seized from her arms the minute she walked in, and Eleanor, ordering Lane to go get dry clothes on, had hurried Sara into her bedroom and got her out of her wet clothes and enveloped her in a fluffy bath towel and applied another vigorously to her long hair.

Now they were all gathered in the kitchen, Sara in her chair clutching Mr. Harris the bear, and the others collected around the table. In the end, she'd been given tea with a good deal of honey and a drop of vinegar, and from somewhere, Eleanor had produced a tiny cup and saucer from a child's tea set, which was set out for Mr. Harris. "I found this upstairs," she said. "I think Lady Armstrong had hoped there would be a girl one day to enjoy it. All the rest of it is over there," she said, pointing to Lane's writing desk. "It will be yours now, Sara." Sara looked to where she pointed and smiled, clutching Mr. Harris closer.

Angela arrived in her car at the same time as Terrell, and both found room to park their vehicles in the already crowded grassy patch beside the barn.

"Horrors!" Angela cried, rushing up to Sara. "Are you all right?" She gave her a kiss on the forehead, and at Sara's shy nod, Angela said, "What a brave little girl! The boys will be mad to hear all about it."

"Here is the hero of the hour," Lane said, indicating Terrell. "Absolutely soaked through! There are towels and whatnot in the bathroom, and I'm sure the inspector won't mind lending you some dry clothes!"

Terrell nodded. "I'll take those towels, ma'am, thank you. I've been ordered to check on you and wait out the rain, which I'm happy to see is beginning to recede. And thanks for the hero comment, but of course, by the time I arrived, Miss Winslow had the fellow at gunpoint." With a slight salute, he went back down the hall in search of a towel.

"Well," said Kenny, looking at Lane with an approving smile. "No surprise, then."

"INSPECTOR DARLING? THIS is Dennis Taylor at the security commission."

"Yes, hello."

"We've had a bit of luck. As I told you, the return of Mrs. Sasaki was already in the works, and I've asked that she be found a place on the earliest ship out. She'll be arriving in three weeks at the port of Vancouver on"—there was rustling of papers—"the *Oriole*. That's a merchant ship. If you can get someone to meet her, you should be able to unite her with her grandchild right away."

Feeling genuine gratitude for this human victory over bureaucracy, Darling thanked Taylor effusively.

Well, he thought, turning his chair toward his window and the comfort of Elephant Mountain, and I know just who that someone will be. Who would not be at least somewhat cheered, after a difficult Pacific crossing, to be met by April McAvity?

"**AND HOW WAS** your day?" he asked Lane, kissing her fondly and patting Sara on the head. Seeing Mr. Harris, the bear, looking expectant, he also gave him a pat on the head.

"It was splendid. We had a busy day. We had a visit from the district nurse, and she pronounced Sara healing very nicely, and was very impressed with Sara's work with the crutches. In fact, we walked over to the post office together and met Alexandra, who I thought would bowl her over, but was in fact very careful with Sara, and then we had tea on the porch. After school let out, the boys came to visit, and they all played outside on the lawn. I think we just might manage a visit to the school tomorrow."

"That should be fun," Darling said, looking fondly at Sara. "I have my own bit of good news." Darling stooped down to Sara's level. "Your grandmother will be coming from Japan in only three weeks!"

Sara knew she had a grandmother, though she did not, of course, know her, and had speculated a good deal about what she might be like. Lane had brought the photo she'd found in the cabin of Sara's mother with her own mother and father, and it lived now in the sitting room on the bookshelf so that Sara could feel the house was a little bit hers.

"I hope she's nice," Sara said.

Lane brought the photo from the sitting room and sat at the kitchen table, gazing at it. "She looks terribly nice. What do you think? She has a very kind smile."

Sara took the photo and nodded. "My mother was very nice. Maybe she got that from my grandma."

"And," said Darling, "you have your great-uncle Akio. You met him, you remember. I'm getting Ames to bring him out on Saturday and drop him off for the afternoon, if that's all right," he said to Lane. "That miracle constable, Terrell, has indeed persuaded his landlady to take in Uncle Sasaki until such time as the family are settled. What do you think of that?"

"Jolly good. Did I tell you Barisoff telephoned this morning? He's very happy because his son is being released, and one of the other men, though not the two remaining friends yet, because they are wanted for something else, apparently."

Darling nodded thoughtfully. "That's something, anyway. And Booker is staying put where we placed him, though he's cross about having to return the jewellery. Did I tell you he got into the jewellery that night when he found the store open? He scooped up what he could and then claimed he'd found it behind the bin. Oh, and you needn't worry that Amesy will be hanging about all afternoon on Saturday. He says he has some sort of business to attend to and will pick Mr. Sasaki up later to take him back to town."

LANE DELIVERED SARA to the school. The girl's reputation had preceded her, thanks to enthusiastic stories from Johnny Bales and the Bertolli boys, so she was welcomed like a conquering hero.

"I shall pick you up after lunch," Lane said to her. "Just for today. I don't want you tired out too much. Will that be all right?"

Sara looked at the desks and books and students all crowding near and said, "I wish I could stay all day."

Lane smiled and gave her a kiss on the forehead. "We'll see."

"WHAT ABOUT THE Anscomb house?" Gladys said. Robin Harris was at their kitchen table slurping tea from his saucer after a busy morning in the upper orchard.

"What about it?"

"Well, why couldn't that family move in there?"

"Are you sure, Mother?" Mabel asked.

"Of course I'm sure," Gladys snapped. "The war's over. You're not suggesting we cling to some sort of race prejudice, are you?" She turned to Harris. "There was all that work done on it by that peculiar woman from Vancouver with the gangland family. You could finish it up, make it shipshape. Who owns the damn thing, anyway? It can't be worth very much, the mess it was left in."

"I expect the gangland woman owns it. Or her husband. She's in prison. They've never succeeded in getting anyone remotely interested. Her husband would be glad to get it off his hands. We should talk to the realtor in town. They'll have it on their books."

"I could run up some curtains," said Gwen, warming to the idea. "We have all that cloth left over from before the war, and with a few odd bits of furniture from all of us, I bet we could make it very homey!"

"I wasn't implying we should have some sort of race prejudice, Mother, only that it is a very gloomy house. I feel like it would crush that lovely little child," Mabel said, stung by her mother's accusation.

"Oh," exclaimed Gwen, "I bet we could make it really

lovely. And then she could go to school here, with children she knows."

Harris nodded. "They could stay at mine till the work is finished. Someone's going to have to get hold of that woman's husband and buy the place. We could pass the hat at church."

AT THE PORT of Vancouver, April, having decided against advice by the chief of police to wear her uniform, was wondering how she was ever to find Mrs. Sasaki. She saw that there were what looked like some scores of people waiting to disembark. Thinking it logical that they might have to go through some sort of customs procedure, April finally was shown to the desk past which the returnees would have to go.

"Excuse me. My name is April McAvity and I've been sent to meet a Mrs. Mary Sasaki. I'm with the Vancouver Police." Truish, she thought. "Would she be coming through here?"

The official, looking harried before the process had even started, said, "Why aren't you in uniform?"

"I thought it might be alarming for her." She wanted to add "after all she's been through," but didn't want to annoy this man. She reached into her purse and pulled out her temporary warrant card. "My warrant card."

Shaking his head, he pointed at a bench along the wall. "Well, la-di-da. Sit over there. It's likely to take a long time. I'll send every Mary Sasaki that comes through over to you. Now get out of the way!"

The line had begun to move down the gangplank and into the customs shed.

474

She was looking away toward the door where people were moving slowly out, back into the country they had left, or been sent from, carrying suitcases and bags. She had listened to the customs man ask for what seemed like the hundredth time, "Do you have enough money to proceed to your next port of call?" as if to emphasize that they were prohibited from staying in Vancouver. She was surprised that his zeal for the task did not seem to diminish. Suddenly she heard, "Hello? Miss?" and a slender woman of no more than fifty, April thought, dressed in a dark suit and a blue felt hat with a narrow brim stood before her. She had put down a heavy brown suitcase and regarded her now with dark, tired eyes. April jumped up and asked, "Mrs. Mary Sasaki?"

The woman gave something between a nod and a bow, and said, "Yes. You are here to meet me? That is so kind."

"No trouble at all," April said, seizing the woman's suitcase. She was relieved that the woman spoke perfect English. "My name is April McAvity; please call me April. How was your journey?"

"Long," said Mrs. Sasaki. "But I am happy to be home. I truly believed I would never see Canada again."

"I bet your granddaughter will be excited to meet you! Come on, let's get out of this crowd. We'll be taking a train this evening, if you don't mind continuing your travels? You must be excited to meet her."

"I am happy to continue if I may see my granddaughter sooner. My brother-in-law told me when she was born, and I have not seen so much as a photo. Have you seen her?"

April smiled and shook her head. "Not yet. I've been in Vancouver doing a course with the police department, so I haven't met her yet. But I did the investigation here when we wanted to learn more about her." She stopped. "I'm very sorry about your daughter, ma'am."

Mrs. Sasaki only nodded. They'd arrived out on the street, and she took a deep breath and closed her eyes. "I came here for a short time when I was only five," she said. "We went back when I was a teenager and I married there before we came back to stay, but I always thought of Vancouver as home, even after all those years in Japan."

April stood undecided for a moment, and then said, "I'll get a cab, and we can go to the station. It's comfortable, and there's a nice place to have something to eat. I've already bought the tickets to Nelson."

In the taxi, Mrs. Sasaki looked eagerly out the window. "It has not changed so very much," she said.

Once at the lunch counter at the Pacific Central Station, Mrs. Sasaki asked, "How did she come to die, my daughter? Please tell me the whole story."

"Ma'am, I'm not completely sure. I think it was some sort of unexploded bomb. The police there will know more, I think." She wished she knew more and felt a great weight of sadness in her chest. She'd lost her own mother when she was a teenager, and now here was a mother who'd lost her daughter. "It must be awful," she added.

The woman nodded. "And where is little Sara now? Who is looking after her?"

"Oh, that's all right," April said, cheering a bit. "She's staying with this wonderful lady called Miss Winslow.

I mean, she's the wife of the police chief, Inspector Darling, so I guess she's Mrs. Darling, but everyone calls her Miss Winslow. She's ever so nice!"

Later, on the train, Mrs. Sasaki dozed, and April watched the passing country until it became dark. She wanted to sleep, but she was excited. Her police course wasn't quite finished, but she'd been given the certificate early so that she could accompany Mrs. Sasaki to Nelson, and in a few more hours she would be home and could see Constable Terrell. And Daddy, she added quickly in her head. *He'd* been writing pathetic letters about how much he missed her and what terrible meals he'd been making for himself.

Terrell had written, too. She sighed about these letters, which she had tucked in her suitcase and tied with string. They took no risks, these letters. Polite, warm even. But they certainly would not qualify for a ribbon. Decidedly not love letters. How maddening he was!

LANE STOOD IN the doorway of Sara's now abandoned log cabin home. Akio Sasaki was behind her, outside. She had offered to go and recover the rest of Sara's clothes and schoolbooks, and Akio had said he wanted to come with her, to see where his niece had spent the war. With a sigh at how empty the place already felt, as if its last inhabitants had been there forty years before, Lane went in and pulled the apple boxes out from under the bed, put all the clothing into one box and took the other to the table so she could collect all the school supplies. She had begun to corral the higher-grade books into a pile when something caught her eye in the bottom of the box.

She reached inside, feeling the bottom. It had a little give. She lifted the box. There was at least an inch between the inside base of the box and the bottom of it. A false bottom!

She went to the sink and found a knife that had been dropped there with all the other cutlery when the RCMP had gone through the cabin, and brought it back. Very carefully she began to pry the false bottom of the box out. With a little cry of "Yes!" she lifted the floor of the box out and was astonished to find a large hard-covered notebook. The clever RCMP had missed this on their visit, she thought with a little tingle of triumph. But this was nothing to the thrill she felt when she opened the notebook and a single page fluttered out onto the floor.

In beautiful, precise handwriting, it began:

> *November 1947*
>
> *My dearest Sara. This is for you. I began to write in it when we first arrived at this beautiful place, because one day you will have this, and you will know who you are. You will know about your beautiful father, whom I still miss every day, and your grandparents and your uncles. You will know where you came from, and how much you are loved. Uncle Ron says we must think about leaving, that he will find us someplace because the war is long over. I know we should leave, for you. But I cannot bring myself to contemplate it just yet. I have grown to love it here, to feel*

*safe. Yet I sense our time here is ending, and
in my heart I know that I must somehow face
the world, give you a normal life. I do not
know what will happen when the authorities
discover we did not comply with the rules, and
I know from the papers Uncle Ron brings that
things are still bad for us. Here I have been
happy enough; there is the work of teaching
you, my clever and beautiful child, and of
keeping this place, and of my writing. What
could I do out there? But here I can write the
most important thing of all: the story of you.*

Lane held this letter for a moment, and then carefully
opened the notebook to read the first page.

*1942. It is evening, and you are asleep, full
of the innocence of childhood. The fire flickers
and is warm. Now I may begin. Your story,
my little one, begins far away and long ago,
in Japan . . .*

Lane slipped the letter in and closed the book. It was
not hers to read. This was Sara's. It was a thick notebook,
made thicker by the meticulous and graceful hand of Ichiko
Harold. Here was something for Sara to have of her mother.
Her heart was pounding with sadness and gratitude. She
sat for some moments, staring out the window that had
developed a mist of cobwebs in its corners. She could see
Akio outside, and understood why he had not yet come in.
He was standing at the edge of the garden, surreptitiously

wiping his eyes. She stood up and took the box of books to the door, causing him to look up.

"I thought my suffering was hard, but what of hers, alone here all these years?" he said, his voice hoarse.

Lane held up the notebook. "She wrote about her life here for Sara to have one day. I only looked at the first page, but I learned that she was reluctant to leave here. She had come to feel safe. Maybe it was not so bad for her, at last."

Akio took the book and held it, nodding, but did not open it. "That would be like her," he said. "That child was the moon and sun to her." He sighed deeply and nodded, squaring his shoulders. "How much is there to take down?"

"Just the box of books, if you'd like to carry that, and I'll bring the clothing. I can wait out here for a few minutes if you'd like to go inside."

Akio shook his head. "I have this now. It will be enough." He patted the notebook that he held in his arms.

THEY HAD A little fire burbling in the Franklin, though they didn't really need it on a warm evening like this. It reminded Lane of the fire in the cabin, Ichiko writing in the twilight, Sara asleep. Perhaps it was because they both missed Sara a little, and the fire provided a dose of extra comfort. Sara, her grandmother, and her great-uncle had indeed moved into Harris's house with him because he had two extra rooms, pending the completion of the renovations at the old Anscomb house, which had in fact been purchased in the end by Mrs. Sasaki. It could shed its tragic past and be called the Sasaki house ever after, Lane thought happily.

Lane picked up the paper and showed Darling where she had folded it open. "Have you seen this? Dodi Cartwright won the day!"

Darling took the paper. "'Balloon Bomb Hazard.' Blah blah blah, blah blah blah, 'do not approach and contact authorities immediately.' How likely are most people to run into these things, though? I'm sure they're sprinkled across millions of acres of unpopulated wilderness."

"Yes, you could be right. But the bombs, if they did not explode on impact, will be a danger in perpetuity. It's a loathsome quality of intelligence services that they think no one is entitled to know anything except them. Look what it says here: the reporter discovered that in Oregon the authorities didn't release any information until someone was killed in 1945. I suppose the authorities knew about the bombs but were reluctant to let the Japanese know they'd even arrived. Wanted them to think the whole thing had been a failure. But even after the war, and the deaths, they were reluctant and were finally forced to by good sense and public opinion. I'm not for all these secrets."

"Says the woman who bristles with the things," Darling said, kissing her. "For myself, I'm just happy we have the unhappy Mr. Humphries in prison and going on trial. You'll be called upon to testify, for your interference. When Ames and Terrell went through his shop, they found several bags of valuables from the store. No doubt part of his escape plan." He paused and turned to her. "Lane . . ."

"It was his impulsiveness that scared me, I think," Lane said with a slight shudder, remembering the tension of having to be careful about anything she said. "I don't know if it's novels, or what, but one imagines killers being cold and calculating, with the kind of intellect that only Sherlock Holmes can best. But I could see that wasn't Humphries at all. He was confused and desperate and, I'm bound to say, not that bright. I rather arrogantly thought at first that he would be easy to manipulate, that I'd be able to play on his uncertainty, and get him to stop whatever he had planned. But then I realized that that was what made him so dangerous. He was uncertain and didn't have a plan. I began to believe he would kill us when he felt trapped and could see no way out."

"I think that's what happened when he went to confront Ron Harold that night," Darling said quietly. "The way he tells it, he'd heard Harold was going out of town again, and he begged him to meet before he left. Reluctantly Harold said he would. He went to tell him he was broke and to get him to give him his share of the inheritance right away. He had his back against the wall and was desperate. He hadn't told his wife anything. Another place he couldn't see a way out, I suppose. All that guff about how well he was doing was a smokescreen. He was hiding his losses from everyone. He'd lost most of his money on the mine and he'd borrowed money so his wife wouldn't find out, kept splashing out to show everything was all right. A fur coat for her, for example. He couldn't think what to do, but he imagined that if Harold died, he'd get the whole lot. It was then he learned that Harold had changed his will, and the money would all go elsewhere when he died. Humphries panicked. Harold refused to tell him where it was going, but he'd said it was too late, he'd already

482

prepared the paperwork, and Humphries hit him a good solid blow on the head."

"Why did Humphries go there with his geological sample hammer? Doesn't that suggest premeditation?"

"Oddly, no. He was furious about being cut out of the will, so he stormed out of the shop, meaning to drive away. He kept this little sample pick on the floor of his car; he'd been given it when he visited 'his' gold mine. According to him, he grabbed the thing and went back in. Harold was working at his desk, apparently having already forgotten their interaction. Perhaps he'd only meant to threaten him, but something snapped. He said Harold was just sitting there going over his papers, like nothing had happened. And the next thing he knew, Harold was dead, and he hadn't meant to do it. But once it was done, he realized that he could still stop the inheritance going elsewhere if he could find the paperwork for the codicil. He was sure it must be somewhere because Harold said he was *going* to give it to Padgett. The irony is that Mrs. Harold, all unknowing, had seen the envelope addressed to Padgett and dropped it off, little realizing that in that envelope was a secret she also knew nothing about: Sara. Padgett already had it and was preparing to act on it. Then Humphries tried to cover the whole thing up by making it look like a robbery gone wrong."

"You know what I don't understand? Why didn't Harold just give Humphries the half he intended for him right away, when he sold the property before the war?"

At this Darling fell silent, for so long that Lane looked at him, puzzled. "What were you going to say?"

"I feel I let you down a bit," said Darling, finally. "I learned something about Humphries that I didn't tell you. If anything worse had happened, I could never have forgiven myself. We should have locked him up at once when I saw that photo. I should never have left you out here unprotected once we knew how violent and impulsive he could be. We just didn't have the final proof!" His frustration was evident.

"Don't be silly! You didn't leave us unprotected—you sent Constable Terrell out on his shiny Triumph. You couldn't possibly have known Humphries would come here to try to kidnap Sara! Besides, his impulsive nature was evident to me almost at once." She reached over and took his hand. "Please, it's not like I'm entitled to know anything, let alone as much as you do tell me. And anyway, all's well that ends well! Everyone is safe and sound. What *did* you find? Something more than the photo of him with the weapon?"

"It was in the painting. It kept nagging at me, that painting. The fact is, I was so horrified when I saw that photo of him actually holding the weapon he'd used, and a vicious-looking thing it is, that I forgot. I went back to get it finally, hoping to see something I missed, when I realized it might be under the backing. I'd seen that the backing was peeling off the first time I'd seen the painting and I thought nothing of it at first, but then I tore it off and there it was: a letter his aunt had written Harold dated October 1919. She said she wanted him to know why she did not want his cousin to get the money, and that he, Harold, should not feel bad because she had given Martin enough money to set himself up. Apparently, Martin had lived with her when he was sixteen and had spent the time pilfering her jewels and silver, but she had overlooked it because she felt awful about how deprived he'd been growing up, but then one day he'd gotten into a fight with one of the local boys and nearly beat him to death over almost nothing. His mother had told her he'd been kicked out of school because he was fighting, but she'd implied they were just childish scuffles. That turned out not to be quite accurate. He had seriously hurt several boys at school, and his mother took him out before it became a matter for the police. The worst part of it, she said in her letter, was that Martin Humphries hadn't known he was doing it. It was a kind of blind rage. She was badly frightened by this and believed that if he ever came into any real money, he would become really destructive, and she couldn't have that on her conscience. I think that's why Ron Harold put off doing anything with the money at all. Then, when Sara was born and his brother died, it became very clear to him what he would do. He would secure Sara's future."

"Goodness! I wonder why he hid the note. It must have been shocking to learn that his friend had such a violent and ungovernable disposition." She shrugged. "Or maybe he knew or suspected and didn't want to destroy the note; maybe he'd have to use it to explain their aunt's change of heart. So he just hid it where there would never be any danger of Humphries finding it. Of course what Humphries really wanted, desperately, was the change-of-will note, and there it was, pushed under Padgett's blotter, where I dare say even Padgett could have forgotten it. And then it didn't matter, because when Bertha told him they had a niece it all fell into place for Humphries. He must have thought in his addled mind that if he couldn't get the codicil, he could eliminate Sara, and somehow he thought he would still get all the money. On what tiny happenstance things can hang," Lane said. She shuddered. "Things, or people."

Darling shrugged. "Not every murderer is hanged. Perhaps it will be a life sentence. He's clearly not in control of his impulses. Maybe for once that will work in his favour."

They sat quietly for some moments and then Darling reached for Lane's hand, the consequence of finding the killer suddenly weighing on them.

"What will happen to Bertha Harold?" Lane said, after a silence.

Darling, his mood lightening, smiled slightly. "Is there no end to your nosiness? As far as I know she is selling up, both shop and house, and moving away to Ontario where she doesn't have to be faced with the painful memories. Or her niece. She is not, I'm afraid, a forgive and forget sort of person. And before you ask, Humphries's wife has gone to the States to stay with one of her sons. There. Are you finished?"

"What was Ames's business when he dropped off Uncle Sasaki that day? Isn't that what he said to you? 'I'll drop him off, I have some business.' Would that have been at the Van Eyck garage? Did the police car need its brakes looked at?"

"I have no idea whatsoever," Darling said. He paused, looking innocently at the ceiling. "But, when we first went to investigate the jewellery store robbery, Ames let slip something. He said, 'I was just here the other day.'"

486

"Getting his watch fixed?" Lane suggested.

"Maybe," Darling said with a smile and a shrug. "If you think Amesy confides in me, you are quite mistaken."

ACKNOWLEDGEMENTS

NO **BOOK IS WRITTEN IN** solitary splendour, including this one. Thank you to my husband, Terry, who is that lovely combination of patient and a kind of genius, the kind who when I'm flapping about in a bind over some detail will say, "Why not just . . ." and it's *always* something clever. To my encouraging son Biski and daughter-in-law Tammy, both Lane Winslow enthusiasts, and the two young men they've provided for me to grandmother, Teo and Tyson.

I am amazed and honoured by the endless kindness of people who want to share their expertise with me. I owe a special debt of gratitude to the now retired historian at the Nikkei National Museum and Cultural Centre in Burnaby, Linda Reid, for the time she took to speak with me about the history of the Japanese internment, and also to Daien Ide, research archivist at the centre. To Dr. Jeff Fine for interesting details of a punctured skull and post-mortem reports; to Royal Navy Leading Diver David Gray, a destroyer of mines and unexploded devices both at sea and on land in the United Kingdom, for his knowledge of unexploded bombs from the second World War and their range of devastation; to Gregory Williams for his deep familiarity with vintage motorbikes, 1940s tire advertisements, and the correct way to ride to someone's rescue in the driving rain on a gravel road; and to Crispin and Jan Elsted for their help with Japanese paper, and—never surprising with the Elsteds—incredibly detailed knowledge about many other things including balloon bombs. Very special gratitude to the amazing Comox Air Force Museum, where the lovely, very knowledgeable, and helpful docents expressed so much interest in this project, and where one can see a real live Japanese balloon bomb on display! It's a top-notch little museum, and I encourage you to visit. Finally, a very special thanks to Loreth Anne White, whose suggestion it was to include the wonderful Dr. Masajiro Miyazaki in this chronicle.

Any errors of detail are mine alone.

If this book can hold up its head at all, it is because of the people who spend time with my manuscripts once I deliver them. Thank you to my wonderful first reader Sasha Bley-Vroman, who is so attuned to period language, and now so familiar with all the regular characters that she can spot an inconsistency at fifty paces. To the glorious TouchWood Editions team, Tori Elliott, delightful and hard-working publisher extraordinaire; editor Kate Kennedy, who so kindly encourages me to write as I want to; and publicist Curtis Samuel, whose charm and reach have been so responsible for the success of the books. Special thanks also to Claire Philipson, as kind and firm and clear-thinking as an editor can be; to Renée Layberry and Meg Yamamoto for their help in making the book sing; and of course to the wonderful Margaret Hanson for her cover art, which delights all who see it.

IONA WHISHAW is the author of the *Globe and Mail* bestselling series The Lane Winslow Mysteries. She is the winner of a Bony Blithe Light Mystery Award, was a finalist for a BC and Yukon Book Prize, and has twice been nominated for a Left Coast Crime Award. The heroine of her series, Lane Winslow, was inspired by Iona's mother, who, like her father before her, was a wartime spy. Born in the Kootenays, Iona spent many years in Mexico, Nicaragua, and the US before settling into Vancouver, BC, where she now lives with her husband, Terry. Throughout her life she has worked as a youth worker, social worker, teacher, and award-winning high school principal, eventually completing her master's in creative writing from the University of British Columbia.

WEBSITE: IONAWHISHAW.COM

FACEBOOK & INSTAGRAM: @IONAWHISHAWAUTHOR

DISCUSSION QUESTIONS: TOUCHWOODEDITIONS.COM/LANEWINSLOW

THE LANE WINSLOW MYSTERY SERIES

THE LANE WINSLOW MYSTERY SERIES